BETRAYED BY
POLITICS

Juan Corrigan

Acknowledgments

I would first like to thank God for everything He has done for me. All the glory and honor belong to Him. I will always put Him first, and doors have always opened—even in my darkest moments—because of Him.

The idea for writing this book came from two projects I worked on after college. The first was my thesis for my master's degree in 1997. I figured if I could write a thesis, I could certainly write a book. The second was in 1999, when I was on the cover of a romance novel titled *Rocky Mountain Romance* by Kathleen Suzanne. That same year, I decided to write a novel.

My first idea was a story about an agent who runs into a labyrinth of corruption, gets accused of a crime for knowing too much, outsmarts two governments, and in the end, gets the girl. My mother, Maria Elba Corrigan, was a great inspiration in writing this book. When I told her I was writing a novel, she encouraged me to use the experiences I've had and assured me the words would come. She was right.

The ideas didn't come all at once. Over time, I would write paragraphs or a few pages. Months and years passed, and life brought new responsibilities—Army schools, obligations, and later deployments. My own experiences, along with those of people I knew in government service, gave me the inspiration to piece together stories and move the novel forward.

When my sons were little, I would tell them that I was working on a book. Both Juan Diego and Gabriel encouraged me to continue. One time, my youngest said, "Why don't you just finish it, Daddy?" That stayed with me, and eventually I decided to do exactly that.

The book was nearly complete during my last deployment, and when I returned from Kuwait in 2024, I decided to finally publish it. I was very fortunate to find New York Book Publishers, where I spoke with John Solomon. He was extremely knowledgeable, explained the process clearly, and assigned me to Jim Banister, who guided me throughout this adventure. Jim was an excellent mentor, and his guidance helped make this book possible.

Many others also contributed to bringing this novel to life. I would like to thank Carolyn Abadie for allowing me to hold my first book signing at her bookstore, Bookmart, in Starkville, MS. I am deeply grateful to her for that opportunity. I also thank Dr. Thomas Pearson for believing in me and sponsoring me to jump-start the process of making this a reality.

I am grateful as well to Sissy Bullock, the director of the New Albany Library, for hosting a book signing in my hometown of New Albany, MS. That was a special moment for me, as New Albany is where I grew up and truly experienced the American way of life. Many teachers, coaches, and mentors also inspired me to study, move forward, and never give up. I thank them all.

May this novel bring well-deserved recognition to all these people. Lastly, I would like to thank America for giving me so many opportunities in all aspects of life, so that we may continue to enjoy the freedoms our forefathers fought for and strive to reach the American Dream.

Table of Contents

About the Author

Juan Antonio Corrigan was born in El Valle de Allende, Chihuahua, Mexico, and grew up in Jimenez, Nuevo Casas Grandes, and Chihuahua City. His stepfather's job brought him to New Albany, Mississippi, when he was seven years old. He quickly adapted to the American way of life and excelled in both academics and sports from elementary through high school.

He attended Mississippi State University, where he graduated with a Bachelor of Science in Kinesiology and a Master of Science in Exercise Science. While in college, he enlisted in the Army National Guard and attended the State Officer Basic Course, where he was commissioned as an officer. He has served for over 38 years, including five deployments to the Middle East. During his military career, he held several occupational specialties, including artillery, engineering, special forces, and military intelligence.

Juan has also appeared as an actor in several films. His life experiences, both in the military and beyond, inspired him to write this novel and let his imagination bring this story to life.

1

Another day passed in the ancient Tenochtitlan, the great city of Mexico. It seemed like a country within itself. There was so much to do without an end in sight. This city is beyond imagination. Ever since the Spanish Conquistadores arrived in this ancient city, it has maintained its mystery and heritage. Its people, so rich in culture, still possess the ways of their ancestors. In terms of cultural richness, it dwarfs any city in the world.

One is struck with awe when seeing the city at night, especially from above. The lights gleam and stretch from one end of the horizon to the other. George Lucas could use the spectacular show of light in his Star Wars movies. Even though it's a cosmopolitan city, it has its own unique sense of Mexico in every corner. The ancient ways and its European influences meld into a dish with endless flavors.

With all that is happening, order is somehow maintained. But when one looks closely, order appears only as an illusion that doesn't come easy. The struggle between good and evil is always present in minute incidents and events. Mexico City was said to be the center of the universe by the ancient Aztec people. In many ways, they were right.

As the sun started to go down, a breeze was felt by a passer-by outside the congressional building. An old Indian man, who was outside selling artifacts, looked toward the sky. There are many Indian-descendent people in Mexico, and many still retain the features of their ancestors. The man's face changed from carrying a look of curiosity to one etched with fear. With a feeling of foreboding, he took a deep breath and began to walk faster, away from the building that was supposed to establish order. It seemed that, somehow, things were about to be shadowed by something diabolical. A storm was coming, and it would be one that would come unexpectedly.

On the fifth floor of the congressional building, congressmen were in their last discussion of a political debate. They had had a late session discussing the usual political arguments. The interior of the room was filled with all sorts of decorations. The Mexican Flag was shown with pride and distinction. Its three colors, red, white, and green, seemed to glow as the great eagle; a symbol of the ancestors who had established this great city and its nation, of the empire of a past kingdom, and of the nation's pride, seemed as if about to take off and soar.

Esteban scanned the room as usual, his eyes moving steadily as he assessed the demeanor of each person present. Nothing seemed out of the ordinary. He'd been in there thousands of times with the same or similar congressmen, diplomats, and even the President.

A senator was on the floor speaking about some economic agenda. The room was less than half full. Esteban barely paid attention to what the congressmen said because it all sounded the same to him. He only dedicated his senses to making sure that nothing was out of the ordinary. The huge room was filled with loud whispers among the senators, and a few people were walking to and from the corridor. In many cases, the person speaking is ignored, but in this case, the Senator's speech was raising voices and even shouts. The senator on the floor had brought up the subject of taxes, and that always brings about a commotion.

Esteban checked his watch. It was finally time to go home, and a good thing because the cabinet meeting that Senator Fernandez led was about to turn into a shouting match.

I just want to go to bed, Esteban thought to himself. Esteban was standing to the right of Senator Fernandez as he shook hands with the last of the congressmen. He was about to be dismissed by his replacement bodyguard, Raul, who was slowly walking toward him.

"Gracias, Raul, I'm so ready to go home," Esteban whispered to his bodyguard replacement.

"I'll see you in a few days," Raul responded as he smiled.

Senator Fernandez was a well-respected congressman. He'd been one of the few politicians who was known for honesty and righteousness. Many had tried to come up with some dirty laundry on him but all had failed. It seemed like he was one of the few politicians who was actually doing what he liked to do, and that was to help his people. It showed whenever he took any stand. The Senator even had cabinet members arrested in the past for attempting to bribe him. He had won the hearts and minds of the people of his state but, in the process, made many enemies within his political circle. Because of this, Senator Fernandez was feared by some and hated by others. Esteban exchanged papers and instructions with Raul and walked out of the meeting room feeling relieved.

As he was leaving the room, he glanced at Senator Sinal, who was whispering to his aide and looking at Senator Fernandez with a glint in his eye. *Senator Fernandez won this argument again, and he didn't even speak*, Esteban thought to himself. Senator Fernandez was a rival of Senator Sinal. They didn't see eye to eye on many issues, and they didn't have any love lost between them. They usually treated each other with respect, but only on the surface; underneath, they harbored a cesspool of hate and jealousy. Senator Sinal was a very powerful man when it came to connections and getting things done his way. Many feared him and with good reason. It was said that he made deals with the Devil; those were the rumors anyway, along with others, that only a few cared to discuss, trouble or ending up missing were, of course, content threats looming over the heads of those who opposed Senator Sinal.

Esteban took the elevator and saw his good friend Javier. Javier was a fairly new agent. He'd only been working in the department for less than a year but had worked with Esteban a few times.

"Hola Javier," Esteban greeted.

"You look beat, Estaban. Must have been another one of those long meetings that politicians like to have," Javier commented. He was all smiles and cheery tones, typical of the men who had not been in the field long.

"It's worse; I actually wanted to shut them up with super glue this time," Esteban replied. "They keep repeating the same thing without a sense of trying to resolve anything. I'm beginning to feel more like a babysitter each time."

"Relax, Esteban, in a year, you'll be making your own rules and writing your own ticket."

"That's all that's keeping me going, Javier, for now anyway."

"I'd like to be in your shoes right now; I still have ways to go before I put in my time and be in your position."

"Well, I better go... the "Woman" finally wants to talk things over about that night." Esteban looked above Javier's head at a clock.

"I bet she does." Javier laughed. "Call me if you need medical help; I know a good short-haired nurse with a fine ass that can ease your pain."

"Ha, ha, you're a barrel of laughs," Esteban replied as Javier wiggled his eyebrows. "See you Monday."

"Adios." Javier waved as he walked past Esteban.

The congressional building was huge. Usually, it was filled with people from all walks of life, especially reporters. Since it was late, it seemed rather empty compared to its usual day.

As Esteban walked to his car, he saw two young kids who appeared to be teenagers. At first, he thought they were just admiring his car, but as he crept closer, he noticed a crowbar in one of their hands.

"Hey! What the hell are you doing!" Esteban broke into a sprint.

The young kids couldn't have been older than 16; they turned around immediately, hands raised as if prepared to attack. One pulled out a knife, while the other one had a crowbar clutched between his sweaty fingers. Esteban quickly anticipated their move and, in a flash, side-kicked the one holding the knife and flipped the other one, swinging the crowbar and slamming him flat on his back. The kids never had a chance.

Sprawled on the ground, they grunted in pain, barely able to breathe. The owner of the knife clutched at his stomach, coughing and dry heaving. His eyes filled with tears. The other was beside him on the cold concrete, slowly moving from side to side as if trying to rock himself into a peaceful slumber.

Esteban pulled his plastic cuffs out and roughly put them on the pathetically struggling kids while they were face down on the pavement. He grabbed his radio and pressed the call button.

"Security! I've captured these pandilleros trying to steal my car! I'm in parking lot B3. Send someone over here. Now!"

Esteban couldn't understand why this was happening. He scanned the parking lot, counting five cameras that would have a perfect view of what had been happening with his car and the young delinquents.

The punk stayed face down; nose pressed on the concrete as they waited for security to arrive. One moved his head to the side, glaring at Esteban until his eyes traveled to his wrists. He looked toward his own and nudged his friend, indicating Esteban's wrist with a nod. The tattoo on Esteban's wrist was the same as theirs.

"How can he have the same mark as us?" one whispered.

"I don't know, but I don't like it... I hope to God they don't kill us now," the other responded.

"Don't say anything, just keep your mouth shut."

They spoke in hushed tones, a tremble in their voice. Their eyes shifted around them quickly as beads of sweat formed on their foreheads.

Esteban noticed their whispers and their tattoos but said nothing.

Clearly furious, he launched into a lecture on the consequences of attempting to steal a car on government property. He barked at them like a drill sergeant, his voice booming at ear level in the middle of the parking lot. The young punks quickly regretted ever trying to steal the man's car, their bravado crumbling as their eyes filled with tears.

Security finally arrived, and the boys were put in the squad car. Five security guards are huffing and puffing, acting like they were late for work.

"I'm glad no one took their own sweet time!" Esteban yelled.

The security officers looked very embarrassed and didn't know what to say. One shuffled his feet awkwardly while another pretended to trace with his fingers where the security cameras were pointed.

"An old, blind, lame dog is better than this multi-million dollar surveillance you all seem to have. Where the hell is security when there is a vehicle being stolen? My car was nearly stolen from underneath your noses, but you don't care, of course!"

The security guards did not meet Esteban's eye. "We saw the whole thing on the video scan, and we were taking measures in apprehending these juveniles, sir," one of the security guards said.

"Oh, so you saw it on video and reacted as slowly as a wart growing on your ass!" Esteban raised his voice. "This day can't get any worse! Who the hell hired you? Listen, I don't have time for this shit! You can bet your ass this will be reported to your superiors, and your badge numbers will be on it!"

Esteban pulled a notepad from his pocket and began writing down the names and badge numbers of the security men. "This is the third incident this month! What the hell is security good for if we keep getting mugged or carjacked? Next time, someone will be murdered, and all that security will be able to say is, 'I'm sorry! I was watching it all on video, but I was too scared to go get the bad guy.'" He pocketed his notepad.

One of the guards was impatiently tapping his foot. Esteban got in his face and continued his tirade of insults. "Well, that's not good enough for the family of the victims! Is it? This is supposed to be a well-guarded facility, the best that this country has to offer, and here I am, almost getting my car stolen by two punk teenage gang members! What if the President was with me?" He turned to face the others. "Do you think he'd be amused if this were to happen while he was escorted to his car? If two kids with no sophisticated training can get in here to steal a car, then any psycho/terrorist can come in here and destroy this facility! What kind of security are you if you can't even protect the area where congressmen or even the President preside every day? I'm glad I'm not in your shoes because your heads are going to roll!"

None of them said a word back to him. None had answers.

"Enjoy your weekend! I'm sure you'll be looking forward to Monday." Esteban opened his car door and gave one last seething look at the guards.

The security guards were shitting bricks, feeling like they were on death row. They looked at each other in distress.

Esteban got in his car, slammed the door, and sped out of the parking lot. His nostrils flared as he rounded a turn way too fast. He kept thinking about why nothing had been done to improve security. It defied all his training and reasoning. It was very difficult for him to tolerate any stupidity that violated security. It was something that came naturally to him, so he resented anyone who was lax in their job, as it meant the protection of lives, property, and secrets.

He called his close friend Chavez, who was one of the men in charge of the Secret Service and security. He picked up the cell phone and waited for Chavez to answer.

Click.

"Chavez, this is Esteban."

"Qué tal amigo," Chavez responded very enthusiastically.

"Chavez, I don't mean to call you at 11 p.m., but there was an incident at the parking lot in the congressional building just minutes ago," Esteban sounded very stern and dissatisfied. "Two snot-nose gangsters almost stole my car."

"Shit, I can't believe it," Chavez said with a surprised tone in his voice, his previous enthusiasm leaving him.

"Well, I caught them and cuffed them. I turned them over to the fat security legion that exists there, but with security's performance record, I'd bet the two gangsters will get away from those idiots."

"I don't know what to say, Esteban. I will make sure someone's ass will be on fire; you can guarantee that," Chavez answered angrily. "Esteban, you know that I'm doing everything possible to make things right. You're the only one I can trust, and I appreciate you calling me first. I know how all this could be blown out of proportion if the media got a hold of it."

"I'm just glad that I have a few days off for now," Esteban said. "I just thought you should know what happened before the news added their shit tactics to it."

"I'm glad you called me, and I'm glad you're alright."

"It takes more than two punks to damage me, you know that, Chavez," Esteban said sarcastically.

"Oh, I know it... and believe me, I'd hate to be the man to really piss you off."

As cocky as Esteban was feeling, he couldn't shake his discomfort with the whole ordeal. "This concerns me, Chavez, because if two punks can just walk in there, what will stop a trained maniac."

"Esteban, I understand, and believe me, this will be dealt with, especially when it comes from you."

"We've been friends a long time, Chavez, and you're one of the few I can trust."

They both knew that their trust in each other went back several years, and they took that trust to heart.

"OK, well, let's get together sometime in the next few days to just talk like friends," Chavez says. "You know that I'll always be there for you, Estaban. You've saved my ass more times than I've pissed, so I'm always in your debt."

"Hey, you're my friend, and I trust you, so don't get sentimental on me." A smile broke through the frown that had been on his face since he saw the thieves. "In this business, trust is more precious than gold."

"OK, amigo, go home, and I'll take care of the whole thing."

"I'll see you later Chavez." Esteban hung up the phone.

I need to just relax, totally be alone for a little while, he thought. *This is a good excuse to try that tequila my cousin sent me. I can use the best drink that Mexico has to offer. I may need several drinks once I've talked things over with Isabel.*

The drive was about an hour long due to traffic and signal lights.

As he labored through the streets at a snail's pace, he began thinking about the two kids. Esteban was a good analyzer and usually figured things out, sometimes in the strangest places. *I can't believe the gang is still active,* he thought. *I shouldn't have been that rough with them, but they pissed me off.*

He kept driving with many questions on his mind; the activity around him seemed to blur as he moved forward, his mind going a million miles a second when his car only moved a few feet. *How the hell did they ever manage to get in? The place is supposed to be so well-guarded. I smell something wrong. I'll let Chavez handle this for now. He's a good friend, and I have no one else I can really trust.*

Esteban was a well-trained agent. Security was always on his mind. He looked at even the most minor details to figure out if there was a threat of any kind. It was his job, and he was extremely good at it. Many clients constantly asked for him whenever they wanted to be totally secure during events. Chavez always kidded around and used to say he was the best that Mexico had to offer as he imitated the tone in one of those famous tequila ads.

Chavez would say, "The best cabron is Esteban mi pinchi amigo... el puede chingar a cualquier cabron." Translated, the phrase says, 'Esteban is the best fucker and the best motherfucker as a friend, and he can kick any motherfucker's ass.' Most of the time, he would say that when he was drunk on the tequila from the ads, but Esteban would always see it as a nice gesture from a friend. At times, he had to calm Chavez down because he'd like to exaggerate things... as any normal drunk would. They had gotten drunk many times together and had gotten in trouble along the way.

As his hands clutched the steering wheel, his eyes moved from the road before him and focused on his wrist, on the tattoo – the Aztec sun.

2

When Esteban was eleven, he lived in a poor neighborhood in Guadalajara, Mexico. His life was a simple one. He had a mother and father who were poor and were not always able to manage from day to day. His father, Rafael, was a quiet man. He didn't really know his father well because he was gone most of the time. He was the kind of man who worked wherever employment was available, mostly in construction, where manual labor was always in demand. His father would write home from time to time, especially when he had to work on various job sites for extended periods. Despite his absence from Esteban's life and home, he would not hesitate to show affection to his son. He would always write to Esteban or say that he loved him and was proud of him.

Esteban's mother was a strong and determined woman named Josefina. She was a maid who spent long hours working for a rich, stuck-up family. His mother was usually overworked and underpaid. She would go to the houses of the wealthy people of her country and watch as they gave no appreciation or acknowledgment of the privileges they held, but worst of all, they did not treat her well. Many times, his mother fell ill, but she had to keep working to support the family when money didn't come in from her husband. Her employers were not kind or compassionate enough to let her take time off to get well. Times were hard, and situations were difficult, but somehow, Esteban's mother made it through, and things worked out.

Esteban learned to accept his way of life like all children his age. He spent a lot of time visiting his grandfather, who happened to be blind. His grandfather's name was Moises, and he was of Mexican Indian descent on his mother's side. He had a lot of stories that he told Esteban. Esteban would visit him every other day, depending on his school and chores. His grandfather used to tell him about all the hunting he did as a young boy and that he fought in the Revolution of 1910 alongside Emiliano Zapata. Esteban was always thrilled to hear his grandfather talk about the revolution. His grandfather said he used to carry out orders from Zapata himself and that, at one time, he was exalted for a job well done on one of the raids. These stories intrigued Esteban every time he visited his grandfather. It seems like there was always a different story to tell every time he visited his grandfather.

Through his stories and teachings, Moises taught him how to always have honor and to seek the truth. "The way to the truth is to follow the heart," is what his grandfather used to say to Esteban. He considered his grandfather a wise man and believed everything he told him. "Esteban, one day when you become a man, you will see things a lot different than now; it's part of growing up," his grandfather used to say as well.

One rainy day, Esteban made his way to his grandfather's house with a heavy heart and a sad expression painted on his face. As he entered and put his school bag down, he said, "I don't think I am very special. I feel so alone in school. No one wants to be around me."

His grandfather had only smiled at the boy. He took out a bead necklace with some stones on it. The stones seemed to shine when the lights hit them; they emitted a bright blue hue and sparkled. His grandfather said, "These stones are blessed by a shaman. They keep away the bad spirits. My father gave me this necklace and now. I want to give them to you."

As Esteban reached his hand out to clasp the necklace, his grandfather continued, "Everyone is special. Especially you. That is why you must have this special necklace. It has saved me from many mortal fights. As you can see, I've lived to tell about it," his grandfather said. "Your grandfather wasn't always like this. I was a very strong man and was afraid of nothing, but as you get older, you realize that courage is a small part of being a man... you must also love and have compassion, above all, be close to God."

Esteban gazed at the necklace in his hands and rubbed his thumb over its stones.

"I want you to be blessed as I was, Esteban." His grandfather put his hand on Esteban's head and blessed him in his own way.

The boy's eyes filled with tears. He knew then that that necklace was one that he would cherish throughout his life.

Sometime later, Esteban had to move to a different school. There, he quickly realized that cliques were something that you had to be in, and some of those cliques were gangs. You had your "prep boys or rich boys," your "want to be popular boys," and the tough "want to be gang boys." Even though all of the kids were only children, the cliques were categorized by family status and the income their families made, just as it was in adult life. Esteban fell to the very bottom where the gang boys were, whether he liked it or not.

His teachers, at times, judged the kids on how they conducted themselves but also on who they hung around with and their economic status. He was picked on and several times ganged up on by other boys making fun of him; the teachers, of course, did nothing about it. Since he didn't have the best clothes or, in fact, didn't even have many clothes, he ended up wearing the same clothes for many days. Naturally, all of the boys made fun of his poor clothes, where he lived, and the way he was. He didn't seem to fit in.

His mother always told him not to get into fights and that she never wanted a bad report from school. He always did his homework and was smart, but being bullied from time to time made it difficult for him to have friends the way he wanted. It didn't take long for him to realize that being in a gang would protect him from getting beaten up by other boys.

He joined the "want-to-be gang" of "Los Panchitos." They seemed to welcome him since they were poor themselves and they lived in the same barrio. This gang was notorious for being cruel and tough; most of its members were in the higher age groups of sixteen and up. The older gang activity actually involved people getting seriously hurt and sometimes killed. Elementary and middle school kids tried to imitate them because of all the things they heard about them. They considered "Los Panchitos" like Robin Hood heroes, but they never actually mentioned all the robberies and deaths they caused. Esteban considered himself one of the gang. Several days after being in the gang, other boys began to leave him alone. He didn't travel alone anymore, and he felt wanted and respected. He just knew that he wasn't going to be picked on anymore and that he actually had people he could hang around with.

When he was about to turn 13, his gang was about to get into a brawl with another rival gang. It was their first rumble, and he didn't know how things were going to turn out. Inside, he was scared, but at the same time, he felt like he had to fight to protect his friends. The opposing gang was going to meet in an abandoned warehouse, and his gang was going to be there to brawl. They made plans to meet there after school.

When the time came, members of both gangs showed up. The boys held sticks and had logos showing their gang's affinity plastered all over them. They also had symbols showing their level of authority. Each side was trying to show that they were tougher than the other. They stood tall and glared across the space, trying to tell the other gang that they would be losing today. A few cried out, hurling curses and slurs toward the others. They hit their sticks to the floor and tried to look intimidating.

From where they were, they could barely see the edge of the barrio. They were sandwiched in a narrow alleyway beside the abandoned warehouse. Here, they had little visibility of what was happening around them, and so, little did they know that a third party was lurking in the area, observing them.

Suddenly, the boys were thrown for a loop, scrambling and shouting as grown men with real weapons infiltrated their brawl space. Before they could react, both gangs were surrounded by men on bikes and on foot. They revved their engines loud. They screamed and hooted and made gestures of intimidation.

The "want to be panchitos" didn't know what to do. They only saw that they were about to be turned into hamburger meat. They were all trembling, looking around themselves with bloodshot, wide eyes. The real gang made a move, turning and throwing themselves as the opposing gang. They noticed the gang signs plastered over the men; they were the real "Panchitos." Hooting and shouting, they began to attack the other gang. They pulled out knives, sticks, and clubs and raised them as they approached. A few boys were stabbed, and several were badly beaten up.

After the brawl, they turned their attention to the unharmed boys and took the "want-to-be gang" to their place, where they began to question them. They were taken to a section inside the old warehouse. Their money and possessions were taken away. Not a word was said.

A man, tall, dark, and angry-looking, made his way toward the boys. He held his head up high, his shoulders were broad, and his chest looked massive. Before he reached the boys, he spat on the floor. The symbols he had on his vest told the boys that he was the leader.

"I want to know why the hell are you punks using our name! Who the hell are you pretending to be!"

"El Huitre," said one of the gang members, "These punks don't know their place. They have no idea what it means to be a part of "Los Panchitos.""

El Huitre pursed his lips and nodded, locking eyes with one of the smaller boys in the group.

"I want to be just like you," the boy said bravely.

All the boys were shaking and keeping their hands clenched into fists. Some looked down at the floor while others scanned their surroundings, searching for a window or doorway through which they could escape. Some began to cry, saying that they didn't want to die. Los Panchitos' leader was a rough character. His name meant buzzard. He dressed in loose clothing with a chain as a belt and had tattooed stripes on his forearms. He had some gold chains on his neck and a blonde streak across his head. When he spoke, a gold tooth stood out like a sore thumb.

The gang leader, Huitre, said, "Oh, so you want to be like us, huh? Well... only a few brave people get to be in our army, punks. I don't like faggot boys pretending they're us, especially crying faggots. But I'll give you a chance to prove yourself and be like us. You see this," he pointed to his forearm. His forearm has some army-like stripes. "Every mark that I have here is how many motherfuckers I've killed," he says loud and proudly. "Since you want to be one of us, you have to go through the same schooling, and I am your commander-in-chief... you will always do what I say, or else you'll be marked." He jabbed his finger onto one of the tattoos.

The boys were in dead silence, especially Esteban. He didn't know how he could ever get mixed up in this, but it was something that had built up since he was hanging around the gang. All he could think was that his mother would be so hurt if she knew what he was doing.

"Your initiation starts now, and we'll see if you can be worthy to be one of us." Each small boy had to endure being beaten up by three other gang members. If that individual endured the beating and was still able to walk or run away, then they were in. Out of the ten boys, only two were still able to stand up. One of them was Esteban. The "Panchitos" then took both of them and tattooed an Aztec sun on their right wrist. The process was painful, but it was part of the initiation. At this time, the pain didn't quite matter to Esteban. He was just glad that the beating stopped and he was alive. After that, there was no turning back; he was in. The real gang laughed and made fun of them.

The leader then said, "Now that you're in, you do as we say. Especially when I give you orders. You belong to us. We'll come and get you when we need you. When I say come, you come; when I say fetch, you fetch. Oh, by the way, if you tell anyone, especially the police, about this, we'll kill you. It won't end with you... your sister and mother are all up for grabs you understand?"

The gang leader smiled at Esteban and the other boy. El Huitre's tooth stood out every time he smiled. Both boys just nodded. They both were going along so that this would end, and they would be able to get the hell out of there. As they stood there in shock and embarrassment, laughter erupted around them, low, sarcastic, haughty laughter. They knew that their life wasn't going to be the same and that it could mean the difference between living and dying someday.

After some time of talking among the gang members, the real Panchitos finally decided to leave. They spoke among themselves and didn't say a word to the two boys. They all stared at them for about a minute. It was like intimidation, saying that they were serious about what they said. They all turned around and left. They walked out of the warehouse, got in their car, and drove away. All was quiet after that.

Standing in the warehouse as the smaller boys slowly made their way out, holding their injured limbs and sobbing quietly, Esteban was still. He raised up his arm to see the new tattoo that had just been inked onto his wrist. For the amount of pain he went through, it wasn't a bad tattoo, but he knew it was one that would scar him for the rest of his life.

***

Esteban finally arrived at his apartment. He lived in an apartment complex that was very private and luxurious. A friend managed to get him the living arrangements. Esteban has the ability to have people owe him favors. He tended to save their ass most of the time, and the favor was always due. He learned this from previous military experiences and was very good at it.

He usually went to the gym after work, but tonight, he just felt like staying away from people; it was late. After the parking lot incident, he thought it was best to just be home. He had a lot on his mind. He also had to cool his temper down because he had to talk to his girlfriend, Isabel.

Esteban and Isabel had been dating for the past two years. She was a career woman, working for an advertising company as a public relations agent, and was very good at her job. She was also extremely beautiful. She had first caught Esteban's eye at the gym where they were both working out. He saw her several times there and, by coincidence, kept seeing her at big events. They got to know each other through brief meetings until, finally, Esteban couldn't resist any longer and asked her out for dinner. They knew each other fairly well because they kept in contact almost once or twice a week. If they didn't see each other at the gym, they'd see each other at a banquet or at a convention. Since then, they've had a close, intimate relationship. But now, they both seem to feel distant from each other. Things were getting rocky.

Isabel, at times, was a jealous woman, and trust was the issue that began to divide their love. Esteban was trying to understand, but at times, he felt that he was the jealous one, and he also began to judge her trust. This wasn't the issue when they started going out together. Esteban was a very handsome man, and he managed to attract women fairly easily, especially when he didn't want to, but Isabel was also a gorgeous woman who had no trouble making heads turn wherever she went. She used to model in high school and was the beauty queen of her college. She was offered several modeling contracts but refused them to continue her education. Slowly, Isabel noticed that Esteban could also turn some heads. She had always known that; she just never accepted it. At first, it never bothered her, but after being around Esteban, certain things annoyed her, especially when other women started noticing him while they were together.

Esteban checked his mail and then walked up to his apartment. *I should have moved to the first floor; it would have been much easier to be in my apartment,* he grumbled to himself. When he got to his room, 313, he heard the phone ring. He hurried to open it, but they hung up as he opened the door. *I guess they would call back later.* He started his answering machine to check his messages. Most seemed to be friends saying hi, but two of the messages were from Isabel. "Isabel, why are you like this?" he said in a sad, pouting voice.

On the voicemail, Isabel said she was going to arrive from Miami and wanted Esteban to pick her up from the airport.

The problem was that the plane had arrived over an hour ago, and Esteban had no idea he was supposed to pick her up. *So much for the tequila tonight.* He picked up the phone and called Isabel's cell phone. He felt as though he was about to be punished again.

The cell phone rang, and Isabel picked up.

"Isabel? It's Esteban."

"Where have you been, Esteban? I've been here at the airport for almost two hours!" She sounded very frustrated.

Esteban took a deep breath, "I didn't know that I was supposed to come pick you up at the airport; you didn't tell me." Esteban was not in the mood to be in any type of argument.

"I was going to surprise you," she said.

"I was still in a meeting with the Senators, and it went beyond the usual length."

"Please come pick me up; I really want to go home."

"OK, Amor, I'll see you in a few minutes. I'll call you as soon as I arrive at the airport."

He hung up the phone and went to the bedroom to take off his suit and put on some more comfortable clothes. *I don't believe I'll be able to have the talk with Isabel; it will have to wait. We're both in a negative mood. It will be best to talk it over when the right moment comes along. God...please give me patience and strength to deal with this woman.*

As he stepped into the bedroom, he just took a deep breath, getting ready to yell. "Isabel, if I didn't love you, I'd leave you as fast as I could!" he shouted, trying to relieve some tension from all that had happened in the last few hours.

Meanwhile, Isabel was in a cafe inside the airport. She was talking to her mother on the cell phone, confirming that Esteban was picking her up. "Mother, don't worry, Esteban just spoke to me, and he's on his way to pick me up."

"I know, hija, but a mother worries no matter if her daughter is dating Superman."

Isabel laughed. "Well, sometimes I wonder about that too, Mother."

"He thinks he's Superman. I sure hope he understands the new job you might be getting," her mother said.

"Me too, mother, but I believe that Esteban will be understanding; he'll be sort of quiet at first, then he'll slowly see that it's something that will help my career," Isabel said. "This doesn't happen every day, and it could be a chance of a lifetime." Isabel smiled.

"I'm very proud of you, Isabel... if your father was alive, he'd say the same thing," her mother said in a sweet voice.

"I have you and Papa to thank."

"Are you still upset with Esteban from the convention dinner?"

"Mother, I don't want to discuss that right now," Isabel replied sort of angrily.

"I just want you to be happy, that's all."

"We haven't talked, but we'll work on it," Isabel responded.

"You're a great daughter, and speaking of that, did you bring me the things I asked you to bring?"

Isabel smiled, "Yes, Mother, I did. You said they were a few things, but Mother, the list was so long I had to pay extra at customs for all the stuff I brought, and that's not including the search they did."

"You didn't have to get everything," her mother said in an innocent way.

"You know I'd bring anything you asked, but please, next time, make it one or two things, not twenty." They both laughed. "I better go, Mother; my battery is getting low. I'll see you tomorrow morning then, and Mother, I love you."

"Yo te quiero tambien, hija," her mother responded.

Isabel hung up and began to drink her coffee.

Esteban left his apartment and headed to the airport. Traffic in Mexico City was a driver's nightmare. He had to use all five senses just to stay alive on the road. So much went on every time he took the wheel. Esteban saw it as a normal routine. He was a part-time chauffeur in his job, and he was well-trained in how to avoid bad situations in all kinds of traffic. He was thinking about what to say to Isabel. He had had a bad day and he couldn't appear like he was reluctant to pick her up. They were still trying to patch things up from the last incident they just had. *I hope that Isabel is just a little more understanding. She has to realize that looks are not all what they appear.* He began to recall the situation that made Isabel jealous and put doubt in her mind. *If she would only listen to me and see things the logical way... God. Why did you make women so damn stubborn? They always seemed to read more shit into a situation than there was; I know it wasn't an accident; it was an intentional thing, but I wish she would hear me out.*

***

Over four weeks ago, a fundraising event was held in a luxurious hotel. Sports companies were raising funds for charity work, and government officials were there to get some of the spotlight. Congressmen and Senators always seem to be invited to big events when it comes to important athletic functions. Esteban was working as security at the event. A former girlfriend of Esteban, Sara, was at the function. Estaban couldn't quite decide yet if that was a bad thing or not.

Sara used to be a former beauty queen and a model in college. Esteban knew she would be there because she had called and left him two messages at his apartment. He didn't really know how she got his number because he had everything unlisted.

He noticed Sara talking to different people for only a few minutes at a time. Each time she stopped, she would scan the room and almost seemed disheartened when someone else approached her to make small talk. Sara was the kind of pretty that made men turn into idiots when they were close to her. She had no problems with socializing since each man was almost tripping over the next, trying to get a chance to speak with her. Sara had the ability to be an expert flirt, giving her a greater edge. That's how she'd gotten everything she'd wanted. Esteban knew that Sara was prowling for him. He stepped out into the open so she could see him but turned to the side to make it seem as if he had not yet seen her. She spotted him but very politely kept a distance to time her presence just right.

During the mingle part of the party, Sara approaches Esteban.

"Hello Esteban," Sara said.

"What a surprise," Esteban responded, pretending he didn't know she'd be there. "What are you doing here?" Esteban asked her curiously.

"Well, since I'm also in the commercial trade, I am one of the clients that people want to sell things to, and so, I'm here," she replied.

"I must say, you're still as attractive as ever."

"Why, thank you. I didn't think you'd notice anything about me," she responded sarcastically.

"I always knew you were beautiful, Sara, and I'm glad that your trade seems to be working well."

"We all have our things that work."

Esteban heard a buzzing in his earpiece. He was getting a call. "I have to move to another position; excuse me, I may be able to see you later in another part of the building," he said and started to move toward a crowd.

Sara still wanted Esteban. He appeared more handsome and far better looking than ever before. Not that he wasn't handsome when Sara and Esteban were together, but now he was well educated, established, well built, extremely eloquent, and had everything a woman would want from a man like

Esteban. She always desired him, and tonight, she wanted him even more. Sara was eyeing him from a distance and thinking of ways to persuade him to take her. She didn't have any intention of sleeping with him when she first arrived at the function, but after seeing him in person after so many years and witnessing how he worked, she was flabbergasted, like a damsel in distress, desiring her knight and shining armor to sweep her off her feet.

At times, she had to go back a few times to her group and later came back to look for him to start a conversation. She couldn't stay away from him. Esteban was in another area, close to some people, acting as if he were mingling. Since he was a security agent, he would do this a lot so that he'd be able to blend in and not look so suspicious. As a woman approached him, Sara decided that now was the time. She swooped in, grabbing a glass of wine from a tray as she walked and slotted herself between Esteban and the approaching woman.

"My, do you move around a lot?" she said, twirling her hair.

"Well, it's part of my job to guard against the bad guys," he replied.

Sara kept looking at him with seductive eyes. She was using all her femininity to attract her prey. "The bad guys, huh... I'm not one of those bad guys, am I?" she said to see what kind of response Esteban gave her.

"No, you're not one of those bad guys... I don't believe you would be a bad person like the ones I've chased before." Esteban was thrown; he found the question somewhat weird, but as he looked into her mesmerizing eyes, he was too occupied to care.

"Well, at least they're being chased by you, which is more than I can say for me," she said as she licked the rim of her glass.

Esteban grinned a little and tried to change the subject. He started to think about what he should say next, but couldn't stop staring at Sara.

"You have a very lovely dress, Sara; it makes you look very beautiful," Esteban said. "I always knew that you'd be a great sight to see. Tell me, what is it that you do besides your commercial trade?"

She didn't even notice that last sentence. All she heard was the comment about her being beautiful. Almost in a daze, she responded, "Well, Esteban... you know.... that I always tried my best to look good for you even now that I haven't seen you in years." She slowly walked up to him while looking at him very seductively. She was right in front of him, looking at him like she was about to make her move.

Esteban knew what she was doing but felt almost frozen. Plus, he did not want her to stop. He opened his mouth to respond, and she fell onto him, pressing her lips against his softly. She pulled back and smiled at him slowly as Esteban held his mouth open, not knowing what to say.

Her whole body seemed as if being pulled toward him like a magnet. Her eyes were half closed, looking up at him. "Esteban, I want you tonight; I've missed you, and you're the man who can satisfy me right now."

Esteban only looked at her with a blank stare and a blank mind. All he could focus on was the way her hair softly fell against her flushing cheeks.

"Sara, you're very beautiful, but I can't be doing this at a time like this. I'm working, and any little thing I do may be taken the wrong way; besides, I can get in trouble with my job, not to mention that my girlfriend is here as well." He looked around in fear.

Esteban picked up a glass of soda, drank it, and stared at Sara. His heart was beating fast, and he was taken by total surprise. He didn't expect anything like this at all, especially in a public function while he was working as a bodyguard for a Senator who is like a hero to him.

Sara just stared at Esteban in a trance. He didn't like the stare she was giving him. It was a stare of pure sexual desire with magic that would definitely work on him. It was hard for him to resist because she was a good-looking woman, and he'd had her before when he was in the academy. Any other man would take the ball and score it for a touchdown, but he knew the consequences.

"I heard you were married." Esteban tried to change the subject again.

"It's only a formal engagement," Sara responded with little interest. "We don't love each other; we're only together for business and society. You know, appearances have to be kept." Sara then grabbed Esteban by the hand and looked at him closely in his eyes. "After this is over, come to my room. I want you badly, Esteban," she persisted in her seduction. "I want to make love to you as erotically as I can... I will make you beg for more," she whispered with authority. "You don't know how much I've missed you." She looked at him. "I've always desired you and loved you; I was a fool to ever let you go."

Esteban felt like he was in the wrong place for this. His job was to be a security agent with no attention on him, but it felt like the spotlight was beginning to shine on him.

"I have these feelings that only you can satisfy. I know that we've been apart for several years, but I haven't stopped thinking about you. I knew you were going to be here, and I planned it all along to meet you here; I need you, Esteban." She looked at him very passionately and held his hand tight. "I want to take you somewhere in private... please," she said with despair.

"I can't leave my post, Sara, not just for the hell of it," Esteban looked around as he said it.

"We'll pretend that you're helping me to the phone booths over there," she said desperately. She took Esteban by the hand and dragged him into a dark hall where phone booths were available.

"Sara, I can't do this. I have to get back," Esteban said nervously.

"Oh Esteban, don't you remember all the good times we had?" she began to act really sexy, twirling herself around Esteban.

"I can never forget those moments... but that was a long time ago, and we're both different now and have different commitments." Esteban was trying to be professional, but he was getting excited.

She looked at him and caressed his face.

"Sara, you're married." Esteban tried to make it a point.

"My so-called husband is never around, and I know deep in my heart that he has another woman, and I really don't give a damn if he does," she said with no remorse.

"Well, I don't make it a policy to be with married women." Esteban was looking at her, unable to move. She kissed him lightly and then kissed him again, but this time with passion. She grabbed his chest, and then her hands slipped to his butt and then to his crotch.

Esteban didn't put up his defenses.

He took the long, passionate kiss that Sara gave him. He is shocked and froze up. Esteban couldn't help but notice that Sara was looking extremely attractive. Her dress hugged every feminine curve that she had to offer, with no end in sight. He felt like he was drifting into a spell of enchantment with her kisses and moves. She was always extremely sexy. They had a good time being together while he was in the Academy.

Esteban always managed to get the attractive ladies no matter where he went. At times, they came to him, but not all in perfect timing... and the cycle continues. Sara was in the heat of the moment and wanted Esteban all to herself. She regretted every moment of ever letting him go. Esteban tried to reason with her while they were kissing, but she didn't give him a chance to even breathe.

He then broke away from her enough to just say a sentence, "My girlfriend is here, and she wouldn't understand." He said it a little loud. "Isabel is my girlfriend. She's here, and this isn't right. I love Isabel, and I can't do this," Esteban said in a low but almost victimized way.

Sara launched herself and kissed him again more passionately than the last time. As soon as she launched herself toward Esteban, Isabel happened to walk in and was standing directly behind him. Sara opened her eyes while kissing Esteban and saw a woman behind him, and immediately stopped kissing Esteban. Esteban turned around, and Isabel was staring at him with tearful, crying eyes.

She had a terrible, angry, sad look in her eyes. She slapped and screamed at Esteban, "You bastard," and walked toward the crowd, crying. Esteban knew he was in trouble. His heart sank. Esteban felt horrible.

"Sara, look what you've done now," he yelled at Sara. "Now Isabel won't want to understand," he said sadly. He went after her, but he lost her in the crowd. He couldn't stray far because he was still part of security at the function. He went back to his post and endured the rest of the event.

All that time, he looked for Isabel and thought of ways to ask her to forgive him, to hear his side of the story. He kept seeing Isabel's face in shock and humiliation. Esteban felt like he had betrayed someone way closer than a friend. He knew he needed to explain, but Isabel wouldn't have wanted any explanation. He didn't know what to do. All he could do was do his job for now, and that included watching people mingle and form crowds.

Sara hadn't given up so easily. She gave Esteban many clues as to where she was staying. He ignored them all. He hadn't seen Isabel for the rest of the night. After the event, he was not able to get a hold of her. He called her, but no one answered except her answering machine. He hadn't gotten any word from Isabel's mother either. He felt very guilty, especially since he hadn't had a chance to explain. It had been days since he had heard even a word from her.

The next day, all his work colleagues were giving him a hard time. They called him "the stud, Romeo, the lady's man." That's something he didn't want to happen because it could be overblown, especially as a bodyguard in the Secret Service. He knew they were kidding, but that's how nicknames get started. Not only that, many of the people that he had to protect tended to be women, so he certainly didn't want any negativity on that part. He usually worried more than he should in situations like that, but he was afraid to lose Isabel because of a stupid misunderstanding. After several days of giving Esteban the silent treatment, Isabel finally spoke to him. He began to slowly explain his side of the story, but Isabel was inconsolable. He knew he had some hard work ahead but he also knew that he did not want to let Isabel go.

3

He finally arrived at the airport and called her cell phone to tell her that he was there. "Isabel, I'm here, finally," he said. "Are you at the terminal?"

"No, I am in a café about two stores down from there," she responded. "I am in the Colombian Cafe."

"OK, I'll see you there in five minutes." He then hung up the phone. As usual, it was a madhouse. It seemed like the whole world was flying into the city. He parked his car at the very front and headed toward the terminal. *I guess there are some advantages to working for the government.* Most people were not allowed to park directly in front except government officials. He parked the car and told the security guard to keep an eye on it. He began to walk toward the terminal and saw many athletes who were arriving. They appeared to be soccer players. Mexico was a major force in soccer, especially in Mexico City. All the major tournaments and final games were decided in the capital. He wondered if he'd have to work during one of the games. He was usually right on feelings like that. Celebrity athletes needed protection most of the time. He was so used to protecting famous people, but his favorites were athletes. They tended to be easy to talk to and more down-to-earth. He guessed he got along better with them because he had a lot in common with them, especially when it came to training. Esteban loved physical training.

He spotted Isabel sitting at a table in the café. She was sitting and talking to a blonde woman. Esteban's heart leaped when he saw her. *She looks so gorgeous.* Isabel was wearing a short black skirt with a red coat. Her legs were very well shaped and very well defined. She was naturally tan all over with black hair that passed her shoulders. Any place that she puts her legs, men could not help but stare. *And to think she's mine and she likes me for some unknown reason.* The aggravation that he had seemed to pass away to some extent. *Isabel could make any angry man kneel before her.* Her long black hair could have easily been in a shampoo commercial. He walked closer, and she saw him. She got up, smiled, and walked slowly toward him. They hugged and kissed. She made a face at him and said, "I missed you, Esteban."

"I missed you too, Isabel." He took her hand. "I want to apologize for many things, Isabel," he said in a very low, sad voice. "I would like to talk in private about it sometime-" he said.

"I know, for now, let's just enjoy my arrival, and we'll talk about it another time," Isabel cut him short. They made their way back to her table. Isabel looked at the woman that she was sitting with and introduced her to Esteban. "Cindy, this is my novio (boyfriend), who I was still mad at, and Esteban, this is Cindy."

Cindy laughed. "Good to meet you, Esteban, you're more handsome than Isabel described you."

"It's a pleasure to meet you too, Cindy, and thank you,"
Esteban replied. "Isabel is the gorgeous one and very hard to
win arguments with," he added.

"I like him," she stared at Isabel, "do you have a brother I
might be able to meet?"

Isabel and Esteban laughed. "If he did, I would've found
out a long time ago." Isabel looked at Esteban. "Cindy and I
met in Miami, and we were working on the same advertising
job. We had a lot of things in common, and we became friends.
She is here for the advertising of the soccer game for Nike. She
is staying at the Hilton Hotel. I told her we'd give her a ride
because, you know, I don't trust taxis. I'd told her it would be
OK," Isabel looked at him like it should be an instant approval.

"That's fine." He looked at her in a sarcastic way and
smiled. "I'll be happy to take her anywhere she wishes... any
friend of yours is a friend of mine," replied Esteban. He turned
to Cindy. "Well, are you ready to go?"

"Yes, we had to go get our bags," Cindy said.

"Let's go then," Esteban said. Esteban didn't expect to be a
chauffeur, but he was willing to help anyone that Isabel knew.
Taxis in Mexico City had recently developed a bad reputation
for posing as real taxis and then turning out to be impostors
robbing innocent tourists. He understood why Isabel wanted
him to give Cindy a ride.

They walked toward the baggage claim. Isabel and Cindy
kept the conversation going as they moved closer. They mostly
talked about their trip to Miami. Cindy was an American
woman, and her Spanish was very good. Esteban knew she had
lived in a Spanish-speaking country because no one could just

speak a language like that without the constant practice of everyday use. The women talked and mentioned all the things they had seen and gone through. They both worked for an advertising agency so that alone gave them plenty of topics.

"You don't know how glad I am to be home, Esteban," Isabel said as she raised her arms to hug him. "I love traveling, but I always miss my family and, most of all, you."

As Isabel was still squeezing him, Cindy chimed in. "All she talked about was 'Esteban, Esteban, Esteban.' I feel like I know you already." She gave Esteban a smile.

"I hope she kept her innermost secrets private," Esteban replied. "A man can feel like he has nowhere to hide if his secrets are exposed," he joked, but with a different tone, a more serious one.

"I believe she only told me the good things about you. Believe me, I wanted to know more about the secret stuff, but she wouldn't tell me." Cindy laughed.

"We all need a good night's sleep then?" Esteban said, trying to change the subject.

They finally reached the baggage claim. Isabel had four big suitcases and a large box. Esteban laughed and said, "I can't believe all these are yours, Isabel."

"Well, my mother wanted me to bring some things, and I didn't realize how much until I actually packed them."

"I need a van, not a car, to take all this," Esteban replied. "We'll just have to squeeze in real tight. I'm sure we can make it fit."

"You're good at that, aren't you?" Isabel replied, giving him a playful, suggestive look.

Esteban made a face at her to signal her to stop before Cindy overheard. He managed to get all the luggage in the car, and they all got in. They were finally on their way to drop off Cindy. The hotel where Cindy was staying was very fancy, and at night, it looked like something out of a movie set in Las Vegas.

"Ever been to Mexico City, Cindy?" Esteban asked.

"I did when I was a teenager, but it seems so much bigger now," she replied.

"Well, being the largest city in the world, it has every right to look big," Esteban said.

As they drove, Cindy admired all the lights and buildings that she didn't recall from her last trip. "It was like being in a sci-fi movie here," said Cindy.

"You ought to have tried going to work every morning through this traffic, and you will wish it was just a movie," replied Esteban. "You speak Spanish very well, Cindy; where did you learn to speak the language?"

"I took it ever since I was in middle school and I came to different parts of Mexico and Central America as I was growing up, so I managed to learn it in that way," she replied.

"That was a great way to learn it. It was good to see people making an effort to know other people's language and way of life. We needed more people like that all the time."

They arrived at the Hilton. They stopped and unloaded Cindy's bags. They got out, and Cindy said, "I greatly appreciate the lift." As she was picking up a bag, she said, "You were very kind, Isabel, and your boyfriend was very nice and good-looking."

"I hope you might know someone that you might introduce me to so that I might practice my Spanish," smiled Cindy.

"Well, you wouldn't have had any problem finding admirers," replied Isabel. Cindy was your typical all-American-looking girl with her long blonde hair and sparkling blue eyes.

Esteban got a bellboy to attend to the baggage. "Cindy, it was a pleasure to meet you, and I hope you have a nice stay," Esteban said. "If there is anything that I could do for you while you are here, please don't hesitate to ask."

"With my approval, of course," Isabel interjected sarcastically.

"Don't take any candy from any strangers," said Esteban, wagging his finger at Cindy.

"Don't worry, I'm on a diet," replied Cindy. "Thank you, Isabel, and I'll call you tomorrow so that we can plan our interview with the ad companies," Cindy said to Isabel.

"Yes, I planned to sleep late, so I'll call you after lunch," Isabel said.

"OK, you both have a good night." Cindy waved goodbye.

"You too," Esteban and Isabel waved back at the same time. Esteban and Isabel got in the car and headed toward Isabel's place.

After a couple of seconds of awkward silence, Isabel finally spoke. In a quiet voice, she said, "You know I left a message for you to pick me up tonight."

"I didn't get your message; today was a hectic day, and I barely had time to go to the bathroom," Esteban replied.

Esteban didn't know if Isabel was going to start an argument or was just asking. Ever since he had the incident with Sara, she had been acting very defensive, and Esteban usually had to sit and take the lecture that Isabel gave him.

"Esteban, I missed you terribly, and I wanted to be as close as I could," Isabel responded.

"So did I, mi amor, but we needed to talk and speak our minds," Esteban said and thought to himself that that's exactly what he wanted to hear from her. "Tomorrow or Sunday, we can go somewhere, and it will be just you and me, OK," Esteban smiled with his eyes.

"OK...," said Isabel.

They were both tired from their long day. Esteban was in no mood to discuss any type of emotional feelings. He was barely over his angry feelings from the earlier stolen car incident that evening. Both stared into the traffic as they drove. They reached Isabel's place. She lived close to her mother, but since it was late, she wasn't going to go see her that night. She decided to just call when she was in her apartment. Esteban parked the car and unloaded the baggage. She had four large suitcases and a big box. He looked at Isabel as he was unloading; she strained against the weight of the luggage; his face looked pretty cute while she did it. The amount of luggage made it seem like she had bought all of Miami.

When the last suitcase was in the apartment, Esteban turned towards Isabel, looked her in the eye, and said, "Isabel, I have to go and... I wanted to tell you that I missed you very much. It was only a little over a week, but I thought of you a lot. I'll call you tomorrow."

Isabel wanted to tell him that she loved him, but she was still slightly annoyed by the memory of him kissing that other woman. She kissed him and said, "You are my man, Esteban, and I am your woman." It sounded like dialogue out of a Tarzan movie, and Esteban didn't quite get it. She stared into his eyes. He smiled like he was looking at an angel and took her hand in his.

As he kissed her hand, Isabel seemed to melt. She smiled at him and said, "Goodbye, Esteban."

"Bye, Isabel," he said and left.

He drove back to his apartment. He definitely wanted to go to bed and rest. He began to think about Isabel. *I'm glad that we didn't get into any argument. I'm sure if Cindy wasn't around, the situation probably would've been different. She did look extremely good though.* He smiled. *I think that she is able to tame a Lion straight after a kill. I knew that as soon as I saw her at the airport, most of my anger melted.* "Isabel, I want to be close to you. I truly love you," he said calmly in a whisper.

Trust was something that Esteban valued greatly. So many times, in the past, he had been betrayed. Trust had become a value worth more than money and love itself. Isabel was the only one so far who had defied all his past experiences in keeping it, along with Chavez. He had lost a few friends' lives due to people's mistrust. He realized that life was something that could not be predicted and bad things sometimes happened. People were the ones that made the choices. He put down his car visor where he had placed a picture of Isabel. As he stared at it, he felt warmth. He knew and felt that he didn't want to lose the bond he had with her. He drove the rest of the way with the visor down.

When he reached his apartment, he kicked off his shoes and immediately made his way to his bed. Within minutes, he was fast asleep.

The next day, he woke up at 9:10 a.m. His usual sleep time ranged from 5 to 6 hours so anything else over that he considered a luxury. He went to the bathroom to freshen up and started making his morning coffee. He remembered to call Isabel and wake her up because he wanted to talk and perhaps plan something later on. He decided to wait until 10 a.m. to give Isabel a chance to get some extra sleep.

As he started to shave, he began to think of some incidents that had happened yesterday. He realized that everything was as normal as usual but he began to put things into perspective. He didn't like the way Senator Sinal was staring at Senator Fernandez. It was more than a stare. He didn't like Senator Sinal because of things that he had heard he did, and his personality seemed to be very pushy and arrogant. He then realized that his car, the one that was almost stolen, was next to Senator Fernandez's car. *Why didn't I see that before?* he asked himself. *It's very strange for that to happen. It could be a coincidence, but I don't have that feeling. I also don't like the way those two punks got into the facility. How did they ever get by security? Even someone with half a brain would have spotted them unless...*

He then grabbed the phone, called the congressional building and began to ask about the incident that happened last night. After being put on hold, he talked to the designated people in charge and found out that no incident had ever been reported, so it never happened. *What the hell...this is very strange,* he thought. *I know that sometimes, during the weekend, things get delayed, but it shouldn't be delayed because of that.* He began to make a note to call his friend Chavez.

I don't know why I hadn't thought of it before. I need to keep a tighter grip on protecting the Senator. I don't like what might happen if I don't. After he shaved and ate a quick breakfast, Esteban called Isabel. She answered the phone.

"Hello."

"Good morning, Amor; how are you this morning?" Esteban asked.

"I'm fine," she said.

"I didn't want to call you too early because you seemed tired from your flight."

"That's fine. I needed to get up anyway," she replied.

"Well, I thought about taking you somewhere in the park, maybe even outside the city. I want to find a place where we can both be alone without anyone getting in the way."

"I'd like that, Amor, but I do need to be here later today," she said.

"I thought of that, too. How about we go somewhere tomorrow instead? That way, you can relax, unpack, and do whatever you need."

"That sounds great. I need to do all those things," Isabel said, sounding excited.

Esteban smiled. "OK, call me when you're unpacked and settled so we can plan something."

"I will, amor, but I'll be taking my time. I've got a lot to unpack.'

"That's alright. I've got a few things to do as well," Esteban responded.

"I'll call you soon, then," Isabel said, hanging up the phone.

Esteban decided to watch TV. He hated politics, so he usually tried to avoid news that dealt with it. Yet, because of his job protecting government officials, he often found himself watching politicians. As he flipped through the channels, he noticed a news report about a drug bust in Veracruz. This wasn't unusual, but when the camera zoomed in on one of the detainees, he saw a tattoo on the man's wrist, one that looked like his own. Though the picture wasn't clear, Esteban could easily identify it. It had to be the same tattoo. He was stunned.

"What the hell is going on here?" he muttered, his face twisting in confusion. "Something's happening, and I don't know what it is, but I'm going to find out," he said, determined.

Esteban started to feel like there was more going on than he had realized. For some reason, he felt compelled to speak with Senator Fernandez. He had protected many government officials before and always trusted his instincts. He never liked leaving anything to chance. In his line of work, one second of neglect could cost someone their life, even his own. He made a note to call Chavez again before picking up the phone to call the Senator. The phone rang.

"Senator Fernandez's residence," a voice answered.

"I'd like to speak with the Senator if he's available. This is Agent Esteban Galindo."

"Let me check; hold on, please," the man said, putting him on hold.

I hope I didn't interrupt anything, Esteban thought to himself.

A voice came on the line. "This is Senator Fernandez speaking."

"Senator, this is Agent Esteban Galindo. I'm sorry to call you on your day off."

"That's alright," the Senator replied.

"Senator, I'd like to discuss a few things with you before you head to the congressional building on Monday. There are some things I believe you should know."

"Like what?" the Senator asked.

"Well, right now, I'm working off hunches, but I've learned to trust my instincts, and I think you should be aware of certain situations that might develop. I'd prefer to tell you in person, in a private and secure place," Esteban said.

"That's fine. We can talk for thirty minutes after you pick me up on Monday," the Senator said.

"Actually, sir, I'd like to speak with you now," Esteban replied.

"Is there a problem?" the Senator asked.

"I'm not sure, Senator, but it's my job to secure all potential dangers, and I need to speak with you privately."

"Well, you can come to my house now, and we'll get the talk over there. I also like to spend time with my family like everyone else," the Senator said.

"Good. I'm just doing my job, sir," Esteban said.

"And I appreciate it. I thank you and all the agents for what you do for the congressmen," the Senator replied.

"I'll see you in a few minutes, sir."

"See you then," the Senator said, hanging up.

Esteban turned off the television and headed out to see the Senator. "The Senator sure likes to cut me off at his discretion," he muttered with some annoyance. He got in his car and took off, beginning to think about things that seemed insignificant but might make sense. He didn't like how certain things were turning out: teenagers getting into the facility, the tattoos on their wrists, and the tattoos seen during the drug bust. These things didn't feel right to him.

He arrived in an upscale subdivision, the kind that required special permission to enter. Security guards were stationed at the gate to welcome residents and keep strangers out. As he approached the Senator's house, the guards at the door asked for his identification. He showed it and was let in. Driving up the long driveway, he parked in front of the house. A man came out to escort him to the Senator. The house looked like a mansion, easily resembling a hotel with its grand size. Once inside, he was led to the living room, where the Senator sat reading a newspaper and drinking coffee.

"Afternoon, Senator," Esteban greeted.

"Afternoon, Esteban. Please, have a seat," the Senator replied, shaking his hand.

They both sat down. "This must be something very concerning," the Senator said.

"It is to me, Senator, because it concerns your safety," Esteban replied.

"My safety? How so?" the Senator asked, staring at him.

"I'm not sure yet, Senator, but certain things have happened that don't seem to be in their proper place."

"Tell me," the Senator prompted.

"Is it safe to speak here, Senator?" Esteban asked, concerned.

"If you're asking if there are loose ears, it's perfectly safe, Agent Esteban," the Senator assured him.

Esteban leaned forward toward the Senator. "Senator, yesterday, after I was dismissed from guarding you, I was heading to my car when I caught two teenage thugs trying to steal it. I apprehended them, but it took forever for security to come to pick them up. The whole situation didn't sit right with me," Esteban explained.

"I wasn't informed of this by security," the Senator said, sounding confused and picking up his cell phone.

"No, Senator, and when I called this morning to check on the incident, I was told that no one had heard anything about it," Esteban said.

"That's odd," the Senator remarked, putting his phone back down.

"I'm also concerned about how they even got in. Another thing I realized this morning was that the car next to mine was yours, sir."

"Mine?" the Senator said, surprised.

"Yes, sir. I don't know if that was a coincidence or planned, but in my line of work, there are no coincidences," Esteban said, looking the Senator straight in the eye. "I usually park close to whoever I'm guarding, but this is one coincidence worth noting." He laced his fingers together before him. "I took the names of the security men, and they'll be reported for the incident. Their excuses were the lamest I've ever heard. This should have never happened. By Monday, I should have their names and badge numbers," Esteban added.

"I see," the Senator said.

"Another thing, Senator: this morning, I was watching the news, and there was a big drug bust in Veracruz. Several hundred pounds of cocaine were seized," Esteban continued.

"That's nothing unusual these days," the Senator remarked.

"One of the men arrested had a tattoo on his wrist—the same tattoo that the teenagers had when they tried to steal my car," Esteban said.

The Senator's expression grew more serious as he listened.

"Senator, I want to share something personal with you so that you understand what I'm trying to say." Esteban's tone shifted, and he hesitated before saying, "I came from a poor family, and as a teenager, I was coerced into joining a gang for protection—both for myself and my family. It's not something I'm proud of, but in my neighborhood, it was a choice I had to make. Gangs use symbols to identify themselves, and the tattoo that those teenagers had, along with the man arrested in Veracruz, is the same one I got when I was in the gang many years ago." Esteban rolled up his sleeve to show the tattoo to the Senator.

"There's more going on here than meets the eye, sir," Esteban said.

The Senator looked off to the side, deep in thought.

"I don't want you to feel uncomfortable with me, Senator. I just want to tell you what I'm seeing so we can take precautions," Esteban said earnestly. "I've been trained to recognize potential dangers, and I believe someone is testing the security. Those teenagers were probably allowed in to steal a car to see if it could be done. They were 'testing the waters' to gauge how strong our security is."

"In the process, they almost got away with it," Esteban remarked. "We have hundreds of cameras, and it's hard to believe they weren't seen." He paused for a minute. "Another thing—why steal a car that was parked next to yours? If that can happen, Senator, someone could easily place a bomb in your vehicle or anywhere else in the facility." His tone grew more serious. "Senator, I don't like these incidents, and I'm concerned about your safety."

They stared at each other for a moment before the Senator stood up and walked toward the fireplace mantle. He turned around and looked at Esteban. "Agent Esteban, I don't know what to make of this," the Senator said. "I haven't heard of any incident like the one you're describing." He paced around the room. "I do admire you for coming here to tell me this; it shows me you're doing your job well and that you care about what happens within the government and to its officials."

Esteban began to feel like he was being patronized; he grabbed the armrests of his chair. The Senator continued, "Agent Esteban, I have my own sources in Congress." He stared at Esteban. "I'm aware that you had to tell me this, and believe me, we'll talk again. But for now, I have other matters to attend to," the Senator said, signaling that the conversation was coming to an end. "I'd like to talk more about this with you. You may be a good ally, and that's always good to have."

Esteban felt puzzled but understood that the Senator wanted him to leave. "Yes, sir, I'm here to help," Esteban replied.

"I'm glad you have a decent heart. I believe we can be a good team," the Senator said. "I'll talk to you more next week, and keep me informed if anything else happens." The Senator pushed a button, and a man entered the room.

"I will, sir, and thank you for letting me come on such short notice to inform you," Esteban said.

"I'm glad you did," the Senator smiled. "I'll be seeing you again, Agent Esteban."

"Thank you, sir," Esteban replied as he was escorted to the door and seen to his car. He drove away, heading back to his apartment.

As he drove, he felt like he had wasted the Senator's time. *I don't understand this—how could this not have been reported to the Senator? Chavez has a lot of explaining to do.* He continued driving in silence, listening to the radio. Upon arriving at his apartment, he called Chavez.

Meanwhile, the Senator made a call. The phone rang, and someone answered, "Hello."

"Mi amigo... El Zorro, I had a visitor today," the Senator began. "He's an agent and seemed very concerned...I wonder if this agent is trustworthy."

The voice on the other end asked, "Who's the agent?"

"His name is Esteban Galindo. Do you know him?" the Senator asked.

"Yes, I do. In fact, I know him better than most people," the other person replied.

"Is he trustworthy?"

The voice on the other end laughed. "Let me put it this way—he's the best I've seen, and I'd trust him with my life," the voice said confidently.

The Senator raised his eyebrows and nodded. "Well, that's a high recommendation coming from you."

"I've known him half my life, and I'm still alive because of him."

"Then I believe he's going to have to join our team."

"I'd highly recommend it," the voice replied.

"I just wanted to ask before anything is brought out in the open," the Senator said, his tone mysterious.

"It would be very wise."

"I'll stay in contact. Keep me informed on everything," the Senator instructed.

"You can count on it," the voice replied.

The Senator hung up the phone and went to join his family for brunch.

4

Back in the apartment, Esteban called Chavez.

A woman picked up the phone. "Bueno."

"May I speak to Mr. Chavez," Esteban said.

"May I say who's calling, please?" the lady replied.

"This is his friend, Esteban," Esteban said.

"One moment, please." The lady went to get Chavez.

Chavez then answered the phone. "Bueno."

"Chavez, this is Esteban."

"Que tal, Esteban? What's the big surprise... calling me here?" said Chavez.

"Well, I needed to talk to you about last night and about something that happened today," Esteban said.

"Go ahead, amigo," Chavez said.

"Well, I called the congressional building to see about the stolen car incident, and they told me they didn't know anything about it. Not only that, but I just came back from seeing Senator Fernandez, and he also told me he knew nothing about it either." Esteban paced around the room as he spoke, his tone growing agitated. "Now, why is this happening, Chavez?" Esteban asked, shaking his fist in the air. "Of all the people that should know, it should be the Senator, who happened to have his car next to mine—the car that almost got stolen," he said in a louder voice.

"I told you I'd take care of it, Esteban," Chavez responded.

"Well, it didn't seem like this was taking care of it, and it seemed like everyone was acting like it didn't happen," he said, holding his hand to his head. "For the Senator not to know, now come on!" Esteban was almost yelling at this point.

"Esteban, I know all this seems crazy right now, but you'll just have to trust me on this," Chavez said. "I cannot explain nothing to you right now, especially on the phone, but all in good time, things will turn out fine." Chavez kept his voice low as he spoke.

"All in good time?" Esteban raised his voice. "What kind of an answer is that?"

"Esteban, I have trusted you with my life many times, so please trust me on this one. I'm doing what I can, and I'll tell you more about it later on." Chavez paused. "That's all I can tell you for now…"

"Well, I'm in the dark, Chavez. I just didn't want to be in the dark when someone's life is about to be put out because I'm the one responsible," Esteban said.

"No one's life is going to be put out. Things will work out, trust me," Chavez said.

"At least keep me informed when you can." Esteban had begun to calm down. He knew that Chavez would never betray him and so, he trusted that he had good reasons for keeping information from him.

"Esteban, you have been my close friend for years. I will not let it go bad. Relax. Enjoy your weekend and go see Isabel like you said you were going to," Chavez said.

"I'll be calling you to see what you've been doing to improve this, Chavez," Esteban said sarcastically.

"You know I will help you, amigo," Chavez replied.

"OK then, call me in a day or two to give me an update. One that I can feel satisfied with."

"I will, and please trust me. I am your closest friend. I owe you many favors, Esteban. Just trust me." Chavez sounded earnest.

Esteban nodded. "By the way, who is that woman who answered the phone?"

"She's my date... we've been going out for two weeks now," Chavez commented.

Esteban began to think it was probably a woman from work. Chavez liked to ask secretaries out, especially new ones. "OK, I'll call you later on." Esteban hung up the phone.

Esteban decided to just listen to music for now and perhaps go to the gym later to work out some of the piling aggression. He rested on the couch and steadily fell asleep.

He woke up two hours later and decided to go to the gym immediately. He usually worked out four times a week as he constantly had to stay in shape and keep his hand-to-hand combat skills at their peak. He also went to the shooting gallery every other day, depending on his schedule.

Throwing some of his workout clothes into a bag hastily, he made his way out to his car.

I really need this workout. It seems like the best workouts I ever have are the ones where I have so much on my mind that my body just seems to put up with the stress I give it. It's all good, though.

He arrived and parked the car. The place was called Gold's Gym; it was a fairly popular spot in that part of Mexico City. That particular gym was typically full of people hoping to get some more gains. Most of its popularity could be credited to the fact that Arnold Schwarzenegger went to promote fitness there, and a movie was also filmed in that location. Esteban admired Arnold for the things he had accomplished. He felt that something about Arnold's life was similar to his own- they both overcame the challenges that came their way.

He went in and changed into his gym clothes. The first thing on his gym agenda was to punch the bag. He spent 40 minutes on the bag and then decided to lift some weights.

"This workout brings back memories," he thought to himself. "Seems that I've been working out all my life, but I enjoy it quite a bit."

As he was about to start working out, he saw Javier.

"Hi, Esteban," Javier smiled and approached him.

"Que tal, Javier," Esteban responded.

"So, you're trying to stay in shape, huh?" Javier said sarcastically.

"I'm always trying to do that," Esteban responded. "I don't think there's an end to this being in shape thing." He smiled at Javier as he grabbed a couple of 30 kg dumbbells.

"I totally agree with that," Javier laughed.

"I'm about to do that new tai-box workout I've heard so much about," Javier said. "Some Mexican-American is supposed to be doing a class exposition here in a few days. He's supposed to be a real fit guy. I think his name is Juan Antonio.

I'm not sure. It's supposed to be one of the ultimate types of workouts."

"Well, all workouts are the ultimate if you do them right," Esteban said, starting his first set.

"I'll tell you how it is after I come out of there all sore," Javier laughed.

"Just don't hurt yourself and pull a groin muscle." Esteban elbowed his friend as he balanced the weight of the dumbbell in his hand.

"Yeah, that would be my luck," Javier responded, looking worriedly at his crotch area.

"Hey, have you talked to your girlfriend yet?" Javier asked.

"You mean about our misunderstanding from that night?" Esteban turned his face away from Javier and tried to play dumb.

"Yeah, the misunderstanding where you were chasing her for forgiveness in front of the whole audience," Javier put it more in the light with a slight comedy.

"Well, you don't have to elaborate so vastly there, Mr. Jerry Springer," Esteban said, dropping the weights.

"I was just curious. I like you better when things are going your way," Javier said. "I certainly wouldn't want you mad. People are afraid of you sometimes, you know."

"Afraid? Now, why are they afraid?" Esteban asked.

"Oh please, Esteban. Of all the things we've heard about you... of course, we are afraid of you."

"Well, stop reading the tabloids like the American National Enquirer. It's bad enough we have newspapers like that in

Mexico. You might finally get some truth then... instead, read something that makes sense."

"Well, anyway, I'm just glad to be on your good side."

"You better hurry up for your class. I think it just started, and you'll be late," Esteban pointed to the room where people were moving.

"Oh damn, thanks," Javier looked around and ran.

"Don't pull no groin muscle," Esteban yelled and laughed.

Esteban finally finished his workout and changed to go back to his apartment. When he reached, he put his clothes in the hamper and took a shower. After cleaning up, he turned on the TV and sat to browse some channels. He saw a commercial about a mom giving her son some sandwiches, and he thought to himself, *I better call my mother to see how she's doing.*

He called his mother. She was the world to him; he loved her so much and would do anything for her. He knew and realized all the things she did for him and all the sacrifices she had to make in order for him to get where he was.

The phone rang.

"Bueno," a lady answered the phone.

"Mama, it's your son Esteban."

"Hijo, how are you? It's so good to hear from you."

"I'm sorry, Mama, that I haven't called. Sometimes, my job keeps me from calling you, but I try to make it up by writing to you."

"That's alright. I got your letter yesterday, and I loved it," she said warmly.

"How have you been feeling, mama?" he asked.

"Well, I'm doing O.K. for an old woman. I can't clean and move as well as I used to, but I manage as much as I can," she answered.

"Don't overdo anything like you're used to. You know that the doctor doesn't want you to overexert yourself picking up heavy things," he said. "Have you gone to the pool like I told you and exercised there?" he asked with concern.

"Hijo, I go sometimes, but I just don't like to go with men following me. I feel like I can't do anything without asking permission."

"Mother, they're only there to protect you. Besides, it's only one man, and he should always be at a distance," he said.

"Well, why would anyone try to hurt me?" she asked. "I'm just an old woman with no great riches."

Esteban smiled and said, "Mama, you're a great wealth to me. I love you and just wanted to check up on you. I also wanted to tell you that Isabel is in town. She'll be here for a good while."

"That's wonderful." She paused, and the silence got heavy. "So, when are you going to ask her to marry you?" she said firmly.

"Mother... I am not ready for that right now," he said with emphasis on "not ready."

"Well, you better get ready. I don't want to end up an old woman without any grandchildren. You should've been married a long time ago," she began to nag him.

"O.K., mama, I get the point. We've been through this before... I just wanted to check up on you and tell you that I love you," he said like a little boy.

"You be sure and marry that girl, or she'll go away," she said.

"Yes... mother," he responded sarcastically.

Esteban realized this was going nowhere. "Mama, I have to go. I will call you soon," he said, trying to get off the phone.

"You listen to your mother and marry that girl."

Esteban heard this from his mother all the time. Doña Elba was always worried about his love life. She wanted him to finally settle down and marry a sweet girl, as well as have grandchildren like all mothers her age did.

"Oh, when are you going to visit me?" she asked.

"Soon, mother. I have to find out my schedule."

"You bring Isabel with you. I like talking to my future daughter-in-law."

Esteban's mother knew how to maneuver her son, and he always fell for it.

"Ok, ok, Mom, I get the point. I love you, and I'll send you some more money," he said.

"Tell Isabel I said hello," Doña Elba said.

"Yes, I'll tell her," Esteban sighed. "Adios, Mama, and te quiero mucho," he said warmly.

"Te quiero yo también, hijo," she responded in the same way.

They both hung up and as usual, Esteban was speechless. He took a deep breath. *When will my mother ever stop pressuring me to get married? Must be a senior citizen syndrome to push their sons into getting married.*

He made himself stop thinking because he didn't really ever think about marriage except when he talked to his mother. He then began to think about what happened at the parking lot. He studied the situation a little more, wondering how the teenagers could've gotten in.

The only way I can think that they got in is through the front gate, and no one seemed to notice or care, he thought to himself.

He looked at a copy of the building on the computer and made a few notes while he looked at it. He then called Isabel to see how her unpacking was going.

She answered the phone, "Hello."

"Isabel, have you unpacked most of your stuff?" he asked.

"Well, to tell you the truth, half of it is my mother's." She kind of laughed when she said it.

"Hmmm, I should've guessed on that. No wonder you had so much luggage," he said. He already knew this information because she told him when he had picked her up, but he went along with it anyway.

"Well, I did my errands and even worked out at the gym. I wanted to call you to see if you still want to do something tonight," he suggested.

"I would love to, but I do want to see my mother and have a long talk with her. Also, Cindy and I have a lot of things we have to discuss for our upcoming advertising events," she replied.

"Let's just see each other tomorrow like we planned," said Esteban.

"That's the best thing, amor," Isabel agreed.

"OK then, I'll call you tomorrow around 10 a.m., and we can move on from there," Esteban said.

"I like that; call me then, amor," she said.

"I'll see you tomorrow then," he said smoothly, then hung up.

Esteban continued to study the building on his computer. He was just trying to make sense of it all, and by doing some detective work, he hoped things would become clearer. He studied it for a few hours until his eyes were red and his stomach was growling. After eating, he decided to get some rest.

***

The alarm went off at 8 a.m. It was a beautiful Sunday morning; the sun was shining just right with only a few clouds in the sky, and the city was as busy as usual. It was hard to tell what day it was because every day, the streets were full and bustling with busy people going to work. It never seemed to stop. The only real way to tell it was Sunday was by listening to the nearby church bells. The traffic continued to flow, and people still moved from place to place like any other day. It seemed like only the elderly took their time and enjoyed life as they walked through the park; the rest were all walking with purpose, quickly, without stopping to admire the beautiful day.

Esteban decided to get up and run a few miles. He always had to exercise in some form or other. It was the only way to gain an edge when it came to fitness. After the run, he cleaned up and ate some breakfast. It was almost 10 a.m. He finished up in the kitchen and went out of his apartment. He got into his car and called Isabel on his cell phone to tell her he was on his way. She replied that she would be ready.

Esteban began to think about the car incident again. *Something isn't right, it's just a gut feeling I have.* He tried to block it out as he didn't want to think about business right now. This was, in a way, becoming an obsession for him. It was all he seemed to think about. He just wanted to think of Isabel for now, and he concentrated on that. As he approached her apartment, he saw Cindy knocking on her door. Esteban was a bit surprised to see Cindy there. He parked the car and stepped out.

"Hi Cindy, how are you this morning?" Esteban asked as he pulled up beside her.

"Hello, Mr. Handsome," Cindy replied, putting her hand on the roof of the car.

"Are you surprising my girlfriend this morning?" Esteban asked.

"Actually, Isabel called me and wanted me to come see her," Cindy said, smiling.

"Well, I see," he responded, smiling but with doubt in his mind.

"While you and her go out, she wants to introduce me to her mother, and later on, we can do our girl thing," she said.

"Well, we can't go through the day without doing the girl thing," Esteban said jokingly.

Cindy laughed.

"Ah, you women are very cunning," Esteban smiled. "Her mother is a very sweet woman. You'll like her," Esteban proclaimed. "I have to warn you, though, she'll put you to work and will tell you all the things you need to know in order to capture a man."

"Is that so? Well, I like her already," Cindy laughed along.

Isabel opened the door and popped her head out. "Well, when company comes, it comes in twos," she said with a big smile. Esteban entered and kissed her on the lips.

"Hola, mi amor." She hugged him. "Hmmmm, you smell gooood," she said sensually.

"You don't have to tell me," Cindy replied.

"How are you, Cindy? Come on in," Isabel said. "Please excuse my mess; I'm still not through unpacking."

Estaban looked around at the piles of suitcases, bags, and clothes. "I believe it will take you a week to unpack," he remarked.

"Oh, stop. Most of this stuff is my mother's," Isabel gently hit him on the arm.

"Cindy, let me just get through with this, and we can take you to my mother's. I told her that I was taking you there and that we've become good friends," Isabel said.

"Esteban told me all about her," Cindy said.

"Oh, he did? Well, don't believe a word he says. He's still all uptight because my mother puts him to work," she said sarcastically.

"She would make a good warden," Esteban said.

Cindy laughed.

"I'm going to tell her you said that," Isabel said in a defiant tone.

"I'm just joking. You know I like your mother." He smiled at her innocently. "She made this beautiful woman that only the angels could adore," Esteban sweet-talked her.

"You better bow down to me," she laughed.

"Where can I find a man like you?" Cindy said.

"There are plenty at Wal-Mart, 5 for a dollar," Esteban said jokingly.

Isabel and Cindy looked at each other, shaking their heads and smiling.

"Well, we better go, or the day will fly by," Esteban said.

"Let me get my things, and we'll be on our way," Isabel went into the bedroom.

Esteban had to load up all of Isabel's mother's stuff in the car. He felt like he had just unloaded it the other night for nothing. They left the apartment and headed to Isabel's mother's house. Isabel and Cindy acted like they had been friends forever. All Esteban said was yes, no, ah huh, and you're right—the usual male responses when two women in conversation were asking him questions. He enjoyed it, though; he liked being around Isabel when she was in a good mood.

They arrived at Mrs. Diaz's house. "Well, here we are," Esteban said. They went in, and Isabel introduced Cindy to her mother. Esteban then unloaded all the stuff Isabel had brought her mother from Miami.

"I'm glad there are no rocks in these suitcases," he grumbled to himself.

"Buenos días, Señora Diaz... it's good to see you," Esteban said.

"Buenos días, Esteban... It's good to see you too," she said happily.

Mrs. Diaz had always liked Esteban. She really accepted him and wanted Isabel to marry him eventually. She knew that he loved her daughter, and she had a good relationship with his mother as well.

"Mama, this is Cindy, my American friend that I met in Miami... she's really been a big help, and I believe we'll be seeing each other a lot when I go to Florida," Isabel said.

"Well, it is very good to meet you, Cindy," Mrs. Diaz said.

"The pleasure is all mine... Isabel told me a lot about you, and I feel like I know you already," Cindy said in Spanish.

Mrs. Diaz was very surprised. "My my, you speak Spanish, and you speak it very well."

"Muchas gracias, I used to spend the summers in Mexico and Central America when I was a little girl," Cindy said.

"We're going to get along just fine," Mrs. Diaz said, smiling.

They went inside and began talking about their trip and how they met. Mrs. Diaz had a very nice living room where they sat and had their conversation. Esteban just smiled and said the minimum because he knew it was girl talk.

After the introductions and small talk about getting to know Mexico, Esteban and Isabel made their move to go out for a ride while Cindy and Mrs. Diaz stayed to get to know each other. They both got up and went outside to Esteban's car to go for a ride and have time for themselves.

"We'll be back in a few hours, mother," Isabel said.

"O.K., hija, you be careful."

"Adios," Esteban and Isabel waved as they left the house.

Esteban drove toward the park that was located outside the city. It resembled New York's Central Park but with certain stands selling magazines and people making a living by showing off their talents. The drive was well over thirty minutes. Esteban looked at Isabel.

"Amor, why didn't you tell me that Cindy was coming over?" Esteban asked.

"I tried to call you, but you must have left. I couldn't leave her alone all by herself at the hotel, so I invited her to go to my mother's," she said. "Since you love me, I knew you wouldn't mind." She smiled at him.

He looked at her and made a face. "You're a very surprising woman, Isabel," he said. "I don't mind doing it. I just don't want to be put in a position where I have to say no, and you'll be mad at me."

"I'll understand; I know that your job can be very unpredictable. I won't get mad," she devilishly smiled.

"O.K., you heard it, ladies and gentlemen, it's a sworn testimony from the Queen of the Nile... she will not get upset," Esteban said sarcastically.

"Keep that up, and I won't tell you what I brought you from Miami," she smirked, raising a brow.

"I'm sorry, Your Highness... forgive this humble peasant who drove you from the jungles of the airport at midnight without notice."

They reached the park and parked near some big oak trees. "This looks like a safe place for the car," Esteban said. "Where do you want to go?" He looked at Isabel.

"Let's walk, and we can choose a bench," she said.

They began walking, holding hands. They both had so much to talk about, but neither knew how to approach it, especially regarding his encounter with Sara.

They walked and saw people strolling by and kids playing. The park was very beautiful when there wasn't a cloud in the sky. Esteban thought about how he could begin talking about the things he wanted to tell Isabel. Words didn't always come easy to him, especially to the people that he loved. He began to brainstorm in his head as he walked with Isabel.

"Isabel, I've been wanting to talk to you for a long time now. We've never really had the chance, and circumstances have never been ideal," Esteban said.

"I know, amor. There are many things that I've been wanting to tell you as well," Isabel said, looking at him very patiently. They both stopped and sat on a bench.

"Isabel, I have to explain about Sara." He looked at her and squeezed her hand.

"You don't have to..." Isabel tried to speak, but Esteban put his finger on her mouth.

"Yes, I do, Isabel. It's been eating at me all this time."

"I have to tell you." He looked at her seriously. "Sara was a former girlfriend, and I had no idea how she got my phone number at home." He looked into her eyes. "I believe she got it from my mother because she knew my mother liked her just like she likes you, and she got along with her as well." He ran his hand through his hair, feeling the sweat accumulating on his forehead. "Anyway, I didn't know that she was going to be at that particular event; she took me by surprise." He fixed his eyes on her. Isabel was looking upwards at a tree branch. "When I saw her, she just wanted to talk. I had no idea that she wanted to have a relationship with me, much less kiss me behind the phone booths."

Isabel closed her eyes slowly and pursed her lips. "Well, you didn't seem to run away when she kissed you," she said in a low voice. "She had her hands on your ass..." She paused, and when she spoke next, Esteban almost jumped. "So what am I supposed to think when I see something like that?!"

"It may have seemed that way, but I was as surprised as you were," he said. Isabel let out a "huh" expression.

"I didn't know her intentions," Esteban responded, trying to hold Isabel's hand.

She pulled it away. "Well, I could've told you what her intentions were," she huffed.

"She told me that she wanted me and that she made a mistake in leaving me," he said. "I don't know if she was saying this to make me feel better or to make me look like an idiot in front of everyone close to me." He looked at Isabel, concerned. She had her arms crossed. "I knew that it was a bad situation to be in, but I wanted to know what she was doing and how her life had been going... just like seeing an old friend. I'm sure you'd be curious if an old boyfriend popped out of nowhere," he added, making an analytical point.

"I wouldn't go around kissing him and grabbing his ass in the middle of an event like that," she said with a sour tone.

"Isabel, I hadn't seen her in years, so it was innocent talk until she started to push her kisses and suggestions on me," he said.

"Oh, she did that all right," Isabel said, kind of jealously.

"That's the part that you got to see. You didn't see the part where I told her I had a beautiful girlfriend and that we've been happy together for a long time," Esteban said very honestly.

Isabel began to pay more attention to him now. "The part you missed was when I said you were my girlfriend and that I didn't want to get involved with married women." He tried to grab her hand again, and this time, she gave in. "Isabel, I don't want anyone to come between us. I love you very much; I would do anything for you and would never hurt you." He put his hand under her chin and pulled her face up toward his own. "This was all a misunderstanding, but I know that it looked like I was really cheating on you, and I would have questioned it myself if our situations were reversed."

She remained silent, her eyes filling with tears.

"It's not like I could've just left the place or called security to escort Sara away. I was part of that security, and she also put me in a bad situation with my job. Her husband is a rich, powerful man, and a big scene would've been created."

Isabel pulled away. "Oh, Esteban, I was so hurt when I saw you kissing her," she said. "You have no idea what went through my mind and the instant feeling I had in my heart." She was looking at him. "Why were you in the phone booths in a dark area?" she asked. She still wasn't through with the questions. "It just looked like you wanted to be with her!" She slowly began to cry. "Do you have any idea how terrible I felt?" she cried.

"I'm very sorry, Isabel. Please forgive me. I take all the blame. I don't like to see you cry," he kissed her hand.

"I was bragging about you the whole night... about how good of a boyfriend you've been to me and how much you showed me that you love me," she said, barely able to talk. "All my girlfriends tell me that they are so jealous of me for having a boyfriend like you. They all say that you're one in a million and to not let you go." Her voice came in racked sobs as tears came down her cheeks. "My mother thinks the world of you. And when I saw you kiss that woman, I felt that you betrayed me. I felt like you'd been using me." Her tears rolled down, and she couldn't help herself. She was hurt. Terribly. "I began to wonder how many other women you might have been with besides her, how many other times you had affairs behind my back... I felt like I was made a fool of in front of the world," Isabel's red eyes looked at him. "I just wanted to die," she cried hysterically.

Esteban didn't know what to say. He held her, and she cried on his shoulder. With those comments, he felt like he too wanted to cry, especially when he heard that word—betrayed.

He felt like a traitor, the bad guy, the boyfriend who didn't deserve an angel like Isabel. He knew that feeling too well, and it was the worst feeling he could ever feel. He felt hollow and empty for giving the feeling of betrayal to the woman he loved. They both took a few moments in silence and hugged each other. Esteban could not help but shed some tears. He wanted to speak but couldn't because her words had feeling and power behind them. He felt guilty and hurt to see the woman he adored crying because of him. She was so beautiful and lovely; even when she was sad, she still looked like an angel.

After a few moments, he looked at her and kissed her on the cheeks and forehead. "I don't want to hurt you in any way, amor. You are the best thing in my life, and I haven't betrayed you," he said, looking at her as tears ran down her cheeks. He smiled. Without thinking and acting out of instinct, he sat in front of her to see her straight in the eyes and said, "Isabel, you are the love of my life, the woman of my dreams. I love you with all my heart. I pledge myself to you, to be your other half and to be your closest friend. All my life, I never knew love. I never knew what it was to desire or want to be with someone until I met you. You are my entire reason for loving this world."

Isabel had stopped crying and now looked surprised and touched. Her eyes were soft but still red. Her hands trembled a little as they held Estaban's more tightly.

"God has blessed me so much to give me a woman like you. Ever since I saw you at the gym for the first time, it was hard to keep my eyes off you. I thought of you all the time, and I wanted to be with you for the rest of my life. God has a purpose for every human being and a reason for things to happen, and sometimes we ignore them."

Esteban looked down at the floor. His heart felt flooded with emotion: pain, love, hurt, adoration.

"I've ignored many things in my life that I knew could have been better or made a bigger difference. I didn't want to lose the opportunities that God gave me for being negligent. You're a gift sent from heaven that I know...I will not let time pass by."

He knelt in front of her, holding her hand.

"Isabel... would you marry me and be my wife and take me as your humble husband?" Esteban asked her and stared into her eyes. "I will love you for the rest of your life and do my best to make you happy," he said, holding her hands. He took out a small box with a ring and gave it to her.

Isabel didn't know what to say. She was in shock. She began to cry again. Esteban just stayed there, kneeling without moving. He didn't know what to think. He was holding his breath in nervous tension.

Finally, Isabel hugged him and kissed him all over his face.

"Yes, yes, yes, I'll marry you... you ignorant bastard," she shouted without even knowing what she was saying. "God, I love you sooo much, Esteban."

She stood up and began jumping. "I never expected you to ask me today, but I've been dreaming of you asking me for so long," she smiled and hugged him. "I love you. God, I love you," she yelled out, smiling and laughing as she cried.

Esteban felt so relieved. They both acted like small children hearing good news. She didn't even look at the ring the excitement. It was hard to tell if she was crying from the talk or the proposal. A small crowd gathered and witnessed the whole proposal. Some women cried from what they had seen. They received a standing ovation, and all were shouting, "Congratulations!"

Isabel opened the small black box and saw a big diamond ring. She looked like a little girl opening up a Christmas gift. She began to cry even more. She ran to Esteban and jumped into his arms.

"I never in a million years would have guessed you'd ask me to marry you today, amor. How did you manage to have the ring with you today?" she asked him, playing around while still kissing his face.

He held tightly onto her. "I always carry it because I never knew if I would ever ask you, and by carrying it, I could at least feel comfortable with the thought...also, I was waiting for the right moment and the courage to do it," he smiled as he said it.

Isabel hit him jokingly.

"It felt right today, and I just had to ask you. I guess I was only following my heart," Esteban smiled.

With her legs still around his waist, Isabel kissed Esteban deeply as the crowds around them cheered and applauded.

5

They finally left the park and headed to Isabel's mother's house. She couldn't wait to tell her mother.

"I love you, Esteban! You've made me the happiest woman in the whole world," she shouted for joy.

"I love you too, Isabel, and I want you more than anything." Esteban looked at her smiling face, and it made him feel as if he was the luckiest man in the world.

They arrived at the house, and Isabel acted like a schoolgirl rushing into the house; she skipped and hopped toward the door, shouting, "Mama, mama, come here quick!"

Mrs. Diaz came outside running; all stirred up. Cindy was right behind her. "What's wrong, hija? Are you OK?"

"Mama, I have something to tell you," Isabel just couldn't wait.

"Well, what is it?" her mother impatiently asked.

"Mama, Esteban asked me to marry him!!!!" She showed her mother the ring. "...and I said YES!!!!" She jumped around and shouted.

"Oh, Dios mio, I'm so relieved," her mother said, holding her chest. Then she became stern and put her hands on her hips. "You almost gave your mama a heart attack shouting like that," Mrs. Diaz hollered. "I thought something terrible happened."

Cindy was excited as well, squealing and throwing up her arms. She hugged Isabel and kissed her, congratulating her.

Esteban walked up to them and said, "Well, don't I get a hug too?" They all laughed.

"Yes, you get a big hug, too; she's marrying you, right?" Mrs. Diaz said, laughing.

Cindy hugged Esteban as well.

"I'm so happy for both of you. I feel younger already from all this excitement," Mrs. Diaz said. "I hope I didn't put too much salt in the casserole; I jumped frightened when you yelled." They all laughed at that.

"Come, let us eat and celebrate this moment. I even have some wine somewhere in storage; I happen to have lunch ready just in time," Mrs. Diaz said very happily.

They all walked in. Esteban told Isabel that he was calling his mother to tell her the news. He used his cell phone and called Doña Elba. The phone rang, and his mother answered, "Bueno."

"Madre, it's your son, and I have some good news," he said.

"Good news, what is it, mi hijo?"

"Mama, I asked Isabel to marry me, and she accepted!"

"Madre de Dios santisimo, I have to sit down for this," she said, very surprised.

Esteban could tell that his mother wasn't expecting this. "Hijo, I'm so happy for you, and I'm very happy...you have no idea how much I've been praying for you to find the right woman...Isabel will make a fine wife for you," she said. Esteban knew that this would make his mother happy because she had been wanting him to get married for the longest time.

It was just a few days ago she was encouraging him to marry Isabel, but she really didn't know it was going to be this soon. "You have my blessing, mi hijo...I'm happy for you both," she said. They had some more words, and then Doña Elba congratulated Isabel.

They seemed to talk forever and cried over their happiness, and then Mrs. Diaz got on the phone, and they exchanged their happiness as well. Esteban was the man of the hour, but all the glory went to the women. He knew it and was happy it did. It was part of the tradition that he was accustomed to. After everyone finished talking on the phone, they started preparing to celebrate and eat at Mrs. Diaz's house. Music was put on the stereo, and the atmosphere was full of celebration. Mrs. Diaz went into the kitchen, and everyone followed along.

"You know, Cindy is a good helper; she might make a good Mexican cook someday," Mrs. Diaz looked at Cindy as she began to go into the kitchen. Esteban and Isabel laughed. They all went into the kitchen and began to eat. They spent the rest of the time just talking about the proposal and when the wedding might be. Isabel bragged about Esteban's proposal. Esteban was embarrassed, and Isabel knew it but laid it on thick every time.

Esteban had no idea that he was going to propose to her that day. Either way, the wheels were in motion, and a wedding was going to take place in the near future.

After their good dinner, Mrs. Diaz commented on Isabel's new position in her new job. "Did you tell Esteban about your promotion, hija?" Mrs. Diaz said so innocently.

Isabel gave her a blank stare for a moment before remembering. "No... I didn't; it has totally slipped my mind," she looked at Esteban in a fearful daze.

"What new position?" Esteban asked.

"Hija, tell him now; he needs to know," Mrs. Diaz said.

"Well... I was offered a job in the Florida region, and I sort of told them I would take it," she acted like she was about to get hit with a bat.

"So, what does that mean? I hope it's a good move for your career," Esteban said.

"Well... I would have to move to Florida permanently until I would get transferred by the company. That might take at least two years," she said very unhappily. "But now I don't know if I want to go; all of this changes things for me, Esteban," Isabel said, a little unsure.

"Hmmm, sounds like you had it planned at the beginning, but you have time to think about it," Esteban said. She looked at him sadly with her big eyes. "I just want you to be happy, Isabel," he said.

"I don't want to be away from you, Esteban, especially now," she said in a desperate way. "I...I don't know what I want anymore." She seemed confused.

"I'm sure we have time to talk it out. I'm willing to compromise with your career," said Esteban.

Esteban knew how things could be. He didn't know that he was going to propose, and she obviously didn't know that her life would change in a day. Esteban wanted time to digest all this and realized that Isabel needed to do the same thing. It was a big step that both were taking, and the dust had to settle before making any more decisions.

"I agree; let's just talk this over later and enjoy this moment, Amor," she smiled and made a face at him. Her mother stared at the food while she ate, hearing them talk, and Cindy did the same. There was a tense awkwardness in the air. They didn't know how this would affect their current plans, but it was plain to see that this had caught both of them by surprise.

Esteban kissed her and continued talking about the wedding plans. Everyone continued to enjoy the moment and kept talking about how the whole day had evolved. The night passed, and it was time for everyone to go home.

It seemed that most of the day had been devoted to celebrating their engagement. It was a once-in-a-lifetime experience that everyone enjoyed in the moment.

"Well, Mama, I think it's time for me to head home and get ready for work tomorrow," Isabel said.

"I have to do the same," Esteban added.

"I guess I'm just tagging along," Cindy replied.

"I'm very grateful to God for allowing all of this to happen," Mrs. Diaz said warmly. "My daughter is finally marrying a wonderful young man like you, Esteban."

"Your daughter is a gift from heaven, Mrs. Diaz," Esteban responded as he held up her hand and kissed it, "and I will always take care of her for as long as I live."

"Alright, that's it!" Cindy chimed in with a grin. "I need to find someone like Esteban before I leave Mexico City, or else I'll have to clone him!"

"I enjoyed the dinner, Mrs. Diaz, and I look forward to seeing more of you," Esteban said.

"I enjoyed it too, and I love the way you cook," Cindy added, addressing Mrs. Diaz with a smile.

"Well, we better get going then," Isabel said. "Goodnight, Mama. I'll call you tomorrow."

"Goodnight, hija. I'm so happy for you," Mrs. Diaz replied, tears welling in her eyes.

All three women exchanged happy tears before heading outside to Esteban's car. They waved goodbye to Mrs. Diaz and set off.

"I never thought I'd be part of a proposal when I came to Mexico City," Cindy said, looking delighted.

"It just goes to show you how life can surprise you," Esteban replied, chuckling.

"I think you two will make a wonderful couple for many years," Cindy smiled. "Just don't forget to invite me to the wedding, okay?"

"I'd never forget that, Cindy," Isabel assured her. "You'll be one of my maids of honor."

"Really? Oh... thank you, Isabel!" Cindy hugged her friend tightly.

They arrived at the Hilton and dropped Cindy off. Then, Esteban drove Isabel back to her apartment, where she invited him in. Overflowing with happiness, all Isabel wanted was to hold and kiss Esteban.

"I love you so much, Amor," she whispered. They kissed deeply, savoring the moment together. All other thoughts faded, and they lost themselves in the bliss of being alone and in love.

After a while, Esteban pulled back gently. "I would love to stay, Isabel, but I have to be up early to see the Senator."

"I understand," Isabel replied. "I have a lot to do at the agency as well."

"I love you, Isabel," Esteban said, gazing into her eyes.

"I love you too, mi amor," she replied, looking at him like he was her prince.

Finally, Esteban left and returned to his apartment. Isabel was in a dreamy spell, still processing that she had just accepted a marriage proposal. All her previous doubts had melted away. All she could think about now was Esteban, their love, and the happiness awaiting them in the future.

***

The night passed, and morning came. Esteban woke up and realized he had to get ready for work. He got up, ate a small breakfast, and headed out the door. As he was pulling into the parking lot, he spotted the place where he had parked last Friday. *I wonder what excuses they'll have for the thugs who tried to steal my car,* he thought to himself. "Chavez better have a good explanation for all this," he muttered under his breath.

He got out and went inside the congressional building, greeting the janitor and some secretaries along the way. Esteban walked toward Senator Fernandez's office, as he still needed to discuss the events he had observed. *I just hope the senator doesn't act like he did last time...he seemed like he wanted to get rid of me that morning,* he thought. *He acted like he didn't care, as if I was making all this up... I didn't like that.*

He arrived at the office and knocked on the door. The secretary answered and told him to come in. "May I help you?" the secretary asked.

"Yes, I'm Agent Esteban Galindo, and I came to see Senator Fernandez... he's expecting me," Esteban replied.

"Please have a seat, and he'll be with you in just a moment," the secretary said. Esteban sat down and waited to be called in.

After waiting for ten minutes, the secretary looked at Esteban. "The senator will see you now," she told him.

"Thank you," Esteban said, standing up.

Esteban walked in as the senator was just hanging up the phone. "Come on in, Agent Esteban, and have a seat," the senator said, sounding somewhat pleased.

"Thank you, senator," Esteban replied. "I hope I'm not taking too much of your time, senator."

"No, by all means, you're not." The senator paused, straightening out the papers before him. "I wanted to talk to you privately here and tell you that I've thought a lot about your visit and what you told me." He looked straight at Esteban who was listening attentively. "I'll be honest with you, Agent Esteban, I knew about the incident that happened Friday evening involving you."

Esteban looked puzzled.

"In fact, it was all kept secret because it would only cause a scandal with the press and raise concerns about our premises' security," the senator explained. "I don't know how this happened, but I have men working on it, and we'll get to the bottom of it," he assured Esteban. "When you came to see me at my house, I wasn't sure if you were coming with false information or trying to misguide me," he admitted.

"I wouldn't do that, senator... I serve to protect whoever I'm assigned to," Esteban said.

"I realize that now, and that's what I like about you," the senator replied. "I did some checking up on you because I take security very seriously too; I hope you understand."

Esteban wondered what this was leading to. "Agent Esteban, I've been in politics for over twenty-five years, and the way things work is by 'I rub your back, and you rub mine'; otherwise, you get nothing done on your own," the senator said. "I realize that your job is to protect whoever is assigned to you, but even the best agents have been bought for a price."

"Sir... I am not for sale, and no one buys me," Esteban replied firmly.

"I've come to realize that, Agent Esteban and that's why you're here," the senator said. "I've spoken to my best source, and he highly recommended you above everyone in the agency. In fact, he recommended you for a full-time bodyguard position. For this person to make such a recommendation, I have to take his word as law."

Esteban was a bit confused but felt proud at the same time.

"I want you on my team, working solely for me. You won't need to worry about other congressmen or diplomats to protect," the senator said. "You'll handle every case or job that helps the people I represent and contribute to making this government a respected institution rather than a corrupt one." His tone was almost like he was giving a speech. "This also means you'll answer only to me and take orders from no one else unless I instruct you to," the senator said firmly.

Esteban simply nodded.

"You might think I'm making myself a totalitarian figure here, but I would never abuse my power or go against the constitution, in case you're worried about that," the senator said. "It won't be easy because I play by the rules, but I play to win, and I don't take bribes or threats from anyone. Everything I do is for the people who elected me," he stated. "I choose only the best, and I'm choosing you, Agent Esteban, to be on my team," the senator concluded.

Esteban looked down at his hands. So much was changing so fast. He could not keep track. His life was being turned upside-down.

"Are you up for the challenge?"

Esteban looked down at his feet, weighing the situation at hand.

"You don't have to decide now, but I do need to know soon... there are situations that are happening, and I need someone like you... the government is an ever-changing entity that has to be controlled, or it will create chaos. It has great rewards but with great amounts of responsibility and consequences if done wrong." The Senator picked up a file that had Esteban's name on it. "I don't have to tell you about that; you've experienced that yourself." He opened it and scanned the pages. "I have a feeling that you would be good, and you could work with me to help make a better government for the people of Mexico."

Esteban eyed the file, wondering what kind of information the Senator had on him.

"All I can promise you is that you'll be in a clean atmosphere where honor, integrity, and justice will be done as intended when this nation was formed... I need people with those qualifications, and you, Agent Esteban, have them," the Senator said. He paused, waiting for Esteban to speak.

"Your salary will stay the same for now, but since this is a promotion, you will also get a raise in a month," the Senator added.

Esteban felt like he was being recruited for the military again, but he knew that coming from the Senator, it was honest and sincere. "Sir, I don't need to wait... I will work for you and help with whatever needs to be done. I believe in your work, and I believe in you," Esteban said. "I've also seen many politicians in my five years here, and you're the only one I've seen who doesn't have a bad background in corruption and the only one with the courage to do what is right, not what others want you to do... I'll be more than honored to be on your team."

"Great, that settles that then," the Senator said. He stood up from his seat, and Esteban followed. He reached his hand out and smiled warmly. Esteban happily took it and gave him a firm handshake.

"My secretary will arrange all the paperwork, and you'll only need to report to me or my office. You'll start as soon as that's taken care of," he said. "Meanwhile, you can take care of other matters you might need to, and we'll be seeing each other quite often."

"Yes, sir. Thanks again, Senator. I'll do my best to help in any way," Esteban replied.

They shook hands again, and Esteban left the Senator's office, heading toward the main floor. The Senator watched him as he went. The secretary guided Esteban to her desk to start working on his paperwork and to transfer everything to the Senator's department.

"It might take four days or even more than a week to do this paperwork," he thought to himself. "I know; I'll call Isabel and see what she's doing."

The secretary told him, "I'll need these papers from you first, then you'll have to fill out the rest here before we start transferring the rest," she said. She showed and pointed to him which papers applied to him, which ones he had to get signed, and so forth. She continued, "Please come here tomorrow, and I will guide you on where to start. Some you'll have to do here, and others you can do at home."

"You're very kind. I'll just get what you need from the other offices... I'll be back," he said as he headed out the door.

He got his cell phone as he walked out into the hall. He stepped to one side to let others pass by. The phone rang.

"Hello," Isabel answered.

"Morning, Amor, how are you?" Esteban asked.

"I'm surprised you called me this early; you usually call me closer to lunch," she said.

"Well, I couldn't stop thinking about you, and I also wanted to give you some good news," he said.

"I love you, you know that," she said in a joking manner. "What's the good news?"

"Well, I met with Senator Fernandez this morning, and I'm going to be working for him permanently," Esteban said.

"Is that good?" Isabel asked.

"Yes, that's very good... that means I don't have to go around like a puppy dog wondering who I'm going to protect or take care of," he said. "Sometimes the people I get assigned to are real assholes or complete idiots... I'll know for sure who I'll be with, and the job will seem more tolerable... but I know I'll have more honor here than with the rest of my other clients."

"I'm happy for you, Amor, as long as we can be together."

"We'll always be together, Isabel," he replied. "Well, I do have to cut this short because I have a mountain of paperwork. I'll call you later today when I get off work."

"Esteban, I also want to talk to you about this job I was offered. I want to hear your view on it." She seemed very upset and unsure as she spoke.

"Of course, you know you can tell me, especially if it means you are going away," he said in an assuring voice.

"Don't say that; I am not going anywhere. I want to stay close to you." Her voice shook as she spoke.

Esteban did not want to make her more upset, so he made it a point to keep his tone calm and even. "OK, tell me all about it when you have all the details, and we'll work it out."

"Alright, I miss you already," she said.

"Adios, Amor," he said and hung up.

I feel like I've been on the phone for twenty minutes, and all I wanted to know was how she was doing. Seems like time flies when I talk to her on the phone. He smiled.

He headed to the office where the transfer papers would be processed for him to work solely for Senator Fernandez. He knew that he would have to rely on the secretary's guidance. All the paperwork was in "lawyer language" that only a translator could understand. He got his file and presented it to the secretary there, then spent the rest of the time waiting and signing documents.

"Everything is paperwork," he whispered softly.

After about two hours, he went to the break room to get a cup of coffee. In the break room, he saw Chavez.

"Chavez, what are you doing here?" Esteban asked.

"Hola, amigo, I was just thinking of you," Chavez replied.

"It's good to see you... I've never seen you in this part of the government wing," Esteban said.

"Well, I sometimes wander off from my office to see what's going on in other departments... smell the roses, you could say," Chavez joked. "I wanted to talk to you about the call you made the other day about the parking lot incident."

"I know about it already. The Senator told me some details on how he wanted it kept quiet," Esteban replied.

"Well, you seem to know more than I do now," Chavez said, chuckling.

"I have some news for you, Chavez," Esteban said, looking at him.

"What is it?" Chavez asked.

"I'm going to be working solely for Senator Fernandez," Esteban said.

"You are?" Chavez acted surprised. "That's a great honor, Esteban."

"Well, he is a good senator, and it would be nice to just focus on one person instead of being like a blind date all the time, guarding God knows who," Esteban joked.

"It's a great honor, Esteban. You may not realize it, but it's rare these days to have just one bodyguard, especially for a senator," Chavez said.

"What do you mean?" Esteban asked.

"Today, you were given an honor that few have shared—to be the sole bodyguard for Senator Fernandez on a permanent basis."

"I didn't know it was such a high level of prestige," Esteban replied, feeling shocked.

"It is, and you deserve it. The Secret Service isn't always well trusted, and even if someone has a bodyguard, that doesn't mean they're not vulnerable to betrayal," Chavez added.

"Damn, Chavez, you sure know how to make a guy feel like he's on a bad Gestapo team," Esteban joked.

"I'm just telling you what I know. I'd never let you go in the wrong direction. I owe you too much," Chavez replied, recalling an incident where Esteban had saved him in a firefight by pulling him to safety and getting him to a helicopter while they were under attack by guerrillas. "Congratulations on protecting Senator Fernandez... this means we have to celebrate, you know." Chavez grinned.

"I don't know about that," Esteban hesitated.

"A celebration is always good!" Chavez said.

"The last time I celebrated with you, I had a headache from hell!"

"I didn't make you drink all those shots," Chavez replied innocently.

"Whatever." Esteban laughed. "Oh, I have more news."

"What are you, a journalist now?" Chavez raised an eyebrow.

"No, but I do deal with them from time to time... I'm marrying Isabel," Esteban announced.

"You proposed to her?" Chavez's eyes widened. "Oh my God! That's hard for me to believe." He eyed Esteban.

"Yes, I asked her to marry me yesterday."

"Well, I'll be damned! I never thought I'd see the day..." Chavez shook his head, smiling.

"I'm still surprised myself—it hasn't hit me yet," Esteban said with his eyes wide.

"Oh, it'll hit you... like a pile of bricks, believe me. But congratulations anyway." Chavez shook Esteban's hand. "Now we definitely have to celebrate!" Chavez beamed as he wagged a finger at Esteban. "I don't want to hear 'no.' You're coming with me for beers and tequila shots."

"I don't know, Chavez..." Esteban hesitated.

"No arguments. We'll have fun, that's that. We're getting together this Friday, and we're going to celebrate before you become one of those husbands who never leaves the house without his wife's approval," Chavez teased. "I'll come pick you up, no other plans made. Got it, my almost-gone bachelor friend?"

Esteban smiled. "Alright, alright. But I have to get back to the office and complete the transfer papers."

"I have to go too," Chavez replied. "Good to see you. And remember, I'm coming to pick you up Friday. Just you and me, no excuses."

"Alright, I'll be there," Esteban replied, laughing.

"Great! See you then," Chavez said, waving as he left.

Esteban thought for a moment. "You did say just you and me, right?" he asked Chavez with a raised eyebrow.

"What, you want me to reveal all my secrets? I'm the head of security, remember?" Chavez said with a mischievous grin.

Esteban smiled. *Shit... he'll never change... he better not get me in trouble.*

"Adios!" Chavez called as he left.

Esteban waved back and returned to the office to finish his paperwork.

After being in office for most of the day, Esteban felt a bit overwhelmed and restless, so he left a little early and headed to the gym. He hated being in offices all day; he wasn't born to sit behind a desk. As he walked toward the parking lot, he took out his cell phone and called Isabel.

Isabel answered, "Hello."

"It's me, Amor," Esteban said.

"Hola cariño, are you still at work?" she asked.

"No, actually, I'm getting off a little early so I can go work out at the gym," he replied. "What about you?"

"Well, I'm still here, going over the details of my Miami trip with Cindy. We've been having a great time showing all the different types of advertising we can do and the market we can target," she said. "I'll probably be out of here by six-thirty tonight."

"Great. Would you like to go out for dinner tonight? I feel like celebrating a little because of my work with Senator Fernandez," he asked.

"I'd love to, but don't be mad if I go a little over time. I'm only guessing when I'll get out," she said cautiously. "Would you be upset if I suggested we go another time?" Isabel asked, sounding careful.

"Well, this is spontaneous, but so is life. Let's just go have something quick to eat—I just want to celebrate the moment and share it with you," Esteban said.

"Oh Amor, you know I want to be with you. Just be patient and wait for me to be through, and we'll go out together," she replied in a soft, affectionate voice.

"That's fine. It'll give me time to work that much harder at the gym," he added.

"OK, call me before you come to pick me up," she said.

"I will," he replied.

"Adios Amor," she whispered, kissing the phone.

"Adios," he kissed back and hung up.

He was halfway to the gym now, and his mind drifted to his new client, Senator Fernandez, and the responsibility of protecting him. Esteban planned to do more research on the issues surrounding the so-called "gang." When he arrived at the gym, he changed into his workout clothes and got ready to exercise.

***

Meanwhile, Isabel was still in a meeting with some of the directors. Her company represented Nike, Gatorade, and other sports-related brands, and her job was to boost

92

advertising in the Central Mexico region. The meeting was going well. Cindy was a big help, explaining the U.S. perspective and the skills needed to expand advertising in Mexico. They worked well together. The meeting lasted past six-thirty, and though Isabel and Cindy were tired, they were happy with how it went.

"I'm so glad you're here, Cindy. You've made this whole ordeal so much easier than it could have been," Isabel told her.

"I'm more than happy to help, Isabel. You're good at what you do—it's almost like the work we did in Miami when we first met," Cindy replied.

"You're right; we make a good team," Isabel smiled. "Many of the clients here wouldn't have listened as closely if you weren't here, Cindy. It's because you're American and work for an American company; they take what you say to heart," Isabel added. "It also makes me look good that you have confidence in me and give me some credit on the proposals."

"Now, Isabel, most of the ideas are yours, and you're being too modest. I'm just here helping out," Cindy said. "I'm just happy I got invited to Mexico to help with advertising and making money... you can't beat that," Cindy smiled. "Besides, I'm also working for my company, so it works both ways."

"Well, we make a great team," Isabel repeated. She looked at Cindy to gauge her mood before asking her next question. "Cindy, I'm going out to eat with Esteban tonight," Isabel told her. "He wants to celebrate a promotion he received, and I told him I'd go after I finish here."

"That's great! He looks like he could be a big boss someday," Cindy smiled.

"I just don't want to make you feel like I'm leaving you alone or ignoring you right after work," Isabel said.

"Oh, don't be silly. Go with Esteban and have a good time; you're not doing anything wrong," Cindy replied. "I'd expect you two to be constantly together after the proposal this weekend." Cindy smiled. "I'll be in Mexico City for two weeks, so we'll see each other quite a bit every day."

"Well, I'll call you after I get home, and we can discuss more about the presentation we have to do this week," Isabel said.

"OK, I'll still be up watching some TV. I need to stay updated on all the new trends anyway," Cindy joked.

"Great! Well, let's go—I'll drop you off at your hotel."

"Let's go then."

***

Esteban did his usual workout and even took an abdominal class because he had some spare time. He did his best thinking when he was busy doing something. Most of his ideas came when he was doing other activities or exercising. He then had an idea of where to take Isabel. *Right now, Isabel is probably tired and ready for some relaxation, something that's not too fancy or dressed up,* he thought to himself. *I have it! I'll take her to one of those diners like the ones they have in New York, where you can eat a sandwich and just be yourself. I remember them from the last time I was there; I hope she wants to go there.* He smiled as he thought this.

After he finished his workout, he showered and headed toward her place. He called her on the cellphone.

"Bueno," Isabel answered.

"Hola, Amor, I'm coming to pick you up at your place," Esteban said.

"Well, if you get there before I do, just go on in. I just got through dropping off Cindy at the hotel, and I'm also on my way there," she said.

"If I beat you here, you owe me a big favor," Esteban laughed.

"Oh, is that so? Well, if we're going by favors, then you'll have to double mine if I beat you."

"My, my, aren't we greedy, huh?" Esteban smiled. "I'll see you there then, Amor."

They both hung up and headed toward the apartment.

Esteban beat her there. He waited outside for her. As Isabel arrived, he shot her a smile as she drove up toward him. She got out and said, "So you beat me; why didn't you go in and wait for me here?"

Esteban looked at her and said, "Because I wanted to see you drive in."

"That's very sweet and, hmm... you smell good." She kissed him passionately.

"Actually, I don't have a key to the apartment." He kicked the pavement and smiled sheepishly.

Isabel put her hands on her hips and glared at Esteban. She looked as if she was scolding a child but she had a small smile playing at the corners of her mouth. "Did you lose the one I gave you?"

"No, I just managed to leave it in your apartment last time I was here... I think I hung it up by the refrigerator."

Isabel shook her head.

They both went in, and Isabel went off to get ready. Esteban went to the refrigerator, and sure enough, the key was there. "I found the key," he said. He then headed to the living room and watched a little television.

"Amor, I won't be able to stay too long. Cindy and I have to talk a lot about the presentations that we have to do this week," Isabel said.

He felt a bit disappointed at that but decided to take it in stride. "We won't stay long. We'll just have something to eat and be right back."

Isabel fixed her hair and put on another blouse. She came out and said, "I'm ready."

"Hmmm... you always look so good no matter what you wear, cariño," Esteban said, looking at her; she was a knockout.

She smiled. They both left and headed to a diner called 'Phillies.' They chatted about their day and how far behind they both seemed to be in paperwork. They finally arrived and went in.

They both ordered a "Philadelphia special" with hot sauce and a soft drink. Esteban had a Carta Blanca beer also.

"Mmmm, this tastes almost as good as the ones they have in New York City," Esteban claimed.

"It is good, but the cheese sure is sticky. I can't seem to break it off; it keeps stretching," Isabel laughed.

After they finished eating, Isabel told Esteban what she'd been thinking all day.

"Esteban, all I've been thinking about is you, and I'm kind of glad we're here because I wanted to ask you about the job situation that I was offered," she said.

"Well, don't let me stop you. I don't want to be the cause for you not to reach what you've been fighting to do all these years," Esteban said.

"It's not that easy, Esteban. I love you, and I really never wanted to leave in the first place, but it's only for a year if I do. I would start next year in Florida, but now they're talking about Los Angeles," she said. "I don't want to leave you, especially now... I don't want to leave your side," she looked at him while they held hands.

"I don't want you to go either... I feel so close to you, Isabel, and you are the closest thing to my heart. I would do anything to keep you and make you mine, but I don't want to spoil your goals either," he said. "We can work things out if we plan them right; we just have to have lots of patience and sincerity. Don't you agree?"

She nodded her head. "I'm yours always."

He leaned over and gave her a good, long kiss. He knew he would miss her intensely but he did not want to keep her from her dreams.

"Let's do this then. See if you can work things out with your company where you're able to stay in Los Angeles or Florida for a shorter time, and you can do more traveling back and forth. You know, that way, I come to see you as often as I can. It might work out where I may even go there on business trips all the time," he said. "We have worked things out so far, haven't we?" Esteban said positively.

"Yes, we have," she looked at him in his eyes.

"God, what have I done to deserve you, Esteban," she said, throwing her arms around Esteban and kissing his cheek.

"Please, Isabel, I'm the lucky one to have you. Any man here would kneel and worship you; you're a goddess come alive. I'm the one that asks myself what you see in me." He smiled as she kept kissing him.

She leaned over and kissed him on the lips for a long time. After kissing, Esteban said, "I almost forgot to tell you. You know that I'll be working for Senator Fernandez from now on," he said. "What I didn't know was that it's also a promotion within itself. I will also be getting a raise in a month."

"That's great, Amor; I'm glad that it's turned out the way you wanted."

"Well, I wasn't expecting that. In fact, I wasn't expecting anything. I'm just glad it's turned out like this so far... I believe that this will be a good place to work, and the Senator is a fine man," Esteban said. "I'll have to introduce you to him when we have the chance."

"I'll be happy to meet him for taking care of my man," she smiled and laughed.

"What do you mean! I will be the one taking care of him."

They both laughed and enjoyed the beautiful night.

6

A few days passed, and Esteban was getting the hang of working with the Senator. So far, it had been very easy, and he tended to feel like he wasn't doing much work. Esteban was essentially acting as a butler to the Senator's guests. He didn't mind, though; he liked going beyond his job to improve things and to make the Senator look good. He knew that the Senator had chosen him, something he had never done for any other agent in his career. The Senator didn't seem to be taking advantage of his work, and Esteban appreciated that. He sensed that the Senator was still testing him out; Esteban would have done the same if he were in the Senator's shoes. All of this didn't really matter because Esteban felt honored. He used every opportunity to reflect on the things the Senator had done and to observe him in action, performing his duties—duties he had sworn to uphold: serving his people and representing them. Esteban admired him more than ever because the Senator took the time to listen to important issues concerning education, low wages, crime, and more.

The Senator was a great speaker and had natural charisma. Mexico had many problems in various economic areas. The government could only do so much, but many times, officials paid attention to these issues only when election time came around. The rest of the time, they circled the issues, and somehow, their bank accounts mysteriously grew. Politicians were infamous for stealing money from the government. It was all legal, of course, but either way, the money disappeared from the government's reserves; this was the people's money that was being taken. It was politics as usual, and little tended to change.

The Senator promised and delivered running water, electricity, and schools in areas where no one else had bothered to help. He made an effort to bring industries to his state, raising the standard of living for his people. His state viewed him as a hero, and nothing could change that, given all he had done. No other senator accomplished as much. Now that the entire nation had seen his work, he was constantly named as a potential candidate for the Presidency. The Senator was also invited to Washington, D.C., by various departments honoring him for the employment opportunities he had created and the difference he had made in Mexico. The U.S. recognized his efforts and credited him with improving ties between the two countries. He enhanced the lives of poor Mexican villagers with the help of U.S. advisory programs and factories.

The Senator had also learned quite a bit about Agent Esteban. As he sat in his office, he reviewed his personal profile and discovered that Esteban had attended a public high school in Guadalajara, enlisted in the Army for two years, and was the best in his class, excelling in physical fitness and infantry tactics. He was offered a full scholarship to the military academy of Mexico and graduated at the top of his class in Engineering. His excellent performance had earned him the chance to choose almost any area of duty, and he chose Special Forces. After his commission, Esteban served in different areas and attended many infantry schools, including the U.S. Army Infantry School in Fort Benning, Georgia, and the Israeli S.W.A.T. course. He completed nearly all infantry schools in Mexico, as well as the Ranger and Special Forces schools in the United States. He was sent to France and Italy for additional training. He was fluent in English and could understand Italian and French as well. He had been involved in twenty-three conflicts, with seventy-eight confirmed kills. Other governments had used his services through Mexican authorities, with some missions classified. He was a black belt in Taekwondo and Jujitsu. Esteban had saved several comrades during firefights and had been awarded many medals for his bravery.

He was involved in an incident where he disobeyed direct orders to save the lives of his men. His men were about to be ambushed, and they were too exhausted and outmanned to counterattack. The orders were to continue the mission and destroy the enemy. However, there had been bad intelligence during the mission planning from higher up, and the enemy was waiting for them. Two of his men were wounded, and another was killed. Esteban disobeyed the order by aborting the mission to save the rest of his men. He knew they would never come out alive if they stayed and engaged in a firefight. They barely made it out alive. The wounded men survived and lived to see another day. None would have survived if they had continued with the mission. For his actions, he was given the choice of court-martial or resignation, and he chose to resign.

All of this impressed the Senator, who was very happy that he had chosen Agent Esteban to be by his side. He felt it was more than coincidence—that God was working to help him.

I've made a good choice in choosing Agent Esteban to work for me. Chavez was right about him, the Senator thought to himself. "This man has seen a lot of bloodshed, and even with the raw deal he was given, he's still doing the right thing... Agent Esteban will be my right-hand man," he said to himself, almost in a whisper.

He then put the file back on his desk, looked around, and went on about his business.

The Senator had other things to worry about. There was a bill that had been nagging at him since the start. He had been pushing for this bill to pass, which called for auditing government officials and their sources of income. Many were opposed to it because it would scrutinize the salaries of government officials. Senator Fernandez supported it because it was a way to show which congressmen and senators were earning more than they were supposed to and to examine their assets. It all came down to who was getting bribed and who was earning their money honestly. This, of course, was strongly opposed by Senator Sinal, who was a millionaire and by no means wanted to disclose how he earned his money or where it came from. It was all based on an honor system, with a supposed audit agenda reporting on what government officials earned. However, this system was usually controlled by the officials themselves, so there was no real oversight. No one wanted to rock the boat, but the ones who pushed for it were the people and Senator Fernandez.

"If you have nothing to hide, then everything should be clean, and no one should have anything to worry about," Senator Fernandez stated to the people. Others viewed it as an invasion of privacy and resented the idea of answering to bipartisan inspectors. Since this was politics, everyone had much to worry about—even the President.

The bill seemed stagnant and hadn't progressed since its introduction. Senator Fernandez didn't necessarily want it to pass but hoped to incorporate enough of its contents to make a dent in how government officials earned their money. He wanted to remind them that the voting public cared about where their taxes were being spent or deposited. Politicians stole money from the government so frequently that it barely made big news anymore. When exposed, they usually fled the country and never returned to Mexico due to shame or fear for their lives.

Senator Sinal realized that Senator Fernandez was using this bill to send a message: he wasn't playing by the rules. The two had been rivals ever since they came to office and had confronted each other. While they respected each other, they were enemies to the core. Senator Sinal was like Darth Vader when it came to underhanded dealings. He was patriotic—for a price—but wouldn't hesitate to abandon that patriotism if he could get away with it.

All of this was a never-ending debate.

***

Friday finally arrived, and Esteban received a call on his cellphone from Chavez. It was 9 a.m., and Esteban stood outside Senator Fernandez's office. He knew that only a few people had his phone number, and the caller ID confirmed who it was.

"Hello," Esteban answered.

"Esteban, how's my favorite bachelor?" Chavez greeted him.

"Hi, Chavez. I was expecting your call sometime today," Esteban replied.

"I'm sure you were. I'm surprised you didn't turn off your cell phone or leave it at home," Chavez said, laughing.

"The thought crossed my mind."

"Oh, come on! You're not still sore from the last time we had a few drinks, are you?"

"Me? Sore? Nawww. Now, why would I be sore about a buddy who leaves me with an ugly-ass woman in the middle of God knows where? Oh, may I add that I was blind, ass drunk?" Esteban said sarcastically.

"She wasn't ugly! She was a good-looking woman... She had great, big tits and a fine ass," Chavez argued.

"Yeah, but she was a prostitute, and I have no idea how she looked if I'd seen her sober," Esteban shot back. "What if I had already known Isabel at the time? You think she would've understood? I don't think so. She doesn't know I've been with a prostitute, and if you tell her, she will definitely dump me and kill me afterward."

"Relax! You had a good time, and no one will tell. We were younger and just wanted to get laid anyway," Chavez said.

"Do you know how long it took me to explain the incident with Sara? I don't want to go through that again. She still doesn't know the whole truth about Sara or what kind of woman she was," Esteban said, his frustration clear.

"Look, I'm coming to pick you up after work. You and I are going to a great place to talk as friends and celebrate your engagement," Chavez said. "You're my friend, Esteban. You're closer than any brother I ever had, and I want to do things with you now before you finally get tied up and can't do shit with me anymore."

"I appreciate that, but I don't know if I want to go, Chavez," Esteban admitted hesitantly.

"Don't hurt my feelings on this, my man. I love you like a brother, and I won't get you in trouble. Please, let me do this. I owe you, and I want to be friends and take you out for a good time," Chavez pleaded.

"I know things didn't really go as planned last time, but hell, I was drunk too. I'm the one who ended up with two prostitutes, so you have no room to complain," Chavez said sarcastically.

"That makes me feel so much better," Esteban replied, his tone sharp with sarcasm.

"Look, I don't mind having a few drinks. I just don't want to end up in a gutter or waking up with some whore, and Isabel seeing me there with my pants down," Esteban said. "Things are going too well to mess it all up."

"I won't do that to you, I promise. But I do want to throw a party, and I'm not going to promise that you won't have a good time. Hell, I'd rather go to jail myself than let anything happen to you, Esteban. You're my hero," Chavez said earnestly.

Esteban smiled to himself. "Now you are full of bullshit," he said. After a pause, he added, "As long as it doesn't involve prostitutes or excessive drinking by the gallon."

"I'll pick you up at 6 p.m., so be ready," Chavez said, smiling as he hung up.

"Great. I always seem to worry every time Chavez wants to do things like this," Esteban mumbled to himself. "He means well and is my eyes and ears in everything I do, but when it comes to partying, he's unpredictable." He sighed and thought to himself, *How will I explain this to Isabel? All she knows about Chavez is that he's a womanizer and parties all the time.* He paused, considering. *He's nothing like that—well, he is when he parties, but he doesn't do it all the time.* Esteban smiled to himself again.

7

Isabel and Cindy were delivering their final presentation, and things were going well. Their plan and advertising propaganda were a success. With the championship game scheduled to be played in Mexico City in a few months, there was plenty of room for advertising almost anything related to soccer.

One of the games would be played in Los Angeles, and Isabel was informed she would handle advertising there. She was excited but nervous about what it might entail. Finally, she worked up the courage to ask her boss the question she had been dreading about a year-long stay in Los Angeles or Florida.

"Mr. Ramiro, may I speak to you in private?" Isabel asked.

"Sure, let me attend to these gentlemen first. Wait for me in my office," Mr. Ramiro replied.

Isabel walked over to Cindy. "Cindy, I'm worried about what Mr. Ramiro might say if I tell him I don't want to leave the D.F. for a year," Isabel confided.

"Well, you know him better than I do. What would he do if you said no?" Cindy asked.

"I'm supposed to open the contract and negotiations between the U.S. and Mexico. They've been working on this for years. I don't think he can find a replacement this quickly," Isabel said, her face filled with worry.

"Then you're in deep shit," Cindy said bluntly. "Don't say you don't want to go. Just suggest some modifications to your stay. You might be able to work something out, and it won't be as bad as you think. But don't say no." Isabel considered what she said, her enthusiasm and confidence leaving her. Cindy picked up on it and decided to press on harder. "If it were my boss back in Miami, he'd fire me," Cindy added seriously.

"Great. I guess I'll see what he tells me and try to express at least part of how I feel about it," Isabel said, sighing.

"Do you want me to be there with you?" Cindy offered.

"No, I think I'd better do this on my own," Isabel said.

"Okay, but I'll be here if you need me," Cindy assured her.

"Thanks, Cindy," Isabel said with a small smile.

They both returned to organizing their papers before Isabel headed to Mr. Ramiro's office to wait for him.

Mr. Ramiro came into his office, and Isabel was sitting, waiting for him.

"Well, that was a great presentation, Isabel. You and Cindy make a great team. It looks as if you've been working together for years. Hard to believe you've only known each other for a month," Mr. Ramiro said.

"Thank you, Mr. Ramiro. I like Cindy, and we've hit it off great since we met," Isabel replied.

"Now, what is it that you wanted to talk to me about?" Mr. Ramiro asked.

"I wanted to talk to you about the year-long stay in Los Angeles or Florida," she said.

"Oh, well, I hope you really like it. I have big plans for you there. In fact, you've impressed many of the bigwigs there, and they want to do business just based on your presence alone," he said. "You're a beautiful woman and smart. I like that. It shows that we also have women here in Mexico who can do the job as well as anyone else."

He did not notice Isabel's nervousness and continued praising her as she awkwardly moved her feet.

"The Mexican teams that will play there will make a big impact because Los Angeles has a great deal of Mexicans, of course, but it also has a great deal of advertising opportunities for all Hispanics. That's something we need to tap into, especially here from Mexico City."

"I thank you, and I'm very grateful for that," Isabel said. This was harder for her to say now. She felt like she was in a position where too much was on the line, and for her to say anything involving her personal life would be out of place. She didn't know if she should even ask if she could make a few more flights back home. She felt confused momentarily and almost froze.

Mr. Ramiro was completely oblivious to her thought process. He moved about his office, organizing papers and devices as he spoke. "Soccer is a big sport all over the world, and it seems that Mexicans and other Hispanics are making it more popular in the United States. The U.S. is constantly showing us all their sports heroes, and the only heroes that are really seen in the U.S. from Mexico are when we actually play them or when one of our boxers is beating the crap out of theirs." He smiled as he said this. "Well, now it's our turn to show two teams from the Mexican Soccer League playing in one of the biggest stadiums in the United States, watched by Americans with Mexican advertising and Mexican logos. I say it's about time, don't you?"

"Yes, I... I totally agree with you," Isabel responded, still in a daze.

"I'm making sure everything is to your satisfaction, and everything you need will be supplied. Just say the word, and I'll make sure it happens from this end," he said.

"Thank you, sir," she replied. He smiled at her warmly but Isabel had to stop to gather her thoughts. "I do want to ask just a small favor," she added nervously.

"Anything. Just name it," he said.

"Well... since I'll be staying for a whole year there, I was wondering if I'd be given time to come see my family more frequently than just on holidays. The holidays seem to be months apart, making the visits about three times a year," she asked, her voice shy and nervous.

"Why, of course. In fact, you might be coming home once a month or maybe even twice a month. I'll need reports and statistics on how we're doing. I know everything is on computers nowadays, but some things will have to be presented in person. Computers will never replace that," he said.

Isabel was stunned and didn't know what to say. It was more than she had expected, and she was extremely happy with what Mr. Ramiro had just said.

"Oh, I'm very happy to hear that, sir. I was... was concerned for my mother and my new fiancé," she said, smiling from ear to ear.

"Well, don't worry about that anymore. You've worked hard to get where you're at, and I need you now more than ever. So does this company, and I'm not going to let you go," he smiled. "Is there anything else on your mind?"

Isabel was wide-eyed, smiling, and not knowing what to say. "No, sir, that's all I wanted to ask. Thank you for everything you've done to help me."

"It is I who should thank you. With presentations like the one you did today, you'll have my job someday... when I retire first, of course," he laughed.

She laughed as well. "Thank you. I'm glad you let me talk to you about this. It was really on my mind," she said.

"No problem at all. Please come and talk anytime you need to. My door is always open," he said.

"Wait, did you say you had a fiancée?" Mr. Ramiro said. "Yes I do", responded Isabel. "Well congratulations!!; you need to bring him here so I can congratulate him as well, I'd like to meet him. Have a great rest of the day."

"Thank you, Mr. Ramiro," she said and walked out of his office. She took a deep breath, feeling so relieved it had worked out so well. She was very happy and went to Cindy to tell her all about it. She almost ran to her friend's desk, and as soon as she was out of view of her boss, she started jumping and smiling wide. "I can't believe that I'll be able to be here once a month at least," Isabel almost yelled, acting like a little girl in excitement.

"I'm happy for you. Just don't forget to come see me or invite me when you do," Cindy said as they hugged. She moved away from her screen to give Isabel her full attention.

"Well, I feel like doing something tonight," Isabel said.

"Are you and Esteban going out somewhere?" Cindy asked.

"I was thinking of you and me going out by ourselves to celebrate. What do you think?" Isabel asked, holding Cindy's hands in her own.

"Hey, I'm game. I'm dying to go out," Cindy replied with excitement.

"I might invite another girlfriend of mine that I haven't seen in weeks. You'll like her; she's fun to be around," Isabel said as she pulled her hands back.

"Let's do it, then. *Tus amigas son mis amigas*," Cindy replied without hesitation.

Isabel laughed. "I'll have to tell Esteban that tonight is ladies' night out," she said with a playful look.

"He doesn't mind?" Cindy asked curiously.

"No. We sometimes go out with our friends. It's not like we're searching for other dates," Isabel said.

"What a man! Please clone him. I want someone like Esteban too," Cindy joked. "I'm telling you now, Isabel, if you ever decide to dump or get rid of Esteban, please, please, please give him to me. I beg you. I'd do anything for a man like him," Cindy said, acting dramatically.

They both laughed and continued with their work.

***

Senator Fernandez had gone to a local restaurant and was just finishing his meal as Esteban stood nearby on guard. The Senator looked back at Esteban and said, "You can eat now."

Esteban, ever the professional, usually avoided distractions, even during meals, when guarding a client. He shook his head, indicating that he would take his break later, but the Senator was not having it. "Agent Esteban, I know it's your job, but even you need energy to live. Please sit down and eat. I'll be fine here—there are many Senators around, and you can relax for a little while," the Senator urged.

"Thank you, sir, but it wouldn't look right if I didn't guard you," Esteban replied, staring straight ahead as he spoke.

"Nonsense," the Senator insisted. "I want you near me, but I also want you in good shape and full of energy. So, please sit down and have something to eat."

"Yes, sir," Esteban said, finally relenting.

"From now on, when I eat, you eat. I know you can do your job well, no matter the situation," the Senator said firmly.

"I appreciate that, sir," Esteban said. "I just want to be able to make the call when it comes to safety, no matter where we're at. Is that fine with you?"

"That's fine with me," the Senator replied.

Esteban called the waiter, placed an order, and began eating when his plate arrived. Meanwhile, the Senator sat with two congressmen, discussing the controversial auditing bill. The two congressmen opposed the bill—not out of disagreement with its principles but because they didn't want it enforced in its entirety.

When Esteban finished his meal, he returned to his post near the Senator. The congressmen eyed him warily. One of them leaned toward Senator Fernandez and asked, "Is he independent or a government agent?"

The Senator replied, "He's my personal bodyguard. He's government material but only answers to me."

The other congressman pressed, "Can we trust this man around us? How do we know he's not an informant for someone else?"

"Believe me, gentlemen, he's not. Do you honestly think I'd have someone working for me without thoroughly vetting who he is and what he does?" Senator Fernandez said, meeting their gaze.

"I agree. If he's good enough for you, I'll trust him without question," one congressman said.

Both men nodded. They trusted Senator Fernandez, whose reputation for honesty was well-established among his colleagues. "I only ask one thing to keep this between yourselves, do we understand each other?" the senator states. All the men said yes without question or hesitation.

As the political discussion continued, Esteban stepped aside to call Isabel.

"Hello," she answered.

"Isabel, it's me, your secret admirer from France," Esteban teased.

"Hi, amor, I was just thinking about you," Isabel said warmly.

"Well, we must be on the same wavelength," he replied. "I wanted to tell you—a friend wants to take me out for a few drinks tonight. If you had anything planned, we can do it tomorrow."

"Really? Well, I was going to tell you that Cindy and I wanted to go out, just the two of us—maybe another friend too, if she decides to join," Isabel said. "My boss gave me great news. I'll be able to fly back to the D.F. at least once or twice a month! I'm so happy, and since Cindy supported me through this, I feel like celebrating with her. I hope you don't mind."

"Not at all. I'm very happy for you," Esteban said. "This way, we'll see each other more often, and the distance won't feel so far."

"Who's your friend taking you out?" Isabel asked, her tone shifting slightly. She was known to get a little jealous.

"You don't like him much, but he's a good friend of mine," Esteban began cautiously.

"Don't tell me... it's Chavez," Isabel said, her voice flat with recognition.

"I know you don't like him, but he's not that bad," Esteban said defensively.

"Not that bad? He's a womanizer! All my girlfriends say he's trouble. I don't like it—it doesn't sit well with me when you go out with him," Isabel said, clearly annoyed.

"I know, but I've set boundaries, and he'll stick to them," Esteban assured her.

"Boundaries?" Isabel scoffed. "The only thing he knows is how to charm women into bed, and he doesn't even follow those rules!"

"Amor, he's my friend. We're just going to have a few drinks, that's all. If it bothers you, I'll come to your place afterward," Esteban offered.

"No, you don't have to make excuses for him. I just don't want him causing trouble for you. I trust you, Esteban, and I know you trust me. That's what I love about us. But please, don't let him ruin the trust we've built," Isabel said softly.

Esteban knew that she was referring to their most recent fight. "I promise he won't. You're the love of my life, Isabel, and I wanted to tell you about tonight because I value you," Esteban said sincerely. "Chavez may be flawed, but he's been like a brother to me. He feels indebted to me because I've saved his life several times. You and Chavez are the two closest people in my life, but only you have my heart."

"Okay," Isabel said reluctantly. "But call me if you get into any trouble. I don't want to lose you to anyone—not even your best friend."

"You have nothing to worry about," Esteban said, smiling. "You're a gorgeous work of God, and no one could compare to you."

Isabel softened. "Okay, Mr. Charmer. Be careful, okay?"

"I will. You enjoy your time with your friends too. Call me if you need anything—I'll always be there for you," Esteban said.

"I worry more about you than me," Isabel replied. "I love you."

"I love you too," Esteban whispered.

After lunch, Esteban took the Senator back to his office in the congressional building and then stood in front of the door.

He didn't act or behave like a centurion. Instead, he was like a normal employee, acting very casual in a manner where he wasn't as conspicuous as other bodyguards. His philosophy was to blend in and not be a target; "Only when you need to look like a bodyguard should you look like a bodyguard," he always said. It had worked for all his previous clients. It was also part of his prior military training.

I'm always amazed at how all these politicians tend to behave in front of their peers—so straightforward, with the mentality that they are so honest—and behind closed doors, they act like they want to take over the country. It only reminds me of Senator Sinal. I will be glad when I can only be around the Senator and not the other politicians.

Other security men were in the area, but they usually stood outside or by the doorway. It was so obvious that they were bodyguards. Esteban walked around, looking more like a tourist and reading magazines whenever he felt like it.

The Senator finished his lunch and his talk with his peers. He got up and told Esteban that he needed to get back to the congressional building. Esteban had the car prepared to pick up the Senator. The car pulled by the restaurant, and the Senator got in. They all headed back to the main building.

As they drove back, the Senator went over some papers. Esteban looked out the window, getting used to being around the Senator and his way of life. He seemed to be a well-informed man. He was also someone you didn't underestimate. He might have appeared as though he didn't know or didn't have a clue, but he was already several steps ahead of you by the time you made a move.

Esteban liked that. He liked men with leadership, initiative, and the intention to do right. So many times in the past, he had been around men similar to the Senator but with the wrong intentions. He had seen too much and too many dead men from greedy tyrants. He was still reserved and held back because he hadn't given the Senator his total trust. It was probably instinct, but it was something that Esteban didn't give freely, and neither did the Senator. It was going to take some time for both to completely trust each other. In this type of work, trust could mean the difference between life and death, politically or literally.

They arrived at the congressional building, and Esteban got out first. They went back to the Senator's office, and Esteban did his job by hanging around the office. After five o'clock, the Senator finished his work, and Esteban took him back to his house. Few words were exchanged because the Senator was on the phone most of the time. It seemed like everyone needed to talk or arrange a meeting with him. It was surprising how he got anything done. He was constantly interrupted by people wanting to present their pleas or suggestions on all matters.

The Senator and Esteban exchanged goodbyes as the Senator was dropped off at his home. Esteban wasn't sure yet of the attitude the Senator had toward him, but he felt positive about it. He then drove off with the chauffeur back to the congressional building to pick up his car and finally went home.

He arrived where his car was parked and sighed with relief, knowing his day was done. It was also a Friday night, and he knew Chavez would be coming to pick him up in a couple of hours. He smiled, thinking about how Isabel reacted every time he mentioned Chavez. Chavez wasn't a bad guy; he just liked women and wasn't ready to commit to one yet. Esteban never thought he would commit either, but sometimes, things came along that weren't part of the plan he thought he had.

Esteban could also have been considered a womanizer. He had dated many women in his life, and women seemed to be attracted to him. He had learned that women could be trouble because he had found himself in difficult situations a few times. When he first joined the agency, there was a secretary who was very attractive. They became well acquainted and later started going out. He slept with her several times, only to discover she was the mistress of another Senator. He hadn't known until they almost got caught. He found out when he saw the Senator and her in his office. They didn't see him, but he saw them before he entered. He hadn't been in love with her—they had simply shared great moments together. She told him that she had been using the Senator to get what she wanted, but it wasn't going to work with Esteban. He later moved to another place and had only seen her a few times since then.

Another incident involved the wife of another agent, who had come on to him on several occasions. Esteban knew she was married, but she claimed to be separated and in the process of divorcing. She also said that only Esteban knew about it. She was very attractive, and one thing led to another—they became lovers. It ended when Esteban found out about the affair the hard way. He had been playing racquetball with the woman's husband. During their conversation about relationships, the man said he had a great wife. He talked about how he didn't know what she saw in him and how good of a mother she was. Esteban didn't realize who he was talking about. After the game, they chatted more, and the husband showed a picture of her. Esteban was stunned. He had been having an affair with a married woman from a good family. He was in shock. The husband always seemed to brag about how good-looking she was. There had never been any intention for a divorce, and they had never been separated. Esteban had a rude awakening about marriage at that moment.

All that was in the past. He tried to focus only on the future, but it still lingered in the back of his mind. He had learned some hard lessons in relationships that hadn't worked out as he thought they would. He had never had his heart broken like some of his friends, but his feelings had been hurt many times. Isabel was the only woman who had truly won his heart, and that scared him at times. He didn't always know how to deal with it, but he realized he would do anything for her. He had to trust her just as she trusted him. He wanted her to be the one, for the rest of his life.

8

Things began to look like they couldn't get worse with all the suspicions surrounding Senator Sinal's activities.

Companies were facing problems because of employee pay issues. The textile field was in chaos because employees left and right were complaining about their abysmal pay and awful work conditions. At first, the new changes in the system were celebrated; the new wages appeared appealing because they were more than the average man on the street could earn, but it was soon realized that the work was far from glamorous. In fact, it was grueling. The workers had to put in long hours, and if an employee didn't meet the required output, they would be replaced in the blink of an eye. This forced employees to work extra hard out of fear of losing their jobs, which put serious stress on their bodies.

A few employees even accused one company, Maxil, of threatening workers who didn't meet their schedules or work expectations with punishment. In retaliation, the employees began threatening to strike. This, in turn, seemed poised to spark a chain reaction in other states with the same company, as employees elsewhere shared similar grievances. Senator Fernandez received an early tip about the potential strike before the employees began to organize. These textile companies were foreign-owned, and a great deal of pressure was placed on employees to produce a high volume of products within strict deadlines. While the workers appreciated their pay, as it was more than they had ever expected to make, it was still low compared to what Americans or Europeans earned for making the same products.

In one incident, an employee from Maxil, a company that assembles electronics, was interviewed by the press about his position and why he was fired. He responded that he had been working overtime, clocking 70-80 hours a week, and had not received his overtime pay. "I worked to support my wife and children," he said, "and I liked making extra money, but now the company got used to me working like this all the time, and they demanded the same hours with no extra pay.... I was fired because I was told I was insubordinate and didn't want to work." He looked utterly defeated as he spoke to a reporter. "I had several problems with my hands from the difficult work I had to do, and several times I was denied permission to see a doctor unless I had a severe cold or disease... the companies don't believe that employees can get hurt from doing repetitive, manual labor... all they care about is making the product without any problems from their workers." His eyes betrayed the stress he was facing. "We're not robots, and we can get hurt... they don't seem to understand that, and they also don't take any of our concerns seriously."

"What are some of the damages that have occurred to you while working this job?" the reporter asked.

"I can no longer move my fingers like before, and my lower back has a constant ache... I'm not my normal self anymore, and now I don't know how I will support my family," he said sadly, with tears in his eyes.

Meanwhile, many other employees behind him shouted in agreement, anger clear on their faces. The company's spokesperson was also interviewed but denied the allegations to the extent stated by the employees. The spokesperson for Maxil responded, "Our company is a company that cares. We take care of our employees, and they have benefits if they are injured in any of our facilities. We don't deny medical treatment, and we don't lay off employees because they get injured in our company," the spokesperson stated.

The public had heard these kinds of statements before from companies within their own country. To them, this was the same song, only now from foreign companies. The issue was brought to the attention of some government officials. The media shed light on the situation, and the workers for this particular company felt that the only way to be heard was by getting news teams involved. They were beginning to talk about a strike.

Meanwhile, the issue had reached Senator Fernandez and other congressmen. The Senator was briefed on the situation, and his staff brought in a recorded newsreel for him to review. Senator Fernandez watched the recording.

"I see major corruption with this man," the Senator said to his aide. Esteban was in the room, standing guard, his ears primed, listening in. "It's people like these that cause suffering, and then, society pays for it," the Senator said, pointing at the TV. "I've had my share of dealing with companies that don't care for a soul, only wanting to make money and leaving poor, honest men out in the cold with no way of making a decent living," he said with a tone that struck a nerve somewhere with him.

"Foreign companies are good for strengthening our economy here in Mexico; they raise our standard of living, but they also tend to abuse our people for cheap labor they couldn't get in their own country," the Senator said. "I want to know more about this incident because so far, crowds are gathering in many cities, and the people are getting organized. A strike can sometimes lead to people getting hurt and even killed... I don't want it to get that far, especially if it threatens my state," he concluded.

The Senator's other aide took notes on what the Senator said. The Senator then ordered his two aides to find out information to determine if this could get out of hand. The aides nodded to the Senator and then left the room.

"What do you think about all this, Esteban?" the Senator asked.

"Well, Senator, I have to agree with that poor man. He may never be able to move his wrists and his lower back. This will cost him his total way of life because he'll be dependent on his family that he can't support," he said.

"I think we need to get these companies to stop abusing good people and pay for the wrongful abuse of their employees," the Senator said. "If someone has to be the one to throw the shit in the fan... well... I'm not afraid to do it in order to help my brothers trying to make an honest living." The senator folded his arms. "Don't get me wrong, I appreciate foreign companies investing in Mexico and helping our country, but sometimes it's a cost more than a human being can bear if the person is abused."

Esteban admired the words from the Senator. He had other clients that he had to protect, and some didn't give a rat's ass for a poor employee who was screwed by the system.

Another thing that was happening in Mexico was that many foreign companies from the U.S., Japan, and Europe were setting up maquiladoras to assemble products for cheap labor. It benefited the companies and gave jobs to unemployed, low-income Mexicans. However, it also put them in a life where they earned just enough money to stay ahead while risking bodily harm as time went by. Foreign laws didn't apply in Mexico as they did in their own countries, so the companies got away with more when it came to safety. There were no major retirement benefits and very limited room for advancement without the proper education. This all meant that employees would be stuck in a constant cycle, living from paycheck to paycheck.

The laws were changing and improving. Many had made a great living from it, but there was still a long way to go for honest people not to be taken advantage of for their labor. Esteban knew all this because he had seen it firsthand when his father shifted from job to job while he was a little boy. Senator Fernandez knew this as well, and he seemed very convincing in deterring this type of employee abuse.

A few days passed, and suddenly, violence erupted in the streets of Tampico. There were a few maquiladoras in that area, and a strike was established. The company had other employees continue to work, but the striking employees began throwing stones and burning tires, blocking newly hired employees or employees who didn't want to strike.

The workers were protesting against the overwork that was expected of them. The pay didn't seem to be the issue, but eventually, it became part of the protest. Police were sent to calm the situation, and dozens of people ended up being arrested and severely hurt during the demonstrations. Everything began to happen in the manner that Senator Fernandez didn't want it to go. The police began to get out of hand, beating some demonstrators, and that got put on television. The whole thing got blown out of proportion.

The next day, other companies followed in other cities with more violent demonstrations than the first one in Tampico. The media was filled with coverage of all this violence that appeared from nowhere, all for better working conditions and pay. Many of the stories were taken out of context, adding fuel to the fire, as in the first incident.

The Army was put on standby by two governors, and even the President in Los Pinos was ready to give the go-ahead to send troops to the necessary areas. Finally, in the city of Aguascalientes, soldiers were sent to keep order. They wanted to make sure that no riots occurred like they did in the other two cities.

All these clashes captured international attention, making the U.S. more aware of what was happening south of the border. Since it was in the U.S.'s interest to protect their companies, they began monitoring American companies to ensure nothing major happened to them.

A famous reporter from the television station Azteca had always been involved in controversial topics. Many of them had gotten him in trouble and, in one case, arrested. The reporter, Guzman Estrada, seemed to always take on the dangerous news reports where others tended to be very afraid.

In a recent incident, stories had been spread that U.S. companies were using merchant trucks to transport drugs across the United States. Eighteen-wheelers were the lifeline for many companies in transporting assembled products to the U.S. Estrada investigated the matter and found patterns pointing to the American Hollow Company.

Mr. Estrada was a very persistent reporter and kept investigating and asking questions about the American Hollow Company, where electrical equipment was assembled in maquiladoras. Mr. Estrada wanted to get interviews with company officials but was always denied. He then questioned the employees, but none were willing to give any information out of fear of losing their jobs. The workers made good money, and very few ever wanted to leave.

He finally managed to get one employee to be interviewed. The employee decided to talk to Mr. Estrada because he felt that the company was responsible for his brother's disappearance and that nothing was being done to find him. His brother had been missing for over a year, and the last time he was seen was when he was driving some merchandise toward the U.S. border. His brother had told him that packets that looked like drugs were being transported across the border. That was the last he heard of him.

Mr. Estrada was deeply intrigued and captured the interview on tape while protecting the man's identity. Late at night, in a dimly lit hotel room, Mr. Guzman Estrada conducted the secret interview. His camera crew, seasoned and fearless, operated like a combat team, ready to face any danger to document the truth. The video began with Mr. Estrada introducing the interview:

"Hello, I'm Guzman Estrada for Azteca Television Station, and I'm here in secrecy, interviewing Mr. Ramirez—a pseudonym given to protect the identity of a former employee of the Hollow Company."

The camera revealed only a shadowy figure and a disguised voice as Mr. Estrada began his questioning. "Mr. Ramirez's brother is also an employee of the company but has been missing for over a year. Rumors have circulated for years that drug trafficking has been occurring through major companies, but this is the first time we've had the opportunity to interview someone who might shed light on these claims. Now, Mr. Ramirez, you are saying your brother has been missing for a year or so, and nothing has been done to find him?"

"Yes, that is correct. My brother hasn't been seen or heard from since last year, and he was working for the Hollow Company driving a truck," Mr. Ramirez responded in a deep, distorted voice.

"How long have you been working for the company?" the reporter asked.

"For over three years," Mr. Ramirez replied.

"And how long had your brother worked for the same company?" Mr. Estrada asked.

"It would have been the same amount of time if he was found or still here. We both started working at the same time," Mr. Ramirez said, his nervousness obvious.

"Did you speak to your brother at all before he disappeared?" Mr. Estrada pressed further.

"Yes, I did. My brother spoke to me before he left for Nogales," Mr. Ramirez replied.

"What did your brother tell you when you spoke to him?" Mr. Estrada asked more intensely.

"Well, my brother said he found packages of white blocks that looked like baking soda stuffed in his electrical equipment. He knew it was drugs—possibly cocaine—and was afraid to go to the U.S. with it," Mr. Ramirez explained.

"So your brother told you he saw blocks of what appeared to be cocaine in his semi-truck and was afraid of what might happen to him if he crossed the border?" Mr. Estrada clarified.

"Yes, that's right, Mr. Estrada," Mr. Ramirez confirmed.

"Did he go across the border?" Mr. Estrada inquired.

"I don't know. All I know is that my brother was scared because he found out something he shouldn't have. When you know too much, you end up getting hurt. That's what I think happened to him—he ended up getting hurt. Otherwise, we would have heard something by now. It's not like him to go even a week without letting us know where he is. It's been over a year, and he hasn't called. We haven't been able to get hold of him," Mr. Ramirez said, his voice tinged with frustration and sadness.

"Did your brother contact the police or any authorities about this?" the reporter asked.

"No. My brother was afraid to contact anybody. That's why he called me. He knew he was in trouble the minute he found out what the shipment contained," Mr. Ramirez explained. Audiences could not see his face, but they could tell from his voice that his eyes were filling with tears.

Mr. Estrada's tone was serious as he said, "Mr. Ramirez, has your brother ever been in trouble with the law?"

"Never. We've always been hard workers and never had any problems since we were kids."

"Have the authorities or the company made any progress or resolutions regarding your brother's disappearance?"

"The police don't know anything because they haven't received a complaint from the company. And the company says they don't know where my brother is either," Mr. Ramirez replied. "They say my brother just hasn't shown up for work and is considered terminated for not showing up." His words began coming out faster now. "I don't know what to do or who to talk to. You're the only one who has made an effort to even help me with this."

"Are you still working for the company?" Mr. Estrada asked.

"They have put me on suspension because I've made comments about what my brother told me," Mr. Ramirez revealed.

"So, at this time, you are not working at the company?" the reporter clarified.

"No, I'm not. I don't believe they want me to go back to work for them," Mr. Ramirez said.

"Did you mention to the company that your brother found what appeared to be blocks of cocaine?" Guzman asked, leaning in slightly.

"No, sir... you're the first person I've ever told since my brother disappeared. I'm afraid to say anything because I don't know what may happen to me if they find out," Ramirez said.

"Right now, you're anonymous, and the company doesn't know. But speaking out is a step toward finding out what happened to your brother. Perhaps someone out there has information that could help solve this mystery," Mr. Guzman responded. "Have you received any threats for asking about your brother?" the reporter asked.

"Yes, I've received phone calls saying that if I don't shut my mouth, my family will pay for it. They also threatened that I'd never work anywhere again," Ramirez revealed.

"Mr. Ramirez, we thank you for your cooperation. May this case be resolved and your brother found," the reporter concluded.

Turning to the camera, the reporter added, "Now that we have firsthand information on the disappearance of a Hollow Company employee, what other dark secrets might surface from the rumors that have circulated for years?" He ended the broadcast, saying, "This is Guzman Estrada, reporting from a secret location for Azteca Television Station."

A few days later, company officials learned about the interview, and that's when the trouble began for Mr. Estrada. Death threats started pouring in, demanding he return any video or information he might have about the company. The police showed little interest, dismissing the threats as baseless accusations. Law enforcement officers brushed it off, claiming it was likely a prank by kids or someone playing a joke.

But Mr. Estrada was undeterred. He announced that he would air the tapes on national television in his next program. The threats escalated, and soon they became a grim reality. One day, Mr. Estrada failed to show up at work. He was later found dead in his home by his maid. Police and EMS personnel were called, and the story quickly made national headlines.

Other reporters who had worked with Mr. Estrada were kidnapped and beaten. The infamous tape, which many believed contained damning evidence, was never found among Mr. Estrada's possessions.

The incident sparked widespread concern. If Mr. Estrada indeed had proof of drug trafficking within a major corporation, it was now clear that he had paid for it with his life. This raised suspicions that powerful companies could be involved in a drug trade far more extensive than previously imagined.

Mr. Estrada's murder caused an uproar on both sides of the border. Major US news outlets like FOX News and CNN ran stories about the incident, drawing nationwide attention to the matter. Among those who took notice was Senator Fernandez, who decided to assign Esteban to investigate the case.

The next day he received the news, Esteban was heading to work. He picked up a newspaper and began reading as he entered the senator's office. He had caught part of the news the previous night but hadn't given it much thought until now. As he read further, he realized the gravity of the situation. Reputable companies were now being implicated in drug trafficking.

Riding the elevator, he continued reading. When he knocked on the senator's door, he found Senator Fernandez already at his desk, deeply engrossed in the same newspaper.

"Esteban, have you seen what's going on with this drug company ordeal?" the senator asked, pointing to the article.

"Yes, Senator. I just read about it. I hope what the paper is suggesting isn't true," Esteban replied.

"I don't know what this world is coming to," the senator said, shaking his head. "We already have enough problems with the strike developing, and now we have this—an incident that could tarnish the reputation of our biggest companies." He shook his head. "When it rains, it pours," the senator muttered.

"It always seems that way, sir," Esteban agreed.

The senator paused, staring pensively at his desk. Esteban knew he was deep in thought and waited for him to speak. Finally, the senator looked up, his expression serious.

"Esteban, I want you to go and help investigate this matter about the reporter," he said.

Esteban was caught off guard. He wasn't a detective and had never conducted an official government investigation. His only experience was a few assignments in the Army, and even those were rare.

"You will act as a government observer," the senator continued, "to ensure that the case is being handled properly. Step in and give orders if necessary."

"What kind of orders, Senator?" Esteban asked, his brow furrowed.

"Orders to gather evidence from people and places that others might avoid. You're a professional bodyguard with years of experience. You know what it takes for someone to be murdered and why. Use your knowledge to assess how this case is being managed," the senator explained.

"I've heard firsthand accounts of your work. You've helped solve many cases involving foul play, so I know you have what it takes," he added.

"It's crucial, even down to the smallest piece of information. This could involve powerful people we've never suspected—people who might be far more dangerous than we ever imagined," the senator said, his tone firm.

Esteban thought for a moment before replying, "Senator, I'm not a detective, and I don't have the experience of being one, but I'll do as you ask."

"I don't expect you to be Sherlock Holmes," the senator said with a faint smile. "I'll arrange for you to have the status of an Inspector General. You'll have full authority as an observer to detect and gather critical information. Even though it may seem like you're acting as a detective, your primary role will be oversight."

Seeing Esteban's confused expression, he continued, "I'm the head of the committee, and I have the authority to appoint whoever I see fit, especially in emergency situations."

"Yes, sir. I understand. I'll leave as soon as you need me to," Esteban said, nodding.

"I want you to leave tomorrow after lunch, and I'll instruct you more tomorrow morning. Meanwhile, I have to deal with this strike before it becomes a runway fire that can't be controlled," the Senator said.

"I'll leave you to your job, sir, and I'll be out here if you need me," Esteban replied as he headed out the door, closing it behind him. Once outside, he began to make plans to leave the next day. He made a list of the things he needed to do and the items he would take with him. He wasn't sure how long he would be gone, but he estimated a few days. It all depended on how much cooperation he received and what luck he had in finding clues.

I feel like Magnum P.I. every time I have to do this, he thought to himself. "I should've been a detective," he muttered aloud. Esteban had dealt with similar situations before during his time in the Army. He had been an investigator when two soldiers were killed during an exercise and had witnessed how things were handled. This was just another unexpected part of his job, but it felt like the story of his life.

Later that evening, he finally left work and started driving to Isabel's place. He wanted to tell her in person that he'd be leaving for a few days. She always worried, and he wanted to be close to her when he broke the news.

On the way, he called his mother to check in. Everything seemed fine. They had their usual conversation, and he hung up. Then he called Isabel to make sure she was at home.

"Bueno," Isabel answered.

"Hola, amor. I'm glad you're home because I'm heading to your place," Esteban said.

"I've been home for about thirty minutes... did you just get off work?"

"Yes. I'm calling to see if you need me to pick up anything on the way."

"You sure are being nice tonight, but no, I don't need anything from the store," she replied in a playful, sultry tone.

"Well, you know I can't stay away from you," he said. "I'll see you in a few minutes."

"OK, I'll see you soon," she said, kissing the phone before hanging up.

Esteban smiled to himself. *Whatever plans we had for the weekend are shot with this investigation. We'll see how this one goes,* he thought as he drove.

When he arrived, he knocked on the door. Isabel opened it with a smile. They kissed and hugged before he stepped inside.

"Honey, I brought some food from this great restaurant, and there's plenty here. Won't you stay and eat with me?" she asked.

He was surprised by the food—good thing he hadn't picked anything up.

"That sounds really good, but I don't have much time," he said.

She looked at him curiously. "Why are you leaving?" she asked, though her tone suggested she already knew the answer.

"Actually... yes," he said. "I have to go and play secret agent. I'm leaving tomorrow. I just wanted to see you and talk for a few minutes."

"Esteban, you're always extra nice to me when you're about to do something dangerous. You're making it sound like you're going into battle," she said.

"No, it's nothing dangerous. I might just be there longer than I anticipated. I wanted to see you before I go because even a few minutes with you makes my day."

"Now you're making me sad because you're leaving."

"I didn't come here to make you sad. I came here to see you smile. Your smile makes me feel good," he replied, kissing her as they sat on the sofa.

Esteban reassured her that nothing was wrong and that this was just part of his job. He compared it to when she had to leave and stay away for a few days. Once he had lifted her spirits, he began to say goodbye.

"I'm glad you feel better about this now, Isabel," he said.

"I still don't like you going off without knowing what will happen," she replied.

He smiled. "The only thing that will happen is I'll be bored and wish I were with you. I'll call you every day while I'm there."

"Promise?" she asked.

"On my hands and knees," he said with a smile.

They kissed again, and he got up to leave.

"I have to pack and get ready. I leave tomorrow," he said.

They said their goodbyes. Esteban headed back to his apartment to prepare for the next day.

Once home, he began packing. He laid out the necessities: his weapons, communication equipment, and other essentials. He set his alarm and got into bed, though he wasn't particularly sleepy. He lay there for a while before finally drifting off.

The next morning, the alarm clock went off, and he reached over to turn it off.

"It's going to be a long day," he muttered to himself as he got up and started getting ready.

Meanwhile, back in the town where reporter Guzman Estrada had been killed, the police continued their investigation into the mysterious homicide that had captured the headlines. They maintained round-the-clock surveillance of the crime scene to keep unauthorized personnel out and prevent the press from exaggerating the situation.

Esteban headed toward the congressional building to see the Senator. The Senator was supposed to give him more instructions on what he was expected to do. He had an idea, but he was still keeping things under suspicion because the Senator often had other plans.

I don't know exactly what I'll be doing in this case, but I'm sure that the Senator wants to get some answers, he thought to himself. *I wonder what my title will be when I'm there. He did say I would be an Inspector General. I certainly can't be an investigator for the crime scene—that's for the feds to work on. So, this will be a surprise for me.*

He approached the congressional building and drove into the parking lot. After parking his car, he headed inside and walked toward the Senator's office. The Senator hadn't arrived yet, so he waited for him. Usually, Esteban would head to the Senator's home to bring him to work, but this was an unusual situation, and the Senator wanted to change things this time.

The Senator arrived ten minutes later with two bodyguards. Esteban was waiting for him outside the office.

"Morning, Senator," Esteban said.

"Morning, Agent Esteban. Come in, and let's discuss your trip."

They both entered the office while the two bodyguards stayed outside the door.

"Have a seat, Esteban," the Senator said.

Esteban sat down.

"I know this may seem awkward, but I have to know what happened to that reporter," the Senator began. "For several years, I've received reports that major drug loads have been passing through the borders, but we've never really had anything concrete to go by—until now. This report will shed light on what I've been told was only hearsay."

"If this is true and this is happening, it could explain many circumstances and situations that have occurred in the past few years," he continued, looking directly at Esteban. "This is something that the President should be handling, but he's not. I, as a Senator, am doing what I think is best for my country. I may step out of bounds, but I do it to better my state and my nation. This is probably the job of the Secret Service or another law enforcement branch, but I have to find out for myself without the risk of having any moles in my investigation. I've reached this point because I'm losing faith in our judicial system."

The Senator looked at Esteban with a disappointed expression.

"I have to find out what is really going on, and I trust you, Agent Esteban," he said, meeting his eyes.

Esteban stared back quietly. The Senator looked away briefly, then turned back to him.

"I lost a good man when he was told about this trafficking that supposedly is happening, and he was never found," the Senator continued. "He wasn't as well-trained or well-educated as you, but nevertheless, he was a good man. I know how that employee felt when he said he lost his brother."

The Senator got up and walked to his mantle, looking at a picture of his son before turning back to Esteban.

"Esteban, I want you to go to the crime scene and inspect every inch of that place. I want you to gather information as a detective would and see what can be clarified as an independent investigator," the Senator said. "You will probably get a lot of flack, but I will give you the authority and the means to get what you need." He paced around the room. "Another reason I want you to go there is that if someone is trying to cover up anything, they'll have to go through you. I want you to be a fly on the wall—hear as much and see as much as possible."

The Senator looked away, his eyes flashing with grief. "I'll conduct my separate investigation here with the information you supply me, and I'm sure I'll find something that confirms what I've always suspected," he said. "This is to be kept as secret as possible. No one else knows about this operation but you and me, and that's the way I plan on keeping it."

The senator finally sat down. "Do you have any questions?"

"What if they resist giving me information? May I use any means necessary to get it?" Esteban asked.

"Only within reason, Esteban. I don't want you going around beating the hell out of people or shooting them up. It would defeat the purpose, make me and everyone here look bad, and compromise my secret operation. I could even lose my seat here," the Senator replied.

"I understand, sir. That wasn't my intent. I was just asking whether I'd be seen as a criminal if I had to break in or subdue anyone trying to harm me," Esteban asked.

"I'll give you the authority to do practically anything you need, but don't kill anyone, and don't involve the press," the Senator replied. "Do everything within reason, and if you're unsure, don't do it. The objective of this mission is stealth. Do we understand each other?" the Senator asked firmly.

Esteban nodded, fully grasping the weight of the Senator's words. He trusted him enough to interpret "any means necessary" as potentially going beyond what was explicitly permitted, even though the Senator wouldn't say it outright. Esteban knew this assignment skirted the edges of legality. Breaking rules to make something right was not new to him— it was a principle he had lived by before.

"You do realize, if anything goes wrong, I'll have to deny you and this entire situation. Too much is at stake," the Senator said, locking eyes with Esteban. "I need your word, Esteban, that you'll deny everything you know about this mission—including my involvement."

Esteban's heart raced as the Senator's words sank in. He thought about the trust being placed in him and the times he had given his word before, only to be betrayed. Still, he relied on his instincts.

"Yes, Senator. I understand. I give you my word—I won't disclose anything about this mission. You can count on me," Esteban said as his heart beat rapidly.

The Senator let out a small sigh of relief, his trust in Esteban seemingly affirmed.

"Good." The senator smiled. "You can call me if you have questions, but keep it brief—no more than three minutes. Here's a separate cell number for our communication," the Senator said, handing Esteban a slip of paper. "People are always spying on government officials. I don't want anyone to know what you're doing."

Esteban took the number and listened intently.

"You and I are the only ones involved in this investigation," the Senator continued. "I'm trusting you because I believe in your abilities. Sending you is a gamble, but it's worth it to uncover the truth and see if this connects to anyone in the government."

"Yes, Senator. I understand and will follow your orders," Esteban replied.

"Good. I assume you're packed and ready to go. Here are your tickets," the Senator said, handing them over. "You'll be flying to Puebla, where the reporter died in his home. Your plane takes off in an hour. Instructions are in this envelope."

"I'll call you once I'm settled," Esteban said, accepting the documents.

"Good luck, Esteban, and be careful. You're my right-hand man," the Senator said with a small smile.

Esteban felt an odd sense of vulnerability. Usually, he was the one urging caution, but this time, it was directed at him. They shook hands before Esteban left the office.

Outside, Esteban walked briskly through the congressional building, heading to the parking lot. He climbed into his car and drove to the airport. As he navigated the roads, he opened the envelope and glanced at its contents. The first thing he noticed was that it said he would be taking a private plane to avoid the delays and risks associated with commercial flights.

The Senator really wants this to be as covert as possible, Esteban thought to himself. *He said something about that he was suspecting something like this all along. What did he mean by that? I guess I'll find out when I'm there.*

At the airport, Esteban parked in a designated area and retrieved his luggage. A young man approached him near the hangar.

"Agent Esteban?" the young man asked to confirm his identity.

"Yes," Esteban replied.

"I'm Jorge Morales, your pilot. It's a pleasure to meet you," the man said, extending his hand.

"Same here," Esteban responded, shaking his hand.

"Do you need to use the restroom before we take off?" Jorge asked.

"I'm fine. I'm ready to go," Esteban said.

"Let's board, sir. The plane is ready," Jorge said, helping load the suitcases into the small twin-engine airplane.

Once aboard, they took off toward Puebla. Esteban gazed out at the city below as they ascended, marveling at its vastness.

No matter how many times he had seen it from the air, it never failed to amaze him.

Settling into his seat, Esteban pulled out the envelope and read the instructions more thoroughly. He was to check in at the Camino Real Hotel, report to the local police headquarters, and then visit the crime scene. His task was to photograph and record anything that might shed light on the case. He would document everything separately, keeping personal copies of all findings.

Seems straightforward enough, Esteban thought, tucking the papers away.

Meanwhile, the pilot made small talk about the plane and how long the trip would last. Esteban kept his responses short and brief, acting like he was enjoying the trip. After an hour, they reached Puebla and landed at the airport. The plane came to a stop, and they both stepped out. A car was waiting for Esteban.

"Thanks for the ride. You're a good pilot," Esteban said.

"Anytime, Agent Esteban. I'll be here whenever you decide to fly back," the pilot replied.

"Thanks. I'll give you a call when that time comes."

Esteban retrieved his bags, loaded them into the car, and drove off to the hotel. Once there, he called the Senator to inform him of his arrival.

The Senator was in a conference, debating what to do about the strike. Several congressmen were advocating for the use of military power to keep the strike under control. Others, like Senator Fernandez, wanted to avoid making things worse.

As the Senator's device beeped, he glanced at it and saw it was Esteban. He pressed the confirmation keys and instructed Esteban to continue with the plan.

Esteban confirmed and smiled as he finished his sentence. "Technology is great... who would have known you could do all this ten years ago... amazing," he said.

The Senator returned his focus to the ongoing discussion. The debate over using the military as a police force raged on. He realized that deploying the Army would likely be perceived as an act of hostility by both the people and the international community. The Senator was determined to keep the matter at a local police level, even if additional officers from nearby towns had to be brought in. He suggested addressing the issue through a press conference, allowing the strike leaders to discuss their grievances with company officials to reach a resolution.

The debate continued for most of the day, with arguments growing more heated. Senator Sinal, known for his bold opinions and strategic maneuvering, spoke with authority.

"Gentlemen," Senator Sinal began, pounding on the podium. "We all know that situations like these have a tendency to get out of hand. The people are responding to the injustice they believe they've experienced. Now, having the local police is a must, but if some of these thugs and hoodlums start a wide-scale riot, I see no shame in having the Army on standby. Other police from nearby towns don't have the training or equipment to handle something like this."

He paused, scanning the room before continuing. "Some of these people are legitimate in their protest, but many just want to create total chaos and havoc. We've already had two incidents in two of our cities, and look where that's gotten us. The police couldn't control or contain the rioters. We don't need that spreading to our other cities. The military is there to be used when it's needed—and it's needed now. Controlling any riot escalation is our duty for the safety of our fellow Mexicans. No one likes violence, but we have to use whatever means are necessary to maintain order."

The room was already stirring with whispers and teeming with nervousness.

"I'm ready to state my power to send the Army to calm this situation down and get talks back on the table," Senator Sinal declared, his voice commanding and unyielding.

The room fell silent as many congressmen avoided challenging Sinal directly. His reputation for accomplishing his goals through intimidation was well known. No one wanted to cross his path. Though he had done a few commendable things in the past, most of his influence came from instilling fear. Sinal firmly believed that showing force would deter further violence and give him more power.

No one knew what his true intentions were; Sinal had deeper motives. If the military were deployed and violence ensued, he had connections with certain generals who would help him achieve these goals. They could manipulate events and fabricate evidence to twist the narrative in his favor.

On the other side of the debate, Senator Fernandez maintained his stance as a diplomat. He strongly opposed military involvement, knowing that such a move would only be perceived as aggression. He knew this approach would lead to innocent people being hurt or killed. Fernandez argued passionately for negotiations between the people and companies.

His persistence frustrated Senator Sinal, though Sinal tried not to show it. The two had clashed in past debates, and Fernandez never backed down. He understood the consequences of deploying the Army and was resolute in finding a peaceful solution.

The discussion dragged on until the end of the day, with no resolution reached. Many politicians left the room visibly agitated, tempers flaring, and tensions high. As they left the conference, all they could think was, *"What will come next?"*

9

Esteban checked into the hotel. As soon as he got into his room, he put his things away and called the police station. He informed them that he was on his way to talk to the police chief.

"I'm sure they'll be expecting me with open arms," he said to himself sarcastically while rolling his eyes. He used the landline to call the hotel reception and got the information about a rental car that had already been arranged for him. Gathering the things he needed, he headed toward the station.

Puebla was a nice city with a lot of history. Esteban had been there many times. His first visit was during his time at the academy when he attended a banquet. It was here that he had met Sara.

While driving, he looked around and noticed a few new additions to the city; new stores and buildings were constantly being built or established here. He finally arrived at the police station, parked his car, and went inside.

He walked to the front office, where a woman in uniform greeted him.

"May I help you, sir?" she asked.

"Yes, I'm Agent Esteban Galindo from the D.F., and I came here to talk to your police chief..." Esteban read the Chief's name from a paper as he spoke, "...Chief Nava."

"Let me get him for you, sir. Please have a seat; I won't be long," she said.

"I'll stand; that's okay." He looked around the station, taking in his surroundings, noticing it wasn't as busy as he had expected. He saw a few drunk men being questioned, along with some prostitutes. *I'm glad I don't have to deal with that shit every day*, he thought to himself.

The woman returned and said, "Agent Galindo, the Chief will see you now."

"Thank you... and you can just call me Agent Esteban."

The woman nodded, smiling, and led him to the Chief's office. As she escorted him, she kept glancing back at him with her mouth slightly open. She walked close to him and her cheeks were redder than when she had first come in.

"Enjoy your visit," she said.

Esteban smiled and entered the office.

The Chief stood up and said, "Welcome, Agent Galindo. We've been expecting you. I'm Chief Lorenzo Nava, and I'm here at your service. We were informed that an agent was coming to assist us in the murder investigation." The Chief wore a crisp blue suit with a black tie. His hair was neatly cut, and his beard was trimmed short.

"Agent Esteban Galindo, and thank you for the welcome," the Chief said as he shook hands with Esteban. "Well, how can I help you, Agent Galindo?"

"Please, you can call me Agent Esteban."

"And you can call me Chief," the Chief said, smiling.

Esteban let go of the Chief's hand and took a step back, standing at ease. "I know this is out of the ordinary, Chief, and you're probably thinking that I was sent here to make sure you're doing your job right, but that's not the case," Esteban said. "It may seem intimidating at first, having someone from the Capital overlooking your case."

"It won't be the first time we've had the Feds here," the Chief said.

"I was sent here to observe and see if this is at all related to any government security," Esteban explained.

The Chief raised his eyebrows in surprise.

"I can't tell you exactly the situation, but I can say that if it has any relationship to the safety of our government officials, then I'm here to report and assist both you and the federal agents," Esteban continued. "Also, if anything is found that relates to government business, then I'll take over from there. Everything else should follow common operating procedure." "Also, nothing is to be said outside you and me on this. The only thing that should be given to anyone outside you and me is what is found but nothing about me being here to anyone, otherwise it defeats the purpose of me being here."

Esteban noticed the Chief seemed a little uptight but wanted to make it clear he was there on business. "I'm not here to point fingers or determine who's doing their job right or wrong unless it pertains to government security," he said as he put his hand to his chest in sincerity.

"You have to realize that we're all still very curious why a reporter is so important to the Feds," the Chief said.

Esteban could sense the Chief's discomfort.

"I do thank you for telling me this, and as long as we can work together and cooperate, we'll solve this case sooner," the Chief continued.

"That sounds good to me, Chief Nava," Esteban said with an agreeable grin.

"Now, I've been given access to any place I think needs to be seen, but I'm not going to barge in without your awareness or permission," Esteban said. "Before I start observing and writing my report, I'd like to have your approval and hear your views."

"Well... I wouldn't expect that from the Feds. It's good to know I have a say since I am the Chief of police in this city," the Chief said sarcastically, giving him a pointed look as he spoke. "You all have more legal boundaries than we do, and I'm glad you're being upfront with me. Not too many Feds do that; they tend to be arrogant in their procedures."

Esteban understood how some agents could behave. He had dealt with his share of arrogant colleagues and knew it gave the agency a bad rep. "Chief, whatever issues you've had with the agency in the past don't apply to me now," Esteban replied. "I'm willing to work together and cooperate to solve this case so we can all go home and get back to our lives."

They nodded in mutual agreement. They had laid their feelings about each other's organizations on the table and were now able to quickly move on to business.

"Well, what exactly happened to this reporter?" Esteban asked.

"We found him with a bullet in his head 52 hours ago. I believe it was a 9 mm. His name is Guzman Estrada," the Chief said as he adjusted his coat buttons. "He's a famous investigative reporter, one I'm sure you've heard about. He always reports stories that most people would stay away from. He was interviewing a former employee of the Hollow Company," the Chief continued. "He claimed to have a story that would break the news about the company and that he was going to air. That's the last we heard from him until we found his body. The network called us because he didn't show up to work, and he never misses work."

"Does he have any family?" Esteban asked.

"His mother passed away a few months ago, and he only has a brother, but the brother has an alibi—he's in France; he's on his way back to attend his brother's funeral whenever they have it," the Chief replied.

"What about his wife or children?" Esteban asked.

"He never married. He was seeing a woman, though, and she's currently under investigation to see if we can get any information from her."

"Do you know her name?" Esteban inquired.

"I don't know it off the top of my head, but that information—and more—should be in Guzman Estrada's file. We'll give it to you as soon as I appoint an officer to assist you," the Chief said.

Esteban nodded.

"She also seems to have a good alibi because she was out of town as well," the Chief added. "Two of my officers were the first on the scene."

"Do you mind if I talk to them?" Esteban asked.

"Not at all, but don't put them in a position where they have to choose between what they're legally supposed to tell you and what they shouldn't. You understand?"

"I'll just ask simple questions that won't interfere with how the investigation is being handled. I'm not here to inspect, just to observe and gather information," Esteban clarified.

"I know, but I've dealt with the Feds before, and it almost cost me my job because they were assholes..." The Chief gave Esteban a small smile. "No offense."

Esteban smiled. "Well, you're right—they are assholes. But I don't work for the Feds all the time. I'm here to find out certain things about the murder and matters that pertain only to national security. You have nothing to worry about with the Feds."

The Chief chuckled but still wasn't completely at ease with Esteban.

"I'd like to go to the scene, Chief Nava, and see the place," Esteban stated.

"Let me get you an officer to show you where it's at," the Chief replied. He pressed a button on his phone. "Sgt. Correro, report to my office ASAP."

"I'm on my way, sir," came the response.

"Sgt. Correro will get you a good man. You'll need someone to show you around and drive you if that's OK with you," the Chief said.

"I will for today. Thank you for your hospitality, Chief," Esteban responded.

Sgt. Correro entered the office a few moments later. The Chief turned to Esteban. "Agent Esteban, this is Sgt. Correro.

Sgt. Correro, I want you to assign someone to escort Agent Esteban to the crime scene and assist him with anything else he needs.”

“Yes, sir. By when?” the sergeant asked.

“Now. He is to stay with Agent Esteban until the investigation is complete or when Agent Esteban is finished here,” the Chief instructed.

“Yes, sir,” Sgt. Correro replied.

Estaban walked up to the young man and held out his hands. “Good to meet you, Sgt. Correro. I’m sure I’ll be seeing you around.”

“Same to you, sir. It’s a pleasure,” the sergeant said nervously, shaking Esteban’s hand firmly before leaving to carry out the task.

“Chief Nava, how can I contact you if I have questions? Do I call you here at your office, or do you have a cell phone?” Esteban asked.

“This is my direct cell number, but please keep it at a minimum. I got in trouble with the Mayor because my wife called me during a meeting, and the Mayor doesn’t like to be interrupted,” the Chief chuckled.

Esteban smiled, imagining Isabel doing something similar to him. “I totally understand,” he replied.

After a bit more chit-chat, Sgt. Correro brought in a young police officer. The officer looked like a rookie, stepping into the office with the sergeant and looking puzzled.

“Chief, this is Officer Rios,” the sergeant announced.

The rookie stood still, but before he had a chance to speak, the Chief said, "Officer Rios, my sergeant has chosen you for an important mission."

Officer Rios looked around, wide-eyed, surprised.

"I want you to meet Agent Esteban. He's from the Federal District and is here to observe our investigation into the homicide of the reporter Estrada," the Chief explained. "You will accompany him and be his driver and assistant in whatever he needs. If there is anything he requires, you are to make sure he gets it to the best of your ability." He looked the rookie directly in the eye as he spoke.

Esteban looked at Rios and extended his hand. "It's good to meet you, Officer Rios, and I'll try to make things as cooperative as possible."

"The pleasure is all mine, Agent Esteban, and it will be no bother at all," Rios responded surprisingly firmly.

"Sgt., see that there's an unmarked police car at his disposal and have it ready after lunch at the latest," the Chief ordered.

"Yes, sir," the sergeant responded.

"That is all, Sgt., and good to see you, Officer Rios," the Chief added.

"Same here, sir," Rios replied.

Both men stepped out of the office and headed toward the maze of the building. Esteban was grinning. He couldn't help but notice how nervous the young officer looked—almost as though he couldn't decide whether to sit still or jump out of his skin.

"I hope you don't mind the selection of the recruit offered to you, Agent Esteban," the Chief remarked, sensing Esteban's thoughts.

"No, not at all. In fact, it'll be good to have a new person with me. He'll have a completely fresh perspective on how things are done," Esteban said with a smile.

The Chief smiled as well.

"Chief, you don't mind if I look around, do you? I just want to get to know the place, see where everything is, and kind of get familiar with it. You understand," Esteban asked as he slowly moved across the room.

"Not at all, help yourself. I've got to get back to keeping the Mayor happy and preventing these reporters from turning this into a circus," the Chief replied.

"I'll see you later, Chief, and thank you very much for your cooperation in this matter," Esteban said.

"Don't mention it. But it's not over yet," the Chief said.

"True," Esteban agreed, stepping out of the office.

He wandered through the building, observing how many people were working. There were rows of people in each room; most seemed busy at their stations, and some were mingling and getting coffee together. He checked the halls and the front entrance. Then, he visited the jail cells to see where the prisoners were held. The cell was smaller than others he'd seen but seemed sufficient for the town's needs. The detainees appeared to be a mix of random drunks, a few drug addicts, and other troublemakers.

"Nothing new," he muttered to himself.

He headed to the parking lot where the squad cars were parked, noticing a lack of parking spaces and only two security cameras covering the entire lot. He made a mental note of that.

Glancing at his watch, he saw it was almost 11 o'clock. *Hmm, I think I'll get something to eat*, he thought. He decided to find a place where he might overhear gossip about the reporter's murder; a bar and grill seemed like a good choice.

While still in the parking lot, he saw a local bus stop near the police station. On a whim, he decided to catch it and take a look around the city. Just as the bus doors were about to close, Esteban managed to slip inside.

"You almost missed it," the bus driver said.

Esteban smiled and paid the fare. "Where's a good place to eat and have a few drinks?" he asked.

"Well, are you looking for something fancy or just a laid-back spot?" the driver asked.

"Something laid-back."

"That'll be close to downtown. There's a good area there with bars and restaurants to choose from."

"Great, take me there," Esteban said eagerly.

The bus pulled away from the station, and Esteban settled in.

Esteban looked at his watch and saw it was now 11:05 a.m. He decided to give himself two hours for lunch to look around and get some information from the locals. He decided to call Isabel but it went to voicemail.

She must be in a meeting. I'll just tell her I'm OK, he thought to himself.

"Isabel, mi amor, I made it earlier this morning, and things are fine. I wanted to call you and tell you that I'm OK and that I will call you later." He paused, thinking about what she may be up to. "You're probably in a meeting. Hope it's going well. I love you, and I'll talk to you soon." He glanced at his phone screen before hanging up.

The bus was about to pull into the stop where he was supposed to get off. He pulled the cord, got out, and began walking toward the bars.

Esteban looked around as he walked, eventually deciding to go into a bar that looked very tropical. It was called *La Isla*. It looked somewhat Hawaiian. He went in and sat at the bar. He ordered a beer and a menu.

The bartender was friendly and recommended the special of the day. Esteban ordered it. As they talked, Esteban began asking questions about the murder of the reporter.

"So, tell me, what's the deal with the murder of the reporter? I heard about it, but I don't know the whole story," Esteban asked, acting as if he didn't know anything about it.

The bartender leaned across the bar before he spoke in a low voice. "Well, as far as I know, Guzman Estrada, the reporter, was interviewing some guy from the Hollow Company. It was all kept secret because he was suggesting that the company was doing something illegal," the bartender said, looking around at the people around them. "He mentioned that he was going to air a story exposing how corruption was being kept alive, but that's the last we heard of him until they found his body about two days ago."

"Wow, that's some story," Esteban said. "Maybe he saw too much, don't you think?" he asked, making it a point to keep his eyes wide.

"It seems when you know too much, you end up missing or dead," the bartender replied as he placed Esteban's food before him.

"I think you're right," Esteban said, taking a bite of his sandwich.

"Are you new here in Puebla, Mr...?" the bartender asked, also probing for his name.

Esteban wiped his chin after eating some chips and said, "Yes, I'm here on business, and I hate traveling. I rarely get to watch any television, so I'm clueless about what's going on in the world." He avoided giving his name, dodging the question.

"What's your line of work?" the bartender asked with a cocked eyebrow.

"I'm in finances but mostly travel to check things out... kind of like an inspector for banks," Esteban said.

"Wow, sounds very interesting. At least you're where the money is at," the bartender said with a smile.

"Yeah, I guess you could say that, but unfortunately, it's not my money," Esteban said with a frown, trying to be funny.

The bartender laughed.

"This is a good sandwich. I'll have to recommend it to some of my traveling companions," Esteban said with a smile.

"Thanks. My boy works part-time, and he's a good cook," the bartender replied.

"He needs to be a chef," Esteban said.

After finishing his meal, Esteban said goodbye to the bartender and headed back to the police station. He took the bus. After a 15-minute drive around the city, he arrived at the station. He got off and headed inside to see about his vehicle and driver.

He went to Sgt. Corerro's office. The sergeant saw him approaching and got up to meet him.

"Agent Esteban, we have a car for you, and Officer Rios is waiting for you outside in the car," the sergeant said. "If there's anything else you need, please ask," he added.

"You've been very kind, and thank you," Esteban replied.

It's amazing how they treat you when you're a federal agent. I guess they're afraid of losing their job, Esteban thought to himself and smiled.

He walked across the office, where the lady who had greeted him earlier saw him. She glanced at him as he walked. She seemed to like his stride and his physique as she eyed him up and down.

Esteban went outside and spotted the rookie.

"Are you ready, Officer Rios?" Esteban asked as he walked behind the rookie.

Officer Rios was a little surprised and said, "Yes, sir, I'm ready."

"Let's go then," Esteban said.

They both got in the car and drove off, leaving the police station behind.

As they drove, Officer Rios looked puzzled, unsure of their destination. Finally, he asked, "Sir, where do you want to go?"

Esteban smiled. "I want you to first drive me around the city so I can see what's new. It's been a while since I've been here, and I want to get familiar with it while I have the time."

"Okay, but do you have any place in particular?" Rios asked.

"We'll start by going north, then west, south, and finally east. That should cover most of the city," Esteban replied.

Rios glanced at him, still looking puzzled. Esteban observed the rookie closely. He wanted to analyze him, to figure out if he might be a spy or just someone the station pulled in at the last minute.

"How long have you been on the force, Officer Rios?" Esteban asked.

"A little over a year, sir," Rios replied.

"Wow, you're practically still new at this," Esteban said. "Have you ever worked with a federal agent before?"

"No, sir. You're my first," Rios said.

"Okay, let's head west now," Esteban instructed. Rios started the car and took off.

A few moments later, Esteban asked, "Do you know anything about the reporter Guzman Estrada?"

"I just know him from watching him on TV once in a while," Rios said.

"I never really saw his show," Esteban said, feigning ignorance. "What exactly made him so famous?"

"Well, he was brave—exposing people and reporting stories about injustice," Rios explained.

"What was the last story you saw him report on?" Esteban asked.

"I saw the one about the insane asylums that were abusing patients while claiming they were providing adequate treatment," Rios said.

"What do you mean?" Esteban asked.

"Those mental hospitals claimed they treated their patients well, but families reported their relatives had injuries. In one case, a girl got pregnant," Rios explained. "Guzman Estrada went undercover and videotaped how the orderlies treated the patients. His footage showed they were being abused."

"I see now. He was a man who went after the truth," Esteban said.

"You could say that," Rios responded.

"Well, I guess men like that aren't well-liked in this world," Esteban remarked.

"He actually helped a lot of people and opened the public's eyes to what was happening in many situations," Rios said.

"It seems so, but somehow his work got him killed," Esteban said, his tone thoughtful. "Let's go south now," he instructed.

Rios turned into a driveway and then headed south. Esteban gazed out the window, taking in more of the city.

"Are you married, Officer Rios?" Esteban asked, wanting to break the ice and encourage Rios to be more open with him.

Rios hesitated before speaking. "N-no, sir, not yet."

"You're like me," Esteban said with a smile. "I'm still waiting for the right moment. But the longer you wait, the longer the moment seems to take."

"Why haven't you married, sir?" Rios asked.

"Well, women are hard to figure out. The older you get, the pickier you become. After a while, you convince yourself you can live without a woman, but deep down, you don't feel complete. I guess it comes to men at different times. It didn't come to me completely until this year," Esteban said. "It's a mystery, I guess."

"Women are a mystery, period," Rios said. "I broke up with my girlfriend, and now my ex wants to get back together. She told me she never wanted to see me again, but now she calls me all the time."

Esteban chuckled, recalling a similar experience. "Well, that's part of being a woman. They change their minds like a strobe light. They don't know what they want until it's gone," he said with a grin.

As they drove, Esteban admired the beauty of the city. It was a shame he was here on business. "Let's go east now," he said.

"Have any other federal agents been here besides me?" Esteban asked.

"Not that I've seen. You're the first, sir," Rios replied.

I wonder why, Esteban thought to himself. In a way, it was good news—it meant he could get unfiltered information on anything that might have been intentionally misplaced.

They continued driving, taking in the scenery. Finally, Esteban said, "Okay, Rios, take me to the crime scene."

"Yes, sir, it's not far from here," Rios responded.

"Do you know the officers who found the body?" Esteban asked.

"I know one of them, but only because I substituted as his partner when his usual partner was sick," Rios replied.

"What's his name?" Esteban asked.

"Officer Miguel Lama," Rios said. Esteban jotted the name down.

"What can you tell me about the crime scene?" Esteban inquired.

"All I know is that Mr. Guzman was shot in the head while he was sleeping. I heard there was no forced entry, and nothing was stolen," Rios explained.

Esteban fell silent, lost in deep thought. *Someone intentionally went in to kill Guzman, and I believe it's because he uncovered the connection between the drug trafficking and the Hollow Company. The next step is proving it,* he thought.

They arrived at the apartment of the famous reporter. A small crowd had gathered outside, mostly reporters, while two police cars were stationed nearby to maintain order and keep people away from the scene. Despite the crime having occurred more than a day ago, the apartment remained a hotspot of public attention. Yellow tape cordoned off the area to keep out unwelcome onlookers. Ever since Mr. Guzman's body had been discovered, the location had drawn considerable attention.

Esteban stepped out of the car and walked toward the apartment. A few officers stood guard near the yellow tape. One of them approached and said, "Excuse me, sir, but you can't come in here. It's a crime scene investigation, and entry is restricted to authorized personnel only."

Esteban pulled out his identification and held it up. "I'm with the Feds, and I'm here to observe and assist as necessary," he said firmly.

The officer glanced at his badge and responded, "Okay... sir... but please don't touch anything." His tone carried a hint of cockiness.

Esteban gave him a hard look. "Don't worry. If I touch anything, it'll be because I need to, and I have the authority to do so without needing your permission," he replied, asserting his authority.

The officer didn't seem pleased but had no choice but to comply. Rios stood quietly behind Esteban.

"That's a hell of a way to make a first impression on a Federal Agent," Esteban remarked, glancing at Rios. Rios remained silent.

The neighborhood appeared affluent, with upscale apartments resembling condominiums—modern and luxurious. Esteban began surveying the area, his eyes scanning for anything unusual. He approached another officer, introduced himself, and checked the name tag.

"Hi, I'm Agent Esteban Galindo. I'm here to assess the scene. Could you direct me to the person in charge so I can get a proper walkthrough?" Esteban asked.

The officer, who had been keeping an eye on the reporters, quickly turned his attention to Esteban. "Good to meet you, sir. I'm Officer Romero," he replied. "Sure, I'll assist you, but let me handle these reporters first. I'll be right with you," Romero added before heading off.

While waiting, Esteban moved closer to the door to examine it. *There's no sign of forced entry. Whoever did this was either skilled at picking locks or had a key,* he thought. He scanned the ground near the door and noticed a faint footprint by the grass, partially concealed. It was easy to miss unless the grass was brushed aside.

Romero returned shortly. "Apologies for not welcoming you more formally, Agent Galindo, but these reporters are relentless," Romero said.

"It's all right. I understand," Esteban replied, pulling out his cell phone.

"I spoke to Detective Zonora; he's leading this case. He asked me to give you a tour," Romero informed him.

Esteban nodded, still holding his cellphone, clocking it so it won't be seen. "Officer Romero, I noticed what looks like a footprint here. Has anyone photographed or documented it yet?" he asked, pointing to the partial print.

Romero leaned closer, examining the print. "I'm not sure," he admitted, sounding puzzled.

"Well, have someone take several pictures of it and make a plaster mold. It wouldn't hurt to be thorough," Esteban instructed. He then took his own set of photos, placing a quarter next to the print for scale. The footprint, located at the edge of the sidewalk, could easily have been overlooked. Esteban's trained eye caught it, thanks to his experience in both investigations and military missions.

Rios looked visibly impressed. They hadn't even been on the scene for ten minutes, and Esteban had already identified a potential clue. Romero quickly made a call to initiate the documentation process.

"Okay, where does the tour begin?" Esteban asked, turning to Romero.

"Of course. Follow me," Romero replied, leading the way.

10

They stepped into the apartment, and Esteban began to look around. The place was very elegant. There were many fine pieces of furniture and sculptures all around the parlor and hall. It looked bigger from the inside than it did from the outside. Esteban looked surprised because it resembled an elegant hotel.

Officer Romero pointed to the stairs. "His room is upstairs."

They started to climb the stairs, noticing pictures of the reporter's family and famous people displayed along the hallway as they ascended the twisted staircase.

I need to have a look at these people in the pictures with him, just in case there are any connections. I'll take some pictures of them before I leave, Esteban thought to himself. "Have they taken the body to forensics?"

Officer Ramos replied, "Yes, they did that about two hours after the body was found. It's only been less than 48 hours since they discovered the body. All the scenes are still fresh and have been touched to a minimum, except the body and sheets."

They reached the room and went in.

"As you can see, this is where the body lay," Ramos said. There was an outline on the bed that traced the body as it was found.

"There was no sign of struggle," he continued. "The body was lying face down, and the bullet was fired at close range to the back of the head. You can tell by the gunpowder marks that were found on the head," Ramos added.

As they were speaking, a man in a suit entered the room. Officer Ramos looked at him and introduced the two men.

"Detective Zonora, this is Agent Esteban Galindo from the D.F."

Esteban responded, "Good to meet you, Detective."

"Same here, Agent Galindo."

"Please, you can call me Agent Esteban," Esteban replied.

"I was just showing Agent Esteban the crime scene here, sir," Officer Ramos said, looking at the detective.

After exchanging greetings, Esteban turned his attention back to the crime scene. There was a picture of an older couple by the side of the bed. Esteban assumed they were the reporter's parents. He also noticed that the lamp was unplugged, as well as the digital clock. He took pictures of the bed from different angles.

"Have they found any shells from the weapon?" Esteban asked as he clicked on the capture button.

"No, but we've learned from the lab that it was a 9mm slug that killed the reporter," Ramos said, following Esteban's movements with his gaze.

Esteban moved closer to the bed where the reporter had lain. He noticed powder marks on the sheets and pillows. He thought to himself, *The killer must have gotten in here without a sound, at a very close range.*

"Agent Esteban, we don't have much to go on... so far, this seems like a homicide, but there are very few clues."

Esteban turned to the detective. "What was Mr. Guzman wearing when he was killed?"

The detective gave him a quizzical look. "He was wearing light blue pajamas."

"May I see the photographs that were taken of the body as it lay?" Esteban asked, trying to assert his authority.

"Sure, they're all at headquarters now. Everything that was initially taken from the crime scene is there."

"How long was Mr. Guzman's body lying before it was found?" Esteban asked.

"Hmm, the coroner said about ten hours or more. It's believed he was killed around 12 a.m. to 1 a.m. Friday morning. His body wasn't found until 10:15 a.m. that morning."

"Who found him?"

"It was two of our officers."

"Can you give me more details?" Esteban looked at Ramos, puzzled as to why two officers would have found him.

"He was late reporting to work, which Mr. Guzman never is. He wasn't answering any of his calls. His friends at work suspected something must be wrong and insisted on having the police check his house. That's how our officers found his body," Officer Ramos explained.

"That clears things up a little better." Esteban nodded as he finished listening to the officer.

"Does he have a cleaning lady?" Esteban asked.

"Yes, he does."

"Has she been questioned?"

"She had the day off and was at home with her family. She's already been questioned at the police station."

Esteban nodded and continued looking around to see if he had overlooked anything.

"Someone must have known that the maid was off and took advantage of that," Esteban thought to himself. He entered the bathroom, crossed the room, and looked down at the carpet. Reaching the window, he examined it closely to see if anything could be detected.

"Have the windows been checked for fingerprints?" Esteban asked the detective.

"Yes, the ones here in this room and the ones in the other bedrooms," Ramos replied, seeming slightly annoyed at this point. "But no prints were found other than his own. Well, there are other prints, but they could belong to the maid. We're attempting to contact her to confirm."

"And downstairs?" Esteban inquired.

"Checked as well—nothing has come up there either."

"There were no broken locks or any sign of forced entry then?" Esteban pressed further.

"None that we've found," Ramos confirmed.

Esteban moved to the closets to look around. He noticed a faint, strange smell that puzzled him. Curious, he proceeded to check the closets in the other rooms and faintly detected the same odor.

Officer Rios noticed his reaction. "What's the matter?" he asked. He was at full attention now.

"I've smelled this before," Esteban replied, narrowing his eyes.

Ramos and the detective sniffed around the area but seemed confused. "I don't smell anything," they both said.

"Is it alright for me to take a shirt from each closet? It has nothing to do with the murder scene in this room," Esteban asked.

Detective Zonora looked puzzled. He slowly shifted his gaze to the cupboard. "Why do you want his shirts?"

"I'd like to have these shirts analyzed and checked out," Esteban explained.

"Sure, it doesn't seem to interfere with the crime scene, so go ahead," the detective replied.

Esteban carefully placed the shirts in plastic, zip-lock bags. He then walked to the bathroom and opened the medicine cabinet.

"Detective Zonora, have your men checked his medical profile? Something might come up that we're not aware of," Esteban suggested.

The detective nodded. "They've checked in there and are verifying if he was allergic to any medication."

Esteban decided to head downstairs to inspect the other rooms. The detective, appearing preoccupied, turned to him. "Agent Esteban, feel free to ask anything. I have to attend to other matters here. Contact me if you have questions."

"Thank you, Detective Zonora, and I appreciate your cooperation. I'll do that," Esteban replied politely before signaling to Rios to follow him downstairs.

The detective stayed upstairs to continue speaking with the other officers examining the crime scene while Esteban and the two officers began descending the staircase.

"Everything seems so expensive here. He must have made a lot of money," Esteban remarked to the rookie officer.

"Yes, he was very rich. A good reporter and very influential with powerful men," Rios replied as he looked around the home.

As Esteban walked down, he glanced at the pictures on the walls. Mr. Guzman was photographed with numerous people, and one image, in particular, caught Esteban's attention. It showed Guzman alongside a few congressmen, one of whom had a known connection to Senator Sinal.

Esteban pulled out a small camera and snapped a picture of the photograph. He wasn't sure, but he thought he'd seen that man before—though he had seen thousands of people with congressmen. Just to be thorough, he took pictures of the other framed photos as well.

Ramos and the rookie exchanged glances, clearly puzzled by Esteban's actions.

In the living room, Esteban spotted a picture frame on a coffee table. It featured a woman—someone Guzman had been seeing. Esteban studied her face for a moment to remember it and took a picture of the frame.

From there, he headed into the kitchen with Rios and Ramos trailing behind.

"We didn't find anything here," Ramos said. "Everything seems to be in its place."

"Were the doors locked here as well?" Esteban asked.

"Every door in the apartment was locked when we got here," Ramos responded.

"Someone knew exactly what they were doing," Ramos added with a hint of frustration.

Esteban stepped outside through the kitchen door and surveyed the area. His eyes landed on the air conditioning coolant system. Walking toward it, he inspected the hose and noticed a small hole in one of the lines. He snapped a picture of it and smirked.

Scanning the ground, he spotted a cigarette butt nearby. He photographed it, picked it up carefully, and placed it in a plastic bag.

As he put the cigarette butt in the bag, Esteban looked at Officer Ramos and asked, "Does the cleaning lady smoke by any chance?"

"We're not positive on that. I don't believe that question was asked... but Mr. Guzman was a nonsmoker and wouldn't approve of anyone smoking in his house," Officer Rios replied.

"How do you know that?" Esteban asked.

"Mr. Guzman was well-known for being against smoking. He even had a show on the corruption of tobacco companies," Ramos said.

"Good for Mr. Guzman. There's nothing positive about smoking—remember that, Rios," Esteban said with a smile.

Esteban then began inspecting the area around the air conditioner. After a moment, he said, "If this guy is smart, he would never have smoked. I wonder if he's as dumb as I think he is."

Ramos and Rios exchanged glances, unsure of what to say. Esteban kept looking around some bushes and suddenly exclaimed, "Ha, there it is! This guy is an idiot for doing this, but it'll definitely help us."

"What are you talking about, Agent Esteban? What's the big deal?" Rios asked, visibly confused.

Esteban smiled. "Well, let's just say the man who could've visited Mr. Guzman might've been waiting out here. I have a hunch that he smokes. And he was stupid enough to open a new pack of cigarettes, toss the plastic cover into the shrubs, and leave his cigarette butt near the air conditioner."

The other two looked at the cigarette butt and the plastic in awe.

"So much for his professionalism," Esteban said with a smirk. "See, that's what happens when a dirty habit interferes with your job. The man could've gotten away with it, but now he's compromised his mission."

Esteban took a picture of the plastic wrapper. "All this is hypothetical, but it still compromises whatever he was trying to accomplish."

Ramos and Rios just looked at each other in amazement.

"You're going to let our lab analyze that, aren't you, Agent Esteban?" Ramos asked.

"Of course. I'm here to assist and observe. I'll only take copies back with me—you keep the original," Esteban replied.

"Here is an agent who's been here for about thirty minutes and already has enough clues to come up with a suspect while the police have been searching for almost two days with no leads in sight," Rios said, clearly impressed.

Esteban smiled humbly, picked up the plastic wrapper, and put it into a plastic bag as evidence. "I guess it's time to leave, Rios," he said.

"Thank you very much for your help, Officer Ramos. I'll mention your cooperation to your superiors," Esteban added.

"Well, I didn't think I helped much—I only gave you a tour," Ramos said innocently.

"That was enough for me to get the ball rolling. And believe me, the ball is rolling," Esteban assured him.

"Thank you, Agent Esteban," Ramos said.

"By the way," Esteban said, pointing toward the front of the condominium, "tell that other officer of yours to improve his attitude. Otherwise, he might stay at the same rank until he retires."

Ramos smiled knowingly. "I will. You just have to get to know him."

Esteban looked at him seriously. "We all have bad days and good ones, but wearing the badge comes with the responsibility of showing common courtesy and kindness— something your fellow officer could learn from a Girl Scout."

Rios burst out laughing while Ramos said nothing.

"Thank the detective for me again as well. He was very cooperative, and I appreciate that," Esteban added.

"I will," Ramos replied.

Esteban waved and signaled to Rios to leave with him. They exited the scene and headed back to the station.

Rios couldn't hide his admiration. It wasn't every day that a federal agent came to a crime scene and, in a matter of minutes, found clues the entire police department had missed for nearly two days.

As they drove back, Rios asked, "Is there anything else you'd like to do, Agent Esteban?"

"Nah, I think that's all for today. It's best to let it sink in and study the situation a little more," Esteban responded.

They arrived at the station and headed to the Chief's office. The Chief was seated at his desk, writing some papers. He looked up as they entered.

"How are things at the crime scene?" the Chief asked.

"Better than I expected," Esteban replied.

Rios couldn't hold back his excitement. "Chief, this man is a real professional," he said, his voice full of adulation. "It wasn't twenty minutes before he discovered several clues that the department overlooked altogether!"

"What clues are those?" the Chief asked, his flat voice contrasting against the rookie's.

Esteban stepped in and explained, "I found that there was a hole in one of the air conditioner hoses, and in that same area, I found a cigarette butt, along with the plastic cover of the package that a suspect could've used. It's a long shot, but it's something that we have to take notice of. I also took two of his shirts from different closets because they had a strange smell that I'm familiar with. I'd like to have it analyzed to see what can be discovered."

"What smell would that be?" the Chief asked.

"A type of gas that can knock someone unconscious," Esteban responded.

The Chief looked surprised when Esteban told him that. "Sounds like you had a full day already, Mr. Sherlock Holmes," the Chief said with a chuckle.

Esteban smiled, and Rios laughed. The Chief didn't want it to seem like their department couldn't even find a clue, but in reality, Esteban had uncovered major ones. To ease the tension, Esteban complimented the department. "I want to say, Chief, that you have a professional staff, and they're doing a good job with the security and inspection of the crime scene."

The Chief nodded, though he knew Esteban had outdone them in the short time he had been there.

"What are your plans now, Agent Esteban?" the Chief asked.

"I'm heading back to the hotel to study the situation a little more," Esteban replied. "I may not hang around as long as I expected, but I'll play it by ear."

"We're here at your service if you need anything," the Chief said. "You haven't been here a day, and you want to leave already... my type of agent," he joked.

Esteban smiled. "I was planning on staying a week, but I may stay only a few days. This is not the only thing I have to do," he said.

"As you wish, but feel free to hang around as long as you want," the Chief replied.

"Well, I think I'm going to go," Esteban said. He turned to Rios. "Thanks for driving me around, Officer Rios. I'll call you tomorrow so we can get back to work on the case."

"I'll be ready anytime you need me," Rios said eagerly.

"You mind giving me a ride back to the hotel?"

Rios smiled. "Of course not."

"Thank you, Chief, and I'll see you tomorrow," Esteban said, addressing the Chief.

"Good work there, Agent Esteban. I'll be here," the Chief said.

The Chief seemed to like Agent Esteban. He'd had bad experiences with federal agents in the past, but with Esteban, he was beginning to see things differently.

Esteban and the rookie left the office and headed toward the unmarked car. As they walked, Esteban suddenly remembered something and hit his forehead with the palm of his hand.

"I almost forgot," Esteban said. "I have a rental car here that I drove." He looked at Rios and added, "I thank you for driving me all over the place anyway."

"The pleasure is all mine, really," Rios said.

Esteban smiled, happy that he had gotten Rios to open up so quickly. The rookie now seemed completely at ease, and anyone could tell that he admired Esteban. "I'll call you tomorrow, but it won't be early. I have other things to do, so just expect my call after lunch sometime," Esteban said.

"Anytime is fine with me," Rios replied.

"One more thing," Esteban said, "don't forget to look at some of the files when you have the chance. Anything that looks out of the ordinary—usually, that's where the clues lie."

"Yes, sir. I'll do that. I'll look over them tonight," Rios said.

"Great. I'll see you tomorrow, then," Esteban said, waving goodbye.

Rios waved back.

Esteban got in his rental car and headed toward the hotel. It was 5:30 p.m., still early enough to get a few more things done.

It's been an interesting day so far, Esteban thought to himself.

11

Esteban drove himself back to the hotel. As he drove, he took out his cell phone and called Isabel. The phone rang, and Isabel answered, "Bueno."

"Hi, amor, how are you?" Esteban asked.

"Esteban!" Isabel responded, her voice full of excitement. "How are you, my love?"

"I'm fine. I was thinking of you and just had to call," Esteban said.

"I was dying from not hearing your voice and not knowing about you. Why didn't you call me earlier?" she asked.

"Well, you know how things can be sometimes. My job occasionally requires me to not call or to call at specific times," he replied, sounding as though he was making an excuse.

"You could have at least beeped me," she said sarcastically.

"Well, Miss Smarty Britches, I'm calling you now," he teased. "I did call you and left you a message. You were probably in a meeting."

They both laughed.

"I'm through for the moment, and I have free time. I wanted to hear your voice. I miss you, Isabel," Esteban said.

"Awwwh, I miss you too. It seems every time we're apart, I miss you more than ever," she replied.

"Does this mean you like me?" Esteban asked, pretending to be shocked.

"You're asking for it," she said, half-laughing.

"Well, right now I'm going to relax a little and then find somewhere to eat... I have no idea where, though," he said.

"Try the restaurant by the movie theater. That's a good place. I've eaten there twice when I've been to Puebla," she suggested.

"I'll check it out. I've never been there," he replied.

"How's your job going?" he asked.

"It's going well. Today was kind of slow compared to yesterday," she said.

"You know, I started to get a little jealous of you and Cindy," she said, abruptly changing the subject.

"Me and Cindy ?" he asked, surprised.

"Yes. You've made a huge impression on her, and now she wants a boyfriend just like you. I started worrying because all she talked about was you," Isabel said, her tone playful but tinged with seriousness.

"I had nothing to do with that. Cindy just needs someone to treat her nicely, that's all. Or maybe she's just looking for sexual satisfaction because she's sexually frustrated," he joked.

"Oh, you're asking for it now," Isabel responded.

Esteban laughed.

"The way she talks about you started to raise eyebrows. If I'd left you alone with her, I think she would have raped you," Isabel said.

"Really?" Esteban replied.

"Well, don't stop a woman from reaching for her goals. You know women have the same rights as men," Esteban teased.

"Esteban... do you want me to whoop your ass?" Isabel said sarcastically. "I'm big enough to pin you down. I don't care how many black belt degrees you have," she added, sounding mockingly assertive.

Esteban just laughed. "What did you tell her about me? That's probably how she started getting ideas, Miss Isabel," he said with a joking tone.

"I'm not mad, just a little jealous. But, actually, I like it," she admitted with a laugh.

"Isabel, Isabel... how is any man supposed to understand a woman?" he asked.

"You're not supposed to. You're a man, and men don't know crap about women," she replied.

Esteban laughed.

"OK, you win as usual," he said. "I hate to go, but I'm still in the car. If I don't hang up, I might run over someone."

"Well, why didn't you say so?" she responded.

"I'll call you later tonight, and we can talk a little longer, OK?" he said.

"OK, amor," she replied.

"I love you. Talk to you in a few hours," Esteban said.

"Love you too," she responded.

They both hung up.

Esteban smiled as he drove. *I have no clue about Isabel. At first, she used to throw a fit if she got jealous. Now she likes it because her friend likes me. There's no understanding that woman*, he thought. *But, for some damn reason, I love her anyway.*

A few minutes later, he arrived at the hotel and went up to his room. Glancing at his watch, he thought, "I believe I'll call the senator in two hours. That way, he'll have time to eat his supper and plenty of time to talk business."

He then went to his car to check out the restaurant Isabel had recommended. *I hope the food there is good,* he thought.

He headed out and enjoyed his meal at the restaurant. Afterward, he returned to the hotel and began organizing the information he had discovered, trying to put it into some sort of pattern.

Esteban got out his laptop, connected to the internet, and began investigating. He researched the reporter and looked at some of the stories Mr. Guzman had written. The results surprised him.

"This man really didn't give up or care what happened as long as he got the story," Esteban said to himself. He was impressed and started to respect the man much more than before.

It was almost 9 P.M. when he checked his watch. "I better call the senator," he said.

He placed a device on the phone to ensure the line was secure. When the indicator turned green, he dialed the number. The phone began to ring.

Someone on the other line answered.

"Bueno," a voice said.

"I would like to speak to Senator Fernandez. This is Agent Esteban," Esteban said.

"Un momento por favor," the voice replied, putting him on hold.

After a brief pause, another person got on the line. "Hello."

"Senator Fernandez?" Esteban asked.

"Yes, Agent Esteban," the senator replied.

"Sir, I'm in the Camino Real Hotel in Puebla. The trip has been good so far, and I've managed to discover a few things," Esteban said.

"Really? Well, that's good to hear. I need good news for a change. The way things have been going lately could drive a man crazy," the senator said.

"Sir, I've found out a few things from the murder scene," Esteban began. "I suspect that the murderer had access to the reporter's home because there were no signs of forced entry, and no fingerprints have been found. I believe this was a professional job, but with some slight errors that were overlooked."

"I knew you were the one who could find things," the senator said.

Esteban continued, mentioning the partial footprint he had found in front of the house and how it was in a particular spot. "Sir, I believe the reporter was gassed to knock him unconscious while he was sleeping. The clothes in his closet smell like carbon monoxide or some type of knockout gas—similar to anesthesia... I recall from my time in the army. They'll need to be examined in the lab," Esteban explained. "This method would have allowed the murderer to work without creating any noise. He could have turned the alarm off, walked up the stairs to the reporter's room, pointed the weapon at Mr. Guzman's head, and pulled the trigger. There were no signs of struggle. If the autopsy and the clothes confirm the presence of carbon monoxide or knockout gas, then he was definitely gassed before being murdered."

"Hmm, ok go on."

"I also checked the air conditioner and found a hole in the hose carrying air into the house," Esteban added. "Additionally, I found a cigarette butt by the air conditioning unit. That might contain some saliva or DNA evidence. The police confirmed that the maid doesn't smoke, so it's a strong indication someone else was there. It also occurred to me that the person could've run out of cigarettes and discarded the plastic wrapper. I searched further and, to my surprise, found one by some bushes. That could hold fingerprints and give us a solid clue about the suspect."

"All we have to do now is wait for the lab analysis to confirm these findings," Esteban concluded.

"That is extraordinary work, Agent Esteban," the senator said. "I'm sure glad you're on my side." The senator chuckled before continuing. "Carry on, and once you think you've done what you can, take the liberty to come back to D.F."

"Yes, sir," Esteban responded.

"Well, carry on and make sure no one knows you're doing this outside agency grounds," the senator emphasized.

"You have my word, sir," Esteban assured him.

"Good. Stay in touch and keep up the good work," the senator said before hanging up.

Esteban hung up as well. He felt proud of making the senator feel good. He respected the senator quite a bit, and it gave him the motivation to continue his work.

He then thought of Isabel and dialed her number. They talked, exchanging words about how much they missed each other, just like earlier that day. After hanging up, Esteban set his alarm for 6 A.M. He expected to have some answers by the next day, which might even allow him to return home earlier than planned. He prepared his things for the next day and went to bed.

***

The next morning, Esteban woke up to the sound of the alarm clock. He got up and began getting ready for breakfast at the hotel downstairs. He turned on the television to hear the news while he shaved. After finishing, he got dressed and headed to the hotel's restaurant to eat and go over some case details.

When he arrived, he chose a private spot where he wouldn't be disturbed. As he ate, he went through some papers by his side. He read files from the police department about the reporter.

"This guy really wasn't afraid when it came to his job," he muttered to himself. Many of the reporters' stories exposed criminal activities.

"It's amazing how he was never killed before, with all these interviews and writing about drug dealers," Esteban thought.

As he continued reading, his cell phone rang. He picked it up and answered, "Hello."

"Agent Esteban," a familiar voice said.

"Yes," Esteban responded.

"It's Chavez," the voice revealed. "What are you doing up so early? I figured you'd still be in bed," Chavez added sarcastically.

"Good one, amigo, but you're not the only one that gets up early, you know," Esteban responded.

"So what's up?" Esteban asked.

"That's why I'm calling you. I wanted to see how you're doing," Chavez said.

"Well, so far, it's going good. I'm doing an errand for my boss, you know, the usual... and I'm glad that you called," Esteban replied.

Esteban hesitated, unsure whether to tell Chavez what was going on. The Senator had instructed him that no one should know about the investigation. Thinking quickly, he decided to keep the conversation casual.

"Listen, I may need your help in a few days... actually, I may need your help sooner than that, like today," Esteban said.

"Anytime, you know I'm here to help," Chavez replied.

"Where are you?" Chavez asked.

Esteban didn't want to give himself away just yet, so he answered vaguely, "I'm outside the D.F. I'll be closer to town soon enough."

Chavez, however, suspected Esteban wasn't anywhere near Mexico City. "Is that so?"

Esteban's tone grew more serious. "Chavez, I will need someone to go over some things in the lab, and they have to be confidential. Is there any way you can help me with that?"

"Of course I can. You know I will," Chavez said. He understood that Esteban didn't need to tell him everything, and sometimes, it was better not to know.

"Thanks, amigo. I'll tell you more about it, but for now, I have to please my boss," Esteban said.

"Well, since I haven't heard from you, I was just seeing where you were. Maybe we can grab a beer sometime again," Chavez suggested.

Esteban smiled, knowing where the conversation was heading. "We will. I'll just have to tell Isabel I'm drinking with someone else," he joked.

"Now, why does that woman hate me so much?" Chavez asked.

"Well, one reason is that you've slept with a few of her girlfriends, and... you were sleeping with a married woman," Esteban replied casually as if it were a minor detail.

"It's not as bad as it seems," Chavez said defensively.

Esteban laughed. "I'd hate to be your attorney in court if you said that."

"Isabel is just going to have to think I'm with someone else when I go out drinking with you... at least for a little while," Esteban added.

"Well, since I have no attorney, I can't really defend myself on that. But I'm just glad you don't take things like she does," Chavez said.

"Chavez, you're my friend, and you're single. I understand. Just don't get caught with your pants down—women can be vicious, you know," Esteban said.

"I know," Chavez replied.

"Listen, before I hang up, I need a way for someone to get me into the television station XEZ in Puebla, so I can talk to someone about a reporter. Can you arrange that, like today?" Esteban asked.

"You mean like some type of pass or access to their TV station?" Chavez clarified.

"You're outside the D.F.," Chavez noted.

"Are you going to help me or not?" Esteban pressed.

"Just asking... I have to have a point of reference," Chavez said. "So, what do you need?"

"Anything that will let them accept me without thinking I'm some kind of cop or law enforcement agent," Esteban explained.

Chavez thought for a moment and said, "Sure. You'll have to give me some time to come up with something, and I'll get in touch with you."

"Well, it has to be today. It can't wait; otherwise, it won't work. Oh, and the pass has to be given to me at the station if I decide to go there," Esteban insisted.

"In Puebla, of course," Chavez said.

"Okay, I'll call you as soon as I have something before the day is over, but like I said, it might take some time," Chavez replied.

"Thanks, Chavez. It'll really help," Esteban said, sounding relieved.

"Feels good to help you, my friend," Chavez said.

"Well, I really have to go. I'll get in touch with you soon," Esteban said, wanting to end the conversation.

"All right. I'll call you as soon as I can," Chavez promised.

They both said goodbye and hung up.

Esteban knew Chavez would come through for him. As he thought over the situation, Esteban began forming a plan. "The only way to get more information is by going to the reporter's office and searching his computer and papers," he mused.

Nothing significant had been found at the reporter's house, and Mr. Guzman hadn't had his computer with him. The only other place to find clues had to be his office at work.

"Chavez will give me the green light to go in and check things out. That's all I need to do, and I'll have to do it without looking suspicious," Esteban thought to himself.

He was ready to get things done and head back. He didn't like leaving the Senator by himself for too long.

With that, Esteban headed out the door to the parking garage and drove to the police station.

He arrived at the police station around 7:15 AM and headed toward the chief's office. He met the young policewoman and greeted her.

"Buenos días," Esteban said.

"Buenos días, Agent Esteban," she responded.

"Is the Chief around this morning?"

"He should be in any moment now," she replied.

"Do you mind getting a hold of Officer Rios, please?" Esteban asked politely.

"Yes, no problem," she said as she picked up the phone.

"Thanks."

"You're welcome."

He then went and sat by the door of the chief's office. He didn't wait five minutes before Officer Rios arrived.

"Morning, Agent Esteban. I hope you haven't been waiting long," Rios said.

Esteban smiled. "No, I just got here."

"Did you go over some of the files last night?" Esteban asked.

"Yes, sir, but I wanted to show you instead of just calling because I really didn't know if they were important," Rios said.

"Well, we'll have time to go over them this morning," Esteban said. "I want to talk to the Chief before we get started, but we can go over it first. Let's go to a private office and see what you came up with," Esteban remarked.

"OK, I'll find one... follow me," Officer Rios said.

They walked to a private office, where Rios laid some folders out to analyze them.

"Today, I want to talk to the two officers who found the body as well as the cleaning lady. Then we'll see what we can come up with," Esteban said. "Now, show me what you found."

Officer Rios didn't really know how to tell Esteban the information. He was still intimidated as a rookie. It didn't help that Esteban looked so much like a professional, finding all those clues in a matter of minutes while they were at the reporter's condominium.

Rios took some of his files and began to give his input. His voice was slightly shaky as he spoke.

"Sir, the thing that I saw that was out of the ordinary was that there was no mention of phone calls to or from the reporter's home," Rios explained. "There are calls that he made, but no numbers were put in the report," he continued. "I looked some of them up, and some tend to be people that he knew, while others are not known," Rios added. "I don't know if this can be interpreted as a clue," he said.

Esteban began to think about that. He realized that if some of these numbers belonged to someone or a company, they could lead to something bigger. He then looked at Rios, giving him a surprised, happy grin.

"This is very good, Rios... it didn't even enter my mind to look at his phone records. I want you to look up all the phone numbers that were called to and from his place. Make sure there are verifications on them so we can start narrowing down who could've called him—perhaps the killer himself. The killer could've left a clue where he least expected," Esteban said.

Rios felt pretty good hearing this from Esteban. It was now very obvious that Officer Rios would believe in and follow Esteban on this case until the end. Esteban had made a lasting impression and had truly implanted his detective skills since his arrival at the police station.

Esteban then said, "I believe this is what I was looking for to get started."

Officer Rios looked puzzled.

"I want you to get started on the phone numbers. If you find anything like companies, names, places, or anything that doesn't seem right, take note of it and then call me," Esteban instructed. "Do you know who should've put the numbers in the file?"

"No… sometimes they're not put in the file. If we need them, we just look them up like I did, but I thought it was strange because it was a homicide, and I expected phone numbers to be listed in the files," the rookie said.

Esteban looked at him with a smile. "Rios… you just made a very smart decision, and that is precisely the way you should think when it comes to doing an investigation. You have the right mindset for this, and you will make a good detective."

Officer Rios smiled. "Thanks."

"Now, I'm going to give you my cell number, and this is very important to me. I have to trust you enough never to give this number away to anyone, no matter the circumstances. Do you understand?" Esteban told Rios.

"After I leave here, delete it from your records and forget the number. You understand?" Esteban said, monotoned and serious.

Rios looked a little scared when he heard that from Esteban. He felt like a little kid hearing a teacher's warning for the first time.

"Very few people have this number, and I get extremely important calls. But in this case, I need to know the numbers, and I trust you to call me when you get information on this. I just need to put trust in you never to give this number out. I can trust you, Officer Rios, am I right?" Esteban put him on the spot.

Officer Rios felt like he was about to make one of the most important decisions of his life, but he responded, "Yes, Agent Esteban. You can trust me."

Esteban smiled. "Good. Trust is very important, and with it, we'll help solve this case."

Rios felt like he had been underwater, holding his breath during that talk.

"OK, then. I have to go interview the other parties who saw the reporter while you look up the phone numbers. You know what to do when you collect enough information on that," Esteban said. "Where can I call you?"

"I'll be at extension 35. You can call the police station and just dial 35, and it will automatically connect you to the office I'll be in," Rios said.

"Great. Well, I guess we've made progress. Do you mind getting the two officers who found the reporter, as well as finding out where I can locate the cleaning lady?" Esteban asked.

"Sure, I can do that, but they're probably on patrol," Rios said.

"That's fine. This will be more of a casual conversation. I can meet them anywhere," Esteban said.

"I'll be right back and tell you where they're at," Rios replied, then stepped out of the office and headed to the control center to find out their whereabouts.

Esteban was glad that Officer Rios had managed to think of checking the phone numbers. He knew that someone had to verify whether the reporter had been at his home before he was killed.

Officer Rios returned and said, "They're by the mall at the east end of the city."

"Great, I'll go ahead and take care of that while you look up the numbers," Esteban said. "I'll see you in a few hours."

Gathering his things, Esteban headed out.

"See you then, sir," Officer Rios responded.

Esteban decided to check if the Chief was in but, instead of waiting, chose to call him. Then, he headed to the mall where the officers were stationed.

He took his rental car and drove, his mind occupied with thoughts about the phone numbers and what he might find in the victim's computer. His hunch was that all of it was linked and could provide insight into what may have occurred. More than anything, he wanted enough information to hand over to the Senator so he could go back and protect him. He didn't want to think that the Senator was vulnerable, but the more he dwelled on it, the more his conscience told him otherwise.

When he arrived at the mall, he wasn't sure what to expect from the two officers. It could have been a routine meeting, but he kept an open mind—after all, even officers could have been involved in the reporter's murder. He had dealt with situations like that in the past.

He drove through the parking lot, scanning the area. Usually, the officers would be parked nearby, patrolling. As he got closer to the mall, he spotted a patrol car but saw no one inside. Continuing his search, he spotted another patrol car, this one closer to the stores. He pulled up beside it and parked.

"I'll look around and see if they're eating somewhere," he thought to himself.

Stepping out of the car, he entered the mall. The usual crowd filled the space, people walking from store to store, chatting, shopping. He made his way toward the food court, scanning the area. A smile crossed his face when he spotted the two officers sitting at a table in the distance.

As he walked toward them, he considered how he would question them. By the time he reached conversational distance, they noticed him and waved.

He acknowledged them with a nod. "Hello… good to see you both."

"Hello, Agent Esteban," they said in unison.

"I guess you know why I'm here, and I'll make it as painless as possible," Esteban said.

They smiled in response. After ordering their meals, they moved to a private booth to talk. Esteban ordered a cup of coffee and waited as the officers ate and chatted. Once they finished, he began his questioning.

"I know you're both used to asking the questions, but I have to ask what you saw," Esteban said. "Can you walk me through what happened from the time you got the call to go to the reporter's place?" His tone was polite, with no hint of intimidation.

Officer 1 began. "Well, we got a call from the TV station that Mr. Guzman hadn't shown up for work and that we needed to check on him. My partner and I headed to his house, thinking it was just a routine call.

"When we got there, we saw his car parked outside, and everything seemed normal. There were two other people waiting for us, who turned out to be his coworkers."

"Do you remember their names?" Esteban asked.

"I don't recall, but it's in the report."

"Go ahead, continue," Esteban said.

"We all walked up to the front door and rang the doorbell. No one answered. His coworkers knocked on the windows, growing more concerned. They kept insisting that he never missed work and that something must have happened. We decided to enter the house. One of the coworkers had a spare key but wanted the police there in case there was a burglar inside. He told us they were very close, and when Mr. Guzman was out of town, he would house-sit for him," the officer explained.

"How was the door opened? Did you open the door? Did you believe you had the legal authority to enter?" Esteban asked.

"The coworker used his spare key," the officer clarified. "Like I said, we opened the door and started calling Mr. Guzman's name, but he never answered. My partner and I split up—he went to the living room and kitchen while I headed upstairs."

Esteban turned to Officer 2 and asked, "Why did you all decide to just go into the house?"

Officer 2 responded, "His coworkers were acting like something was terribly wrong, and that made us very suspicious—like something was going on. That influenced our decision to go in."

"Why did you choose to go to the kitchen and not the living room?" Esteban asked.

"I was closer to the kitchen from where I was in the living room," he answered.

Esteban then turned to Officer 1 and asked, "What did you do when you got upstairs?"

Officer 1 took a deep breath and said, "I looked around the hall and called his name. I went to the guest room and then to the bathroom in the hall, but I didn't see anything suspicious. Then I went into his bedroom and saw him lying face down like he was sleeping."

"Could you tell that he was shot when you first saw him?" Esteban asked.

"No, his back was toward me, and it was a little dark."

"Did you call his name when you entered?" Esteban asked.

"Yes, I did, right when I saw him," Officer 1 replied.

"Then what happened?" Esteban asked.

"Well, I approached him, calling his name, but he wouldn't move. I shook him, and that's when I knew something was wrong because I saw blood on the pillow, near the center of the bed. I shouted for my partner and called the police station. I checked for vital signs, but there were none. The blood was already dried, so we left everything as it was and waited for backup."

"Did his coworkers see the body or go upstairs?" Esteban asked Officer 2.

"No, they did not. I kept them downstairs and told them to go outside and not to touch anything," he said. "Then I went upstairs to see what was going on and saw Mr. Guzman lying on the bed, just as my partner described—dried blood by his head."

"The rest is in the police report," he added.

"Has the cleaning lady been thoroughly investigated?" Esteban asked.

"Yes. She was nowhere near the place when the murder took place. She has been his maid for many years and had no motive to harm him," Officer 2 stated.

Esteban decided this was enough to go on. "Well, I do thank you, gentlemen. I know this has already been done, but it's part of my process as well."

"One more question—what about the coworkers who were there with you? Did anyone question them?" Esteban asked.

"Yes, and they've been cleared," Officer 1 said.

"Thank you both. Let's hope this is settled sooner rather than later. You gentlemen have a good day."

Esteban shook their hands and headed back to the station.

At the police station, some patrol cars were leaving for their usual rounds. Esteban parked in the designated police parking area and went inside. He recognized the female officer from yesterday, working at the front desk.

"Morning, sir," she greeted him.

"Morning," Esteban replied. "Is the Chief in?"

"He's usually in around eight, so he should be here any moment," she said.

"Do you mind paging Officer Rios at extension 35 and asking him to meet me at the Chief's office?" Esteban asked.

"No problem at all. I'll do that now," she responded with a flirtatious smile.

Esteban smiled back and thanked her before heading toward the Chief's office to wait for Rios. As he stood there, he thought about the murder and how things were starting to connect. The pieces of the puzzle weren't fully in place, but he could see the outline taking shape.

"I know that Mr. Guzman was killed because he was about to uncover a story on the Hollow Company," Esteban thought to himself. "I need to know more about this company and who's involved. Somehow, I have a feeling that Senator Sinal is connected. Otherwise, why would Senator Fernandez have sent me here to investigate a murder?"

At that moment, Officer Rios walked in.

"Morning, Agent Esteban. I hope you haven't been waiting long," Rios said.

"No, not at all. I just got here myself," Esteban replied.

"Today, we're going to be doing research," Esteban said, looking at Rios.

"Research?" Rios asked, puzzled.

"Yes. Let's find a good computer and start digging into Mr. Guzman, the Hollow Company, and anything related."

Rios was surprised—he had expected they'd be heading back to the crime scene for more detective work. Nonetheless, he guided Esteban to the computer room, where they began searching for information on the newspaper Mr. Guzman worked for, his interviews concerning the Hollow Company, and the company itself.

As they worked, Esteban examined the crime scene photos. He analyzed them carefully, making copies for himself. He focused on the body and the disconnected lamp. Something about it seemed odd—why would someone unplug a bedside lamp used for reading? The photos only strengthened his suspicions.

Meanwhile, Rios was making progress. "The Hollow Company assembles electronic parts and is also connected to a company that cans and bottles coffee and juice products. They export and import goods worldwide, mainly to the United States," Rios reported.

This new information brought more clarity to Mr. Guzman's death.

"Anything on the phone records?" Esteban asked.

"Yes, sir. There was a call made to an unlisted number around the approximate time of death. Also, two days before his murder, several calls were made to the Congressional Building in the D.F. Mr. Guzman also called the Hollow Company multiple times throughout the month," Rios said.

This intrigued Esteban. He took the information from the rookie, nodding in approval.

"Good work, Rios. You're thinking—and that's very good," Esteban said, offering a rare compliment.

He began to focus on the Hollow Company, downloading all the information onto his thumb drive. He would only tell the Chief what he needed to know.

The morning turned into noon, and the two of them headed out for lunch. Esteban kept his research close, treating it like a strategic game he was playing. Officer Rios, on the other hand, was like an eager child around Esteban. The rookie was so impressed that he practically believed everything

Esteban told him and was willing to follow his lead. Esteban knew Rios was in good hands—he wouldn't steer him wrong.

After lunch, they returned to the station and continued their research. By 3 PM, Esteban decided to call it a day. He needed to investigate some things on his own and couldn't take the rookie with him.

"Rios... it's almost time to wrap up," Esteban said.

Officer Rios looked like he had been watching TV for hours—he was clearly not used to sitting in front of a computer all day.

"I was just starting to get the hang of it," Rios replied.

Esteban smiled. "Well, now that we have this information, we need to decipher it," he said. "I want you to analyze what we found on the Hollow Company and see if you notice any patterns or anything out of the ordinary."

"You just have to look for something that doesn't seem right," he added.

"I'll do that," Rios responded.

"Good. We may not find anything, but we definitely won't if we don't look," Esteban said. "I need to check in with my superiors, so I'll leave you here. If you find anything, call me at this number." He handed Rios the hotel's contact information.

Esteban stretched and headed out into the hallway. As he walked past the Chief's office, he noticed it was empty. He made his way to the front desk and asked the officer on duty, "Do you know where the Chief is?"

"He's out talking with the press and won't be back until late," she replied.

Esteban checked his cell phone for any missed messages. "Nothing," he thought to himself.

He began to plan his next move—visiting the television station and hoping Chavez had come through.

12

Senator Fernandez was still battling with what to do about the strike. His advisors laid out the advantages of both sides until he finally decided that he would agree to a meeting if the strikers and the company were willing to sit and talk about the situation.

The leaders of both sides were contacted and informed that the senator was willing to be present to negotiate a peaceful solution. The strikers were pleased and knew that if the senator was willing to help, they were willing to make the effort. The company, however, was hesitant, as they did not want any government interference. However, they seemed to cave in under media pressure.

The media began to put heat on the company until, officially, the company gave in. The following day, a meeting was scheduled, and the leaders of both sides were set to meet at the city's convention center. The senator would fly in and make an appearance to help settle the situation.

The Senate was not thrilled when it heard what the senator was doing. They did not want to be seen as interfering in a private company's business, especially a foreign company, and not allowing the law to take its course. However, the senator was very popular with the people, and they felt he would be able to handle himself as long as he portrayed himself as a figurehead rather than an initiator.

There was a great deal of unrest. The congressmen were set to hold their usual meeting in the main chamber, where one of the topics to be discussed was the gathering of leaders from both sides of the spectrum to resolve the potential strike.

Senator Fernandez was in the Senate, listening to the disagreement over his stance. Most senators did not want him to meet with the strikers and company representatives. Anything could happen, and many felt it was best to leave the matter alone and let the company and laborers settle things themselves.

After hearing the arguments, Senator Fernandez took the floor.

"Gentlemen, some of you here have always considered me someone who likes to go against the grain or just seeks attention," the senator spoke loudly and directly. "I've heard so many rumors that some don't even sound so bad—if you're Fidel Castro," he added sarcastically.

Laughter rippled through the room as he looked around.

"Well, I didn't get elected senator just to follow along and do what the flock does to satisfy the Senate's self-interest," he said with a chiseled sternness. "I got elected so that I could help my state and my country—to make a difference and improve things."

"This strike is something that could be handled within the means of the people and the company, but at times, leaders must step in as peacemakers and negotiators. I am called to assist in this dilemma we are facing."

"This strike could harm the state of Mexico to the point of bringing chaos that we do not need." He glanced around, locking eyes with Senator Sinal.

"Many other workers are watching this, seeing what will happen and how their government will respond. Others are already on the verge of striking because they are tired of low wages, budget cuts, and long hours—promises made but not yet fully delivered."

"Yes, we've prospered, but we've prospered with a hidden agenda." He paused before continuing.

"We have foreign companies that have chosen Mexico for business, and that is a great blessing... but that does not mean we should not be treated with dignity and respect in our own country."

"That agenda includes treating people as expendable."

"The eyes of Mexico's working class are on this strike, and now they are watching what their government will do to help—what their government will do to defend its fellow Mexican citizens."

"We do not want a domino effect of strikes, especially when it comes to our economy, our safety, and our national security. We already have enough problems. If every senator and representative did their part—listened to their people and helped as much as they could—we would face fewer crises like this. We would see more productivity and success in the future."

"We have thousands of our fellow brothers crossing the border into the United States to find work, better living conditions, and the opportunity to feed their families—opportunities they cannot find here, in our own homeland.”

The senator's words struck a chord, and the room listened intently, though many wore dissatisfied expressions.

“That reality hurts and embarrasses me because Mexico has everything a nation needs to prosper. We are blessed with many natural resources that could make us an economic world power, surpassing even Japan. Yet, we seem more concerned with political party interests and who gets a job through politics.”

“Our oil alone could rival Middle Eastern countries, yet we bicker over not having enough gas stations.”

He turned toward the cameras, knowing they were capturing every word.

“Our brothers even sacrifice their liberty, their freedom, and their lives so their families can have a one-bedroom house or money for their children's education.”

The senator struck a nerve—one that directly addressed the economy itself. Senator Fernandez had never been afraid to speak his mind, and now, he was boldly voicing what many had only dared to whisper.

“So I say to you, as a citizen and son of Mexico, I am going to be the mediator in this strike conference because my people, my state, have called me and because it's my duty,” Senator Fernandez declared.

“I want this country to succeed, with the working people as the top priority. I owe it to everyone who voted for me and to what this nation originally stood for—liberty and freedom.

I am a son of Mexico, and I will do anything to protect its existence. Viva Mexico!"

As he finished speaking, he looked around, waiting for the Senate's reaction. For a moment, there was silence. Then, two janitors at the back of the room began clapping profoundly. Slowly, others joined in until the entire chamber erupted into loud cheers and roars. The applause steadily grew until it turned into a standing ovation. The whole Senate began chanting, "Viva! Viva!"

Senator Sinal observed the scene with an evil smile. He pretended to clap, but all he could do was watch as the Senate hailed Senator Fernandez. Inside, he seethed, thinking about how much he wanted to get rid of him.

After leaving the Senate, Senator Fernandez returned to his office, where a pile of messages awaited him. Strike leaders had been calling nonstop, desperate to meet with him. After speaking with several key figures, he agreed that a meeting with both sides was the only way to resolve the issue.

The senator made it clear—he would not make decisions or interfere with negotiations. He wanted to remain neutral, providing input only as needed. He knew it would be difficult, as both sides would push their own accusations and perspectives. But what they didn't realize was that he was as clever as a fox.

Next, he reached out to company representatives. Their leaders agreed to meet in four days at the convention center, a neutral ground where both sides could talk it out. The senator was pleased and immediately began making preparations for the talks.

Meanwhile, the media was in a frenzy. Every major news network covered the senator's speech in the Senate. They couldn't get enough of Senator Fernandez. Reporters scrambled for inside information on the upcoming meeting, eager to know what he would say. The media attention put him in a favorable spotlight, strengthening both his position in government and his public image. If there was ever a perfect time to be on television, this was it.

Though the situation had the potential to benefit the government, Senator Fernandez remained cautious. His advisors were analyzing the demands of the strikers, who mainly sought better pay and improved working conditions. On the other hand, the company refused to increase wages due to lost profits. The senator carefully weighed the situation, with a small team assisting him in formulating a strategy.

While he was in his office, several urgent calls came through, demanding his attention. His secretary approached him.

"Senator, this man has called multiple times. He says it's urgent. He's with one of the major television stations and insists he must speak with you."

Senator Fernandez sighed, looking up from his desk. "I don't want to take calls right now. Tell them to contact me later."

"Senator, he's been very persistent. His name is Marcos Marti. He's an anchorman for Ojo En Vivo news station, and he says he has something important to tell you—something that could impact your meeting."

The senator hesitated, then nodded. "Fine. Put him through."

As he picked up the phone, his voice was firm. "This better be good."

"Senator Fernandez?" the voice on the other end asked.

"This is Senator Fernandez," he replied.

"Senator, my name is Marcos Marti. I'm an anchorman for Ojo En Vivo, and I need to tell you about a video recording we obtained. It might make a difference in your meeting."

Senator Fernandez's expression hardened. He didn't trust reporters. More than likely, this was just another attempt to fish for information.

"Look, Mr. Marti, I'm very busy," he said impatiently. "I don't have time to watch a video."

"Sir, I understand, and forgive me for the intrusion," Marti said earnestly. "But I'm not trying to trick you into an interview. This video is vital evidence. It clearly exposes the company's wrongdoing. Please, just take a look. If you decide it's important, we can talk more later."

The senator remained skeptical. "I don't make deals with reporters. If I did, I'd have to do the same for everyone."

Marti, however, was persistent. He was a respected journalist, known throughout Mexico and Latin America for his integrity.

"Senator, I can't discuss the details over the phone. I don't want this information to be overheard. You need to see it for yourself. Then, you can decide."

After listening to what Mr. Marti had to say, the senator finally gave in and told him to send it to one of his aides at the congressional building. He would look at it and decide for himself. The anchorman was very pleased and thanked him.

"Thank you, sir. You won't regret it," Mr. Marti said.

"You're welcome, and please don't let this get out, or the whole nation will want to call me for things like this," the senator replied.

"Yes, sir, and thanks again," Mr. Marti said.

The senator hung up and went back to his staff. As he sat down, he told his aides, "I do not want to take any calls from anyone unless it's related to the government, family, or Agent Esteban. Is that understood?"

Everyone nodded and went on with their work.

While all this was happening, Senator Sinal was very irritated because Senator Fernandez was getting good publicity from all aspects. He was the one who always liked to be in the spotlight, pretending to do good while making dirty deals behind closed doors.

During the hearing in the Senate, his blood boiled with rage. He had wanted the Senate to ridicule Fernandez and denounce him as a lunatic for taking such measures, but instead, they applauded and cheered him. The senators rarely agreed on many things, but within Congress, it was well known that they did not like each other.

Senator Sinal sat in his office and called his aides for a small meeting. The secretary paged five men, and within five minutes, they all knew the senator wanted to see them as soon as possible.

Sinal sat in his office, thinking about his next move. "This man is getting too much attention," he thought to himself. He kept replaying the image of the entire Senate clapping for Senator Fernandez, making him angrier each time.

After fifteen minutes, all his aides were in his office. The five men sat, waiting to hear what the senator had to say. They all feared him because he was an intimidating man. He had a way of making people feel worthless, but he carefully selected his men—those with the same mentality and greed as him—for his service.

"Lock the door, and everyone listen—listen good," he said. "Men, today I saw something I haven't seen in a long time... and that is the entire Senate, looking as if they agreed with one man," he continued. "The reason this concerns me is because that's the type of attention that I am looking for, and that man should be me!"

His voice grew louder as he looked at them.

"I have high ambitions, and my ambitions don't just settle for the mere normal line. I settle for the highest line—the biggest chunk that can be offered."

He walked around the front of his desk; his irritation was evident.

"Now, I want to know why so many people are demanding Senator Fernandez do deeds like this," he said. "I don't care what other senators do to get attention, but it's through attention that we get elected. Senators and representatives choose leaders."

"My job here is to do the same, but somehow, I'm not getting through to the people or being shown for what I do for them." He looked at them intensely.

"That's where you gentlemen come in."

He took a deep breath and continued, "I want to know and do everything possible to make my time here very noticeable and appealing. I have higher goals in mind, gentlemen. Being a senator is just one step, but it's not enough."

He paused, then spoke firmly.

"I want to be able to run for the presidency and win—without worrying about getting called for some striker's meeting. You men are my men, and we are a team. We're in this together. You are getting paid to put me in the good light, to put me in a position where I am important and to seek opportunities to make a difference. That's why you're getting paid."

"I pay every one of you more than you ever deserve, and I don't want to have to run second to some senator from a hick state, following his coat tails," he shouted.

"Our operation is sound and profits everyone. None of you complain when it comes to payday. Why? Because we do a good job and we do business," he said, looking at them.

"The whole purpose of this meeting is to get your asses in gear and start finding out what we need to do to better our image—especially mine!"

"All of you work for me. Remember that!"

"What do I need to do to make the people notice me as the next president? That is an important issue! I don't care what you have to do, but do it," he ordered.

"Even though we control most of the strings here, we can't control all the strings with the people. I don't want to constantly be embarrassed where nothing I do counts as much as Senator Fernandez. Is that understood?" he barked like a drill sergeant.

"Yes, Senator," they all responded in a calm, yet fearful manner.

"I want you to find the dirtiest laundry, the filthiest gossip you can on him," he said. "In twenty months, everyone will start talking about the candidacy for the President of Mexico, and I want everyone in Mexico thinking of me," he added, pointing to himself.

"Crime seems to be an issue—expand on it, and any other issue that comes up. Make it the center of how this country is being overrun with crime and give me answers to the problems we are facing."

"Your asses are on the line. I want results, not excuses," he said, looking at each of them.

The aides remain silent, motionless, listening intently to the senator. Though they've never attended a meeting of this nature, they know to expect anything when it comes to fulfilling his demands.

"With all that said, continue what you were doing and get me some positive propaganda—sooner rather than later," he orders. "Now go. Do what I said and get things moving before I lose my patience."

Relieved that the meeting was over, the aides quickly rose from their seats and left. The senator, now alone, returned to his desk and opened his email, resuming his usual business. His "projects" consisted of arranging secret meetings with his trusted narcotics agents and drug traffickers. Every name in his system was carefully coded—only he knew who was who and where they operated.

Few were aware of the full extent of his operations, and he ensured that details were often left until the last minute to avoid suspicion. Senator Sinal was feared, even by those closest to him. His subordinates had little choice but to obey, knowing that defiance was met with blackmail—or worse.

As he typed, his mind drifted back to Senator Fernandez. The standing ovation in the Senate still haunted him. The man had managed to steal the attention Sinal craved, and that was something he could not allow.

13

Another day passed by, and Esteban was on his third day as an observer for the reporter's homicide. He and Officer Rios researched some of Guzman's interviews and biography, looking for clues to his murder. They worked on it for most of the day until Esteban felt he had gathered enough information to call it a day.

Esteban became Rios' mentor. Ever since Esteban noticed the footprint when he arrived at the scene, Rios had become a disciple of the agent from the D.F. The young officer would later pursue a career in the secret service.

Esteban made sure they were working on different computers. He wanted to download anything he wished to keep to himself onto his thumb drive. Several things caught his eye. One was that the last man interviewed by Mr. Guzman had not been heard from—not even by the police. Esteban found it odd but assumed the man was either dead or in hiding. Another was that Guzman had already interviewed people who had rumored ties to drug trafficking from a sister company. A small pattern was beginning to form.

What Esteban needed was access to Mr. Guzman's work computer. The police had already secured it, but he was certain Guzman had a personal computer outside the office. He needed to find out before returning to the D.F. He decided he would have to question Guzman's coworkers to get some answers. He'd have to be tactful, as reporters tended to keep everything to themselves, especially from anyone connected to the government. They trusted the government about as much as they trusted Russian roulette. Esteban would need a different approach.

Officer Rios was not a computer expert, but he was glad that Esteban had gathered enough of the research they were looking for.

"Officer Rios, thanks for everything that you've done," Esteban said.

"The pleasure is all mine, sir. I'm here to assist you and work on this case," the young officer said proudly.

Esteban smiled internally because he knew what it felt like to be in Rios' shoes.

"Well, I believe that's all we can do for today. I'll have to work on this alone and sort things out in my room to get some perspective, but I'll give you a call sometime tomorrow, perhaps," Esteban said.

"Anytime, sir," Officer Rios replied.

"Well, I'd better get back to the hotel and relax because it's going to be a long night going over pictures like we've been doing," he said.

The young officer looked at him with an expression that suggested he wanted to say something. Esteban noticed and asked, "Is there something you want to say, Rios?"

The young officer hesitated but managed to speak. "Yes, sir... I was just wondering if... well... I wanted to know if..."

Esteban could tell it was something difficult for him to ask. "Well, what is it?" he pressed.

"Sir, I just wanted to know if I could continue the research with you at your place... I'm very interested in what you're doing, and I'm learning a lot... I just wanted to know if I could hang around so I could learn from you," Rios finally managed to ask.

Esteban thought about it. Under different circumstances, he wouldn't have minded, but in this case, the fewer people knew what he was doing, the better.

"Rios, you've been a great help, but at this stage of the investigation, your help would only slow me down," Esteban responded.

Rios looked somewhat disappointed.

"But... let me sort things out, and I'll teach you some tricks of the trade that will make you a better investigator. Is that a deal?" Esteban said.

Officer Rios' face changed from sad to surprised and excited. "Yes, sir! Anything to learn from you... I'd be honored just to see how you do things and how you even come up with it," he said.

Esteban laughed. "Good, then. I'll give you a call and share some pointers."

"Right now, I need to get back and speak to my superiors. I'm not alone in this—I still have bosses, just like you, who expect results," Esteban added.

They said their goodbyes, and Esteban headed to his car and drove back to his hotel.

Not even the police knew what room he was in because he didn't want them to know what his real mission was, and the less they knew, the better. He went off and got in his car, not telling anyone except Officer Rios that he was leaving. This research, he would have to do alone.

He headed back to the hotel and began using his computer. Esteban downloaded his findings onto his computer and then started going over the information he had acquired at the police station. He looked and browsed, searching for some type of clue or something out of the ordinary that he could use. Nothing really jumped out. He continued to browse.

There were many interviews that the famous reporter had done. Mr. Estrada had a variety of interviews that were controversial and, at times, politically incorrect. Some dealt with drug trafficking from several years ago, while others focused on prostitution. Esteban smiled because he remembered hearing about some of these scandals.

"This guy must have seen some very weird stuff through his lifetime," he said to himself.

Then, all of a sudden, he thought of something.

"Hmmm," he murmured.

He began to realize that the man Mr. Guzman had interviewed was connected to the Hollow Company. He remembered months ago when he was watching the news and saw an arrest in Veracruz, where a man had the same tattoo marking as him. That was what had sparked the need to visit Senator Fernandez.

In that newsreel, he vaguely remembered that he might have seen a vessel with the words *Hollow Company*. He wasn't sure at all, but he could swear that there were words that had "H..o..l..l" in some sort of way. This changed his perspective on things, and Esteban began to feel inspired. He definitely felt that he was on the right track.

He began to look over old videos that Mr. Guzman had recorded in Veracruz, and sure enough, there was the vessel with the *Hollow Company*. This started to close the puzzle. Now, it was time to somehow talk to Mr. Guzman's coworkers. They had access to newsreels and other information that Esteban needed.

"There must be somebody that knows somebody that would want to talk to me on this," he thought to himself.

"He wonders if Chavez's help will be coming through soon," he thought again.

"All he knows is military intel or politics," he continued thinking.

Esteban knew he was stuck in a bind. He knew that Chavez was a very trustworthy guy, but Senator Fernandez didn't want anyone else to know what Esteban was doing in investigating this murder. This was something that was left to federal agents who were assigned to the case. Senator Fernandez had pulled strings to make it seem like Esteban was there on legitimate observation, but it was nowhere on paper.

Esteban didn't want to jeopardize that by telling anyone else, even his close and trusted friend. He would have to think about it, but he didn't have much time. He needed to talk to the reporters by tomorrow at the latest and find answers before he is suspected of being an imposter back at the D.F.

He took some time from his browsing to think it over, analyzing all aspects of his investigation.

Esteban remembered from his training that when a puzzle didn't seem to fit and the pieces weren't quite right, it meant that he was missing something very obvious. He started to think about the phone records. Guzman had a lead on the *Hollow Company* and had called the company and the inside people he interviewed. He also had a lead on a business or someone outside the *Hollow Company*. The unlisted numbers were a mystery.

He looked up the names of the coworkers. Their names were Lola Calveran, Manuel Alvarez, and Rigo Vargas.

"That will come in handy tomorrow," he said to himself.

He then looked at other numbers. The numbers that were called to the congressional building were also a mystery, but his gut feeling told him it was someone in the government. Someone inside knew something; otherwise, Guzman wouldn't have called there.

"What would drive someone to kill this man?" Esteban thought to himself.

He pondered and believed that Guzman must have found out something he wasn't supposed to find or know.

"That's the only thing I can think of," he said to himself.

"The last of the answers will come from Guzman's office at his work... I feel and know this," he thought.

After reviewing and reading his material, he had a positive view that Guzman had discovered an operation involving the transportation of something illegal and that the government was mixed up in it. He went with his instincts. That was what had saved his life through all his near-death experiences.

He then turned off his computer and called Isabel to wish her a good night. He couldn't wait until this was over so that he could go back to see her.

The next morning, he got up and finished getting dressed. He thought about the passes he would need to get into the television station. His own badge would work if he flashed it to get in, but he was thinking ahead. He wanted a solid front so that the station wouldn't think he was there to investigate other news people that Guzman had confidentially contacted. It had to be a good sell.

He went to eat breakfast at a restaurant near the hotel. Then, he headed to the television station and called Chavez on his way.

Chavez answered, "Hello."

"Buenos días, amigo," Esteban said.

"Hey... how are your errands coming along?" Chavez asked.

"Well, they could always use your help," Esteban responded.

Chavez laughed. "Did you manage to get me what I needed?" Esteban asked.

Chavez began acting like a smartass. "Naww, I just got back from a hot tub full of girls and forgot about it."

"Seriously... did you?" Esteban asked with some seriousness.

"Yes, amigo, I did. All you have to do is go to the TV station, and if they give you any problems, there will be a file with passes and enough sugar-coated information that they'll want you to work for them," Chavez said sarcastically.

"You're really something, you know that?" Esteban said.

"Well, what can I say?" Chavez replied.

"I appreciate this, Chavez. It really helps," Esteban said.

"You're my friend, and you know I'm there for you," Chavez replied.

"Well, I'm almost at the TV station. I'll call you when I'm closer, and we'll have a few beers," Esteban said.

"Now that's what I wanted to hear," Chavez laughed.

They said their goodbyes, and Esteban arrived at the TV station.

He parked his car half a block away so that they wouldn't know where he was walking from. When he arrived, he asked for the name of one of Guzman's co-workers.

"Do you know where I can find Miss Lola Calveran?" Esteban asked the lady at the front office.

The lady said, "She's in her office. Do you have an appointment?"

"No, but I would really like to talk to her about a very important matter. Tell her that it's about Mr. Guzman," Esteban said secretly.

The lady's eyes widened. She got up and walked to Miss Calveran's office. A moment later, she came out and told him that Miss Calveran would see him now.

Esteban thanked her and walked in.

Miss Calveran was a middle-aged woman and looked concerned. Esteban approached her and introduced himself.

"Hello, Miss Calveran. I'm Esteban."

"Good to meet you, Esteban. I'm Lola Calveran," she replied. "How do you know my name?" she asked.

Esteban thought quickly and said, "There should be a file that was brought here, and it should answer your questions."

Miss Calveran looked puzzled and paged her secretary.

"Is there a file that was brought in?" she asked.

"Yes, it was brought in yesterday," the secretary responded.

"Bring it here, please," Miss Calveran said.

The file was brought in and handed to the curious woman.

"Come on in. We'll talk better in my office," she said.

They both went in, and Miss Calveran sat in her seat while Esteban took a seat in front of her. She looked through the file, and her expression showed surprise.

"So, you knew Mr. Guzman?" Miss Calveran asked.

"I've had dealings with him, and after I heard about his death, I needed to know what happened," Esteban said.

She seemed a little concerned and asked more questions.

"Why are you here, and how can I help you?" she asked.

"Mr. Guzman had some information that I gave him, and it was only half the puzzle. I'm here to solve the other half because it might be what got him killed," Esteban lied through his teeth.

"I feel partially responsible... He trusted me, and I trusted him. I felt like he was a good friend," he continued.

"He told me he would keep it safe in his computer system, and that's why I'm here," Esteban said.

Miss Calveran studied him.

"Mr. Esteban, I don't know who you are, but it does seem that Mr. Guzman knew you... He never mentioned you in my presence, but he kept a lot of things to himself. Why should I help you and not go to the police?" she asked, giving him a straight look.

"The police cannot help and would only make matters worse. You know that as a reporter. Mr. Guzman put his life on the line to do the right thing, and that's worth his effort," Esteban stated.

"I know this is strangely out of the blue, and you have every reason to doubt me. I would too in your situation. But what I gave him will help save lives—lives the police can't save," he continued.

"Mr. Guzman was a very good friend of mine. We were like... family... and—" she began to cry.

Esteban moved closer and tried to console her.

"You have to believe me. I only want to help, and the only way to do that is to retrieve the information he was storing for me," he said.

She managed to fight back her tears.

"I don't even know who you work for. And why is this information so important?" she asked.

"I work as a freelancer and a private investigator. I gather information that people want, and sometimes it's dangerous. I need to break this case so no more people die," he explained.

"I know he had to have a computer or some system that he put it in," he added.

Miss Calveran controlled her emotions and looked straight at Esteban. For a brief moment, she believed him.

"I will help you. What are you looking for?" she asked.

"I know he put the information on a computer. Did he have one here or somewhere else?" he asked.

"Yes. I kept his laptop because I know it has confidential references. I'll have to give them to you, but you can't go into his private references," she said.

"I am one of his private references, but that's fine. I just want what I gave him," he replied.

Esteban knew he needed all the information he could get, so he would have to search carefully without looking suspicious.

She opened the drawer in her desk and pulled out a laptop. Turning it on, she navigated to Guzman's files.

"What did you give him to store?" she asked.

Esteban thought of the Hollow Company.

"Look for Hollow Company. I don't know where he could have stored it, but I do know that's the company," he said.

There were about ten files on the company.

"Open the first one," he instructed.

She opened it, revealing information on packaging cans in semi-trucks.

"Perfect," he thought.

"I'll need all the files on the company. He could have spread them out so they couldn't be used separately," he said.

"Why is this company so important?" she asked.

"I don't have the full answer. All I know is that the company was in trouble, and Mr. Guzman was investigating its employees. I gave him information on it and told him it was only half of what I had. I also told him to spread it out so it couldn't be seen in one file. I believe he did a good job," he said.

"Well, I can't just give it to you. We need a copy for ourselves," she said.

"I only need one copy, and you can keep yours. We can both help solve this case," he said.

She nodded in agreement. Esteban got a copy, knowing this information would bring his investigation in the city to an end. He spoke highly of Mr. Guzman and the conversations they had.

They were all lies, of course.

After saying all those good things about the deceased, he made it quite noticeable that he needed to get going to solve the case.

"Miss Calveran, I really appreciate your help. We can work together on this and bring whoever did this to justice," he said.

"I hope so. He always fought for justice and wanted to get rid of corruption," she said sadly.

Esteban handed her his work number, which was actually his home number.

"Don't hesitate to call me anytime but please don't give this number to anyone. Only you can call me if you need me," he said.

"Thank you, Esteban—if I can call you that."

"Of course you can. Mr. Guzman did," he replied.

"I must go, and I hope to hear from you soon," he added as he stood up.

"You can count on it," she said.

They shook hands, and he left the building.

As he walked to his car, he thought about some of the lies he had told to get the files he needed. Not all of it was false, but in the end, it got the job done. He believed he had enough information and a good idea of what the reporter had discovered.

He needed to go back to the police station and get the last update from Officer Rios before heading back to the D.F.

He was amazed at knowing that asking the right questions made all the difference in getting people to meet his needs. Chavez had helped with the file that had been delivered.

"I don't know what was in it, but it made Miss Calveran very cooperative," he thought to himself with a smile.

He knew that when it came to handling something out of the ordinary with paperwork, Chavez was the man to call.

He went to get something to eat. He stopped at a fast-food restaurant and ordered something light that wouldn't fill him up. As he waited, he called Senator Fernandez.

The phone rang, and someone answered, "Hello."

"This is Agent Esteban," he said plainly.

"Please hold," a voice replied.

A moment later, the senator's voice came through. "Agent Esteban."

"Sir, I believe I have enough information to tell you what happened," Esteban responded.

"Good to hear... I knew you would be able to get some valuable data on the man," the senator said.

"I will brief you when I get to D.F.," Esteban said.

"Do you need to stay until tomorrow?" the senator asked.

"No, I can leave today. The sooner I leave, the better it is for us," he stated.

"If that suits you. But do what you think is best," the senator said.

"I appreciate that, sir, but I'd rather get there sooner than later," Esteban replied.

"Sounds good. I will expect you when you get here... I'll see you then," the senator said.

"Yes, sir." Esteban hung up.

He knew that once he opened the files, he could put everything together. The evidence was all there, and now, instead of relying on hunches, he would have proof. He picked up his food and then left for the police station.

He arrived shortly after noon and got hold of Officer Rios. They went to a private room, where Esteban waited until Rios walked in.

"Hello, Agent Esteban," Rios greeted.

"Hi, Rios," he responded.

"Did you find anything that looked out of the ordinary?" Esteban asked.

"The only odd thing was that Mr. Guzman knew a lot of politicians, and he was investigating corruption within the government," Rios said.

That made Esteban think. He remembered taking pictures of Guzman's portraits back at his house. Some of them included politicians—three presidents, countless senators, and representatives. This was connecting to a significant point of interest.

"I believe that is going to help, Officer Rios," Esteban said. "Sometimes, the things that seem meaningless to us are the ones that matter the most."

They discussed the politicians and which ones were involved in issues pertaining to the nation's agenda. Rios was a great help, and in turn, he learned from Esteban. They talked for nearly an hour, exchanging information, until Esteban realized there was nothing more he needed. He had enough to put everything together and brief the senator.

It was time to end his visit.

"Officer Rios, I have to get back home. I've observed and assisted in this case, and you have been a tremendous help in everything you've done," he said to the rookie.

"Sir, you have been an inspiration, and I have learned so much from you. I would like to go into your line of work," Rios said proudly.

"When the time comes for you to make that choice, I say do it. You will be a good agent, and I'm willing to help you as much as I can," Esteban stated, knowing the rookie was both skilled and motivated.

Officer Rios truly appreciated the words of wisdom and never forgot Esteban's advice.

"I have to see the Chief and thank him for his help," Esteban told Rios.

"I'll get him, sir," Rios responded.

They both headed to the Chief's office while Rios went to find him. As Esteban waited, he reflected on how this case had twisted through both government and private enterprises. He was glad to be done here.

A few moments later, the Chief and Rios arrived.

Esteban got up and said, "Chief, I just want to tell you that I've appreciated all the cooperation you've given me. I did my best not to interfere and not to stir any major waves."

The Chief smiled. "You did no such thing, and by the way... you have helped beyond what we could've done in a short period of time. Thank you, Agent Esteban."

"I will be leaving, but before I go, I need the results of the clothes that were taken from Mr. Guzman's closet and a few other forms of information," Esteban asked.

"Of course, it's in the reports, and we'll more than willingly assist," the Chief said.

"Thank you, sir... I'll get it before I leave," Esteban replied.

"If there's anything else you need, don't hesitate to ask... we're here to help," the Chief said.

"Same here, sir," Esteban said.

They shook hands, and Esteban headed to the records room. Rios went with him. They gathered the information he needed and said goodbye to each other.

"Take care, Officer Rios. Keep in touch," Esteban said.

"You too, sir, and thank you for being here," Rios responded.

Esteban got his stuff and left the station. He headed toward the hotel and checked out. Then, he went to the airport, where the senator's connections arranged a flight for him. He boarded the plane and took off for Mexico City.

"It's always good to be done with something like this," he thought to himself.

His pilot was the same one who had taken him to Puebla.

"Jorge Morales, I'm ready to go home," Esteban said.

"You remembered my name," the pilot said.

"Old habits are hard to break," Esteban said.

He didn't get to talk much because he was organizing his notes. He arrived in the big metropolis before 10 P.M. and called the senator from the airport. The senator acknowledged him and planned to see him in two days. Then, Esteban called Isabel.

He stared out the window of the plane as he called his love and future wife. He was lost in a daze, reflecting on everything that had happened, and he was glad things had turned out the way they did.

The phone rang, and Isabel picked up. "Bueno."

"Hola, mi amor. How are you?" Esteban said romantically.

"Esteban!!! I'm so glad to hear your voice! Why haven't you called me?" she said loudly and excitedly.

Esteban laughed because he was excited too. "Well, I know it sounds like an excuse, but I was very busy and in situations where I couldn't call... I have missed you so much, though," he said with meaning.

"Ohh, not as much as I have! All I can think about is you and when I can see you. The more you're gone, the more I want to be with you forever," she said seductively.

"Me too, mi amor... but now I'm here, and I'll see you very soon," he said.

"Listen, I'll go to your place so you won't have to come pick me up. I know that you're very tired, and I don't want you to overdo yourself," she said sarcastically.

"Anything to be with you."

“I’ll be arriving in about three hours or so,” he said.

“OK then, I will see you at your place when you get here… big kiss,” she said and kissed the phone.

“Gracias, and a kiss for my gorgeous girl,” he responded.

They talked for a bit longer and then hung up. Isabel would arrive before Esteban got to his apartment. He was happy that he had a beautiful bride-to-be who was crazy about him.

He arrived at his apartment, and Isabel was waiting for him.

14

Esteban and Isabel woke up all snuggled up. Feeling the warmth of each other and the love between them, neither of them wanted to get up. They had both had a peaceful sleep, and Isabel seemed to be having a good dream. Esteban finally decided to check the time—it was 11 a.m. He knew he had to prepare to brief the Senator, and he needed to report in that day, even if it was just a phone call.

Isabel looked so beautiful while sleeping that he decided not to wake her. She smiled a bit as she slept, which made Esteban's heart melt. Carefully, he got out of bed and went into the bathroom to shower and shave, then headed to the kitchen to fix something to eat.

The smell of something cooking woke Isabel.

"Mi amor, what are you doing?" she asked, walking into the kitchen while rubbing her eyes.

"I'm making some brunch, and there's plenty here for both of us," he said.

She smiled and nodded.

"Isabel, I have to get started on a briefing that I have to give to the Senator tomorrow, and I was wondering if you would do me a favor," he asked.

"Of course," she nodded.

"Contact your friend at the TV station and see if he can confirm if the Hollow Company was in a news report several months ago in the port of Veracruz, where there was a major drug bust."

She looked at him seductively and said, "That's going to cost you big time, and I'm not cheap... You might have to give up your body for it."

He raised an eyebrow and said, "My body has plenty of credit... in fact, it's unlimited."

They both laughed.

After they finished eating, Isabel went to her apartment, and Esteban began working on his briefing. He put together all the data he had gathered and started to organize it like a jigsaw puzzle. He knew Guzman had been murdered for uncovering what the Hollow Company was doing—but more importantly, for discovering who was behind it.

His confirmation would come when he reviewed Guzman's computer records and received Isabel's call about the news report he remembered seeing a few months ago.

As the hours passed, he got into the zone, completely focused on the Hollow Company. He knew drug traffickers would use anything to smuggle drugs into the U.S. and Europe. Nothing was sacred to the cartels. They would kill their own mothers for money and power. He had seen it many times during his time in the Army. He was glad he no longer had to deal with that directly and had been eager to get out at the time.

The Hollow Company had many subcontractors that dealt with it indirectly. It branched off in many directions, but the nerve center was the company itself—there was no denying that.

He looked at his watch and realized he needed to call the Senator. He picked up the phone and dialed.

"Senator Fernandez Residence," a voice answered.

Esteban replied, "This is Agent Esteban. Is the Senator available?"

"One moment," the man said, and then went to get the Senator.

"Agent Esteban, it's good to hear from you," the Senator said.

Esteban was taken by surprise—he had never received that kind of response from the Senator before.

"Yes, sir, I wanted to call and see what time you wanted me to brief you tomorrow."

"It would be good to have it after lunch. I have to meet with several other leaders in the morning and need some good news for a change," the Senator said, sounding like he'd had nothing but bad news lately.

"After lunch, it will be, sir. I'll be there at 14:00 and we'll take it from there," he said with confidence.

"Good. I'll see you here then... adios," the Senator said and hung up.

Esteban then gathered his papers and called his mother.

The phone rang, and his mother answered, "Bueno."

"Mama, cómo estás," he said.

"Mi hijo, qué gusto en oír tu voz," she said joyfully. "Why haven't you called me lately?"

"Mom, you know that when I'm away, it's sometimes hard to call because of my job," he said, even though he sometimes just forgot to call but didn't want to admit it.

"Well, I'm very happy that you did call. Are you here for a long stay? You know you sometimes come and go and don't even tell me until you're gone again," she said, just like any other mom would.

Esteban smiled. She had always been like that, and he wouldn't have it any other way.

"Yes, Mom, I'm here for a while," he said. "I wanted to come see you tonight, if that's OK."

"You know this is your house. You can come and stay anytime... I'll cook you a good supper," she said excitedly.

"You don't have to, Mom. I just want to come spend time with you," he said.

"Nonsense. I cook—that's what I do. And is Isabel coming, or is she out of town too?" she asked.

"I'll see. She might have something going on, but she loves your cooking, so be prepared just in case," he replied.

"Where did you go? I had no clue where you've been. You could be kidnapped and not even Saint Antonio would know where you're at because you don't tell anybody," she said worriedly.

"Well, sometimes everything happens at the last minute, and at times I can't say where I'm going," he said reluctantly.

He had told his mother many times that working for government officials meant traveling and secrecy. She knew this, but she still liked to have a general idea of where her little boy was, just to have a frame of reference. Señora Josefina had always been protective of him growing up—and even as an adult, she still told him what to do, as only a mother could.

"Well, I'll see you here for supper then. I have enough if you want to bring more friends, not just Isabel," she said.

"OK, Mom. I'll see you around 7 p.m. tonight."

"OK then. See you soon."

They both said goodbye and hung up. Esteban could talk to his mom about one topic, and she would always extend the conversation. That was just how she was. She liked to make conversations last—especially if she hadn't seen him in a while. He loved his mom more than anything in the world, and lately, he'd been thinking about that more than ever.

He had come to realize his mother wasn't that young anymore. He'd always taken her for granted, but recently there were moments when he noticed she wasn't as agile as before. He knew she would need him more as time passed. She had always known where he was, but now things were different. As people age, they tend to feel lonely, sometimes even unwanted. Señora Josefina had always been surrounded by friends and family, and she didn't like being alone.

She had endured her son's long military schools and missions, which usually lasted no more than four to six months. During those times, he always called and kept in touch, so she never truly felt like he was gone. Esteban had always been very close to his mother—a bond born from the way he was raised and the love she had poured into him.

He hadn't heard from Isabel, so he called her cell. It rang, but there was no answer. He left a message reminding her about the news report. It wouldn't make or break his briefing for the Senator, but it would definitely strengthen his credibility if his hunch turned out to be right.

As time passed, he realized that everything might be leading to something much bigger than he had imagined. He knew politics were dirty—full of backstabbing that most people would consider betrayal. He'd had his fair share of that just by trying to fit in. He avoided being anyone's favorite, whether in the Army or in government. But sometimes, he had to play the game. That's why Senator Fernandez had been the exception—someone Esteban actually looked up to.

While going over his notes, he got a call from Isabel.

Esteban answered with anticipation, "Hola, mi amor."

"You were right, amor... the Hollow Company is involved, and I have some interesting information," she said. "The Hollow Company was there at the drug bust. And as it turns out, attorneys who used to work for the company were the ones who represented two of the people arrested."

"They were sentenced, but it was practically nothing. They were fined $100,000 and made a deal for house arrest. Can you believe that?" she said, clearly frustrated.

Isabel had seen her share of high-class thugs getting away with almost anything illegal by simply buying themselves out.

"That carves things more in stone. The Senator will be happy to hear this," Esteban said. "That was great work, mi amor. I knew you could help me out."

"Anything for you, mi amor. I want you to finish whatever you're doing so we can be together," Isabel said.

"This will definitely help. I'll see the Senator tomorrow and explain everything," he said. Then he shifted the conversation to something more personal. "After I'm done, I'd like for you and me to go to a restaurant. I want to take you out so we can spend some time together."

Isabel was rarely one to say no to him—unless she was mad at him, which wasn't often, but it had happened before.

She smiled. "That would be great. I was thinking about going somewhere. Can I pick the place?"

"No, you can't," he said sarcastically. He heard the sound Isabel usually made when she pouted on the line. Then he chuckled. "Of course you can."

"Good. I'll make it a surprise then," she said, her voice playful.

"Well, I'd better get this brief done. I'll call you after I'm finished at my mother's. Are you sure you don't want to come with me to see her?" he asked.

"You know I would, but I want you and your mother to catch up. She's always talking about you and saying that you go in and out without spending much time with her. I don't want to be in the way," she said, concerned.

Esteban knew she was right. He thought back to what he'd reflected on earlier about his mom.

"You're right. I'll spend time with her. She needs my attention, and I want to be with her too. I'll call you after I'm done," he said.

"I'll be here," she replied.

They said their goodbyes and hung up. Esteban finished his briefing and set it aside, ready for the Senator the next day. Then he took a shower and got ready to eat supper with his mother.

When he got there, his mom did not even say hi. "I thought Isabel was coming with you," she said as she opened the door.

"Well, things came up for work at the last moment, but she'll make it next time."

They went inside and talked about his current adventures and the ones from when he was a little boy. His mother always brought up stories she remembered and reminded him that his father had been the same way. Sometimes, that almost brought tears to Esteban's eyes because he had always wanted to be closer to his father, but it didn't turn out that way. He hid it well and had been doing so for many years, but it still got to him when he had heart-to-heart talks like that with his mom.

He couldn't get enough of his mother's cooking. She cooked like no other and was often asked about her recipes. She never took anyone seriously, but occasionally, she mentioned it to Esteban.

Isabel was also a great cook. She had learned from her own mother and had even exchanged dishes with Esteban's mom. He knew there would never be a problem between his soon-to-be wife and his mother. They got along wonderfully and were both genuinely happy when he proposed to Isabel. He still remembered their reactions when he told his mother the news—they were thrilled with each other.

They talked for several hours, covering many topics, until Esteban noticed it was getting late.

"Mama, it's getting late and I'm going to have to go. It's going to be a long day tomorrow, and I need to be fresh to see the Senator," he said.

"Está bien, hijo. I know you need to go. I'm just so happy you came to see me—and ate like you used to when you were a little boy," she said, smiling.

"I miss you very much, and I know I won't be around that much longer. Anything I can do, I want to do it while I still have my health," she said sincerely.

"Mama, don't talk like that. You will be here a long time—and that's that. Don't say anything less," he replied. He didn't like it when she brought up the "I won't last forever" routine.

"Well, God has His ways. I just want to see you married so that someone can take care of you," she said.

"Mother, I love you. God knows what He's doing. Let's just live and enjoy life. That's what He wants, and so do I," he said, trying to steer the conversation away from the idea of losing her. He didn't want to talk about death or imagine life without his mother.

Esteban said goodbye, left his mother's house, and drove home. As he drove, her words lingered in his mind. He knew that eventually, she would pass away, but he couldn't bring himself to accept that. He didn't want to think about it. He preferred to focus on how things had always been.

He arrived at his apartment and went to bed, carrying the weight of her words into his dreams.

The next day, Esteban woke up early enough to shower, eat, and review his briefing. He had all the information stored in his computer and was prepared to present his findings to the Senator. He believed it was something significant, though he knew the Senator had his own way of thinking.

He went over several key facts he had gathered on the case, then headed out to the Senator's office. It was still early enough to call Isabel and see how she was doing. The day was clear, and the city buzzed with its usual rhythm. Everyone seemed caught up in their own worlds, moving through their routines.

Sometimes, Esteban wished he had a job where all he had to worry about was himself—nothing more, nothing less. On impulse, he decided to stop at a coffee shop and call Isabel from there.

He pulled out his cell phone and dialed.

"Bueno," she answered.

"Buenos días, my princess," Esteban replied warmly.

"What are you doing this morning?" she asked.

"I'm having some coffee and toast before I meet with my boss... and you."

"I'm working on some ideas for a client's advertising strategy," she said.

"I wanted to tell you—I really enjoyed being with my mother last night. You were right. I needed to spend that time with her, to listen, to just enjoy her company."

"I knew you would. It's been a while since you've done that, and I get it. It's the same way with my mom," she said.

"Are you going to have to travel for this client?" he asked, knowing that sometimes her work took her across the state and occasionally to other parts of Mexico.

"No, this client wants to focus their ads in the capital first and then expand throughout the country. They're pretty new but have big plans."

"Well, you know a lot more about that than I do. I wouldn't even know where to start with advertising—but everything has its own system."

"When do you meet the Senator?"

"Sometime around 1:00 p.m., but I'll get there earlier—just in case he wants to start ahead of schedule," he stated. "I'll call you later, and we'll get together after everything's done. I want to take my girl out, remember?" he said cheerfully.

Isabel smiled. "I can't wait."

They said their goodbyes, and Esteban sat in the café sipping his coffee, his thoughts drifting to the case he had just returned from.

He had come to realize that the deceased—Mr. Estrada—was a very influential journalist, someone highly respected, even if not widely accepted in elite media circles. He had the same drive and persona as those at the top, but he remained a loner by choice. Estrada had always aimed to report the truth as it unfolded—unbiased, unfiltered, and free of hidden agendas.

He had often faced criticism for speaking out against the government and its corrupt officials. Few reporters were as bold, but Estrada knew how to walk the fine line between bravery and recklessness. Esteban saw reflections of himself in that courage—the missions he had undertaken, the risks he had accepted. He would've liked to have met Mr. Estrada. Now, all he could do was read about his life, study his work, and try to understand why someone would want him dead.

He took another sip of coffee and stared out the window, watching the steady stream of people passing by.

Back at the Senator's office, the Senator was meeting with sub-leaders of several companies. There was growing tension over a rumored strike that could cause a major disruption across the state. The sub-leaders had been persistent in requesting a meeting, hoping to arrange a larger discussion with their own leaders later on. But the Senator's schedule had been packed, and this meeting had to be squeezed in where time allowed.

The Senator had become a trusted point of contact for many. He carried the kind of charisma and steady presence that inspired respect. People wanted him in the room—not just because of his position, but because of his reputation for fairness. That same presence, however, had made his role complicated. He walked a fine line between observer and mediator, and that duality was a double-edged sword.

He checked the time and wrapped up his conversations. After shaking hands and offering parting words, he dismissed the group.

Knowing he had to meet with Agent Esteban soon, the Senator called his team and suggested they grab lunch. There was a dining facility next to the building, and he headed there to eat before his important meeting.

He was eager to hear what his best source had uncovered about the murder of Mr. Estrada.

The day was sunny, and the city seemed as active as ever. Esteban was in a daze, reflecting on how his trip had been. He realized that Guzman Estrada had been a good man. He thought about how everything could come to an end. In the blink of an eye, one's world could change.

Mr. Estrada had made many politicians and criminals angry for exposing their dirty laundry. He had been used to death threats and was one of the few who would dive into the pool of fear to tell the truth about corruption. His bravery had earned him world fame and all the admiration a journalist could aspire to.

"All this, just to be murdered in his own house with no remorse and no reason," Esteban thought to himself.

He remained in a daze as traffic and people passed by. Then he snapped out of it and looked at his watch. It was 12:15 p.m.

"I better get going... I need to get ready so that the Senator won't have to wait on me," he said.

He called the waitress for the check and paid for his lunch. He got up, left the café, and headed toward the government building. Not far away, a woman and a man watched him leave. They looked at each other and began to follow him to the building. Esteban didn't realize he was being followed.

He arrived at the gate, where the guard checked his ID and let him in. He parked in his usual spot and walked to the Senator's office. He saw the secretary and smiled.

"Hola, señorita."

The secretary looked up and smiled back.

"Oh, Agent Esteban... the Senator is still at lunch, but he told me he'd be back real soon. You can go right in if you'd like."

"Good. I need to prepare before he arrives," he replied.

"Gracias," he added, smiling as he walked into the office.

Esteban took out his computer and some papers for the Senator to review during the briefing. Twenty minutes passed before he heard the secretary say, "Senator, Esteban is waiting for you in your office."

"Gracias," the Senator responded as he opened the door.

Esteban stood up and greeted him. "Buenos días, Senator." They shook hands.

"Good to see you, Agent Esteban. You have no idea how happy I am to see you," the Senator said. "I've had nothing but nagging and tug-o-wars with companies these days you've been gone. I can't seem to escape them—not even in my own home. Please, have a seat and tell me what you found out about your investigation."

"Yes, sir. I put it all in a presentation, and here are some papers so you can follow along," Esteban said, handing them over.

The Senator looked at the papers while putting on his glasses.

As the Senator reviewed them, Esteban directed his attention to the computer.

"When I spoke to you the first day I arrived, I gave you most of the information on the initial crime, but I'll expand more in the brief I've prepared," Esteban began. "If you have any questions at any time, please ask, and I'll explain." He straightened his posture. "Senator, I'd like to begin by telling you what I first found when I arrived at the scene. I didn't know anything about the journalist until I arrived at his home. I wanted to see what I could find by being as objective as possible and not have anything that would give me a motive to target the crime."

The Senator nodded as he listened.

"When I first arrived, I met the Chief of Police. He wasn't very glad to see me. He thought I was inspecting the way he runs his job. He's had several bad experiences with the Feds and assumed I would be another one. He reluctantly cooperated and assigned me a rookie cop to help out. I was taken to the crime scene and met Detective Zonora, who was in charge of it. I examined the crime scene and noticed small things that seemed out of the ordinary but started to make sense.

"Mr. Guzman was murdered by someone who knew his schedule—at work and at home. He was a man who took every precaution you could think of. He had been threatened before, so it was nothing new for him to receive threats when he covered hot stories on politics or drugs.

"There was a footprint in front of his house that the police had initially overlooked. The killer could've been observing Mr. Guzman's movements from outside. In his bedroom, there was no sign of struggle. Mr. Guzman was sleeping when he was shot point blank in the head with a 9mm handgun. We know it was a 9mm because of the two shells found behind his bed and the bullets found during the autopsy. The lamp and digital clock had been unplugged. This was done so that no time could be linked to the murder, and so no one could see the murderer from a distance because of the lamp's light.

"Mr. Guzman had a security system that only he had access to. The killer had to know something about it. The killer also managed to get in without waking Mr. Guzman. That would've been hard to do unless he had been in a drugged state. We know he didn't use any controlled substances, and none were found in his home. I got curious about the smell on some of his clothes, so I went downstairs to where the air conditioner was located. It turned out to be outside, near the kitchen. I found that the hose had a hole cut into it and footprints nearby that matched the ones in front of the house. I also found cigarette butts and the peeling of a cigarette pack not far from the footprints.

"Now, all this is important because Mr. Guzman didn't smoke—and neither did his maid. In fact, he prohibited anyone from smoking in his house. His maid didn't smoke and had the day off, so the killer knew when to make his move. His girlfriend was in France and had a stable relationship. She had no motive to kill Mr. Estrada, and she was also a non-smoker.

"The killer would've been the smoker."

The Senator looked at Esteban, impressed.

"I assess that the killer used some kind of gas to knock out Mr. Guzman long enough to get into the house without worrying about the noise," Esteban explained. "The killer disabled the security system and went upstairs, then murdered Mr. Guzman by shooting him at point-blank range. The security system wasn't even turned on. According to the maid, Mr. Guzman never left it off—not even when he was home. I had some of his clothes analyzed for traces of any chemical agents, and they found remnants of the same gas used to put patients to sleep before surgery. This suggests the killer pumped the gas through the air conditioner—just enough to knock Mr. Guzman out or at least make him too groggy to get out of bed. I also had the plastic wrapping we found checked for fingerprints, and it came back linked to a former convict named Doremus Craft. He had served 20 years for murder and extortion but was released a few months ago for good behavior. He only served a little under 12 years of his sentence."

The Senator listened closely, paying strict attention to everything Esteban said.

"Now that we know how he died," Esteban continued, "let's move to why he may have been murdered."

He switched to a PowerPoint presentation on his laptop, showing photos he had taken of Guzman Estrada's house. Esteban guided the Senator through each room, explaining the photos on the walls and the daily activities of the late reporter like a museum docent giving a tour.

The Senator asked, "Did you get all this from the police, or was it your own work?"

"A combination of both," Esteban replied. "The police were cooperative, but there were some things they didn't know about—things I found on my own. I didn't share everything with them. I left just enough clues so they could discover the rest themselves. Every police force has its red tape, and I didn't have time for that. I got what we needed."

The Senator looked at him and smiled. Esteban continued his report.

"I'll begin with the photos I just showed you. Mr. Estrada was a well-known journalist and a respected figure in his field. He had a passion for uncovering the truth behind every story, especially those involving political corruption—which he believed affected his community directly. Many of his stories involved crime, drugs, and, more often than not, politics."

He pointed to the images on the screen.

"The pictures on his walls were of politicians, athletes, and celebrities he had interviewed or worked with. The politicians, in particular, are the ones I'll focus on later. Mr. Estrada started seeing patterns—connections between people who were getting hurt or killed and a particular company. One of those companies turned out to be the Hollow Company.

"Mr. Guzman began investigating Hollow Company when he learned of a missing man who had disappeared more than a year ago. The man's brother told Estrada that the missing man vanished after a shipment—he had discovered that the cargo he was hauling, which appeared to be baking soda, was actually blocks of cocaine.

"The brother told him he didn't want to cross the border into the U.S. with that shipment. He feared getting caught, taking the fall, or worse—getting killed. That was the last conversation they ever had. His brother disappeared soon after. That was over a year ago."

Esteban paused, then went on.

"The brother, who goes by Ramirez for his own protection, said he was suspended after repeatedly asking about what happened. He didn't know where to turn—until Mr. Estrada found out and encouraged him to share his story, hoping it would lead to answers about his brother's disappearance and the drug trafficking operation."

The Senator leaned forward. "But we don't know for certain that the Hollow Company—or any other company—

is actually involved in this, do we? I mean, there's no hard evidence yet, right?"

The Senator knew the answer but was playing the Devil's advocate.

"No, Senator, we only have circumstantial evidence and rumors. But when all these unproven claims point in the same direction, something must be happening," Esteban said. "All these people can't be lying, and all these coincidences aren't just random chance."

"I know," the Senator replied. "And I'm very glad that you were able to go see this and extract whatever clues can be pieced into the bigger puzzle. Go ahead, continue, Esteban—this is all very good."

"The Hollow Company assembles electronic parts in this country and in parts of Asia," Esteban continued. "They also have indirect connections with pharmaceuticals that import prescription drugs to the U.S."

This raised an eyebrow from the Senator.

"In all, this company is indirectly connected with companies here in Mexico, the U.S., and Europe. Mr. Estrada was preparing to interview the Hollow Company, but he was also trying to reach out to politicians he believed were connected to the company—or to other similar companies. He made several calls to government buildings—some were unlisted and I could only get limited information on them. Others I couldn't trace, but I suspect they were from confidential sources.

"The ones I did manage to contact were his colleagues. I met one of them, Miss Lola Calveran—she gave me access to information about the Hollow Company, and that's how I'm able to present this to you.

"The other colleagues are Manuel Alvarez and Rigo Vargas. These were the same people the police called when Mr. Estrada didn't show up for work. They knew something was wrong when he didn't answer his phone, and they were involved every step of the way during his investigation into political corruption. I suspect one of them has the original interview on video—one that contains enough information to justify a formal investigation into the Hollow Company. The phone numbers Mr. Estrada dialed belonged to main government lines. Calls get transferred internally, which makes it difficult to trace exactly who he was contacting."

The Senator was absorbing it all like a sponge. He realized this was exactly what he'd been fighting against his entire political career. Corruption was a part of politics—but when it appeared this blatantly, something had to be done. It had to be exposed.

"I'd now like to direct your attention to some of the pictures I saw in Mr. Estrada's residence," Esteban continued. "He had photographs of everyone he met who was famous in some way. But some of them were indirectly connected to politicians who have long been suspected of illegal activity."

Senator Fernandez had a strong feeling about where this was heading.

"One of the pictures includes this man," Esteban said, pointing. "His name is Humberto Abdujal. He was born in Mexico, but his parents are from Jordan. He's Senator Sinal's attorney. His name also came up in connection with the

Hollow Company when I was researching its export activity to the U.S.

"It appears that Mr. Abdujal has a much bigger role in this game than he lets on. When Mr. Estrada was investigating political corruption, he began connecting the dots. He believed the Hollow Company—and others—were indirectly involved. He identified one employee who was being threatened for digging too deep, and another who went missing. The company made no effort to look into it. When you put those two things together, something was bound to come out of it—and something did: Mr. Estrada's death."

The Senator nodded.

"I believe he was murdered because he had proof—something concrete—linking the Hollow Company and others to corruption. Politicians who supported or contributed to the company didn't want their names smeared, so eliminating Mr. Estrada served them too.

"But they underestimated him—he had a tape, potentially containing evidence that could expose the company and the politicians involved. I would also like to add that I discovered the drug bust in Veracruz several months ago involved a ship owned by the Hollow Company. That was the time I saw the report on TV and spotted one of the detained individuals with a tattoo similar to mine... I believe that's when I first spoke to you at your house and explained how I believed something was going on with the former gang I used to be in. It's also a big coincidence that former attorneys of the company represented the individuals who were arrested. The individuals pled guilty and made a deal to be under house arrest for a minimal time, with a $100,000 bail (dollar equivalent) paid by an unknown source."

The Senator looked at the pictures and sat quietly for a few moments.

Esteban then said, "Sir... this is all I have, and I hope it was enough for what you were looking for. The police station is just now putting things together and will likely arrive at the same conclusion, but I'm sure some of it will be covered up—especially when it comes to the politicians."

The Senator said, "Esteban, you have done a marvelous job. You have gathered a great deal of information in just a few days—more than I had anticipated. I've been noticing corruption since I was elected, and many unusual things have occurred that I'm not proud of... I want those things to slow down and come to a stop before this country gets so overwhelmed that nothing will be able to save it."

Esteban looked at him, already aware that corruption existed. The Senator then stood up and began to tell Esteban his story.

"Esteban, this nation was in political turmoil... it had been like that for years, but recently it had gotten worse. From the outside, it seemed like business as usual, but for those of us on the inside, we saw what was really happening. The problem was, no one seemed willing to do something about it to make things better because everyone was scared—for their political future and sometimes their lives. Politicians were dealing with the scum of the earth to make bad things happen or to make extra money, while citizens suffered from a lack of funds for education, medical insurance, and so on. I've got to get to the bottom of this and stop it before this country goes under. Your investigation had opened the door wider, and it would help accomplish justice."

Esteban didn't know what to say. He was just doing his job and helping the Senator. One thing was for sure—the Senator was now that much closer to leading the charge he had always talked about: that someone had to do something.

"Thank you, Agent Esteban. All this information was more helpful than you can imagine," the Senator said.

"You're very welcome, sir. I am here to serve," Esteban replied. "I could download all of this to your computer, sir, and you could keep the copies," Esteban added.

The Senator nodded, and Esteban began transferring the files to the Senator's computer.

"Esteban, go ahead and take a few days off—you've earned it. All I'll be going into this meeting with people here anyway. I'll call you when I have to go anywhere important," the Senator said.

Esteban noticed that the Senator wanted to be alone, to analyze the work and perhaps go over other things. He didn't want to leave the Senator by himself, but the Senator's gestures made it clear.

Esteban answered, "Yes, sir—but call me if you go somewhere or need me."

"I will. You can be sure of that," the Senator responded.

Esteban got up, and they both shook hands and said goodbye. The Senator returned to his seat and pondered Esteban's investigation. Esteban left and went back to his apartment.

<h1 style="text-align:center">15</h1>

As Esteban did his usual work with the Senator, Chavez worked behind the scenes. Chavez had been his eyes and ears since he became a National Security Advisor. He had been a devoted friend and had every reason to be. Chavez first met Esteban when they started in the Academy together. They had both been best friends and had managed to work together indirectly after they left the military. Chavez branched out into a similar path in law enforcement and made it up the ladder to assistant to the National Security. It didn't hurt that one of his uncles was in politics. In that position, he had been able to keep Esteban informed on what was happening constantly with senators and events that only people with inside information would know. Esteban also gave him information that Chavez had used to put criminals behind bars. They both worked well as a team, but in different departments.

Chavez had seen a pattern that seemed to be taking shape. There had been unplanned meetings between politicians and lots of inside rumors about who was not running for office and who needed to stay out of office. He still hadn't forgotten the time when Esteban called him when two teenagers infiltrated the government parking lot and attempted to steal his car. That made Chavez laugh, but he knew that Esteban was dead serious about the incident. Any other time, Esteban would've barely given the teenagers their lives. He had seen Esteban in action, and no man could compare to how the man could handle himself under mortal danger. He knew firsthand because he had been there with him on numerous firefights in assigned missions when they were in the Army. Chavez took care of the people responsible for letting the teenagers into the government parking lot. It turned out that there had been a breach in security where the security guards exchanged shifts, and two of them were paid to turn off security systems, allowing the teenagers to come in without being detected. The individuals didn't know for what reason the time gap would be used and weren't told. They were only given a certain amount to do it, and they did it. The money was traced to someone in banking who dealt with congressional personnel. There wasn't a clear culprit, but a link had been identified, and the agency was monitoring it. He remembered Esteban saying that they could've been testing the system to plan a future crime against a politician or the building itself.

For the past several days that Esteban had been doing his investigation, Chavez had been looking at how drug trafficking had increased in certain areas of the country. There had also been an increase in assault weapons directly linked to some drug busts that had been acquired. He studied this and knew that there was a direct connection. The only thing was that the weapons tended to be new, and they were from Asia and Russia. But there had been an increase from the US. That concerned him, and he wondered where this was heading. He hadn't told Esteban some of these things because they really didn't apply to him, and he had to keep things to himself because of his job. At times, he had indirectly asked Esteban for his advice because Esteban had knowledge of certain subjects. Chavez also looked at the Guzman Estrada case to see what connections he could come up with. He knew there was something to it and that Esteban would give him information on what he found when he had the opportunity.

Chavez had a direct connection with Senator Fernández. When the Senator needed Chavez, he called for el "Coyote." The Senator relied on him when it came to his every move. In time, Esteban would realize what connection his best friend and his boss had in common. Meanwhile, everything seemed to be working behind the scenes, and everyone knew enough to do their job without a suspicious agenda. It was part of working in politics and in the secret business. It was all about who you knew and what you knew that counted, as well as whom you could trust. Chavez knew that this was what was most important to Esteban. He knew him too well, and that was something that he would never cross. He'd give his life to save Esteban. It was the least he could do for the man who had saved his life numerous times without asking for any favor or reward in return. He was a modern-day knight with true values. He knew Esteban was a true friend, and he could never find another like him.

For someone who had so much responsibility, Chavez always seemed to be in a decent mood. He didn't have that police, law-enforcement look. He smiled a lot and kidded around when it was appropriate. He loved to date different women, and in small circles, was considered a womanizer. To the people who knew him, he wasn't. That was just the way he was. He was a gentleman at heart and loved to enchant women. His problems were that he'd done it with the women from his work area or other politicians' secretaries. People tended to talk in work areas or work stations. It was human nature. In every part of the political game, Chavez was there to keep an eye on what was happening and how he could prevent any mishap that might develop with government officials. He was a call away to keep his best friend informed of whatever happened that might affect him. He didn't need to call him, and sometimes he didn't, but only if he believed that Esteban might be in danger or if he could assist him in helping someone directly.

16

Esteban took the Senator's word and decided to take a few days off. It was the first time he had ever been given extra days off that weren't part of his vacation. He did need some time off to be with Isabel and his mother, but he also needed time for himself. The best decisions and ideas had always come to him when he was alone, where he could analyze the situations around him. He had always had that gift since he was a young boy. As he pondered, a flashback to his grandfather's words surfaced.

His grandfather was sitting on the porch, making something out of wood. Esteban, still a boy, went over to see what his grandfather was making.

"Abuelito, what are you making?" Esteban asked.

"It's a flute," the old man replied.

"Why are you making it?" Esteban asked again.

"It helps me think and see things more clearly," his grandfather explained.

"I don't understand," Esteban said, still puzzled.

"There are times when every man has to come up with answers," his grandfather continued, "and many times, we don't know where to look for them. Most of the answers to our questions come from within us, but we're too busy or worried to see them. It helps to be alone and let your mind wander, to find how to answer some of these questions."

Esteban looked at him, still confused. His grandfather, knowing he was too young to understand fully, gave him an example.

"Now, you were worried about where your puppy went, weren't you?" his grandfather asked.

Esteban nodded. He had been frantic because his new puppy had gone missing, and he hadn't found him for over a day.

"Just sit here and think about where you last saw him," his grandfather suggested.

Esteban thought for a moment and answered, "I was playing with him before I went to bed."

"What else?" his grandfather prodded.

"I couldn't find him the next morning," Esteban said.

"Do you think the puppy could've gone far by himself?" his grandfather asked.

"No, he was little," Esteban replied.

"That's right, he was just old enough to be away from his mother, and he depended on you," his grandfather said. "Where do you think he went?"

"In the shed, where all the stuff is," Esteban said, a thought occurring to him.

"That's right," his grandfather said. "Do you know why I agree?"

Esteban shook his head.

"Because that's where I found him," his grandfather said with a smile, getting up to go inside and return with the puppy. He handed it to Esteban. Esteban's eyes widened with excitement. He had never really known if his grandfather had found the puppy in the shed, but now he understood. Analyzing situations and simply looking at what was there could often reveal answers.

With that memory still in his mind, Esteban decided to head to the gym for a workout before calling Isabel. He felt like he was falling behind on his fitness routine and needed to catch up. He went back to his apartment to grab his gym clothes before heading out. The gym, open 24 hours, was a convenient choice, especially for people with irregular schedules. After his workout, he called Isabel while driving back to his apartment. The phone rang, and Isabel answered.

"Bueno?" she said.

"Hola, it's your loverboy," Esteban replied with a grin.

Isabel smiled. "I have a very jealous boyfriend who doesn't like men flirting with me."

"Is that right? Tell your boyfriend he has good taste and that it's a sin not to flirt with you," Esteban teased.

She laughed. "What are you doing?"

"Well, I was given a few days off and decided to hit the gym before we go out to eat tonight," he said.

"A few days off? How did that happen?" she asked.

"The Senator likes me and thinks I needed it," Esteban replied. "I also think he's busy with meetings and needs to sort things out himself."

"I'm glad you got some time off, and I'm glad you're going to share it with me," she said, with a hint of sarcasm.

Esteban smiled, knowing she loved to joke around.

"You know I am. Listen, what time will you be ready tonight?" he asked.

"I should be done by 7:30," she said.

"Okay, I'll be there a few minutes before. You can pick the place, like you wanted," he said.

"Done. I'll see you by then... I love you," Isabel said, her voice full of affection.

"I love you too," Esteban replied, smiling. They hung up, and Esteban continued driving home.

"I wonder how many days I have off... The Senator said a few days, but that could mean two or seven," Esteban thought to himself. "I won't take more than three unless he insists or doesn't need me."

He arrived at his apartment, preparing himself for the evening ahead.

Meanwhile, Isabel was still at work. She also enjoyed going to the gym, but her schedule depended on how much work she had. Several times, she and Esteban had worked out together. Before they started dating, they used to see each other at the gym, either arriving or leaving at different times. It wasn't planned, but over several weeks, they'd crossed paths so often that they began to feel like they knew each other. They'd also met at conventions and elegant dinners for VIPs. Isabel was still excited and enchanted by the ring Esteban had given her. She loved showing it off at work and whenever she traveled. She prepared to go to her apartment and wait for Esteban, eager to go out for dinner.

Esteban arrived at his apartment and got ready for the evening. *The Senator was right... I do need some time off,* he thought to himself. *All this traveling and investigation can really take a toll if you don't ground yourself,* he continued. He knew the Senator would likely call on him for other matters, perhaps more investigations. This one, he figured, was just a stepping stone to better his future assignments. But for now, all he wanted to focus on was Isabel. She was the dream girl he had always wanted. Their connection had deepened since his encounter with his ex-girlfriend.

After finishing his preparations and getting dressed, he grabbed his car keys and headed to Isabel's apartment. The night sky was clear, with stars shining brightly. He called Isabel to let her know he was on his way to pick her up.

When he arrived, Isabel was already outside. She walked over to the car, kissed him, and said, "Hola, mi amor."

Hmm, you look and smell so good, he said, admiring her. She smiled.

"I know," she replied, "I knew you'd like it."

He grinned, agreeing with her completely. "Well, where to, my princess? You said you wanted to decide where to go."

"I was thinking about that restaurant we went to several months ago... or maybe it's been a year now," she said.

Esteban wasn't sure which one she meant. "Which one?" he asked, having been to so many in the past month alone.

"The one where you first asked me to go on a trip with you," she said with a knowing look.

Esteban's face lit up. "Ah, yes, the Italian place by the fragrance stores."

"Yes, that one," she confirmed.

"Good choice," he said, smiling. "Let's go. I want to show off my beautiful fiancée to the world so everyone can be jealous."

She smiled in return as they drove through the busy streets of Mexico City.

The city was alive with energy. As they passed the famous Golden Angel, they chatted about their day. Isabel was doing well at work. She had been to the United States three times in the past four months, her language skills, beauty, and creativity earning her recognition. Her boss had acknowledged her growing importance to the company, and Isabel had seen the fruits of her labor.

They arrived at the restaurant and parked close to the entrance. Esteban got out and opened the door for Isabel. She stepped out, looking like a movie star in her dress. Her smile was radiant, knowing she was with the man of her dreams.

They entered the restaurant, where a reservation awaited them. Esteban was surprised. Isabel looked at him and said, "I had everything prepared for you."

They were escorted to their table, sitting across from each other. Esteban turned off his cell phone, and Isabel did the same. They wanted to ensure they wouldn't be interrupted, savoring the moment.

"You're so beautiful, Isabel... I still don't know what I've done to deserve you," Esteban whispered, holding her hand.

"All I can say is that I love you, and I'm the lucky one to have you, Esteban. I don't know how I found you, but I'm so blessed to have you in my life," she responded, squeezing his hand.

They gazed at each other for a few moments, simply enjoying the connection. The waiter came over to ask if they wanted drinks. They both picked up their menus, and the waiter, sensing they needed more time, said, "I'll come back in a few minutes."

"What do you feel like drinking?" Esteban asked.

"I feel like some special wine to celebrate us being together," she replied.

"We'll get a bottle then. It's been too long since I've had good wine," he said.

They placed their orders, and the waiter soon returned to take their drink orders. Everything seemed to be going smoothly.

"Esteban, now that we're engaged and things seem to be falling into place, when do you think we'll set a wedding date?" Isabel asked, her voice soft and hopeful.

She was anxious, but she knew there was still much to arrange. Esteban hadn't given it much thought. For him, the big moment had been asking her to marry him, and now he wasn't sure how to approach the next step.

"I'm not sure," he admitted. "I don't know how to go about this. I've never been married before, so I guess we'll choose a date when everything aligns with our schedules and careers."

"I don't want to wait too long, but I agree we need enough time to get everything right," she said, smiling warmly at him.

"If it were up to me, I'd marry you tonight and spend the rest of our lives together," Esteban replied, his voice sincere.

They didn't notice how much time had passed until their food was ready. They enjoyed their meal, continuing to talk about each other and their work. They couldn't stop gazing at each other, completely captivated by one another. They were both so happy and content to be together.

After dinner, they left and walked to Isabel's apartment, enjoying the evening air. They strolled by a small pond, stopping to kiss and savor the moment.

"Will you stay with me tonight?" she asked.

"I'll stay with you anywhere... you're my princess, and I'm forever yours," Esteban responded, his voice full of love.

They headed inside and turned off the lights.

For the next three days, Esteban did nothing but relax, focusing on things he hadn't had time for in a while. He visited his mother every day, worked out at the gym, and spent time with his fiancée. He also reviewed the reports he had written on Mr. Estrada, feeling that there was more to the case than what it appeared. He suspected someone in the government was involved, and there was a cover-up with the Hollow Company. Whether anything would come of it was uncertain, but for now, all he could do was skim through the details and enjoy his time off.

He also daydreamed about the future, realizing that he longed to eventually be his own boss. Politics, he knew, was never-ending, and he had seen enough of it. But for now, he was content to savor his time off, knowing there would be plenty of work awaiting him when he returned.

17

After his leave, Esteban called the Senator to see how he was doing and if he wanted him to come back. The Senator had been busy trying to work out a solution with the employees of companies where there had been accusations of employee abuse. A strike had been pending, and several employees in different cities were planning to strike at the same time to get better working conditions and better treatment. When Esteban called, the Senator had been out of reach, so he waited to call again.

"I don't feel comfortable leaving the Senator like this...I know it's been almost four days, but I'm not used to leaving anyone vulnerable at any time," he thought to himself. "If the Senator begins to find out what is going on and who's behind this Hollow Company or others, he will be in danger, and I'll have to be by his side at all times," he realized.

Esteban had a flashback to when one of his soldiers found out that his commander was stealing weapons and selling them illegally. The soldier had eventually been released early from active duty with a lame excuse, but he was always worried that something might happen to him. The commander had eventually been prosecuted and given the option to resign. He had higher connections that kept him from getting court-martialed and was able to get out of the military honorably. It was all politics, and there was nothing that anyone could have done to change the situation.

After waiting a few hours, Esteban finally got hold of the Senator.

"Sir, just checking to see how you are doing and when you want me to come back," Esteban said.

"I'm doing fine, Agent Esteban, and you can come in tomorrow...today seems to be a little hectic, but business as usual can start tomorrow," the Senator replied.

"Yes, sir, I'll be there, sir... and sir... thank you for the leave. I really appreciate that," Esteban said in a thankful tone.

"Of course, until then," the Senator responded.

They hung up, and Esteban knew that he'd start his routine after today. He managed to have time to read and catch up on the news, which he was informed about through television and the internet. These were habits he would never lose from his training. He liked to know what was going on and see if he could get a head start on anything that could threaten the people he was protecting. The day passed, and another day arose.

Esteban got up early to go for a run. He then got ready and headed to the Senator's office. He didn't want to be away from the Senator that long again; it was just too dangerous for him. He had a feeling that the Senator was being watched closely, perhaps indirectly. Esteban went to the Senator's house to pick him up. The Senator was getting ready. He waited for him to finish his breakfast. When the Senator was done, he walked toward the hall where Esteban was waiting.

"Morning," the Senator said.

"Good morning, sir," Esteban replied.

"We'll be going to my office at first, and then we'll be going to a few other places that I have to be," the Senator explained.

"Sir, which places... I just need to know the security status of the areas that we're going to," Esteban said.

"Don't worry, they're government facilities and they're well secured," the Senator reassured him.

"Just doing my job, sir," Esteban responded.

"Indeed, you are, and I'm very glad you're working for me."

"Now, after I'm done with the person that I'm going to see, I'll tell you more about some of the things that are coming together in the puzzle that we call corruption... for now, let's just do one thing at a time," the Senator said.

Esteban nodded, and they both went toward the car. They got into the Senator's vehicle and headed toward the congressional building. The Senator was going over some papers that he had brought. Esteban was thinking about what the Senator had said about the puzzle of corruption. This was a vague statement because all governments were corrupt to a certain degree. He knew that the Senator was working on something—something that he probably didn't want to deal with, but felt that no one else would.

They arrived at the building, and Esteban escorted the Senator to his office. Everyone checked in, and the Senator went into his office and waited for the person he had an appointment with. Esteban waited outside in his usual spot. The secretary began some small talk.

"Good to see you, Agent Esteban... long time no see," she said.

"Good to see you too," he replied.

"Where have you been? I haven't seen you in a while. Did you take a vacation?" she asked mysteriously, looking for some answers.

"Not exactly. Had to do some bodyguard training. It's part of a continuous school process we all have to go through... it's part of the package in this job," he explained.

"I see... well, at least you get to go out of this place... it can give you cabin fever," she remarked.

"Yes, I can see what you mean," he responded. They continued to chat until several calls came in, and she had to attend to them. The secretary had been with the Senator for over six years and was very devoted to him. Almost everyone who worked for the Senator was happy and honored to be part of his team. He was very popular and cared about his staff just as much as he cared about the people who had elected him.

The Senator spent about an hour with his visitor until their meeting was finished. The man left, and the Senator waved for Esteban to come in. Esteban smiled at the secretary and went into the office.

"Sit down, Agent Esteban. I have a few things I want to discuss with you," the Senator said.

Esteban sat down, expecting anything from the Senator.

"The information you brought me was extremely useful," the Senator continued. "I didn't expect such detailed information in such a short period. I know you're not a detective, but you have the ability to see what's wrong with events, and you're damn good at it... that's the same thing a detective does."

Esteban didn't know where the Senator was going with this.

"Agent Esteban, I don't know if you've heard about some reporters who were kidnapped here in the D. F.," the Senator said. "They were very fortunate to have been released by the kidnappers. They were after some video that involved a drug bust... they had a ransom, but it all ties up very mysteriously."

"I don't understand," Esteban said.

"Esteban, what I want you to do is find out why these reporters were kidnapped and what they knew about the drug bust behind the scenes," the Senator said. "Nothing like this happens without a reason... there's something bigger than what it appears."

"You want me to be a detective again?" Esteban asked.

"Yes, I do... you've proven yourself very good at it, and I need some answers that no one else can really get," he said. "That's one of the reasons I gave you time off, so you could recharge and unwind."

Esteban thought for a moment and felt like he needed to ask why, but the Senator beat him to the question.

"Now, I know you have questions, and I want to answer most of them. Let me begin to tell you the why on this one," the Senator said, and Esteban smiled inwardly because it was what he wanted to know.

"I've told you some of the reasons I wanted you to investigate the murder of Mr. Guzman Estrada, and that all seems to start fitting a pattern," the Senator continued. "These kidnapped reporters are another example of what has happened and also have a link to the murder. The link is that there are government officials involved in this, and this has to be stopped before it gets so big that civil unrest could evolve."

Esteban didn't expect him to mention civil unrest. He had expected him to talk about corrupt politicians or even a government scandal.

"Drugs come with weapons and lots of deaths... it's part of the package. But with that, they also come with drug deals that can cause an imbalance of power to organizations and even government stability," the Senator said. "We see that with Colombia and other Latin American countries. We haven't experienced it like they have, but if things keep going in the same direction, the effect could be worse than Colombia at its worst."

"I don't know how many politicians are involved, but what I do know is that there are a number of them involved. They're probably in it for the money, but mainly for power. The Hollow Company is involved, and they cover their tracks extremely well. There's no real proof in any of the crimes directed at them. They're getting help from our politicians and possibly the law enforcement system."

"That's why I need you to see what you can investigate about these reporters," the Senator said. "Anything could put another piece into the puzzle that has been created."

"I've spoken to the President about this, but I still have to be very careful because I don't know who's mixed up in it... he agreed with me," the Senator added. "He doesn't know I'm doing this, and this is still highly illegal, but legal in the sense that I'm trying to do the right thing... you understand?"

Esteban saw that the Senator was very concerned, and he knew that he'd been working on this longer than he had been working for the Senator.

"OK, sir, when do you want me to investigate the case?" Esteban asked.

"I want you to begin in two days. You can do some research on the first day to get an awareness of the crime and to see how you can talk to the reporters who were kidnapped," the Senator said.

"It made sense," Esteban thought to himself.

"Good, I have to go to another meeting, and we'll talk along the way," the Senator said. They both headed to the limousine and drove out to another government building. The Senator would discuss business with other politicians. On the way, the Senator and Esteban continued their conversation.

"Esteban, those reporters were lucky they escaped with their lives."

"I believe they were let go because the criminals wanted to make a point. That they could bully the media or anyone who got in their way."

"I know the reporters have some kind of clue that will help in this conspiracy, you could say," the Senator said.

Esteban began to acknowledge that it was some type of conspiracy. Why else would all of this be happening, and no real clues be known? He had thought of it as corruption and nothing more, but this was the first time he took the word *conspiracy* and looked at it more deeply.

'This is like some kind of novel or movie plot,' he thought to himself. *'But maybe it's not.'*

He definitely didn't laugh about it anymore. Some things just started falling into place when viewed from a different perspective.

"I'll be here most of the day, and afterward I'll give you some information about the reporters. Most of it is simple, but with the initiative and intuitive mind you've shown, I know you'll find more answers when you talk to the reporters," the Senator said.

They arrived at the building and got out to attend the meeting. Esteban conducted his usual security check and remained vigilant at every entrance, as well as with each agent guarding the premises. The Senator met with the other politicians, and the meeting began.

Esteban kept a lookout and maintained his thoughts to himself. He was trying to sort things out in his head, figuring out how everything fit together and what might come of it.

The meeting lasted over three hours, and Esteban could tell the congressmen were growing tired. Finally, it seemed they had finished all their discussions. The Senator shook hands with the other officials, and he and Esteban walked out toward the limousine.

"I don't believe we'll have time to attend to the other officials. I'll just postpone our meeting for another day," he told Esteban.

The Senator instructed Esteban to call his secretary and reschedule his other appointment for two days later. Esteban called and informed the secretary, who was always kind to him. He knew she liked him.

They both headed back to the Senator's office to finish some work the Senator needed to complete. Traffic was normal, and the day seemed to fly by. In a couple of hours, it would be 5 p.m.

They arrived at the congressional building and entered the Senator's office.

"Sit down, please. There are some things I still want to discuss," the Senator said.

Esteban sat down across from his desk. The Senator pulled out some files and handed them to him.

"These are the people who were kidnapped and beaten. These two reporters were led to believe they had a story. Someone called them and lured them to a plaza where they were kidnapped in the middle of the day. They were put in a van and taken to an undisclosed location. There, they were beaten and made to think they were going to die. Meanwhile, the station received a call demanding that a news clip be removed, one involving a drug bust. I believe that the news clip provides some indication of who might have been involved, or more. They went to a lot of trouble to arrange this, and that's where you come in. As you'll read, they were released and used as an example to deter the media and anyone else. The network was devastated; they didn't believe anyone would harm a reporter over a story like this. Of course, we don't have more details, but I'm sure you'll be able to get them," the Senator said.

Esteban reviewed the files the Senator had given him and understood that he would need to gather more information, just as he had with the Estrada case.

"Senator, I'm concerned about leaving you again... It's not my place to say how you want me to serve you, but I have to disagree with constantly leaving you vulnerable," he said.

"You won't have to travel anywhere with this. The investigation will be here in the D.F. If I go anywhere, I'll call, and you'll be with me," the Senator said.

"What if I'm in the middle of questioning the reporters?" he asked.

"For the next three days, I'll mostly be in my office. I have several people I'll be seeing, and I don't plan on going anywhere," the Senator replied.

"That's good, sir. I'll agree with that then," Esteban said.

The Senator returned to his phone calls, and Esteban stepped outside to take his post as the bodyguard he was.

When 6 p.m. approached, the Senator began closing things down for the day. The secretary had already left at 5 p.m., and only the agents and a few other congressmen remained in the building. The Senator grabbed his briefcase and headed to the door.

"Well, Agent Esteban, let's call it a day," he said.

"Yes, sir," Esteban responded.

They both got into the limousine, and Esteban took him to his house. He then returned to the congressional building to retrieve his own car and headed to his apartment.

He planned to review the files the senator had given him and begin working on the case the next day. It didn't seem like it would be as involved as the Estrada case, but either way, it was still a case.

It was still early enough for him to call Isabel. He dialed her apartment number.

"Bueno," she answered.

"May I speak to the beautiful princess of the house?" he asked playfully.

She smiled. "Esteban, what are you up to?"

"Just wanted to talk to you and see how your day has been," he said.

"It's been fine. I think my boss wants to send me to Mérida, Yucatán, in a few days," she replied.

"Is that right? It's a nice city... I haven't been there in a long time," he said.

"Well, it'll only be for a couple of days. Just long enough to get some clients to sign the contracts. Then I'll fly home," she said.

"Please be careful and call me if you need anything... I mean that," he said, this time in a different tone.

"They're actually talking about using some pictures of the pyramids for advertising watches... It's a contract we've been trying to get for almost a year," she said excitedly.

"I hope you all get it. Could they use a bodyguard somewhere in the background?" he asked sarcastically.

Isabel laughed. "I'll see what I can do."

They discussed their day and schedules in more detail. Isabel knew she'd be doing a lot of traveling as time went by. Esteban believed he would too, but they managed to see each other whenever they could. He called her as often as possible, even just to leave a message.

"I also want to tell you that I'll be busy doing some work for the Senator. The good news is I won't be going anywhere, just staying here and working," he said. "I'll leave you a message if I can't reach you."

"I also have some good news; I might be getting a raise," she added.

"That's great! Now you can take me out more," he said, smiling.

They laughed and finally said their goodbyes. They both had things to do, and Esteban needed to get ready for the next day. He headed back to his place and called it a night.

***

The Senator was at home with his family. He was a family man who always tried his best to be present. His kids had grown up knowing their father as a politician; they knew no other life but living in the background of his public service. His wife had always been supportive and was actively involved in his campaigns and efforts to help the people of his state. She had delivered several speeches on behalf of various organizations, supporting different causes, mostly charities and humanitarian projects. She was well-liked and had been a great asset to her husband.

His wife asked, "How was your day?"

"It was busy... I've been seeing many leaders and colleagues about the strike," he said.

"I know that's been on your mind a lot. If you want me to help, you know I will," she said.

"Gracias, but this is something I'll have to handle myself... it just seems like I'm the only one in the government who wants to do anything about it. No other politician wants to touch this," he said.

"That's what's so wonderful about you. You've always been there and willing to help your fellow citizens. I love you for that, and so do the people... they'll do anything for you and they trust you," she said.

Just then, their daughter came in. "Hi, Daddy."

"Mi hija... where are you going?" he asked.

"Nowhere. I just got back from swimming practice," she said. She kissed him and went upstairs to her room.

The Senator went to his desk and checked his email. Afterwards, he returned to the den to talk to his wife before retiring for bed. He wanted to spend as much time with his family as possible because he had often missed birthdays and celebrations due to his job. The lights went out, and everyone headed to their rooms.

***

The next day, Esteban got up and began getting ready for work. After preparing, he drove to the Senator's house. They greeted each other as usual.

On the way to the congressional building, the Senator said, "I prefer you working outside the government building for this. I want it kept under wraps."

It was information that Esteban would be tasked with gathering without anyone else's awareness. He understood. After dropping the Senator at his office and ensuring his safety, Esteban drove to the university. There, he could blend in like any other student. He went to the library and began reading through the files.

The two reporters who had been kidnapped had worked at the station for four years: one as a cameraman and the other as an interviewer. They had received a tip about a potential scandal and were en route to meet the source. According to the report, while waiting in a plaza, blue vans pulled up and forced them inside. They were blindfolded and taken to a house, the location of which they couldn't recall. There, they were beaten and interrogated.

The kidnappers wanted a news clip containing footage of a drug bust that had taken place three weeks before Mr. Guzman Estrada was murdered. Esteban kept that detail in mind. It could be connected. He remembered the Senator mentioning the possibility of a link.

He continued reading and found that the reporters were released two days after their arrest.

'How could they just release them without bargaining?' he thought to himself.

The report said the kidnappers had warned that anyone would be killed if the story was aired again or given to the police.

'I wonder if they did give it to the police,' he thought.

"That's something I'll have to find out, and more." He went to the computer room and began searching the internet for information about the news station. He looked up the staff and tried to locate the reporters who had been kidnapped. They were still on staff. He wrote down their address and phone number.

"I'll be paying them a visit soon enough."

While he was looking at the computer, he got a call on his cellphone. He looked at the ID and saw it was Chavez.

"Hello."

"Amigo, why have you been ignoring me?" Chavez said.

"Hi, Chavez. I haven't been ignoring you. I've just been enjoying some time off," Esteban replied.

"What, you're on vacation?" Chavez asked.

"The Senator decided to give me some days off after the last job. But I'm working again now," Esteban said.

"Well, you ought to let your best friend know! I started to worry about you."

"Listen, there's a very important diplomat coming to town, and I was wondering if you'd like to make some extra money," Chavez said.

"What do you mean?" Esteban asked, a hint of mystery in his voice.

"This guy is sort of like royalty... Actually, he's a king from Norway, and we need a few more bodyguards. I told his staff I could count on you. You'll make a month's salary in a day," Chavez said, sounding confident Esteban would take the bait.

"Chavez, I don't know if I can do that anymore. Besides, I'm the Senator's personal bodyguard, twenty-four seven. Asking him to let me off would be too much," Esteban said.

"You can ask for one night off. Heck, he gave you a few days. Why not make some extra money on your own time?" Chavez said.

"I can't promise you anything, but for now, the answer is no. If you can convince the Senator, then I'll do it. But I'm not going to mention anything to him. This is your show, not mine," Esteban said.

"Ouch, you're playing cruel. I only want to make the king safer and make you some money," Chavez replied, half-serious.

"I appreciate it, but the Senator's safety is more important to me. You know that," Esteban said.

"Okay... but will you do it if the Senator approves?" Chavez asked.

"I will and see if I can bring someone," Esteban said.

"Like Isabel?" Chavez asked sarcastically.

"Yes, like Isabel," Esteban answered.

"Deal, then. I knew I could count on you," Chavez said.

"Now... I need a favor from you," Esteban said.

Chavez made a face, but Esteban couldn't see it on the other end of the line.

"I'll call you with what I need, once I'm sure. Then you can inform me of what you find out," Esteban said.

"Sounds mysterious," Chavez said.

"Only business," Esteban replied.

"Done. That's what friends are for," Chavez said.

They both agreed and hung up. Chavez would now indirectly ask the Senator to see if he could "borrow" Esteban for the King of Norway. The rest would be up to the Senator.

18

Esteban felt he had enough information and decided to visit the news station to see if he could speak with the reporters. He gathered his papers, left the library, and headed to his car. He then drove to the news station, hoping to get some answers or at least set up an appointment.

He arrived twenty minutes later and parked on the side of the news building. Getting out of his car, he walked inside. A lady at the desk looked up and said, "May I help you?"

Esteban looked around the place. He had never really been inside a news station before. Then he turned to the lady and said, "Yes, I'm trying to get some information, and I was wondering if I could speak to someone who supervises the on-location reporters."

She looked at him, a bit puzzled. "Well, Mr. Gonzales is the one you need to see. Do you have an appointment?" she asked.

"No, but I'd still like to talk to him if he's available. My name is Esteban Galindo," he said.

She looked like she was about to give him a negative answer, but Esteban beat her to it.

"It's about the reporters who were kidnapped."

That got her attention. She picked up the phone and made a call.

"Mr. Gonzales, there's someone here I believe you need to see," she said.

She then got up and walked down the hall to his office. A few minutes later, she returned.

"Mr. Gonzales will see you now."

Esteban walked toward the office, knocked on the door, and was told to enter.

Mr. Gonzales was a middle-aged man who looked agitated, though Esteban couldn't tell if it was because he'd come unannounced or because of the story involving the kidnapped reporters. Esteban walked in and extended his hand.

"Mr. Gonzales, I'm Esteban Galindo, and I do appreciate your time," Esteban said.

Mr. Gonzales shook his hand and introduced himself. "I'm Mr. Gonzales, and how can I help you?"

They both sat down, and Esteban got straight to the point.

"Mr. Gonzales, I won't waste your time. I'm here to find the reporters who were kidnapped and ask them a few questions," he said.

"The police have already questioned them. Why do you need to question them? And who are you?" Mr. Gonzales asked. He clearly had no idea who Esteban was or what he wanted.

"I work for the government, and I know they've been questioned by the police, but there are certain things I need to know," Esteban said as he showed his ID.

"What kind of things? And why is the government concerned?" Mr. Gonzales continued pressing.

Esteban realized this conversation wouldn't go far if Mr. Gonzales felt threatened.

"Mr. Gonzales, kidnapping has always been a concern for any government official. We want to learn from this particular incident. The police can only provide the official story, but we need the complete story so we can train our officials more effectively in case something like this ever happens again."

"I believe these reporters could be a great help because they're in the public eye, like politicians, and could relate more to the people working in public service," he added, making it sound like part of an important government study.

Mr. Gonzales began to lower his guard, visibly more open now.

"I can see that, and I believe you're absolutely right," he said. "The government just wants to learn from this and maybe do something about it."

"I'd really like to talk to your reporters and just ask them simple questions about their ordeal," Esteban said.

"I'll have to talk to them, but it'll have to be tomorrow. They're out of town and won't be back until the morning," Mr. Gonzales replied. "I can have them call you when they get back and are rested."

"That would be great. This will be extremely helpful for our security," Esteban said. "Well, I won't waste any more of your time. Thank you, and I look forward to hearing from the reporters tomorrow."

They stood, shook hands, and bid each other goodbye.

Esteban could tell he wasn't exactly welcome. Often, reporters and the police didn't get along. The press often published stories without fully understanding the consequences, particularly for law enforcement. It was a never-ending battle.

He left the station and headed toward the Senator's office.

As he drove, he thought about Mr. Gonzales's demeanor.

'He didn't really want to see me, but he was curious about what I wanted. I don't think he was going to give me any information until I mentioned it involved people in the public eye," he thought. *"I should have more information soon, and maybe it'll be all I need when I talk to those reporters.'*

He passed a line of children on their way to school. They looked like they were in elementary school. A smile formed on his face as he remembered his own childhood.

Traffic was congested, but it didn't matter. He wasn't in a rush to get back to the Senator. His day was done until tomorrow.

He finally arrived at the government building and walked toward the Senator's office. He smiled at the secretary.

"Miss, would you mind telling the Senator that Agent Esteban is back and outside his door?"

"I don't mind at all," she said with a big smile and called the Senator.

She nodded to confirm that the Senator knew and returned to typing her memos.

Esteban waited outside, reviewing some notes on his computer. When the Senator had a chance, he asked how things were going.

"I'll be talking to the reporters. Tomorrow, they're out of town," Esteban said.

"Excellent. Today's going to be one of those meeting days," the Senator replied.

They exchanged some small talk before the Senator returned to his work. Esteban resumed his role as the Senator's guard until the day was over.

At six o'clock, he took the Senator home. Then Esteban returned to his apartment and started thinking more about the reporters. He realized they would probably only tell him a fraction of what he wanted to know, but even that might make all the difference.

The night passed, and Esteban turned in. Another day behind him.

19

Esteban woke up early and was eager to talk to the reporters. The Senator would be meeting fewer people that day, and Esteban would be able to take his time finding out what the newsmen had to say. He picked up the Senator and took him to his office. They said their goodbyes, and Esteban went to the news station.

He arrived early because he wanted to see how the news people worked and what went into it. The lady at the office recognized him and said, "Hello again... you're looking for Mr. Gonzales again, aren't you?"

Esteban smiled and said, "Yes, but actually I will also be seeing someone else."

"Well, have a seat and I'll call you when they're ready," she said.

Esteban then asked, "You think that I could be given a tour while I wait... I've always been interested in what goes on in the news business."

She looked at him strangely and then said, "You'll still have to wait, but you can take a look for yourself and ask someone... just don't go where it says staff only."

Esteban thanked the lady and walked to the broadcast room. He admired the camera crew and everyone who worked there. About an hour passed by, and he was paged to the front office.

He went back to his starting point, and the lady at the front desk pointed to him and said, "Mr. Gonzales will see you now, and he's got some company for you."

"Thank you very much, you've been very kind," he said.

He walked into the office, and Mr. Gonzales was there with the reporters who had been kidnapped.

Esteban walked in, and all three men stared at him. Mr. Gonzales introduced the men to Esteban. The reporters' names were Raul Coronado, Hector Ortega, and Ted Sylva. Esteban returned the gestures.

"Is this a good place where we could talk?" asked Esteban.

"No, I have a better room where we can have more privacy... let's walk to it and we can get started there," Mr. Gonzales said.

The room they went into was the boardroom, and there was plenty of space for them to discuss their ordeal. They got comfortable, and Mr. Gonzales excused himself from the talk.

"I'll leave you gentlemen alone... I'll be in my office if you need me."

"Thank you, sir... I truly appreciate this," Esteban said.

The three men faced Esteban, and he began to ask them questions. Esteban wanted to make them feel at ease and not act like he was some type of cop.

"I know all of you have already been questioned, but I have to know certain things that can help some of our government officials on how they can handle being kidnapped. I'd like to first talk a little about me. I work for the government, and I've been chosen to find out how people react to kidnappings. Also, to answer questions on how you were able to survive the ordeal and how the victim can control the situation without the knowledge of the kidnapper. Your input will be a great help for government personnel security," Esteban said.

The reporters began to feel more at ease as they stared at Esteban from their seats.

"Now, let's begin with some questions," Esteban said. "What persuaded you all to meet them in a public area?" Esteban asked like he didn't know.

Raul was the one who started the story.

"We got a tip about a murder that occurred a few days before our incident, and we were told that he would meet in a public area. He gave us the place, and we went there."

Esteban looked at the other guy to see if he concurred.

"Yeah, it's like he says... we went after a so-called hot tip, and that's where we went," Ted said.

"What happened after you got to the place?" Esteban asked.

"Well, we waited for over 30 minutes thinking this guy isn't going to show up... then a blue van came by and asked if we wanted to know about the murder... so we approached it, and three men got out with hoods and threw us in the van. They hit us many times and then put a bag over our heads, and I have no clue where they took us," he said.

Esteban analyzed this.

"Can you estimate how long you rode before stopping at the place they took you?" he asked.

"I'd say over an hour."

The other guys nodded in agreement.

"After you got there, what happened?" Esteban asked.

"They took us and put us in separate rooms... we were then given a blindfold and told that we were going to die if the news station didn't make a trade," Ted said.

"What trade was that?" Esteban was anxious for the answer.

"A trade about some news clip where a drug bust happened days prior to our capture," Raul said.

"Did you know anything about it?" Esteban asked.

"Yes, but I didn't know that it was that important to them... every time we said we didn't know, we got slapped or beaten," Ted said.

"So was there an exchange made with these kidnappers?" Esteban asked.

They hesitated in answering, and Esteban said, "It seems that there was. What was so important about this news clip?"

They acted like they didn't want to tell.

"I need to know, gentlemen... other lives could be at stake and you may be able to help," Esteban said.

Raul then slowly said, "We believe that it shows who was in the drug bust, and they didn't want the identity revealed."

"Do you have copies of this clip?" Esteban asked.

They nodded yes.

"Is there any other significant thing that you can remember about these men? Because we really have nothing on them... they're going to get off scot-free. Anything like a mole or a deformed hand-" He was interrupted by Ted.

"Yes, one had a ring because I managed to see it when he was hitting me," Ted said.

"How did you react when he hit you?" Esteban asked.

"I didn't, I just took it," Ted said.

"What kind of ring and can you describe it?" Esteban asked.

"I didn't really think about it until you just mentioned his hand... it was gold with a scorpion on it," Ted said.

"Can you identify it if you saw it again?" Esteban asked.

"Yes," he said.

The discussion didn't last that long. They basically were kidnapped and used as a bargaining chip to get a news clip where some bad guys got filmed. In the process, Esteban got some form of clue about what one of the guys had on when they were beaten.

"I want to get a sketch artist to draw what you saw. Is that fine with you?" Esteban asked.

"That's fine with me," Ted responded.

He felt like there was nothing else they could tell him that would be of any use. All other questions, they couldn't answer. They didn't know where they were taken or where they were beaten until they were unconscious, and their camera equipment was destroyed. The ring was the only clue that he had to go by, and he thought that it might be a shot.

He asked them other questions—what they were given to eat and drink, where they slept, and if they were given any information to confuse them on what the other reporter might say. The reporters responded with nothing significant, the usual victim-type answer that they weren't sure.

"Did the men give any clue on who the man was they didn't want to be shown on the video?" Esteban asked.

"No, the video shows several people all randomly. But one of the men in the video looked clean-cut. Everything else seemed normal," Hector Ortega said.

"Is it hard to find him in the video?" Esteban asked.

"It's the beginning and end of the video. It's panning, so you have to look fast. Nothing extraordinary," Hector Ortega responded.

"Well, thank you, gentlemen. I'll arrange a sketch artist to come by later today... I would like to see the clip that was given to the kidnappers," Esteban said.

Raul looked at him and said, "It'll have to be a few days... it's in a safe place."

"That's fine with me... I just want to prevent any further crimes like this from happening, and perhaps there might be a bigger story brewing," Esteban said.

"OK, in three days I'll come back and see the video. We want to prevent this from happening, but mostly to learn how to survive like you gentlemen did. We don't want this to happen to reporters or anyone else," Esteban said.

They shook hands and said goodbye, and Esteban walked out of the news station. He really didn't have much, but perhaps by watching the video, he'd get a clue of who or what organization was behind this.

"If you gentlemen don't mind, I'll see if I can get a sketch artist today and we can get the ring going so we can be ahead of the curve. You mind if I come back later today?" Esteban asked.

"That's fine," they said. "We'll be working here, so we'll do our best," they all responded.

"Sounds good. I should be back in a few hours before it starts getting late," Esteban responded.

The reporters went to their workstations, while Esteban started walking down the news station's hall. His cellphone rang, and he answered.

"Hello."

"What'cha doing, my love?" Isabel said.

"Isabel... what a surprise," he said.

He really wasn't expecting her call.

"Well, I wanted to tell you that I'll be going to Merida sooner than I expected," she said.

"Really, when?" he asked.

"Like today... plans have changed, and they need me there before the clients leave, and that means I have to do the contracts tomorrow... it really puts the pressure on," she said, sounding unsatisfied.

"I can understand that... do you need a ride to the airport? I have time to take you," he said.

"You read my mind... I'll be ready to go in an hour," she said, comforted.

"OK, I'll be on my way... I love you, and I'll see you soon," he said.

He then went to an area where no one was around and called Chavez.

"Hello," Chavez answered.

"Que tal, Chavez... what's the latest in the intel business?" Esteban asked.

"The usual, nothing that we already don't know... what's up?" Chavez said.

"I need a favor... I need a sketch artist by today," Esteban said.

"Wow, are you looking for someone?" Chavez asked.

"Actually, it's more like someone's ring, and it would help to have a sketch artist draw it up," Esteban said.

"OK, I can arrange that. You'll have to pick the guy up at the police station," Chavez said.

"I can do that. I'll do that before 5 p.m. today," Esteban said.

"What else is going on?" Chavez asked curiously.

"Isabel is going on a business trip to Merida, and I'll be taking her to the airport in a few minutes," he said.

"That sounds like it would be fun. Why don't you go?" Chavez said.

"I would if I didn't have to do any work," Esteban said.

"I don't blame you," Chavez said.

"Well, thanks, Chavez, for this... it really helps, and I'll tell you how it all comes out. If you're free in a day or so, we'll have a few drinks," Esteban said.

Chavez was surprised and said, "Am I hearing this right... you're not making excuses to drink with me?"

Esteban laughed. "No... I just feel like having a few drinks like we used to, that's all."

"It's because Isabel is out of town and you don't have to tell her, huh?" Chavez said sarcastically.

"That does help, but it's not just that," Esteban said.

"Hey, sounds good to me... we'll be in touch then," Chavez said.

They said goodbye, and Esteban was on his way to pick up Isabel.

Esteban drove and was glad that he had the sketch artist lined up to see the reporters.

"Anything to come up with a clue," he thought to himself.

Isabel was almost ready with her packing. She hated to be called to travel like this at the last moment. It had happened once before, and it got her all riled up when she came back from the trip. Esteban was hoping that it wouldn't happen this time.

He was almost at her apartment and parked in front of her door. He got out and knocked. She opened the door and saw Esteban.

"I'm so glad you're here. I've had to pack everything at the last moment, and I hope I have enough for three days. The plane leaves in four hours, and I want to be there early... I cannot miss the plane or I'll be in huge trouble with the company," she said.

Esteban smiled and put her bags in the car.

"You have everything you need, don't you?" Esteban asked.

"I hope so. I just want to go and get this over with... it's been a long morning," she said, frustrated.

"Come, let's go then." Esteban looked over the living room, and then they both got in the car.

They got out of the driveway and headed toward the airport.

"Why the sudden change of plans at the last moment with your client?" he asked.

"I have no idea... something came up, and they're not going to be there a week like they planned, and I wasn't supposed to go in the first place," she said. "I got called at the last moment, and my boss told me I had to pull this through or we could lose them to another advertising company... so here I go," she said, making a face.

Esteban couldn't help but notice her, even when she was mad. She was so beautiful that he kissed her in the middle of traffic.

"What was that for?" she said.

"Because you're so damn beautiful and I love you. Got a problem with that... take it up to the manager," he said jokingly.

She smiled and kissed him back.

They made it to the airport, and he let her off at the front doors. She got a helper and said, "I'll meet you at the terminal... it'll be the Mexicana Airline."

She waved, and Esteban went to park the car.

The airport was busy, and she made it to the terminal. There was a line, and she got in the back to wait her turn. Esteban made it back and found Isabel almost at the front. The line moved quickly. It was Isabel's turn, and she got her tickets worked out.

They had a few moments to talk, but then they started calling for the flight—it was time to board.

"Well, Isabel, call me when you get there and remember that it will be fine... you'll get the contract and you'll be home soon," he said.

"I will. And you call me too," she responded.

They kissed, and she got her handbag and headed toward the plane.

"I love you," they both said at the same time.

He looked at his watch. It was nearly 1 p.m.

"I better get something to eat before I go get the sketch artist," he thought to himself.

He decided to eat at the airport. He got a quick sandwich and then went off to the police station to get the sketch artist and take him to the news station.

It had been a busy morning for him, but he had made progress.

He arrived at the police station but didn't know where to go. He decided to call Chavez because he didn't want to explain what he was doing or get attention. The phone rang and Chavez answered.

"Yes?"

"Chavez, I'm at the police station but where do I find the sketch artist?" he asked.

"He should be outside. He looks like he's a freak, but that's just his style... he knows that you will come pick him up. I told him you'd introduce yourself by Esteban," Chavez said.

"Yeah, but give me more details on what he's wearing or what he looks like," Esteban asked.

"He has thick glasses and brown hair... he looks like a nerd... he also carries a sketch-type pad with him," Chavez said.

At that moment, Esteban was looking at a man who matched the description, sitting on a bench in front of the police station.

"I think I found the guy. Just hang on to see if he's the one," Esteban said.

He walked up to the guy and said, "Hi, I'm Esteban... are you the sketch artist?"

He responded, "Yes, I am."

Esteban picked up the phone and said, "I found him. Thanks, Chavez... I'll see you soon." He hung up.

Esteban then said to the artist, "I'm glad to meet you. What's your name?"

"I'm Cesario Luna," he said.

"Well, an artist indeed... please, I'll take you to the place where you'll be doing the drawing."

"How did you get volunteered to do this?" Esteban asked.

"I'm a freelancer and I got a call from my boss that this was an emergency, and here I am," he said.

"Indeed. Well, you'll be drawing a hand ring... come, let's go and I'll tell you on the way," Esteban said.

Esteban then took him to his car, and they were on their way to the news station. Esteban began to talk to the artist.

"Cesario, what you do here I want you to keep confidential, and you cannot keep any of your drawings."

Cesario looked at him strangely.

"I usually don't disclose any information about what I do for the police."

"Just making sure. I have to do my job, that's all."

"We're going to meet some reporters, and they'll describe a ring. See if you can draw what they say... I know you're used to faces, but a man with your talent should be able to draw a simple thing," Esteban said.

He began to just get to know the artist and made him feel comfortable until they got to the news station.

Once there, Esteban arranged for the reporters to meet in the same private room and describe the ring. Ted then went into the details of the ring.

"The ring was gold and had a scorpion on it. It was sort of like the zodiac sign but in a different position," he said.

"Was it a smooth finish on it or nugget-shaped?" Cesario asked.

"Smooth, and the ring was thick... I remember that because he slapped me several times and I could feel it," he said.

Cesario made a weird face because he didn't know that these men had been beaten. Esteban then asked him a question.

"Was his ring on the right or left hand?"

"His ring was on the right hand, and he had thick hands," Ted said.

Cesario continued drawing as Ted explained his memory. There wasn't much to go on but the ring. Neither reporter had a recollection of the kidnappers. It seemed to be a professional job with no links connected.

Cesario took about 20 minutes, and the drawing was complete. Ted agreed with how the artist drew it, and that was all Cesario could do.

Esteban then said, "Gentlemen, thank you for your cooperation, and I need to know when I can see the show you have for me."

"Yes, we'll call you... it should be available in the days we mentioned," Raul said.

The reporters said goodbye to Cesario as they went back to their workstations. Cesario and Esteban then went out to the car.

"I'll take you home if you want," Esteban addressed Cesario.

"I'd appreciate that. I had a friend drop me at the station and I'd rather get home soon," the artist said.

"No problem then, I'll take you home," Esteban said.

They talked along the way and Cesario was interested in the ring. Esteban just made a cover story to get Cesario interested in a tangent story.

They arrived at Cesario's place twenty minutes later, and Esteban thanked him and gave him one hundred dollars.

"Thanks," Cesario said, smiling.

"It's for a great job, and perhaps I may need your talent again," Esteban said.

"Anytime," he responded.

They waved, and Esteban took off to his place.

Esteban saw that the only thing he had was the ring, and perhaps he could find the random guy in the video when he saw it. He realized that these people were professionals because they did their work with good training and precision.

The kidnappers managed to snatch the reporters in the middle of the day without anyone noticing what was happening, and they got them into the van. The reporters never got a look at them because they were hooded and taken to an undisclosed location. The reporters had no recollection of how many kidnappers were involved. They were subdued with beatings and threats. A ring on the hand of a kidnapper was all Esteban had.

He planned to do some research on the ring. He had a hunch about it, and he was usually right. It was the experience talking to him. He headed toward the government building and intended to get into the secret internet. Maybe he could find some answers there.

The parking lot was full, so he had to go to the upper deck. He parked the car and went in. The standard security measures had to be completed, and then he was in. He saw someone he knew and waved at them. He signed his name and went in to use the secret computer.

He got on the computer and started with "ring-scorpion." He received tons of hits and began to sort through the findings. This went on for two hours before he called it a day. What he found was that rings with scorpions usually represented some kind of zodiac sign, but there was also an organization that used a scorpion as a symbol for a secret type of fraternity. This organization operated in special operations in Latin America.

Esteban planned to do more research on it the next day.

"I'm on to something, and I believe I have some more answers back in my computer," he thought to himself.

He picked up his cellphone and called the Senator. The secretary answered and told Esteban he was in a meeting. He decided he would just go and escort the Senator back to his house after his meetings. He didn't feel as bad now that he was finding some clues—and all from something as simple as a ring.

He arrived at the Senator's office and waited for the day to end so that he could take the Senator home and dig deeper into the mystery. Esteban felt like the case wouldn't take long. It might not solve the identity of the kidnappers, but it would uncover who else might be behind it.

The Senator finished his meeting and greeted Esteban.

"Any headways so far?"

Esteban responded, "We're getting there... I should know more after two days."

"Excellent. I have a man that I must see, and I would like for you to be present," the Senator said.

"Of course, just tell me when, sir," Esteban replied.

"It's supposed to be tomorrow, but it could be delayed because his wife is ill. I'll let you know," the Senator said.

"Yes, sir. I'll be standing by," Esteban said.

"Well, let's go home... it's been a long day," the Senator said.

Esteban took him home, then went to his apartment to relax and search his computer for what he had found. He fixed something to eat and then checked his messages. There was a message from Isabel.

"Esteban, I made it fine with no major problems... I'm in the Radisson Hotel and the contract came through," she said, relieved. "Call me when you get in... I love you," she finished.

Esteban smiled because he knew she did everything at the last minute. He finished his supper and then called Isabel.

The phone rang.

"Bueno."

"Hola, my princess," Esteban said.

"Cariño, I'm glad you called... the day has been full to the rim with things happening," she said.

Esteban felt a long story coming his way.

"I lost my notes somewhere in the airport and I had to give a speech on nothing but sheer imagination. My boss extended me to stay another day to meet another client, and I forgot the dress I was supposed to pack," she said, agitated.

Esteban couldn't help but smile. Even in her aggravated state, Isabel sounded beautiful and lovely to him.

"Mi amor, you've done the best you can, and you've signed a contract all at the last minute... who else could've done that at your agency? Only you," he said.

"I know, but I don't have nothing to wear for my client. I left it at home," she said.

"Tomorrow, when you have the chance, go buy something. They have stores there, and you'll look good in anything," he said, trying to cheer her up.

She hesitated and knew he had a point.

"I'll see what I can find, I guess."

"I'm just glad you're fine and that I have a chance to talk to you."

"I hate not being close to you."

"You're either the one on trips, or I am," he said.

"We need to go on a trip together," she said.

Esteban thought for a moment and nodded his head, like it was a great idea.

"Isabel, that's excellent... let's plan a mini-vacation together, at least for a weekend," he said with excitement.

"That sounds like a great idea... it will give me something to look forward to," she said.

Isabel continued to tell Esteban about her experience, and the conversation went on for thirty minutes. Finally, Esteban had to step in and say, "Isabel, I love you, but I'm going to have to do some research on this thing I'm working on."

"I understand—work, work, work," she said sarcastically.

"I love you, Isabel. And call me to see how your other client works out," he said.

"I will. I love you, Esteban," she said.

They said goodbye and hung up.

Esteban liked the idea of going on a weekend together, even if it was just in the D.F. He went to his computer and went over the information he had found earlier that day. He made a few notes and decided to call it a night.

The next day was like any other day. He got up, did his hygiene, and then went to pick up the Senator. He didn't have time to work out and decided to save it for another day. The Senator seemed agitated and didn't say much until he was in his office.

Esteban still had to wait another day for the reporters to have the video ready for him to see. He waited and did his bodyguard duties outside the Senator's office. Sometimes it was boring, with a lot of standing or sitting around, but during those times one had to stay alert and ensure that security was established at all times.

He thought about what he had found the day before.

"The ring seems to be from some guy that could've been in a professional SWAT or special ops team."

"That could explain their tactics when the reporters were kidnapped."

"Now all I have to do is watch the news clip and see what else I'm able to find," he thought to himself.

The hours passed, and lunchtime came around. The Senator decided to eat within the building and sent Esteban for take-out. They ate at the office, and the Senator continued with his phone calls.

Esteban called the news station to check on their progress with the news clip. The reporter, Raul, told him that he'd have it by tonight and that he'd show it to him the next morning.

This was exactly what Esteban wanted to hear. He planned on finishing this case by the next day.

20

Meanwhile, Isabel was doing fine. She managed to go to a clothing store and bought a knockout business dress for her meeting with her client. Her new client sold computer hardware and was seeking an agency to advertise on their behalf in Latin America. Isabel was a prime choice to show their potential.

The meeting went well, and the company signed with Isabel's agency. This made two clients that the advertising agency was able to close. Isabel made a difference with her experience and beauty. She then went to her hotel and called her boss.

The boss answered the phone, "Bueno."

"Jefe, the deals are done," she said excitedly.

"That's incredible! See, I knew you were perfect for the job," he said happily.

They discussed the trip further and then ended the call. Isabel decided to go out and relax in the sun. How could she pass up being in Merida and not enjoy the accommodations? She called her mother to tell her the news and then called Esteban. She dreamed of being on her honeymoon and having everything settled. The thoughts simply crossed her mind while she talked to her mother.

***

Esteban ended the day by taking the Senator back home. He didn't get much accomplished as the day ended, but sometimes waiting was what made the hunt better. The Senator was not very talkative with Esteban that day. He wasn't mad, just had too many things running through his mind, and he had to sort things out.

Senator Fernandez was a busy man every hour he was awake. His strong character was what enabled him to function and keep going. When he didn't have much to say, it was because he was thinking of ways to solve problems or choosing his battles.

Esteban went home and checked on Isabel. He then called his mother to check on her and went to the gym. Another day ended.

The next day, Esteban looked forward to finishing the case. He wanted to get back to his regular routine. He went and picked up the Senator and took him to his office. He then called the news station. He talked to Raul, and the video was ready. Esteban smiled and headed toward the news station.

He arrived and went in to meet the reporters.

"Buenos días... so the mystery video is finally ready," he said.

"Yes, it is," Ted said.

"Let's go ahead and look at it then," Raul said.

They began to play the video. Nothing significant was initially shown, but in the background, a man appeared on the left side of the screen.

Esteban said, "Freeze it... Now, can you zoom in?"

Ted made the adjustments and zoomed in.

"Now play it very slow," Esteban said.

Ted continued and played the video.

"Now freeze," Esteban said.

The man's face looked familiar to Esteban.

"Now, can I get a print of this guy's face?" he asked anxiously.

"Sure, no problem," Raul said.

They printed one out in color. They continued the video, and nothing else showed but the reporter stating what had happened.

"This is what I believe the kidnappers were looking for, and I'm very glad you made a copy," Esteban said.

Then Esteban thought for a moment and asked,

"You all never aired this, did you?"

"No, that was part of the deal," they both said.

"I see," he responded. "Well, I believe this will complete the questions."

"I would also like some statements on how you all reacted and what you all did to keep from going insane. I'll record your voices and won't reveal any identities... this will help in finding out how to survive when you're kidnapped," Esteban said.

He had to make this look official and not appear as if he was doing nothing but police work. When he ended his charade, he thanked the reporters.

"Thank you, gentlemen, for all your cooperation... this will really help our government leaders," Esteban said.

"I'm glad we could help," the reporters said.

He said goodbye and left the news station. He was off to the government building to use the secret computer. He wasn't sure about that photo, but he believed he had seen that guy before. He would find out in a few more hours.

He wondered how Isabel was doing. He really loved her and thought of her often. He hadn't even taken the time to see when the wedding date would be.

"I guess we'd better start to look at that because time sneaks up and we'll have to do things at the last minute... I don't want that," he thought to himself.

He continued to drive until he arrived at the government building.

This case had turned up more than he expected with a limited amount of clues. He entered the building and went to the secret computer. He accessed the data that he had stored from the last visit and browsed some of the new entries. The picture that he had scanned from the reporter's looked very familiar to him.

He took it out and scanned it into the computer to find a match. The computer took a little while to process it and came up with a find. The man in the picture turned out to be a former Secret Service man. His name was Mario Morales. To Esteban's surprise, he also saw what appeared to be a ring on his right hand. He zoomed in on the finger, but he couldn't get a good image.

Now he had something he could use. He saved the data and logged off the computer.

"I'm done with this. Now I have to get information that only Chavez can provide," he thought to himself.

Esteban headed out of the government building and called Chavez on his way. The phone rang, but Chavez didn't answer. He then called his cell number.

Chavez answered, "Hello."

"Que tal, Chavez? I need to talk to you," Esteban said.

"Well, I don't know if today would be a good time," Chavez said.

"Oh, Chavez, you want to talk when I don't, and now, when I want to talk, it's not a good time?" Esteban said sarcastically.

"I have my security crap I have to do first, but maybe later tonight or early tomorrow, Mr. Smartass," Chavez replied.

Esteban smiled. "OK, tonight will be good... how about 8 p.m.?"

"That sounds fine with me... are you coming over to the house, or do you want to go somewhere?" Chavez asked.

"I'll meet you at your place... thanks, Chavez," Esteban said.

"Anytime... I have to go, a meeting is about to start," Chavez said.

"See you tonight," Esteban hung up and continued to drive through town.

"Well, I guess I can wait until it's time for the Senator to go home, and then I'll go see my friend," Esteban thought to himself.

Esteban decided to head to the shooting range and practice while he waited for the clock to hit 6 p.m. He hadn't gone in many days, and he liked to keep practicing on a regular basis. There were several shooting ranges in the city, and he had shot at all of them. Each one was different and had its own regulations. Most were for law enforcement officials and were located in police academies or government-related agencies.

He went to a familiar range located near a police academy. He entered and followed the procedure by showing his badge and checking for an available time slot to shoot. The staff provided him with a two-hour window, allowing him to practice on both close and distant targets.

Esteban was an expert marksman, and it showed in his practice. He tended to qualify four times and then decided to shoot for the last 30 minutes to see what new moves he could come up with. He was just wasting time now in order to go pick up the Senator.

After practicing to the point of boredom, he checked out and thanked the lady at the desk. It was almost 5:20 p.m., and he headed back to the government facility to take Senator Fernandez home. The Senator was ready to leave and was waiting for Esteban.

When Esteban approached, he said, "Sir, I hope that you weren't waiting too long for me." Esteban felt embarrassed for keeping the Senator waiting.

"No, you haven't. I've only been sitting here for less than five minutes," he said.

Either way, Esteban didn't feel comfortable making the Senator wait for something like that.

They headed to the Senator's home, and Esteban said, "Senator, I believe I should be ready to fill you in soon on this case."

"That's good to hear... Tell me when you have everything ready... I'm still in the middle of meeting a few more VIPs," the Senator said.

"At the latest, two days," Esteban said.

"We'll fit it into the schedule. Also, I want you to be present when that gentleman I spoke about shows up... he might be there tomorrow, so stay flexible," he said.

"Yes, sir, I will," Esteban said.

They reached the Senator's house, and Esteban escorted him in. They said goodbye, and Esteban went to get something to eat before seeing Chavez.

Esteban was confident that Chavez had the missing information. Chavez was familiar with the security personnel, so what he wanted to ask should be common knowledge. This would conclude the investigation, and Esteban could piece everything together the following day.

He went to a nearby taqueria and got some gorditas with a drink. He didn't often eat out like that, but he craved it and went for it. The time was 7:30 p.m., and he finished his drink and went to see Chavez.

Fifteen minutes later, Esteban arrived at Chavez's apartment and noticed that his car wasn't there yet. He decided to wait in his car until Chavez arrived. He relaxed and listened to the radio. Around 8:05 p.m., Chavez rolled in and parked his car.

Esteban got out and yelled, "I could've read a book waiting on you... You're late, soldier." He spoke in a mock menacing tone, imitating an old drill sergeant they had during training.

Chavez smiled and said, "That drill sergeant was an asshole."

Esteban just laughed. He walked over to Chavez and shook his hand. Chavez opened the door and said, "Make yourself at home."

Esteban went to the living room, and Chavez went to the kitchen.

"Want something to drink?" Chavez asked.

"Give me a beer," Esteban said.

"Whooa... Do I hear Esteban wanting to drink while coming off duty on a weekday?" Chavez said it sarcastically.

Esteban just gave him a stupid look, smiling. Chavez came in, and they sat down in the living room.

"Well, what brings you to see me? Because I know it's not about just bullshitting," Chavez said.

Esteban smiled. "True... I wanted to see if you knew something about a ring and to see how things are going... we can talk business and friendship, you know."

Chavez nodded while drinking his beer. He then asked, "What ring... what do you mean?"

Esteban told him that he was interested in learning about a former employee of a secret agent, Mario Morales. He showed him a picture. Chavez took another drink of beer and studied the picture.

"I've met him before, but it was several years ago... I believe I was still new at my job here," Chavez said.

"He looks very familiar to me too," Esteban said. He then asked, "My other question is this ring... I can't make it out, but perhaps you can tell me if agents wear a certain ring... I know I didn't."

Chavez then put his drink on the table and said, "Here's something that I didn't even know until about a year ago... there's a fraternity-type organization in the Secret Service, and one of the things they have in common is a ring."

Esteban looked at him with a mysterious expression and asked, "What does it have on it?"

Chavez was slow at saying it, mostly because he wasn't sure. "I believe, not 100% sure, but I believe it's a scorpion."

This news gave Esteban more confidence in his investigation.

"How come we weren't invited to be in it?" Esteban said.

"From what I've heard, you don't want to be in it, and it's a bunch of bullshit anyway... Besides, you have to be in the business many years and kiss a lot of people's ass before you're considered worthy," Chavez said. "Are you looking for this guy?" Chavez asked.

Esteban looked at him. He knew he could trust him, but he had given his word to the Senator on this.

"I can't tell you all the details right now, but I do need your help if you find out anything else about this guy," Esteban said, looking at him as if he knew he wouldn't get the answer he wanted.

"I understand, no need to say anymore...I'll get on it...I should have some answers by tomorrow," Chavez said.

They both changed subjects and started talking about the good old times they'd had, and drank several more beers. Soon, time passed by, and it was almost midnight. Esteban looked at his watch and said, "Shit, I need to get home…it's a long day tomorrow and I can't be late with the Senator."

"I have to get up as well," Chavez said.

"Listen, this was great…I like talking about our good times and how things are going," Esteban said.

"See, I keep telling you to come have a drink with me but… noooo… Isabel is making me out to be a psycho."

"She hates me…I haven't done anything wrong to her," Chavez said innocently.

"Well, let me see…you've had affairs with three of her girlfriends without their knowledge that you were dating other people, you got caught having sex with a former congressman's secretary, you got away from a scandal of being naked with a prostitute in a bar, and the list goes on," Esteban said.

"Those are minor details blown out of proportion…technicalities that are irrelevant," Chavez said, waving his hand dismissively.

Esteban could do nothing but laugh.

"Look, I don't care, you're my friend for life, but for a woman like Isabel, those are mortal sins, and it won't go away overnight," Esteban said.

They laughed and shook hands.

"I have to go, I enjoyed the talk, and tell me what you find tomorrow when you have the chance," Esteban said.

"You know I will…I'll call your cellphone," Chavez said.

They said goodbye, and Esteban went home.

The next day, Esteban seemed to be wide awake. He got up and ran several miles, his mind preoccupied with the case. He needed to find out what this former secret agent was doing in a drug bust. He also felt 100% sure that he was involved in the kidnapping. All of this was starting to come together, and Esteban felt that Chavez would put the icing on the cake. With Chavez's information, he would be able to brief the Senator on the case and solve it.

He didn't know whether the authorities would take any action or if the Senator intended to pursue it. Sometimes, it worked that way to catch the bigger crook.

Esteban finished working out and was ready to go get the Senator. He left to pick up his boss and take him to his office.

While the Senator was in his office, Esteban patiently waited for Chavez to call him. He would give him until noon, and then Esteban would see what information Chavez had come up with.

The Senator was in his office on the phone, as usual, making the deals that he typically made. Everything seemed to be as it had been the day prior. The secretary was typing up memos and taking phone messages. Other aides were giving the Senator their analysis on his state's economy, agriculture, and so forth.

Esteban ensured that everything was safe and that the Senator's life was never in danger. He checked all possible weak spots where an individual could try to attempt to kill the Senator or any other politician in the Senator's vicinity. He had perfected this since he had started working for the Senator. He was so used to it that it wasn't even part of his job anymore; it came instinctively.

Esteban sat, looking like one of the people waiting to see the Senator. He was always observing how things were and checking for anything out of place.

Time passed, and it was nearing noon. A few minutes later, he got a call from Chavez. Esteban answered his phone, expecting the call.

"I thought you forgot about me."

"You know me better than that," Chavez said.

"Found anything?" Esteban asked.

"Interesting character, this guy with a ring," Chavez said.

"What do you mean?" Esteban asked.

"I'd rather tell you over lunch, not on the phone," Chavez said.

"Let me get the OK from the Senator... hold on," Esteban said.

Esteban knocked on the door and went into the Senator's office. He signaled that he needed to talk, and the Senator held up his hand while still on the phone. The Senator then hung up.

"Sir, I need to get the final details on the errand you wanted," Esteban said, playing it cool.

The Senator understood and said, "By all means, go ahead."

"Yes, sir, and I'll be done as soon as I can," Esteban said.

He stepped out of the office and got back on the phone. "Let's meet at your favorite place."

"See you in 15 minutes," Chavez said.

They hung up, and Esteban took off to see him. Esteban headed to his car and thought about how this case was going. It had all started with two reporters being kidnapped for having videotaped a former secret agent in a drug bust. The secret agent was not arrested or suspected, but only videoed. This made things more suspicious because a lot of trouble had gone into making sure the video wasn't aired.

This all sounded like a big cover-up, and Esteban was about to find out.

Esteban arrived at Hooters. The place was full, and Esteban went inside. He looked around and then saw Chavez waving like a kid at him. Esteban laughed because he knew that Chavez felt at home in places like this.

He walked up to the table.

"I see that you got me a drink already."

"I couldn't resist, and the waitress here told me that it was on the house," Chavez said.

"You must've offered her something like a modeling contract," Esteban said.

He knew how much of a swift talker Chavez could be. They shook hands, and he sat down, and then they began to talk.

"I looked into what you told me and found some interesting facts," Chavez said.

Esteban looked at him and listened.

"The man, Mario Morales, is a secret agent and resigned three years ago. He didn't do it on his own. He was given the choice to resign or face criminal charges of criminal cover-up by the agency," Chavez said as he took his drink.

"What kind of criminal cover-up?" Esteban asked.

"It's not specific, but it deals with homicide and narco-trafficking," Chavez said, wrinkling his nose in disgust.

"I see," Esteban said. He knew that this was the man involved in the kidnapping, and this solidified the case even more.

"Do you know where this guy is living and who he's working for now?" Esteban asked.

"He moved to Mazatlán when he left the agency, and there's no information after that. He's worked for private companies as a bodyguard and security supervisor. The last company was an American company, ALCOA. They deal with agriculture, metals, and other materials," Chavez said.

"Tell me more about this fraternity that we were never invited to attend," Esteban asked, his suspicion growing.

"Well, that's something that is kind of like rumors that are true," Chavez said.

"What do you mean?" Esteban asked.

"Secret agents, bodyguards, and even special ops personnel are sometimes invited to this organization so that they can be part of a group of people that can help one another when the need arises. That includes getting members out of criminal charges or even making disliked people disappear," Chavez said.

"Sounds more like a mafia or a gang," Esteban said.

"Well, it's precisely what it is with a fancier name. Once asked, you can decline, but if you accept and attend their gathering, you won't really be asked to leave. That's what I've heard. I don't know. All I know is that if you don't even consider being part of it, all will be well," Chavez said.

Esteban hadn't realized it was that dangerous an organization.

"What are the benefits, then, in being in?" Esteban asked.

"Protection mostly, and money when the need arises… like you said earlier, it's like a mafia or gang with a fancier name that makes it legal," Chavez said.

Esteban knew that organizations like those rarely provided many good services and tended to prioritize their own interests.

"I'm glad that you enlightened me on this, it really helps," Esteban said.

"It got me curious too, and I learned from it as well," Chavez said.

"Well, let's eat and enjoy the moment," Esteban said.

They drank, placed an order, and chatted about personal matters for the rest of the time. Business only went so far, and their friendship blossomed after much business had been discussed. They finished their lunch and went their separate ways to work. Esteban found it amusing that Chavez had chosen Hooters. Any event that involved attractive women somehow had Chavez in the middle of it.

Esteban then headed back to the Senator's office. All this had added up, and he would brief the Senator when he was through with his scheduled associates. Esteban had thought this was going to be an easier case, but it turned out to have more twists than he expected. He never realized there was a secret organization that dealt with secret service personnel. If these men were to be used for the wrong reason, nothing could ever be secured, and corruption would always exist.

He arrived at the government building, entered, and waited for Senator Fernandez. The Senator was ready to hear

Esteban's brief. The secretary waved Esteban in. Esteban greeted the Senator, and they exchanged handshakes.

"I apologize, Agent Esteban, but people always seem to want to talk to me when I'm about to do something important," the Senator said.

"I understand," Esteban responded.

"I'm ready to hear what you found out," the Senator said.

Esteban set his computer and began his briefing.

"Senator, the video revealed the reason the kidnappers wanted the reporters. It seems that when the journalists were reporting their story, they videotaped this man who was in the area. That man is Mario Morales, a former secret agent who resigned about three years ago. He was given the choice to resign or face criminal charges of conspiracy to cover up the agency's actions. It had something to do with homicide and narco-trafficking. He was last known to be in Mazatlán. His records appear to end, and no further information is known about him after that. In the video, he appears to be wearing a ring that one of the kidnappers recognized. This ring has a scorpion that is associated with a group within the agency that I didn't know existed," Esteban said.

The Senator knew of this group and had kept information about it secret, without anyone else being aware of it.

"With this information, it appears that Mario Morales is one of the ones who kidnapped the reporters and didn't want his face to be seen on TV. This puts an additional twist on the drug bust and why someone like Mario Morales would be at a crime scene with ties to a secret group that only a few know about," Esteban explained to the Senator.

"This is exactly what I needed, Agent Esteban. The picture has become clearer, and things are falling into place. Excellent job, Agent Esteban," the Senator told him.

Both of them made some small talk. The Senator didn't want to tell Esteban about the secret group and that Mario Morales had worked with Senator Sinal. *All in good time*, he thought. The Senator had to attend to other business, and Agent Esteban knew he had to get back to being a bodyguard.

21

Esteban and Isabel had begun seeing less of each other, not because of problems between them, but simply because duty called, and in different directions. Esteban had become more involved in the Senator's investigation, while Isabel had her own commitments pulling her across the border.

Isabel had been assigned a high-profile media coverage in Los Angeles for an upcoming movie featuring two Mexican actors playing the lead roles. It was a major moment for Hispanic representation in Hollywood, and her network had entrusted her with the full coverage. Two Mexican companies sponsored her trip, eager to capitalize on the growing advertising opportunity in the United States. With the rise of Mexican talent in American entertainment, Isabel had naturally become one of the faces leading the charge.

Her boss couldn't have been happier. Isabel's poise, her sharp understanding of media and marketing, and her flawless English gave her an edge no one else in the company quite had. She wasn't just a reporter anymore, she had become one of the most important advertising agents at the firm. As Hispanic markets expanded into the U.S., Isabel was at the center of it, establishing partnerships, negotiating airtime, and creating visibility for Mexican brands in American arenas, particularly in film and sports. She moved through meetings and press events as if she were born for it. Esteban admired her ambition, though he wished their schedules aligned more often.

Back in Mexico, Esteban found himself drawn deeper into political waters. His relationship with Senator Fernandez had grown stronger during the investigation. They were spending more time reviewing files, connecting dots, and chasing leads. They had begun to circle around one name more than once—Senator Sinal.

The evidence against him wasn't direct, but it was building in all the wrong ways. Transactions, phone records, and secret meetings. None of it proved anything, but together it painted a troubling picture. Too many details aligned too perfectly. It suggested that Senator Sinal had ties with known drug warlords and possibly other criminal figures who hadn't yet come to light.

Sinal, for his part, had begun to grow suspicious. He wasn't sure who was onto him yet. He believed it might be internal auditors or some branch of federal inspectors. He hadn't figured out that it was Fernandez leading the quiet hunt. Not yet.

Then strange things started to happen.

First, there was a drive-by shooting downtown. A federal agent, one of the few who had quietly offered information to Fernandez, was hit while getting coffee. He survived, but just barely. A few days later, official government vehicles were targeted in broad daylight. Nothing was stolen; the van was just battered, with windows smashed and tires slashed. It was a message, and Fernandez heard it loud and clear.

The Senator didn't back down. In fact, the attacks only fueled his fire. He called press conferences, condemned the violence, and vowed to uncover the corruption inside their government. The people rallied behind him, and so did the media. His popularity soared.

Esteban, knowing the stakes had risen, increased his vigilance. He stayed closer to the Senator now, watching every entrance, checking every room, inspecting every schedule. He understood that Fernandez was now becoming a symbol. That made him a target.

Weeks passed, and the city began to feel different. There was a tension in the air. There were more reports of crime, high-speed chases that ended in crashes, drug busts happening in upscale neighborhoods, and even an attempted kidnapping of a minor government official. On the surface, they appeared random. The media treated them like isolated incidents.

But Esteban knew better. He was beginning to see something else. A pattern.

The timing. The frequency. The people involved. It was subtle, but it was there, hiding in plain sight. He brought it up during a meeting with the Senator.

"These incidents," Esteban said, "they feel too coordinated to be a coincidence."

"You think they're connected?" the Senator asked, narrowing his eyes.

"I think someone's trying to create chaos. To distract or to cover something up."

The Senator nodded slowly. "Get me everything you can from the police reports. I want to know who's being targeted, what's being taken, and what isn't. We're missing something."

The next day, Esteban requested access to the police department's files. A few officers he trusted pulled strings to get him what he needed. They didn't know everything he was looking for, but they knew better than to ask. Esteban combed through the records with methodical patience.

The Senator was aware that the city was becoming unsafe. Its people were threatened. These were the people he had promised to protect and help. The task of bringing back peace felt overwhelming. But he had Esteban. And he knew that Esteban was more than a bodyguard. He had proven himself to be something more.

A mind that noticed what others didn't.

A man who stood where others stepped aside.

And that was going to be exactly what they needed.

Especially now.

The presidential campaigns had begun, and although voting season was still many months away, campaigns were already underway.

Names were starting to appear on ballots as candidates tried to gain recognition, public appearances increased, and the media was hungry for any news and eager to catch any of the candidates' slip-ups.

Among the early contenders for the Presidency of Mexico was Senator Sinal.

He had been working toward this moment for years, building alliances, calling in favors. Now, he was using every bit of power he had to get noticed. His face was plastered across billboards and TV ads, polished and smiling, with slogans promising strength, prosperity, and reform. But those who knew him understood it was just a mask. Sinal was a master of illusion. He was the great deceiver. He had always wanted the top seat, and now, nothing would stand in his way. Not ethics. Not law. Not people.

But to his dismay, the people had someone else in mind.

Senator Fernandez.

The people were the ones who proclaimed Senator Fernandez as the best candidate for president. The senator himself hasn't decided to run. He wanted to stay a senator, represent his state, and finish what he set out to do. The people were more than eager to see him run and had conducted a few demonstrations to influence his decision. Other states also shouted for his candidacy and encouraged him to run for president. They shouted for change, for honesty, for someone who didn't just speak of justice but acted on it. They shouted for Fernandez.

They had prompted him to take the leap.

Senator Sinal had poured a fortune into his campaign, buying TV spots, glossy flyers, paid influencers, billboards, hiring campaign managers, and more. And still, Fernandez was the popular one.

Sinal was furious. He blamed everything from media bias to political sabotage. But the truth was simple, the people no longer believed in his image. They believed in Fernandez.

Sinal knew he could not win. He knew he had to resort to different, less legal measures. He had to be rid of Fernandez.

***

Part of Esteban's job as a bodyguard was to remain constantly aware of intelligence and rumors regarding Senator Fernandez. Through his research, connections, and work, he received information that groups were mobilizing against Senator Fernandez. There was talk of an attempt on Senator Fernandez's life. The assassins had planned for it to be during a public rally scheduled to take place in a wide-open plaza with thousands of people, minimal screening, and high exposure. It was the perfect setup, and it was set to take place the next day.

Esteban wasted no time.

He met with the Senator late into the night, and told him about the news he had received. It took some convincing. The senator hated to disappoint his supporters. He knew that huge crowds would be gathering for the rally and that all of it was in support of his candidacy. But he agreed.

The senator gave the orders. The event was moved indoors to a secure facility. Attendees were screened. Entrances were tightened. The speech proceeded as scheduled, although many attendees watched it on screens set up outside. It wasn't the ideal political spectacle, but it was safe.

A few days later, during a casual gathering at the Senator's residence, Esteban was introduced to a young man. He was the Senator's nephew, recently assigned to assist with the Senator's security detail during the campaign period. As they exchanged greetings, Esteban recognized the man.

"You're Agent Esteban," the young man said. "We were at the academy together. You knew me. We had a mutual friend. Martín... Martín Vargas."

Martín had been one of his closest friends. He had been smart and brave. They had gone through training side by side, had survived missions together. Martín had died in a betrayal orchestrated by a superior officer during a raid. Esteban hadn't spoken his name aloud in years.

They sat down later that evening and shared stories.

"Martín talked about you a lot," the Senator's nephew said. "Said you were the only one he'd trust to watch his back."

Esteban nodded, his throat tight. "I tried."

They continued to talk about their lives and work. Esteban shared that he was about to get married.

After months of managing schedules, working with the church, and handling their busy jobs, Esteban and Isabel had picked a date. In twelve months, in Mexico City, where their story started, they would get married. They decided to begin their new life in the first place where they met.

They chose one of the grand Catholic cathedrals in the city's center. Invitations were already being printed, and the guest list was growing daily. Friends, family, colleagues, everyone who mattered would be there. Esteban was overjoyed. Isabel could think of nothing else.

***

Across the border in the United States, more pieces were moving across the board. Though happening so far away, they were of great importance to Senator Fernandez and Esteban.

There was a massive drug bust in Dallas, Texas. It was all over the news. It began as a routine traffic stop but escalated into a deadly confrontation. A license check had uncovered a hidden compartment in the truck bed, twenty tons of cocaine, the largest seizure in the region in years. The law and the criminals exchanged gunfire. Four highway patrolmen were wounded. All three assailants were killed.

The driver had a tattoo on his right wrist. Esteban recognized it immediately from the reports. It was the same sign used by his former gang, the one he had left behind when he joined the academy. This wasn't just smuggling. This was personal. Someone from his past was still connected to the larger chain they were chasing.

One of the dead men was Colombian, while the other two were former U.S. Customs agents. That detail sent chills down Senator Fernandez's spine. The corruption wasn't isolated to Mexico; it was happening across the border too.

It became more apparent with every passing week that they were dealing with something huge. This wasn't just about drugs or weapons. This was a syndicate that reached into the highest levels of law enforcement and politics on both sides of the border.

Things were moving so fast, and although Esteban had some of the pieces, the entire puzzle still couldn't be put together.

***

The next day, Senator Fernandez called Esteban into his office with a tone that was quieter than usual, more weighted. "I need you to do something discreet," he said. "No phones. No backup. Just you." He handed Esteban a folded slip of paper with an address and time. "There will be a package under a bench in Chapultepec Park. Retrieve it."

Esteban went dressed casually, walking with the ease of someone enjoying a day off. He moved slowly through the park, eyes scanning but never lingering. When he reached the bench, he sat down, leaned back, and casually slid his hand under the wooden slats. His fingers brushed against something. Taped to the underside was a thick padded envelope.

He tucked it into the inside of his coat, stayed for a few more minutes, watching people walk their dogs and feed pigeons, then left as quietly as he'd arrived.

Back at the Senator's office, the envelope was opened. Inside was a disk. It was unmarked, innocuous-looking. But when they loaded it onto the encrypted laptop, the truth spilled out like poison from a cracked vial.

Millions of dollars were exchanged with banks around the world and with companies that bought and sold weapons. Some of the money came from countries such as China, Iran, and Russia. Other accounts were traced to Colombia, Venezuela, and the United States.

The Senator had this information analyzed, and it was confirmed: Senator Sinal was, in fact, smuggling drugs into the U.S. and other countries. He was also purchasing illegal weapons from terrorist-affiliated countries and supplying certain groups with these arms; groups operating in Latin America and the Middle East were mentioned. Some of these organizations had links to Hamas and Hezbollah.

Senator Sinal was also profiting millions through bank transfers and kickbacks from people within these networks. The investigation uncovered that U.S. personnel were also involved. Among them were high-ranking officials and agents from the DEA and FBI, as well as congressional committee members and military officers.

The documents also contained lists of missing persons and individuals who had been found dead. This was the smoking gun the Senator had been searching for.

He shared everything he knew with Esteban. Information from the day he hired him, to all the assignments he had given him, including investigating the murder of the reporter and the kidnapping of others. He revealed the existence of a secret society, a powerful ring responsible for these crimes.

He told Esteban that Senator Sinal was deeply involved, but warned that proving the existence of this society would be nearly impossible. Everyone connected to it would deny its existence, and no concrete evidence had ever surfaced.

The Senator explained that exposing too much could mean certain death, not only for the person revealing the truth, but also for their family. Esteban understood the gravity of the situation. He knew that possessing this information put the Senator and himself in constant danger.

He also knew the disk was highly confidential and was never meant to be copied. If anyone found out they had it, they would become targets.

The Senator finally came clean with Esteban and revealed the identity of his source. It turned out to be Chavez, Esteban's best friend. Esteban was stunned, but also relieved. He was glad they were all on the same team.

"Senator, your life is in greater danger, more now than ever before. Do you have a plan to expose this information? Who can you trust?" Esteban asked.

"I have a few close government officials who are aware of this," the Senator replied, "but they won't come forward until everything is in place. There's too much at stake if this isn't done right. Esteban, you and I are the only ones who know what's actually on that disk. Chavez doesn't even know. He just downloaded the information. He's been my mole in the government, helping me uncover what's been going on."

"We have to be careful in every aspect," said Esteban. "Our situational awareness must increase in everything we do."

The Senator nodded in agreement. Then he said, "I want you to make a copy and keep it. If anything happens to me, I want you to have it so this corruption can be exposed. Mexico needs to be cleansed of this rot. This is the leverage we need. If there's only one copy, and it's lost, nothing will ever change."

"I will, Senator," Esteban replied. "With your permission, I'll do this and I'll keep it safe. I swear on my life."

22

The streets of Mexico City were alive with excitement.

News outlets flashed headlines in bold: *Senator Fernandez to Run for President.*

People of all ages, genders, socio-economic backgrounds, and situations shouted from the crowded barrios, upscale districts, and the grand avenues where history and modernity blended together. Half of Mexico was celebrating, with horns blaring and flags waving. These were the people who had long since become disillusioned with corruption and injustice. They were those who still hoped for change, for a better Mexico. And now, they placed all of their hope in one man: Senator Fernandez.

For months, Senator Fernandez had been against running for president. But now, he had made a decision to help his people. He knew that leadership of the nation would be a great burden, one that would bring many dangers and attacks. But Esteban's warnings and the evidence of Senator Sinal's web of deceit and sinister ambition had convinced him to give it a shot. Fernandez knew too much about Sinal's hidden dealings and secrets. He knew that if he became President, Sinal would claim that he was bringing order, but he would actually make the nation plunge into chaos. Martial law, a fabricated revolution. These would be the tools Sinal would use to destroy the nation and increase his power and wealth.

Fernandez could no longer sit by and watch the country he loved be destroyed. He could not let it be ravaged by corruption and criminal powers.

Fernandez addressed this when he announced his candidacy for the election. He stood before a sea of supporters who chanted his name. His voice was calm but determined.

"I do not seek power for myself," he began, his words carried by loudspeakers across the square. "I seek it because the people have asked me to stand. I seek it because the time for silence is over. Mexico deserves a leader who serves the people, not one who rules them by fear."

The cheers that followed were deafening. Somewhere in the crowd, Esteban stood silently, his arms crossed, watching not only the Senator but the perimeter, always alert.

But not everyone shared the joy.

In his opulent mansion, Senator Ignacio Sinal was reluctantly watching his enemy. He stared out at the city below through a window in his study. His knuckles were white against the armrest of his leather chair. The television before him replayed Fernandez's speech. He smiled a thin, venomous smile.

"So," he murmured, "he's finally taken the bait."

The announcement was not unexpected, but the public's reaction was what bothered him. The people adored

Fernandez. His clean record, his defiance of corruption, and his genuine concern for the poor. It all made him a dangerous opponent. Too dangerous.

Sinal knew that without the power of the presidency, his larger plans could not unfold. If Fernandez won, it would ruin all of his plans. It would dismantle his web of allies, his power, and his wealth.

Turning to his most trusted aide, he spoke.

"Prepare the contingency," Sinal said. "If Fernandez draws too close to victory, I want it handled. Quietly...and permanently."

The aide nodded. This was not the first time a political opponent had been "handled." But this time, Sinal seemed more on edge than usual.

"I want a team assembled. International, not local," Sinal continued. "The job must have layers of separation. And I want an American involved. If we must make this ugly, it will serve us better to direct the blame elsewhere. Let the public hate the northern neighbor more than they hate their own leaders."

"Understood, Senator," the aide said.

That night, many secret calls were made, large amounts of money were transferred, and a group of mercenaries were being assembled. They met in a secluded compound miles from the capital. Among them, one man stood out: an ex-military American with a record of covert operations and no allegiance except to the highest bidder.

His name was Clay Mercer...or so they said. He had cold eyes, steady hands. He was the perfect ghost killer.

The instructions were simple: If Senator Fernandez appeared to be winning, if the tides could not be reversed through propaganda, slander, or manipulation, he was to be eliminated. The timing would be precise. The blame would fall, not on Sinal, but on foreign influence, on the USA.

Esteban sat in his modest apartment, unaware of the storm brewing. He was still thinking about the tapes and the fact that now, he had to work even harder to protect the Senator.

The game had begun.

***

The noise of Mexico's presidential campaign was starting to reach far beyond its borders. In Washington D.C., behind closed doors, the name "Senator Fernandez" was coming up more and more in government meetings. Reports from the U.S. embassy in Mexico City were getting more detailed and more urgent. The State Department was hearing about rising tension in the Mexican elections, especially with Senator Fernandez's rapid rise and the dark rumors surrounding his main rival, Senator Sinal.

The President of the United States, though silent in public, paid close attention during his briefings. Unrest in Mexico was the last thing the U.S. wanted. Trade, immigration, and drug trafficking...all of it was tied to the political instability of the country right across the border. If Sinal won, or worse, if something happened to Fernandez before the election, it could cause a disaster that might spill over and harm U.S. interests.

Things were already shaky, but a political assassination could set off a chain reaction that no one could control.

Quietly and without public attention, the White House sent aides and intelligence officers to Mexico City. Officially, nothing was happening. But behind the scenes, the U.S. government was on high alert.

23

Back in Mexico, the whole nation was on its toes. They were eager for the elections to begin. People waved campaign banners from their balconies, music blared from speakers, and crowds gathered to cheer on their favorite candidates. There were many rallies, and the news seemed to play nothing other than candidacy updates.

Senator Sinal had launched a full-scale smear campaign against Senator Fernandez. He was determined to destroy his opponent's growing popularity. He accused Fernandez of corruption, claiming that the senator had secretly accepted money from foreign businesses and criminal organizations. Sinal's camp spread rumors through social media, radio, and television, saying that Fernandez was a wolf in sheep's clothing. They claimed he was someone who pretended to care for the people while lining his own pockets.

Though many saw through the lies, some began to doubt. The attacks were designed to erode Fernandez's clean image.

But Fernandez, true to his character, refused to stoop to Sinal's level. He stayed focused on the issues that mattered, calling for unity, justice, and an end to the very corruption Sinal accused him of. Because of this, most people still supported him. Some even shifted from supporting Sinal to supporting Fernandez because many of Sinal's claims did not add up.

Esteban knew the smear campaign was only the beginning. Something darker was still to come. The election wasn't just about politics anymore. This was a matter of life or death, not just for Fernandez but for the entire nation.

Since the election was now close, the media and press had already begun taking polls. The top three candidates were:

- Senator Sinal of the P.R.I., representing the old, powerful political machine.
- Senator Fernandez of the P.A.N., the bold reformer who wasn't afraid to speak the truth.
- Congressman Reyes of the P.R.D., popular with academics but trailing far behind the top two.

The first live national debate was held at the Palacio de Bellas Artes. Esteban stood behind the curtain, watching Senator Fernandez adjust his tie and microphone. Esteban had guarded plenty of important people before, but this time it felt different. This time it was personal.

The debate started with polite greetings and the usual political promises.

But then Fernandez leaned forward, looked straight into the camera, and said, "Corruption is killing our country."

The whole place was so silent you could have heard a pin drop.

"No one wants to say it," Fernandez went on, "because saying it risks everything. But I didn't come here to protect my career. I came because I believe Mexico still belongs to the people. And I will not stand by while the rich rob the poor, while drug lords sit in Congress, and while our children grow up thinking this is normal."

Cheers broke out across the country. People clapped in their homes, in parks, and in public squares.

Senator Sinal forced a fake smile.

"That's a nice thought," Sinal said into his own mic. "But if we spent every day chasing ghosts, we'd never get anything done. This isn't a courtroom, it's politics."

Fernandez didn't skip a beat. "Then maybe it's time politics started acting like a courtroom. Because too many criminals are walking free in suits like yours."

The debate ended with Fernandez earning a standing ovation and cheers that seemed to never end.

It was almost as if you could see the steam rising from Senator Sinal's head.

***

That night, Senator Sinal sat alone in his study, tapping his fingers on a half-empty whiskey glass.

"He knows," he whispered. "The bastard knows."

Footage of Fernandez's speech played on the television in front of him. His advisors had warned him to ignore it, to let Fernandez talk himself into a corner. But Sinal wasn't patient. He wanted results.

He picked up a secure phone. "Activate the contingency," he said. "We'll make it look like the work of a lone madman. One shot. No loose ends."

The answer came through the phone: green light.

***

It was a hot afternoon in Puebla, in the middle of what should have been just another campaign rally.

The plaza was packed with thousands of people waving flags, cheering as Senator Fernandez took the stage.

Esteban was on edge from the moment they arrived. Something felt off. This place was too exposed. There were too many unfamiliar faces, too many nervous glances, too many hands staying buried deep in pockets.

Esteban was always on high alert, staying cautious about rumors and whispers so he could keep the Senator safe. But lately, he heard nothing but reports of possible assassination attempts. He knew that most of them were just distractions. Still, there had been many on his radar for this day. His intelligence had informed him that it was a sniper. Senator Fernandez was already wearing a bulletproof vest. The area had been lined with guards and police.

What was strange was that when Esteban made a round through the perimeter, he did not see many of the faces he was used to. The head of the police was a different man. Gonzalvez was the one he knew and was beyond any doubt, loyal to Fernandez, but this man did not have Gonzalvez's white whiskers.

He scanned the rooftops. His time in the military had trained him to notice even the slightest movement. He knew the way in which a sniper rifle, glass-glinted. And that was exactly what he saw.

Esteban knew he had to be absolutely certain. Taking any kind of rash action here would mean ruining the entire rally.

He would not allow the Senator and his team to become laughing stocks.

He moved closer to the Senator. Eyes glued to the spot on the roof that he had noticed before.

Then, he saw it again.

There was no doubt.

He ran.

BOOM!

He collided with the Senator just as the sound of the bullet echoed through the streets.

THUD!

The Senator had been hit.

"Senator!" Esteban yelled. The Senator pushed Esteban off and stared at his chest. The vest had saved him. The bullet was lodged inside its hard foam. Inches from his heart.

Esteban rushed to his feet.

There was chaos. The crows screamed bloody murder. Every guard was on the move, guns cocked, fingers on the trigger. People ran in all directions, yelling out to their loved ones, crying, and screaming the Senator's name.

"Take him," Esteban commanded the Senator's personal guards. "Keep him protected."

They surrounded the Senator and guided him to safety.

Esteban rushed toward the guards who had surrounded the culprit. The sniper was out of rage. They fired upwards, but the shots bounced off the walls of the building, raining bullets down into the crowd itself.

"STOP!" Esteban yelled. "We need him alive!"

Then there was another booming shot. One just like the shot that had hit Fernandez.

The teams entered the building, climbing up to the roof. Esteban ran just behind them. Once he reached the roof, he saw a group of people just by the ledge.

Esteban pushed the men away.

There he was. The sniper. Dead. Bullet through his head.

He had put his rifle into his mouth and pulled the trigger.

Beside him, bullets, a duffle bag, and a journal were scattered.

Esteban picked up the book. It was filled with what looked like mindless, crazed scribbles. One name stood out throughout the book.

Fernandez.

***

Later that night, the official story was released: a lone gunman. A man with a history of mental illness, acting alone, with no clear motive. No ties to any group. No deeper conspiracy. Case closed.

But Esteban knew better. So did Fernandez. The clean-cut narrative made for good television, but it didn't sit right. The timing, the precision, the method—it was too deliberate, too professional. Esteban had seen enough black ops in his day to know when something smelled like a setup. And this reeked.

To Senator Sinal's frustration, the assassination attempt didn't weaken Fernandez. It made him stronger. The people didn't buy the lone madman story, not entirely.

The question spread: *Why would someone try to kill Fernandez unless he was telling the truth?* The more the press tried to downplay it, the more the people believed that Fernandez was not the real threat, not to the people, but to the powerful, to the corrupt criminals.

Fernandez's supporters swelled. His message of fighting corruption gained new significance. He was no longer just a candidate; he was a man who had almost died for standing up to the system. His words now sounded prophetic. And the people loved him more than ever.

Sinal seethed. His plan had backfired. The bullet meant to silence Fernandez had only turned him into something more dangerous: a symbol.

24

Esteban was in his apartment, resting after a long day. He was watching television, his mind occupied with the usual things.

The phone rang, and Esteban glanced at the caller ID. It read *Felipe Muñoz.* He picked up the receiver and answered, "Bueno."

A girl's voice responded on the other end, "Is this Esteban Galindo?"

Esteban's eyes widened in confusion, doubt spreading across his features. "Who wants to know?" he asked, his voice tinged with suspicion and curiosity.

"I need to talk to Esteban. It's very important," the voice said.

"This is Esteban. What's the problem?"

"Esteban," the voice shouted, "It's Alicia, Felipe's sister."

Esteban recognized her voice. "Alicia! How are you? I haven't heard from you in years. This is a big surprise."

Alicia began to cry. "Esteban... I miss you, and I wish I had some great news to tell you, but I don't." Her voice trembled with emotion.

Esteban grew concerned. "What's wrong, Alicia? What's happening?"

"Esteban..." She paused. "My brother has died. He died early this morning outside of Puebla in a car accident." She continued to sob.

Esteban was speechless, overwhelmed with dismay. He had known Felipe for many years; they grew up together and played as kids. He had known their family well and was even considered part of it. He had helped Felipe on several occasions when he was short on money.

As a child, Esteban's mother had been very sick, and it was Felipe's mother who had helped them with money and medicine they couldn't afford. Felipe had been there for him during those hard times, and Esteban had always returned the favor.

Tears began to roll down Esteban's face. He closed his eyes and took a deep breath before speaking.

"Alicia... how did this happen?" he asked.

"I don't know. The officials say he ran off the road. Maybe he fell asleep," she cried. She sounded frantic, on the verge of a breakdown.

"Alicia, take it easy. I know this is hard. It's hard for me to accept too. Your brother was like a brother to me. I can't believe this has happened to him either," he said. "Just try to be calm for your mother. She needs you right now, and you have to be strong for both of you."

"Oh, Esteban, he was the best part of our family. What are we going to do without him?" she cried uncontrollably.

Esteban couldn't bring himself to say anything. His eyes were flooding faster than he could form words. He wiped his tears and took deep breaths.

Finally, he found the strength to speak. "Alicia... hang in there for me. I'll do what I can to be there in the next day or two. Give your mother a big hug and tell her I love her. And not to worry, I'll take care of everything."

Alicia had calmed down somewhat and was able to respond more clearly. "Thank you, Esteban. You're a great person, you're also like a brother to me."

"I'll be there as soon as I'm able to, OK?" he said.

"Gracias. Tell your mother I said hello and that we miss her," she added.

"I will, Alicia. Thanks for calling me. I love you and your mother. Please be strong for her," he said.

"I will," she replied.

"Adios." He hung up.

Esteban sat in shock. He had known Felipe for so many years. It felt surreal, like something out of a movie, when someone you know dies.

He stared silently at the television for a long moment before reaching for his phone. He needed to call his mother to tell her he would be going to Puebla for his friend's funeral.

He took out his cell phone and dialed.

The line clicked. "Bueno," his mother answered.

"Mama, this is your son. How are you?" he asked.

"Hijo!" she exclaimed with delight. "It's a miracle you're calling me at this time. I was just thinking about you," she said warmly.

"How have you been feeling?" he asked.

"Well, at my age, just getting up and doing my daily routine is considered a success," she laughed, and Esteban laughed with her.

"Mama," Esteban paused for a moment. "Felipe, my friend... he died. I was just informed by his sister, Alicia."

"Ay, Dios mío! When did this happen, hijo?" she asked, clearly shocked.

"Early this morning. He died in an automobile accident," Esteban said quietly.

"I pray that God will give him peace... *pobrecito*. His family must be in so much pain," his mother replied.

"I'm going to attend the funeral, and I'll be staying with his family for a few days. I just wanted to call and let you know where I'll be before I leave," Esteban said.

"And when are you leaving, *hijo*?" she asked.

"Tomorrow, sometime, whenever I get approval from the Senator," he said.

"I'll give you my blessing from here, and I'll pray for him. He was such a nice boy," she said sadly. "Please be careful, *hijo*. I don't want anything to happen to you when you leave."

"*Madre*, don't worry about me. I'm only going to the funeral and to console his family. I know they'll want me there. We were very close, and we shared many years of friendship," Esteban reassured her.

"Please tell his mother, Guadalupe, that I will pray the rosary for them, and that I'll call her even after you leave. I also want to send her a gift with you. Maybe it will help her feel a little better," she said.

"I'll be over later tonight. I just need to finish a few things here first," he said.

"I made some *empanadas* for you to take with you," she said.

"Gracias, madre," Esteban smiled and hung up.

After hanging up, he finished writing some papers he needed to complete. Then he grabbed his keys and headed to his mother's house. It was almost midnight, and he didn't want her to stay up too late. He knew the news would worry her, and he was always concerned about her well-being.

Esteban loved his mother more than anything in the world. On many occasions, he had kept things from her just to avoid upsetting or worrying her. He had become a master at it; his time in the Special Forces had trained him to keep secrets. If his mother knew half the things he had done or the dangers he had faced, she would have had a heart attack.

He arrived at her house and knocked on the door. She opened the door almost immediately.

"Mi hijo," she said, hugging him. She smiled, but Esteban could tell that she had been crying. "Come in and stay for the night."

"Mama, I would, but I have to start getting ready for tomorrow. There are things I still need to do," he replied.

"I pray that Felipe is in heaven. Here are the gifts for Señora Guadalupe and Alicia... please give them my condolences."

"I will, madre. And I'll call you as soon as I get there." He hugged and kissed her.

She handed him the bag containing the gifts, gave him her blessing, and then he returned to his apartment.

When he arrived home, he began making plans for the funeral.

Early the next morning, he called the Senator and told him the news. He began to reconsider the situation, wondering whether he should attend the funeral or stay. This was a critical time for the Senator, and there had already been two attempts on his life. Esteban knew that with him gone, the Senator would be in even more danger. But after listening to Esteban, the Senator encouraged him to go and pay his respects.

"Agent Esteban, I understand that you wish to be here and do your job," the Senator said. "But sometimes things in life are more important, especially when it comes to honoring someone's death. Please, on my behalf, see your friend. If he was a good, close friend as you say, I'm sure he'd want you there, and you'll be able to comfort his family."

Esteban didn't want to leave the Senator alone, but the Senator insisted, understanding how close Esteban had been to Felipe. Never before had he seen Esteban looking defeated. Now, the once confident bodyguard, who always seemed as if no one could touch him, stood with his shoulders drooping and his eyes heavy. He was not just defeated... he was broken.

"Senator, I do appreciate this," Esteban replied. "It's just that things are going out of sequence here, and I don't want anything to go wrong while I'm away. I've never left my post under any circumstance, and I don't feel right leaving in the middle of everything that's happening."

The Senator nodded. "Esteban, I understand your loyalty. But I know sincerely that you want to go. I'm not stopping you; in fact, I encourage you. Go, and don't worry about what's happening now. Things will be fine. You'll be back in a few days, and everything will return to normal."

Esteban knew he was right. It would only be a few days, and he'd be back to protect the Senator. But Felipe's family weighed heavily on his mind. He didn't know how he'd deal with it once he arrived in Puebla; he'd just have to face it when he got there.

The Senator told him to be careful and to hurry back. Esteban felt better after their conversation and began to pack for the trip. His flight was scheduled for 8:00 a.m. the next morning, and he needed to be ready.

He didn't know if he'd be expected to say a few words or even help pay for the funeral. All he knew was that he wanted to be there and help in any way he could. He still couldn't believe his friend was gone.

The next morning, he got up and prepared to leave. He called a taxi; he didn't want to leave his car at the airport. When he arrived, he boarded the flight, his thoughts consumed by memories of Felipe.

He looked at a photograph of the two of them together. The image was a simple one: two boys, no older than ten, their faces sunlit and dirty, grinning with slingshots in their back pockets. They had stood shoulder to shoulder, arms slung around each other like brothers. That was how it had always been with Felipe, natural, easy, unbreakable. They had been good friends growing up. He remembered when they got in trouble for playing with slingshots and accidentally broke the neighbor's window. Their parents had made them work to pay for the damage. He could still feel the scratch of a broom in his hands, the sweat sticking to his back, Felipe cracking jokes beside him to make the punishment bearable.

Tears welled in his eyes.

He recalled the time when his mother was sick, lying pale and burning in their bed. They had no money at all to take her to a doctor. Somehow, Filipe's parents managed to buy the medicine that fully cured her. There was no way for Esteban to repay them back then; all he could do was cry in his friend's arms, thanking him and his family for being so kind, so generous, so like angels in disguise. Moments like that were hard to let go.

Felipe had been a true friend.

"I don't know how my life would've been without you, amigo," Esteban thought. "You were always there for me when we were young," he whispered, then stared out the window.

Felipe's family had also been poor, but his father had managed to earn a bit more than Esteban's. Esteban's own father had been rarely around due to work, so he had seen more of Felipe's father growing up. He had learned some carpentry and masonry from him by helping out whenever he had spare time.

In his early teen years, Esteban worked a few jobs, painting and fixing houses to make extra money. Felipe had always helped and kept him company. Esteban never would've imagined that Felipe would die so young. He had been a happy, generous man, always helping others.

Felipe had gone to college, become an engineer, helped his sister become a nurse, and had been taking care of his parents.

"It just doesn't seem fair," Esteban thought.

For the rest of the flight, he simply stared out the window or up at the ceiling.

When the plane landed in Puebla, Esteban prepared himself to meet Felipe's family. He stepped off the plane and saw Alicia and her parents waiting for him.

They were very happy to see him; they saw him as a son. Alicia ran up to him and hugged him as she cried. Her parents were crying as well. It was almost impossible to hold back the tears.

Esteban greeted them and hugged them all.

"Esteban... I'm so happy to see you," Alicia said through her tears.

Her mother couldn't speak at the moment as she embraced him, and Mr. Gama was the same. Tears rolled down his face, though he seemed deeply comforted to see Esteban.

"Come, let us go before I really start crying too," Esteban said.

They made their way toward the baggage claim.

"Esteban, you're looking very good, you've turned out to be a handsome young man," Mrs. Gama said.

"Thank you, Señora Gama. And you look the same as the last time I saw you," Esteban replied.

She smiled.

"Mr. Gama, you look like a soap opera star with your new hair," Esteban added.

"It's called old age," Mr. Gama said.

They all laughed. The moment was filled with a bit of lighthearted humor, something they all needed. The loss of their son had hit them very hard, and Esteban wanted to keep the mood as positive as possible. But he knew it would be difficult; Felipe had been the center of attention in the family for years. He had supported everyone, and his sister had only recently begun to contribute more after becoming a nurse.

After collecting Esteban's bags, they drove home. The family had come a long way since the days when Esteban was a kid. Back then, they had lived in a small two-bedroom, one-bathroom house, just like his own family. There had barely been room for furniture, but they had always been happy just being together. There was always some kind of meal on the table, even if it was just beans.

Esteban's mother had been the same way. Felipe would often spend the night at Esteban's house, and Esteban would do the same. They had shared many good times and were more like brothers than friends. They grew up together until the age of twelve, when Esteban's parents moved to another neighborhood and he had to transfer to a new school. Even then, they kept in touch and remained close.

Esteban had always made sure not to get involved with gangs, and Felipe had been a kid you never wanted to see get in trouble. There was just something about him, his nature, perhaps, that inspired goodness.

They arrived at the house, where some neighbors and relatives were already gathered. Esteban didn't quite know how to act. He felt confused. He hadn't attended many funerals, especially not for close friends. He didn't know what to say to everyone. Still, they all seemed to know who he was, his family had talked about him over the years, and he had kept in touch.

Esteban just hoped he would say the right things.

Everyone gathered in the living room. Alicia brought Esteban something to drink, and they sat down to talk. Some people still had tears in their eyes. Alicia was especially grateful that Esteban had come.

"Esteban, I'm sorry you had to come at a time like this, but we really wanted you to be here," Alicia said.

"Oh, there's no need to apologize. You are all like family to me. We've gone through so much together; we *are* family. Especially Felipe," Esteban replied.

Señora Gama silently wept at his words.

Esteban went to his small bag and took out a wrapped package. He handed it to her.

"Señora Gama, my mother made these *empanadas* for you. She sends her deepest condolences," he said.

Mrs. Gama hugged Esteban tightly, tears in her eyes. The two mothers had once been good neighbors. They had lived less than a block away from each other and had become close friends.

As people filled the living room and kitchen, a gentle hum of quiet conversation filled the house. Most were waiting to hear when the funeral would take place. It was scheduled for the next morning, but some relatives were still expected to arrive later that day or the following morning.

The rest of the day became a time of gathering, sharing memories of Felipe, remembering his laugh, and the way he cared for everyone. As day turned to night, people began heading home.

Esteban was given a room.

"Esteban, I want you to stay here for the night," Mrs. Gama said.

Esteban noticed it was Felipe's old room.

"Are you sure, Mrs. Gama?" he asked.

"Yes, I'm sure. It's what Felipe would've wanted," she said.

Esteban didn't feel entirely comfortable about it, but he respected her decision. That night, everyone went to sleep.

***

The next morning, Mr. Gama woke early, around 6 a.m. Mrs. Gama was already in the kitchen making breakfast. Esteban woke to the sound of movement in the house. He looked at the clock, got out of bed, and went to the bathroom to get ready.

After freshening up, he walked into the kitchen. Seeing Mrs. Gama at the stove brought back memories of when she used to make breakfast during his childhood sleepovers.

Mrs. Gama looked up and smiled. "My, I'm glad you're up. Here, have a seat. I made breakfast for everyone."

Esteban smiled and sat down.

He knew deep down that they all missed Felipe terribly.

"Mrs. Gama, let me help you so that you can sit and eat something," Esteban offered.

"No, I'm not that hungry, *mi hijo*. I'm just used to being busy and staying in the kitchen," she said with a smile.

Esteban understood. She was staying busy to keep her mind occupied and to better manage all the guests arriving for the funeral.

A few minutes later, Mr. Gama and Alicia joined them and sat down to eat some *huevos rancheros*. The conversation turned to Esteban, inquiring about how he was doing and how his new job was progressing. Esteban didn't mind. He would do anything to ease the tension and help them feel a little better while he was there.

After breakfast, everyone began getting ready to go to the church. There would be a mass held in Felipe's honor, followed by the burial at the cemetery.

Esteban knew it was going to be hard, but as a close friend, he had to be there.

More relatives began to arrive at the house. Esteban would be riding with Alicia and a few of their friends, while Mr. and Mrs. Gama would ride with other family members.

Soon, they all got into their cars and headed toward the church.

Everyone arrived at the church around the same time. There was a long line of cars, and most people were dressed in black. They greeted Felipe's parents and Alicia. Esteban had a blank stare, not knowing how to act in front of everyone.

They finally entered the church and sat in their reserved seats. The coffin rested in front of the altar. It had to remain closed because Felipe's body had suffered massive head trauma.

The mass began, and the priest started the ceremony. As it progressed, all Esteban could do was stare at the coffin and remember Felipe as they were growing up. He had seen fellow soldiers die in front of him, but never someone he grew up with, never someone who had felt like a brother to him.

The priest spoke about hope and peace, something Felipe would have from now on. Esteban's tears began to roll down his face. He had all sorts of memory flashes of the times he shared with Felipe. He remembered the first time they met at school, the time they got in trouble for putting tacks on kids' seats, and the day they got caught peeking at their neighbors while they were showering.

He smiled at some of the things they used to do. It hurt him even more to know he would never be able to share those moments with Felipe again. The rest of the time, he simply sat and listened to the priest and the choir sing.

After the ceremony ended, the coffin was taken to the hearse. Everyone got into their vehicles and headed toward the cemetery. The procession moved slowly, but the journey seemed to go quickly with everyone moving together.

The cemetery was several miles away. Everything had happened so suddenly that Felipe's parents didn't really know how to go about burying their son. Felipe had always been prepared; he had already made arrangements in case something ever happened to him or any family members. His family had never imagined that he would be the one to first benefit from this careful planning.

When they arrived at the cemetery, everyone headed toward the burial site. Seats were arranged for the family, and the coffin was placed to one side. The priest began with a blessing and prayers for Felipe's soul and for the family he left behind.

It was both heartwarming and tearful. Not a single person could keep a dry face while listening to the priest's words. When the prayers were finished, the coffin was lowered, and each family member took a handful of dirt and tossed it into the grave. The priest gave his final blessing, and afterward, everyone came to console the family.

Alicia walked over to Esteban, looked at him, and said, "I know that you and Felipe were like brothers, and I know you loved him very much. I just don't understand how he could've died by running off the road. He's been through that path a thousand times. He wasn't the type to speed or just have an accident."

She began to cry. Esteban realized she was reacting just as he would under the same circumstances.

"Alicia, I know that sometimes life doesn't seem fair, but Felipe's death is still keeping your family together," Esteban said. "Right now, we have questions that can't be answered, and I wish I had the answers... We need to just stay close and console your mother and father. It's a time to be together and remember your brother for who he was and all the good things he accomplished."

Alicia hugged him and cried wholeheartedly. Esteban embraced her, tears welling up in his eyes. He had been holding back his own emotions. He wanted to cry, but he needed to be strong.

Memories kept flooding in every time he looked at Felipe's family. They had gone through so many hard times together while growing up, and he had been part of it all. It just didn't seem right for someone like Felipe to die. He had the heart of a priest and rarely did anything wrong.

Esteban remembered all the times he had to defend Felipe because Felipe wouldn't fight back against other boys who took advantage of him. Esteban had been like his big brother, his bodyguard, while Felipe had always been the one with the right answers when everything was going wrong. He missed him deeply.

After everyone had their time with the family, they slowly began returning to the house. There was a long line of cars, but eventually, everyone managed to find a parking spot in the neighborhood without causing too much congestion.

Esteban and the family went inside. It seemed like everyone was whispering, quietly sharing conversations about the funeral. They were all very respectful and offered help in any way they could.

The day dragged on, but Esteban endured it. Alicia stayed close to him wherever he went. She had a crush on him when they were kids, but it had always been innocent. He could see the pain in her eyes. Felipe had been her source of inspiration, and now that he was gone, she would have to find that strength on her own.

25

There was a television on in an office in Washington, D.C. A man sat watching the news. As he picked up the phone, a ring with a scorpion on it gleamed on his finger. The call went directly to Senator Sinal's office.

Senator Sinal answered the phone.

"Bueno," he said.

"This charade has lasted long enough. I thought you were going to take care of this problem, but your compadre is still being a thorn in our side. This has to end, and it ends now. Get rid of him, or we'll have to do it, and you might get caught in the crossfire. Do we understand each other?" the voice from D.C. said.

"It's understood, and it will be done," the Senator said with a certain tone in his voice.

He slammed the phone down and began to make calls. Several hours later, a group began to assemble. Senator Sinal was informed that Agent Esteban would be out of town and that Senator Fernandez had minimal security. The assault group was given orders to go to Senator Fernandez's residence. Two black vans took off into the night, and everything was about to change.

During Esteban's trip to Puebla, hired mercenaries headed to capture Senator Fernandez while he was at home. The checkpoint security was killed without a sound as they advanced toward the residence. The mercenaries tactically surrounded the home, disabling the security systems and neutralizing any guards present.

They entered without being detected, making their way to his office. They tore it apart, searching for a disk or files containing information on Senator Sinal. They checked the computer and took the hard drive.

The Senator, hearing the commotion, walked to his office. He was met by armed, masked men pointing guns at him. They took him and hit him on the head. They sat him on a chair and he slumped down, unconscious.

After a few minutes, the Senator woke up. Senator Fernandez sat in a chair, his hands tied, his mouth gagged, his head still throbbing from where the men had hit him with a heavy, blunt object. His vision swam in and out, and every noise that the men made seemed as if it were an explosion.

The Senator knew that these men were hired mercenaries. They had infiltrated his home; he still did not understand how. He just knew that with Esteban gone, someone had found a crack in the safe and slithered through.

The mercenaries tore his office apart; all of his documents, computers, files, and drawers lay scattered around him. These men did not bother to remain quiet or conceal the signs of their crime. The Senator knew that this meant his life was in great danger. These men had come to finish the job.

Upon finding nothing in the study, they moved on to search the bedrooms and the living room. After what felt like hours, they returned to the study. By this point, Senator

Fenandez was only half-conscious, the blood dripping from his head.

"Where is it?" one of the men questioned, ungagging the Senator.

"Where is what?" The Senator said, struggling to breathe.

"The files! On Sinal!" The second man had a husky voice.

"Sinal?"

"So, all of those assassination attempts had been Sinal's doing after all...If these men are willing to let me know who sent them, then I don't have much time left," the Senator thought. *"I need to outsmart them."*

"Don't act dumb. We know you have it!" The shorter one yelled.

"I have never seen such files." The Senate stayed strong.

The shorter man picked up a baseball bat; probably the same one he had first knocked out the Senator with.

"You sure about what?" he asked menacingly, just before swinging the bat and smashing a vase into pieces.

"Do your worst," the Senator said before spitting at the man.

The two men pounced on him, beating him hard with their fists and the bat.

He refused to reveal any information. Senator Fernandez held his ground, resisting the beatings and humiliation. Fortunately, his wife and family were out of town and avoided the threats and abuse of the hired killers. Had they been here...been tortured...he might have been less strong.

"Where is the disk?" one of the men whispered harshly in his ear.

"You'll never know, and your boss is going to be revealed," the senator responded.

The man slapped him with a gun, cutting the senator's cheek. Fernandez tried to memorize every detail he could about his attackers and made every effort to leave clues behind.

He made a mental list. The first man: about 5 feet 7 inches, squeaky voice, probably smokes, mousy brown hair peeking out of his ski mask, tattoo on his left index finger. The second man: about 6 feet 2 inches, husky voice, definitely smoked cigars, blonde hair, muscular, probably had military training.

Fernandez made sure to bite the men, making them bleed onto the floor. He pulled at their hair and skin to leave evidence around.

The mercenaries acted like they were on a tight schedule and didn't want to be seen or detected. They had entered through the gates pretending to be electrical workers.

"If you don't tell us, we're going to kill your whole family!"

These mercenaries took every precaution. They disconnected the alarm system, phone, and internet. They even had a cover story ready, claiming they were there to repair a telephone pole near the senator's house. They had studied his schedule and knew Agent Esteban wouldn't be guarding him. He'd be almost completely alone at the house. The other servants had been killed during the break-in.

The attackers estimated they had about two hours before anyone would start to notice the senator hadn't called or made contact. Their goal was to make him talk. Still, the senator wouldn't budge.

"You're wasting your time, and all of you will face justice soon enough," the senator said, blood running down his face.

That only made them beat him more brutally. Finally, one of the mercenaries pulled out a 9mm pistol and aimed it at his head.

The Senator laughed. "You can't kill me. If you do, your boss is doomed. The whole Nation will know what he did."

The taller, blonde man removed his mask.

Fernandez's eyes widened. The man was American.

"Oh, but I can," he said, sneering.

He pulled the trigger.

The senator fell from the chair where he had been tortured and died instantly. The pistol had a silencer, and two 9mm shell casings flew across the room.

The mercenaries continued to search for the disk or any kind of file, but they found nothing. After ransacking every room, they staged the scene to look like a robbery, stealing jewelry and other valuables. No one knew a crime had occurred until the family returned from visiting relatives the next morning.

26

As Esteban arrived at the airport in Puebla, he received a call on his cell phone from Chavez. Chavez delivered the terrible news.

"Esteban, listen to me very carefully," Chavez said, using the commanding tone from their Army days.

Esteban immediately sensed something was wrong.

"What's going on?" he asked.

"Just listen and don't interrupt... Senator Fernandez has been assassinated. It happened sometime last night," Chavez said. "His body was found by his family when they came back from visiting relatives."

Esteban stood in total shock.

"I don't have all the details, but you're in great danger. I believe you're going to be blamed for his murder, and you need to get the hell out of Mexico now," Chavez continued. "I don't have time to explain. They're already looking for suspects, and eventually, you'll be the fall guy."

Esteban swallowed.

"You will not get a fair trial, and I believe you'll be killed on sight. So please, leave Mexico. Contact me when things cool down," Chavez urged.

"How did it come down to this?" Esteban asked.

"I don't have much time, and neither do you. Get what you need and go. Esteban, I love you like a brother. Run while you still can, it's your only hope," Chavez pleaded.

The killers had planted fake evidence at the crime scene to implicate Esteban. They had already paid off other people who were also going to lie and claim he was connected to other assassinations and terrorist organizations. Esteban couldn't believe what he was hearing.

"Another thing, don't use any credit cards that can be traced to you. Use cash whenever possible and avoid using your name. It'll leave a trail until they find you," Chavez warned.

"Will you take care of my mother and make sure she gets safely to Los Angeles? I'd greatly appreciate it....I don't know what you can tell Isabel... I'll call her and say I have to go on a trip. But I'd like you to look after her and let her know I'm doing my duty. She won't believe it, but at least she'll have some awareness," Esteban said.

"You know I will. Esteban, be careful. I'm on your side," Chavez replied.

Esteban realized he had to leave the country as quickly as possible. He would never receive a fair trial. He knew that in the case of murdered politicians, suspects were often executed on the spot.

He called his mother and instructed her to go to Los Angeles. He told her Chavez would make all the arrangements and that she shouldn't worry. Then, he called his relatives in Los Angeles to arrange her travel plans.

Esteban knew he couldn't go to Europe or South America because that would involve using airports, and most officials there had been bribed. They'd expect that move. He tried calling Isabel but couldn't reach her, so he left a message.

"Isabel, I love you very much and I have very little time... I'm calling your cell phone, and I won't be calling your house from now on." He held back tears. "Something came up and I have to go, but please call me as soon as you hear this message... I love you with all my heart."

Esteban decided to enter the U.S. as an illegal alien. It wouldn't be the first time he had entered a country without proper documentation.

He went to his bank in Puebla and withdrew $100,000 in cash to start making plans. He decided to head toward Chihuahua, where he had some relatives. He believed the authorities would assume he'd try to flee using airports, rather than crossing by land.

He borrowed a friend's car and took off toward Chihuahua. His friend would later take a bus and return the car. The long drive gave Esteban time to reflect on what had happened.

While driving, he called Isabel. She answered her cellphone. "Bueno."

"Mi amor, I'm so glad I got a hold of you," Esteban said.

"Esteban, you left me a disturbing message. You have me all worried," she replied.

"Isabel, the Senator has been killed, and I have to see what's going on," he said.

He didn't want to tell her that he was a suspect and would likely be killed if detained by the authorities.

"I know. I heard it on the news; that's why I've been so worried," she said.

"Isabel, I need you to be strong. As an agent, there are things I can't tell you, and this is one of them. Right now, I have to see this matter through, and I'll be traveling a lot. I can only call your cellphone. Please, don't let anyone find out I'm contacting you. Also, starting tonight, I want you to use one of your girlfriends' phones instead of your own. You can call my cellphone because it can't be traced, but yours can."

Isabel became alarmed. "Esteban... is something wrong?"

"Isabel, the Senator has been killed, and that's very bad. He was my idol. I have to find out who or what is behind this."

He knew exactly who was responsible and carried all the proof with him, but he couldn't let her know that.

"Esteban, I'm scared... I don't know what to do," she said, beginning to cry.

"Mi amor, don't be scared... I love you with all my heart. This is part of my job, and I'm sorry you have to deal with it, but I need you to be strong. I want you to call me later tonight to confirm you're using a different phone. Don't use your current one again. Buy a new one tomorrow."

"Ok."

"Call me tonight, OK?" he said.

"OK, but..." she began to cry again.

Esteban consoled her and told her everything would be over soon.

"I have to go, mi amor. Call me tonight. I love you," he said.

"I love you too," she replied, and they hung up.

***

After a two-day drive, Esteban arrived in Jiménez, where he stopped for gas and to eat. He kept to himself, remaining discreet so no one would recognize or suspect him.

Jiménez was the town that one of his old Army friends used to talk about. He remembered the friend often mentioning the annual fair on August 6 and the town's famous street, "La Calzada", a straight road lined with shops where everyone walked in the evenings. Memories and thoughts swirled through Esteban's mind as he sat there.

He called his cousin in Chihuahua City. The phone rang.

"Bueno," someone answered.

"Alexandro, it's me, Esteban Galindo," Esteban said.

"No way! What the hell are you doing, cousin? Long time no hear from you, my man!" Alexandro replied.

"It has been a long time. Listen, a lot is happening, and I'm passing through Chihuahua City. I wanted to stop for a day or so," Esteban said.

"Oh, that's great. Everyone here will be happy to see you! When will you get here?"

"In about three or four hours, if that's OK," Esteban replied.

"You're my cousin, of course, it's OK!"

"Great. Listen, I've got the engine running and need to move the car, so I'll just see you there soon," Esteban said.

"See you soon," Alexandro responded.

375

They both hung up. Esteban finished his meal, returned to the car, and continued his journey to Chihuahua City.

When he arrived, he met with Alexandro and explained the situation, though not in full detail. He told him just enough for his cousin to understand that he needed help. Esteban also limited visits from other relatives to avoid wasting time or attracting attention.

Alexandro hadn't expected him, but he understood that Esteban was not the type to not give a heads-up unless it was serious. It was a good thing Esteban had called from Jiménez; Alexandro wouldn't have been home otherwise.

Esteban told him he couldn't reveal where he was going and warned him not to mention he had seen him, for his own safety.

They spoke briefly about family and how everyone was doing. Esteban wished the circumstances were better for a visit, but he had to make do with what he had.

From there, Esteban headed to Ciudad Juárez to cross the border into America.

27

There he met a good friend of his cousin who was going to take him across the border illegally. The man had modified his car to include a hidden space in the back, allowing a person to hide while he drove across the border. His method was tried and tested, and so far, had never aroused suspicion. He crossed the border daily to buy and sell merchandise, and the border patrol agents saw him regularly. They sometimes didn't inspect his vehicle because he always had the same items. He had been searched before, but nothing had ever been found.

The friend put Esteban in the back seat, lying down. A few seconds later, they started their journey, headed across the border.

After going deep into El Paso, they arrived at a warehouse. Esteban got out and immediately thanked the man. He did a few stretches, feeling sore and tense after the long ride in the cramped compartment. He pulled out some money from his bag and paid the man $1,000. The man refused because he was a good friend of his cousin, but Esteban insisted, so he took it. The friend then told him he would take him to a safe haven. Esteban told him to take him to a cheap motel where they didn't ask questions, so the friend did.

He got a room, paid in cash, and went inside. He didn't want to attract too much attention in any way. After getting a good night's sleep, the next day, he headed to the bus station. He had heard there were jobs in Northern Texas and Oklahoma, perhaps on a ranch or somewhere else where he could blend in. So, he asked the motel's manager, who directed him to a bus stop.

During the trip, he heard on the news that there had been a plane crash off the Pacific coast. A private, chartered plane had crashed into the ocean, killing all passengers. Among them were two soccer players from the Mexican league, one baseball player from the Mexican league, and an advertising agent named Isabel Diaz.

Esteban could not believe his ears. His heart sank, and tears rapidly began to form in his eyes. He was at a loss for words. Tears rolled down his cheeks as he cried silently in the back of the bus.

The bus drove for hours until it stopped in a small town. He decided to stay there to recuperate from his girlfriend's death. He wanted to call her mother, but he knew any call could be traced eventually and would compromise his absence.

He stayed in a local hotel, thinking of her and all the great times they had shared. He looked at her picture in his wallet over and over as tears kept running down. He felt like part of him had died, and there was nothing he could do. All the plans they had made, the new life they were going to start, the love he thought he had finally found, were gone. Blown out like a candle, with no way to light it again.

He couldn't understand how this could happen. Everything had been going so well. He had less than a year before leaving the service to be on his own. He was about to marry the woman of his dreams. He was reaching a level of happiness he never thought possible, and now it had all gone sour and down the drain. In an instant, his life felt over.

He cried like a baby and could only think, *Why? Why? Why?* Not even the worst physical pain could match the emotional pain he felt, a pain that ran deep, straight to the heart and into the soul.

After two days, he managed to feel somewhat better. Some of the pain was temporarily out of his system. He went to the bus station and purchased a ticket to continue his journey. The next bus didn't arrive until evening, so he waited. He wasn't in much of a hurry anymore. At that point, he didn't even care if he got caught.

He kept to himself until the bus finally arrived, then boarded and continued his journey.

Arriving outside the city of Amarillo, he stayed in a cheap hotel. He then sought employment to blend in with the other undocumented immigrants. He was taken to a ranch with orchards about sixty miles east of Amarillo. There, he got a job picking fruit. The ranch was huge, with plenty of work, and many illegals were employed there. Most were migrant workers, but everyone knew they were illegal aliens.

He soon found out that the managers, arrogant gringos, treated the aliens terribly. They saw themselves as superior, viewing the workers only as numbers, and they fit the mold of the typical low, uneducated redneck.

***

Meanwhile, back in Mexico, the situation had worsened. The press went wild over the assassination of Senator Fernandez. They had no idea who had done it. All they had was a gun, bullet shells, and a military coin from the academy of Mexico. The problem was that Senator Fernandez had many coins from that academy, and others had been given to him during visits.

No direct suspects had been found, which upset the campaign. The police and government kept a tight lid on everything until they could build a concrete case, but that didn't seem to be happening. They knew it might take a while for things to settle down and for the homicide investigation to move forward.

The people of Mexico suspected foul play, especially in his home state of Jalisco. Senator Sinal used this opportunity to highlight how bad crime had become, promising to eliminate it if elected president. He expressed his sympathy and made a speech honoring Senator Fernandez for his contributions to the state and the country.

The people wanted and demanded justice for their beloved senator. Riots broke out in the streets of Mexico City and in the capital of the senator's state. The U.S. sent special agents to assist in the investigation.

Esteban spent two weeks at the ranch and began to adapt to its life. He wasn't sure if he wanted to move on. He had spent a few days in a vineyard picking strawberries, and now that he was there, he liked it a little better. The work had been hard, but it was therapeutic for Esteban. The more manual labor he did, the more he was able to suppress his feelings about Isabel and Senator Fernandez.

He was just glad that his mother was fine and taken care of by his relatives in Los Angeles. Chavez had helped his mother get there. Still, Esteban had a troubling thought he couldn't ignore. *What if Chavez was somehow mixed up in all this? Would he ever do something like that?* That was one of the many thoughts on his mind as he worked in the fields.

He let his work do the talking, and it was obvious at first that he wanted to stay busy. His fellow workers got along with him and sensed there was something special about Esteban.

***

One day, he was driving a truck full of fruit when it broke down. Esteban was with two other Mexicans in the front seat. The day was hot, and it was around 1 p.m.; they still had about five miles to go before reaching the market. Everyone got out to see what was wrong with the engine.

Just then, another truck carrying two ranch workers approached and saw the broken-down truck by the side of the road. They slowed down and stopped to check what was wrong. The men, who were overseers of the ranch workers, recognized the Mexicans.

The Anglo men were already in a bad mood, and this only added fuel to the fire.

"So you motherfuckers broke the truck again," one of them said, as if the workers had gone at the truck with bats and hammers themselves. "Why is it that you can pick fruit so good but can't take care of a simple-ass truck?"

The truck was thirty years old and in bad shape to begin with. Esteban looked at him and said, "You're right, we're not educated enough to fix something like this, but we're trying to make something that's already broken work."

The gringos looked at each other and told the Mexicans to get out of the way.

As they stood aside, Esteban and the other two Mexicans talked among themselves.

"Esteban, why are they always treating us like that?" one of them asked.

"It's because it makes them feel like they have power over us, and because they don't know any better... Don't worry, people like that will get a taste of their own medicine, to the extreme," Esteban said.

They realized the gringos didn't want the fruit to arrive any later than necessary, as it would also make them look bad. The overseers tried to fix the truck.

By coincidence, the owner of the ranch, Jake Hamilton, drove by and stopped to see what was happening.

"What's going on here, boys?" Jake asked.

Roy, one of the overseers, answered, "Well, howdy boss... these Mexicans broke the truck again, and we were passing by and stopped to see if we could fix it."

"I see. Have you had any luck?" Jake asked.

"We're getting there," Roy replied.

Jake looked at Esteban.

"Who's the new guy?" Jake asked.

Roy answered, "He came here about two weeks ago and has been working in the field."

"Let me talk to him," Jake said.

"Hey, you," Roy pointed at him, "come over here."

Esteban walked toward Jake's truck.

"Howdy, son. I'm Jake Hamilton. What's your name, and how long have you been working for me?"

"I'm Esteban, and I arrived here about two weeks ago," Esteban replied.

Jake was surprised by his good English.

"You speak English well," Jake said.

"I took some lessons when I was in school," Esteban replied, not wanting to give too much of himself away.

"That will come in handy around here. Well, good to have you, and I hope you're a good worker," Jake said.

"I always do my best," Esteban responded.

Meanwhile, the two overseers had been trying to fix the truck for over thirty minutes. Esteban finally stepped in.

"Excuse me, maybe I can help," he said.

Roy glared at him.

"You're a Mexican, you don't know how to fix it. You dumb nut, you're the one who broke it in the first place."

"Actually, when we parked the truck, I didn't even get the chance to look at it because you took over to fix it," Esteban replied.

Roy stared at him like he was crazy.

Jake said, "Why don't you give the guy a chance? He can't do any worse, and besides, he might fix it."

The Anglos reluctantly let him approach the engine. Esteban checked where the problem might be, twisted and turned a few wrenches, and then told his friend to try cranking the engine. The truck started on the first try.

He had fixed it in a matter of minutes, impressing Jake. The overseers shook their heads in anger; they had been working on it for a while without success. Esteban smiled at them and couldn't resist adding,

"You were right, Mexicans definitely don't know how to fix engines..."

Jake liked the way Esteban handled himself and asked, "Do you know anything about tractors?"

"Yes, sir, I've fixed a few in my life," Esteban replied.

"Well then, we'll see if you can fix this tractor I have on my ranch. I had a guy trying to fix it for weeks, and he finally gave up. Maybe you can do better than he. You up for the challenge?"

Esteban thought for a moment.

"I'll do my best, sir," he said.

"I'll arrange for someone to pick you up tomorrow morning around seven and take you to my ranch," Jake said.

The overseers could hardly believe it. *How in the hell could this wetback, who had only been there a little over two weeks, be invited to work at Jake Hamilton's ranch?* That ranch was considered the cream of the crop to work at; it was near his residence and had nothing but the best. They were furious and jealous of Esteban.

Esteban drove the truck to the loading zone, smiling and joking with the other Mexicans as they went.

"Oye, Esteban, how did you manage to fix the truck so quickly?" one of them asked.

Esteban grinned.

"There was nothing really wrong with the engine... It probably needs a new thermostat and was running a little hot. But when I saw those stupid guys wanting to start trouble, I disconnected the distributor cap so it wouldn't crank. I knew they'd give up and eventually let me work on it."

They all laughed.

"You're very smart, you made them look like idiots in front of the patrón," one said.

"Now they know how it feels to be humiliated by their own actions," Esteban said with a smile.

They kept driving until they reached the market to drop off the fruit. After the delivery, they headed back to their area to end the workday.

The next morning, a man in a truck came to pick up Esteban and take him to the ranch. The man was a ranch hand, driving a beat-up white Chevy. Esteban was waiting for him outside his trailer. The driver got out and said, "Are you Esteban?"

"Yes, that's me," Esteban responded.

"I was told to come get you to go to the boss' ranch."

"Let's go," Esteban said.

While they drove, they started chatting and getting to know each other a little more.

"What's your name?" Esteban asked the driver.

"I'm Mario," Mario responded.

"What's so special about this ranch anyway? They make it sound like it's a big deal," Esteban commented.

Mario grinned, realizing Esteban obviously didn't know that this was the nicest ranch in Texas.

"Well, all I can say is that it's the biggest and best ranch I've ever been in my life, and I feel so honored to just live here," Mario said.

Esteban looked at him and thought this guy might be a little strange.

"Where are you from?" Esteban asked.

"I was born in Morelia," Mario answered.

"That's a beautiful city. I've been there several times," Esteban said.

As they got closer to the ranch, Esteban began to understand what Mario was talking about when he said it was the nicest ranch he'd ever seen.

The place seemed like a dream, something out of *Dallas*, the TV series. The barn itself housed about thirty horses, with several cows on the far end. It was well-built, and everything looked new. The horses had better living quarters than most people, especially compared to the illegals' rooms where Esteban was staying. There was some farming close by, and parked by the side of the barn was the tractor that needed fixing.

As they arrived, Esteban saw a woman riding a horse. She appeared to be a very, good-looking blonde, riding a palomino inside a neatly built white fence. Even from a distance, Esteban could still spot beauty. She looked toward the truck as it parked by the tractor.

"Who's that girl?" Esteban asked Mario.

"She's the patrón's daughter, and she's off-limits to everyone, especially Mexicans like you and me," Mario replied.

"Why would that be?" Esteban asked, already knowing the answer.

"For one, you're a wetback, and you're Mexican just like me," Mario said. "The other reason is that you're poor."

Esteban saw that the migrants here had been well-trained to stay in their place.

"Well, so much for trying to exchange a message with her," Esteban said sarcastically.

Mario laughed. He seemed like the kind of guy who had worked most of his life in the fields and was used to taking orders and doing his work.

Mr. Jake Hamilton was called and informed that Esteban had arrived. While waiting, Esteban looked around the ranch like a tourist. It was so nice it almost felt like a theme park, with all the fancy cowboy trappings on display.

Jake finally came out and greeted him.

"Morning. I'm glad you were able to make it," Mr. Hamilton said.

"I'm glad I'm here," Esteban responded.

"Follow me and I'll show you the tractor," Mr. Hamilton said. "In a few weeks, I'll have to use it to plant some crops, and I don't want to wait until the last moment to get it done."

The tractor was parked beside the huge barn, where it had been sitting for several months.

"Well, here it is. Nothing has been done to fix it ever since that no-good mechanic left," Mr. Hamilton said. "I've had two mechanics look at it since it stopped working, and neither of them got it going for more than a few days."

He shook his head in frustration.

"Is there any way it's fixable? I'd hate to buy a new tractor. These babies cost around $300,000 and up, that's not small feed," Jake said bitterly.

"They're not cheap, that's for sure," Esteban responded. "Do you mind if I take a look at it?"

"By all means... I want you to look at it as much as needed. It won't hurt for you to give it a try," Mr. Hamilton said.

Esteban began inspecting it, looking from top to bottom. He opened the engine compartment, studied it for a while, and then said, "Mr. Hamilton, you seem to have problems with the transmission."

"What do you mean?" Mr. Hamilton asked.

"Well, sir, from what I know about engines, you're going to need a new transmission. The gears are stripped, and even if I make it work, it won't last one drive when you go to use it," Esteban explained. "Whoever used this tractor last didn't know what he was doing, and it shows on the gears and engine. I don't know why the other mechanics didn't see this; it's as plain as day for any mechanic."

Mr. Hamilton recalled that his nephew had been working for him and using the tractor a lot.

"That son of a bitch Scott... I knew I should've never given him that damn job!"

Esteban looked at him silently.

"Never mind," Mr. Hamilton said. "I'm just cursing myself for trying to help my sister's son. That boy is just plain retarded. He destroys everything he's ever used that's mine. No wonder he didn't take all the money I offered him for the job."

"Well, is there any way you can fix it?" Mr. Hamilton asked.

"Yes, sir, but it would be better to put in a new transmission than use this old one. This one is dead; it won't come back from the dead. It can be rebuilt, but it will keep tearing up on you, and in the long run, it won't be worth the money," Esteban said.

Mr. Hamilton studied him. He didn't know much about Esteban, but the man had already fixed a truck when his other two men couldn't.

"Can you give me some guarantee that it will work most of the time?" Jake asked.

"Mr. Hamilton, I'm not going to guarantee you it will be like new, because other parts might have been damaged by whoever mishandled it. But it should be good enough to use with only minor problems," Esteban replied.

"So you're saying you can fix it and it will run for a few years?" Jake asked, concerned.

"Yes, sir. I can fix it, and it will be drivable for several years if it's taken care of," Esteban said.

Mr. Hamilton laughed. "Okay, I'll get you anything you want to put in a new one. It'll still cost a lot less than buying a new tractor."

He knew that anything was better than spending hundreds of thousands on a replacement.

"I'll arrange everything so you can start tomorrow. But today, I just want you to see what you can do with it. If you can get this thing fixed and ready to go, I'll make it worth your while, and you won't have to work out in the field," Jake said, almost like issuing a challenge.

"Yes, sir. I'll do my best to get it going," Esteban replied.

***

Two days later, the owner came to see how Esteban's progress was going. Esteban told him that he would need a transmission repair and that some of the wiring had to be redone.

"I'm getting you more parts that you'll need, but if there are others that you think are missing, tell me and I'll get them so you can fix it," Jake said.

"Yes, sir. I made a list, but it might get longer the more I examine the engine. I don't think it's going to be as bad as I thought, but only by working on it will I find out," Esteban replied.

"If you need some help moving things, tell me and I'll get some more men to help you out," Mr. Hamilton said.

"Thank you, sir, but for right now, I'm able to manage. Perhaps when I start moving the transmission, I might need someone to guide the lift," he said, hinting that he might need help later as his work progressed.

During their talk, the beautiful blonde cowgirl approached them on a horse. She dismounted and kissed her father.

"Hi, Daddy. What are you up to?" she asked curiously, clearly wanting to find out who the new man was.

The owner introduced her to Esteban.

"Amanda, this is Esteban, the man who is going to work on my tractor to see if he can get it running again," Mr. Hamilton said.

"Hello, Esteban," she greeted with a slight Texas accent.

Esteban extended his hand. "It is a pleasure to meet you, Señorita Hamilton."

"You can call me Amanda," she replied, shaking his hand.

"Good to meet you, Amanda," he said, addressing her by name.

She noticed the way he spoke and carried himself. She liked his accent and the way he said her name. Amanda found Esteban attractive right away.

Jake had to leave for a business meeting. "Well, I have to meet some people. I'll take your list and get what you need while I'm in town. Amanda, show him around so he knows where everything is around the barn." He said like it was an order. "And then call your aunt because I have a few words to say about that stupid nephew of mi—"

"Daddy," she said, trying to stop him from talking about her cousin that way.

Jake walked off toward his truck on the other side of the barn.

Amanda looked at Esteban. "Well, I guess I'll give you the tour."

"OK, I'll just follow you," he responded.

She started telling him about the barn, how the horses were maintained, and guided him to where the garage was several feet away.

"The garage has a lot of tools and stuff in case you need them," she said, clearly not knowing much about fixing cars.

They continued walking around the area. "That about does it. If you have any questions, I'll try to answer them, but Mario probably knows more about where things are than I do. He's been here the longest and usually gets my dad what he wants when he asks for it."

"I thank you very much, Miss Amanda, and I'll find what I need to fix the tractor," he said.

"Please, just call me Amanda. I'm very plain," she said with a smile.

Esteban noticed she was very attractive and smelled wonderful, probably from some kind of body lotion. "OK, Amanda. Thank you for the tour, and I'll get started on the tractor."

He didn't want to get distracted and certainly didn't want to show that he had noticed her beauty. Isabel was still on his mind, and the heartache from losing her lingered. Amanda reminded him so much of Isabel...similar features, though Amanda was blonde with blue eyes. Esteban cut the conversation short because he just wanted to get away from her. The further she was from him, the less likely he was to think about Isabel.

Amanda felt slightly annoyed. She wasn't used to someone she approached pulling away like that. Esteban had done it politely, but she still felt like she was in the way.

***

The next day, one of the gringos told Esteban he had to come help them dig postholes. Esteban explained that he needed to work on the tractor, but they told him he would do what they said because he was a wetback. Reluctantly, he agreed.

There seemed to be an endless number of postholes to dig, and the gringos knew they had a mechanical posthole digger. They just wanted to wear Esteban out by making him do it by hand. He worked most of the morning by himself, shirtless, every muscle in his body showing as he dug and set posts.

The gringos enjoyed watching him work himself to exhaustion, but Esteban wasn't fazed.

Amanda rode up on horseback and stopped to see what he was doing. She admired his body, he looked like an athlete, strong and well-built. She approached him on her horse.

She asked what he was doing and why he wasn't working on the tractor.

He explained, "I'm digging postholes and putting up fences because your dad's men wanted me to do this first."

The gringos walked up and told him to leave the girl alone.

Amanda said, "He's not bothering me, and my father wants him to fix the tractor."

Esteban agreed to finish the postholes first.

They called him a troublemaker and said this work would make him a better man. Amanda was disturbed by how they treated him.

She told Esteban, "Stop what you're doing and go back to where my father told you to work." She was clearly frustrated with the redneck ranch hands her father employed.

Esteban made a suggestion on how she should brush the horse.

"Maybe you can tell me how after you fix the tractor," she said.

"Maybe," he replied.

After she left, the gringos told him not to get too attached to the girl. They said they didn't want to see any wetback with an American girl and that they'd hate to see a tragedy happen while he was there.

Esteban was used to threats and had been in so many fights that he compared them to a kid trying to take his lunch money. He simply replied, "Whatever makes you happy," and played it off cool.

The next day, Esteban was fixing the tractor when Amanda dropped by. They made small talk. Esteban asked about a certain horse that sometimes acted up.

Amanda said, "He's like that sometimes."

Esteban suggested that the horse needed to be broken in more.

Amanda replied, "I've ridden him twice with no incident."

Esteban advised, "You shouldn't ride him until it's fully safe."

She insisted, "He's tame."

Through their discussion, Amanda decided to prove her point by actually riding the horse. Esteban didn't want her to, but she went ahead anyway. She saddled him up and began riding.

A few meters from the barn, the horse started to act up and broke into a gallop. Amanda was in trouble. The horse charged toward a fence and knocked it down, with Amanda still on him.

Esteban ran toward her, grabbed the reins, and steered the horse into an open area. Amanda fell, but the horse kept kicking. Esteban managed to get on the horse and ride him until he calmed down. Then he returned the horse to the barn.

Amanda was all right, just shaken up. Esteban checked on her and was relieved she was okay. Amanda felt bad and embarrassed about being stubborn. She tried to play it off as if she were mad, saying the horse just had a bad day.

Esteban saw through it and simply advised her, "Be careful next time."

That made Amanda feel even more drawn to him. She began to take a liking to Esteban for saving her life.

"I knew what I was doing," she said, "and the horse never acted like that before."

Esteban replied, "Some horses have to be broken more than once, and they can always be unsafe."

The gringos blamed the incident on Esteban and tried to push him around, but Amanda stepped in and defended him. When the owner returned, he heard about the incident. The gringos told all kinds of lies about Esteban, but Amanda explained that Esteban had saved her life. The other hired hands agreed, except for the gringos. Jake was glad his daughter was safe and that no harm had come to her.

***

The tractor was almost fixed. Esteban had rebuilt the transmission by himself. Once it was done, he cranked it up, and it ran like new. Jake was thrilled; he had thought he would have to buy a new tractor. He rewarded Esteban with money.

Amanda suggested that since Esteban was good with horses, he could also help out with them. Esteban kept Amanda at a distance because he didn't want to get involved with her. He still had Isabel in his mind, and in his heart, and that was already hard enough to let go.

He gave more of his attention to the owner than to Amanda, which upset her. No man had ever ignored her or said no to her, and she couldn't understand why, especially from a handsome man like Esteban.

Amanda really liked Esteban because he was charming, polite, well-mannered, easy to talk to, and had a way of explaining things that always made her feel comfortable. Even though she didn't show much in her actions toward him, she had a real crush on him. His looks appealed to her; he was 5'10", medium-built, muscular, athletic, and handsome, with light brown eyes and dark, wavy, short hair.

Even if their conversations had nothing to do with romance, Esteban kept things professional. It was still difficult for him to forget the love he had lost, the love he thought would last forever. Deep in his heart, he could not forget Isabel, and her image often flashed before him, especially when Amanda approached. She was so much like Isabel, her movements, her gestures, her looks, except Amanda speaks English, has blue eyes, and is blonde.

All he wanted was for this charade to end, but he knew it would not. He was living a life that could change in a matter of seconds. He didn't know when he would leave or where he would go. Every day was preparation for the unexpected.

As the days passed, he felt a little more at ease because Amanda was always around, somewhere nearby to greet him or say hello.

***

Another day came, and it didn't seem any different from the rest. Early in the morning, Esteban had just finished shaving and was heading to breakfast. Breakfast was usually provided by some of the Mexican wives living in the trailers.

He had made friends with most of the migrant workers, and because he was friendly and helped them out, the wives were happy to invite him to eat with them. They often told him about the poor conditions on the ranch, how the gringos sometimes mistreated them, and how they were occasionally cheated out of their pay.

Esteban didn't like what was happening, but there was nothing he could do. He was trying to stay away from any spotlight or trouble.

When breakfast was over, he headed out with the rest of the men toward the main part of the ranch. The others went to pick fruit or tend the fields, while Esteban went to the stables to tend the horses.

As Esteban walked into the barn, one of the gringos made a comment toward him.

"Hey, Mexican, why are you here so clean and shaven, huh? Are you expecting someone?" the gringo asked in a mocking tone, clearly looking for trouble.

Esteban ignored him.

The gringo persisted. "Hey! I'm talking to you, you stupid wetback!"

Esteban kept walking without looking at him. The gringo couldn't believe it didn't faze him. He got out of his truck, walked in front of Esteban, and stopped him, staring him down. He acted like a street punk, the kind who liked to get attention from his gang buddies with gold teeth.

"You seem to have a real bad attitude here, you damn wetback. When I ask you a question, you better answer me. I'm the one that makes things happen here, and you answer to me, you got that?" He jabbed a thumb toward his chest, suggesting he was the boss.

"I better not find out you're even thinking of impressing the boss's daughter, because if you are… well, I guess you don't really care about your health." He gave Esteban a very serious look.

Esteban stared at him like he was crazy. He knew the gringo was looking for a fight, but if he took the bait, it might cost him his job, or worse, blow his cover. Still, he couldn't resist the temptation to say something.

"Well, Mr. Want-to-Be-a-Badass, I don't make the rules. Since nothing gets done without your say-so, I'll be sure to mention that to Mr. Hamilton today," Esteban replied, locking eyes with him. "I'm sure he'll be very impressed with your comments about his authority, especially since he's the one who owns this ranch and you work for him. The boss has given me orders to take care of the horses, and that's what I'll do.

"As far as me expecting anyone, that's none of your concern. If it becomes your concern, I'll let you know. Now, if you'll excuse me, I have work to do with the horses."

He walked past the man without another glance.

The gringo just stood there, silent. Many of the immigrants nearby didn't know what would happen next, but they knew any incident involving the rednecks usually ended badly. They were too afraid to get involved; they didn't want to lose their jobs or risk deportation.

There was doubt in the gringo's eyes as Esteban spoke to him. He looked furious, but deep down, he was afraid Esteban might actually tell Mr. Hamilton. Mr. Hamilton was a fair man, but he was also tough. The men nicknamed him "John Wayne" because he took no nonsense, kind of like the old Army joke about toilet paper.

So far, Esteban had moved up the ladder since arriving at the ranch, and he appeared to be getting close to Mr. Hamilton, at least workwise. That put jealousy into the minds of many of the gringos, especially the redneck ones.

Esteban went to check on the horses and began feeding them. After filling the feed troughs, he prepared to brush them once they finished eating. Then he decided to check the tractor to see how it was running.

***

Meanwhile, Amanda had gone to the city to do some shopping, something she loved and could spend hours doing. She had a gorgeous figure and especially liked looking at swimsuits. She rarely wore them outside her home because she didn't like the ranchers constantly staring at her. Her house had a swimming pool, and she sunbathed whenever she could. She had modeled a few times and even received offers from swimsuit magazines, though nothing serious enough to make a career out of it.

As she browsed the stores, she found herself wondering what kind of swimsuit Esteban might like to see her in. She actually wanted to ask his opinion, but she also knew her father would never approve of her getting close to any ranch hand. Still, she couldn't help herself; there was something about Esteban that drew her in.

She found him very attractive. He was polite, always saying things that made her feel good, even if not romantic. He often spoke of her father with honor and respect, sometimes more than she did. That made her trust him even more.

Esteban was well built, and it was hard for anyone not to notice, especially Amanda. She had seen plenty of buffed-up men in college, including athletes, but Esteban looked like a *real* man to her, strong from hard work.

As she walked through the mall, she kept him in mind. She picked out several swimsuits to try on. Some were extremely skimpy, covering nothing but her private parts, while others left almost nothing to the imagination. She began to imagine Esteban's reaction if she wore one of them while visiting him at his trailer.

Hmm... I wonder how Esteban would welcome me if I wore this when he was finishing his chores at home, she thought, smiling to herself.

She tried on several more, primping and taking her time as she modeled them in the changing room. She finally decided on two: a yellow silky bikini and a pink one, barely held together by strings.

If this doesn't impress him, then I'll have to say he's gay, she thought.

Leaving the store, she wandered into a shoe shop because, in her mind, every outfit needed the right pair of shoes. After buying a few, she thought, *Now that I've bought this, I think I need to go to the salon and see what they can do with my hair. I want something different.*

She left the mall and headed to her usual salon, located just across the street. The owner was a friend of hers. As she walked, she received several lingering stares from men passing by. Amanda was quite a sight, sexy in every way.

She finally reached the salon and stepped inside.

In the salon, there were ladies everywhere. Some were reading magazines, others were having their hair done. It was one of those fancy salons where they seemed to have everything on the menu: hair, nails, facials, tanning, and massages. It was like a combination spa and pleasure center. Amanda liked it here because she could get everything done without having to go to different places.

As she stepped in, one of the hairdressers saw her and said hello. They all seemed to recognize her, partly because she had been there many times, but mostly because her daddy happened to be one of the richest men in Texas.

One of the hairdressers was a Black gay man named Chad. Amanda liked him because he was the best hairdresser they had. She looked at him until he noticed her. She smiled, and they both lit up when their eyes met.

"My God, girl, you are a sight for sore eyes," Chad said with a big, surprised smile.

Amanda walked over to him and hugged him. Chad was a character; he liked to wear very bright clothes and was as openly gay as they came. He talked about being gay, joked about being gay, and loved bragging about all the parades he had been in. This guy was one hundred percent gay and extremely proud of it; he'd tell you so himself.

"Where have you been, and why haven't you called me in weeks?" Chad asked, loud and flirty.

Amanda smiled, unsure where to begin. "I'm so glad to see you, Chad. I have so much to tell you."

"Girl, you know I like all that good gossip, especially when it comes to men," Chad grinned, making Amanda grin too.

"You're here to get your hair done, aren't you? It would be great so we can talk all afternoon," Chad said.

"Yes, I do need a new hairstyle, and my nails done as well," she replied.

"Well, I will always have time for you. How could I turn down the woman who introduced me to the man of my dreams?" Chad said sarcastically, batting his eyes. They both laughed.

"Are you still seeing that guy from Atlanta?" Amanda asked.

"Oh yes! He is something else. He's more of a drag than I could ever dream of," Chad said with a smile.

"I'm glad it's going well for you," Amanda said.

"I owe it all to you," Chad replied, smiling and laughing. "This loverboy makes me feel like the woman I always wanted to be, and the man I always wanted to have," he whispered comically in her ear.

Amanda laughed. Chad always exaggerated his experiences with her, and it was hilarious.

Several months ago, Amanda had told Chad about a man she'd seen in a store looking at women's clothing. He looked puzzled, as though he didn't know what he was looking for. Amanda had been nearby when the man approached her and asked about underwear. At first, she was puzzled, but the way he acted made it clear he was feminine. She helped him out, they had a conversation, Chad's name came up, and eventually, the two met.

Amanda had her hair and nails done. She and Chad talked about clothes, shoes, and fashion. After she was finished, she headed home, happy after having a girls' day.

28

A few days later, Esteban was working with the horses, cleaning the stables and feeding them. It was almost sunset when Amanda came by to check on him. He didn't notice her as she approached while he brushed a horse.

"Hey," she said.

"Whoa! I didn't hear you sneaking up behind me. How long have you been there?" Esteban asked.

"Just a few minutes. I wanted to see you work," she replied.

Esteban had a feeling she was up to something. "Well, I'm just doing what your father told me to do, take care of the horses. They're very fine horses," he said, trying to make small talk while finishing his work so he could go to his trailer.

Amanda stepped closer. "You seem to know so much about everything, and you're very humble. There's more to you than what you show. I've never met a man like you before."

"I'm just an ordinary man, that's all," he said.

"That is not true. You fix trucks, tractors, you know about horses, heck, you saved my life when that horse knocked me down. You always seem to have the right words to say. That's not ordinary."

"I think you're looking too deep into this. I happened to be at the right place, right time, that's all," he replied.

"Well, then you're at the right place, right time now," she said with a smile.

She stepped forward and kissed him, wrapping her arms around his neck. Esteban was surprised but kissed her back for a moment, until he came to his senses and stopped.

"Amanda, we can't be doing this. Your father would not allow it, and I would get fired. He's put too much trust in me." He hesitated, thoughts of Isabel flashing through his mind, bringing a rush of memories. He also realized his cover could be blown, and someone might figure out who he really was.

"I don't care, Esteban. All I can think about is you," she said.

"There's nothing wrong with following your heart, but some things are not meant to be right now. You're a gorgeous woman, and if the circumstances were different, I'd love to be with you. But there's too much at stake for both of us. Let's just stay neutral for now. The future will always be there."

Esteban didn't want to reject her completely; she could get angry, have him fired, or even accuse him of something serious.

"You're right. I'm sorry I put you in this position. Things can always change, you know. And until then, I can wait," she said.

She turned and walked out of the barn, while Esteban took a deep breath, unsure of what to do next, except head back to his trailer.

***

Several days passed, and the Mexicans were loading fruit onto the truck. They were almost done; only one more crate remained. An old man was bringing an extra one when one of the hired hands yelled at him, telling him the truck was full. The old man didn't hear and set the fruit on top anyway. It rolled off.

The hired hand yelled, "Hey, old man, are you deaf?"

He walked up to the old man, grabbed him by the shirt, and said, "Look what you did! Some of the fruit fell. Now pick them up!" Then he shoved him.

As the old man fell, he landed face-first and hit his head on the back bumper of the truck. Blood began to flow from his forehead, and he was knocked out cold.

Esteban happened to be walking by and saw the hired hand push the old man. He ran to help, kneeling to check if the man was all right. Then he stood and faced the hired hand.

"You like picking on old men? Does it make you feel more of a man when someone can't defend himself?"

"Mind your own business," the hired hand snapped.

"This is my business," Esteban replied.

The man swung at Esteban, but he was too slow. Esteban struck him first, and the hired hand collapsed, unconscious. Two other men rushed at Esteban, but with a swift kick and several punches, both were on the ground, groaning.

Esteban carried the old man to his trailer while some of the other Mexicans went to get the women for help. He told the rest of the men to go ahead and deliver the fruit to the market; he would handle things with the boss. But before they could get into the truck, another hired hand took off in it.

That day, the rest of the Mexicans began to respect and admire Esteban.

When the injured men recovered, they went to Mr. Hamilton and claimed the Mexicans had overturned the truck and lost the fruit. The man who had taken the truck had driven somewhere else and dumped the fruit to make it look as though it had fallen off.

Mr. Hamilton was furious and decided to deduct the cost from the Mexicans' pay. This made Esteban angry, but instead of causing trouble, he used some of his own money to make up for their loss. The hired men never found out, but they began plotting against him.

***

Mr. Hamilton noticed Amanda smiling more often and seeming unusually happy. He enjoyed seeing his daughter like that. His wife had died when Amanda was born, so she had never known her mother.

She was raised by her father, Jake Hamilton, along with help from her maternal grandmother and a paternal aunt. Amanda received all the attention a child could want and was spoiled by everyone. Still, she grew into a fine young woman, even though she had always had everything she desired.

Mr. Hamilton decided he needed to have a word with Esteban about the fight. Since the hired men hadn't told him the whole truth, he wanted to hear Esteban's side.

He drove to the barn, parked his truck, and walked toward Esteban, who was feeding the horses.

"Hey, Esteban, I want to talk to you," he called out.

"Yes, sir," Esteban replied.

"I was told you got into a fight with my hired men and beat them up. Why did you do that? I'd better have a good explanation, because something like that will get you fired," Mr. Hamilton said sternly.

"I don't know what they told you, sir," Esteban said, "but one of your men beat an old man just because he put an extra crate of fruit on the truck. He shoved him so hard that the old man hit his head on the bumper and was knocked out. He didn't deserve that. I confronted the man and told him never to treat him like that again. He swung at me, so I put him down. Then the other two came at me, and I put them down as well. I took the old man to my trailer and got help while the others finished loading the fruit. The truck was in good order when I last saw it, but another hired hand drove it away, and that's the last we saw of it. I'm sorry if I caused any trouble, but that's no way to treat an old man."

Listening to Esteban's account changed Mr. Hamilton's perspective on the story. He went to check on the old man himself and saw that his forehead was still badly cut. He arranged for some men to take him to a doctor.

"Look," Mr. Hamilton said, "I wasn't there to see it, but it appears my men were in the wrong. Still, we can't have fights here. Try to get along with them. You're all working for me, and I'm a fair man. I'll deal with the hired men. Thanks for telling me what happened, Esteban."

With that, he climbed into his truck and drove off.

29

Several weeks passed, and life on the ranch settled back into its rhythm. Esteban kept to his work, mostly tending the horses, mending tack, and hauling feed. Sometimes he was called to fix a tractor or tinker with an old truck, but the barn remained his place, the steady sound of hooves and the smell of hay grounding him.

One late afternoon, as he let the horses run in the paddock, a pickup slowed near the fence. Amanda leaned out the window, smiling. "Hey, Esteban. How's it going?"

He wiped his hands on his jeans, shading his eyes from the sun. "Just keeping busy. How about you?"

"Busy too. Always something going on back home." She hesitated a moment as if gathering her courage, then added, "Listen, there's a festival next weekend, Friday night, maybe Saturday too. You should come."

Esteban shook his head. "I'm not much for crowds. Or dancing."

Amanda laughed. "That's the best part. Music, food, dancing, half the town will be there. Come on, it'll do you good."

He thought for a moment. "Well, maybe. If I get through my work, I'll try."

"Good," she said, her smile widening. "If you come, I'll show you around." Then, with a wave, she drove off.

***

When Saturday came, Esteban got ready and borrowed an old truck from one of the men and drove into town. The festival was already alive, lanterns strung between poles, laughter and music spilling into the warm night air. A bar sat at the center of it, with tents and food stalls set up outside since it was 7 o'clock at night. Most of the crowd gathered indoors, where the band played.

Esteban parked, straightened his shirt, and stepped inside. The place smelled of beer and fried food, the air thick with voices and guitar strings. He recognized a few of the Mexicans from the ranch and nodded politely before finding a spot at the bar. He ordered a beer and tried to blend into the background.

Then Amanda walked in.

She wore a black skirt and a fitted blouse, simple but striking. Her blonde hair fell loose over her shoulders, her blue eyes bright in the dim light. For a moment, Esteban was caught off guard. Something in the way she carried herself, the tilt of her head, the grace in her walk, pulled his memory sharply back to Isabel. The resemblance unsettled him, though Amanda's fair features made her different in every other way.

Amanda noticed his distant expression as she came closer. "What's wrong? You look like you've never seen me before."

Esteban blinked and smiled faintly. "Sorry, I was somewhere else. You look... beautiful."

Her eyes lit up, and she blushed. "I never thought you noticed me."

"Of course I notice," he said quietly. "You're gorgeous."

"Really? You never let it show."

"It's not for me to say. But that's the way it is."

Amanda laughed softly and touched his arm. They ordered drinks and found a small table near the edge of the room. Conversation flowed easily, stories of the ranch, Amanda's childhood with her grandmother and aunt, the way she had been spoiled but still learned to hold her own. Esteban listened, nodding, occasionally adding a story of his own, careful never to reveal too much.

After a while, the music slowed, and couples drifted to the dance floor. Amanda leaned closer, her voice teasing. "Come on. One dance won't kill you."

Esteban hesitated, his gaze flickering toward the floor, then back to her. But he changed the subject and continued just talking.

The band struck up another tune, faster this time, the kind that pulled people to their feet without a second thought. Amanda leaned across the table, her eyes sparkling. "Now you have to dance with me. I love this song!"

Esteban raised his hands a little, shaking his head. "I don't know about that."

"Oh, come on," she urged, already standing.

He hesitated, then gave a faint smile. "All right. Just one."

Amanda grabbed his hand before he could change his mind, pulling him onto the floor. The crowd moved in rhythm, laughter echoing above the music. Esteban tried to keep himself reserved, his steps measured. He didn't want to draw attention, didn't want anyone to think he was there to make a scene. But Amanda's energy was contagious, and soon enough, he found himself relaxing, even smiling. It had been a long time since he had let himself enjoy something as simple as a dance.

For a few minutes, the rest of the world disappeared.

When the song ended, they slipped back to their table, laughing softly as they sat down. Esteban ordered another round, and they talked some more. The music played on, but their little corner of the room felt quieter, more private.

Then the door opened, and the mood shifted.

Three of the ranch hands walked in, the same ones who had caused trouble before. Their eyes scanned the room, and when they landed on Esteban and Amanda together, their expressions darkened. They muttered to one another, then leaned against the bar, watching.

Esteban's easy smile faded. He leaned closer to Amanda. "Those men are here. I don't think they came for anything good. I may need to leave."

Amanda frowned. "Don't. They won't try anything with me here. If they do, my father will fire them."

"That may be true," Esteban said quietly, "but I don't want trouble. I already had one discussion with your dad about them."

"And you told him the truth," she reminded him. "He knows what happened."

"Still," Esteban replied, "truth doesn't always stop trouble."

He stood slowly, giving her a reassuring look. "I'll be right back. Just going to the restroom."

As he walked past the bar, he caught the men's eyes. They didn't move, but their stares followed him, sharp and waiting. Esteban kept his face calm, but inside, he knew something was coming.

When Esteban stepped out of the restroom, he noticed Amanda was no longer at the table. She stood at the bar, arms crossed, clearly uncomfortable. The three ranch hands lingered near her, smirking.

One of them leaned in. "Well, what are you doing here?"

Amanda's voice was sharp. "None of your business."

"Oh, I see," another sneered. "You're with that Mexican, huh?"

She shot them a glare. "No. He just happens to be here."

"What a coincidence," the first man said, his tone mocking. They laughed, circling her with words meant to sting. Amanda brushed past them, refusing to let them corner her, and walked toward the bar to distance herself.

Esteban spotted the tension immediately and walked over.

"Oh, if it isn't Mr. Superman himself, huh." One of them mocked.

He kept his voice calm, steady. "Look, I don't know what you all want. First, you pick on an old man, and now you're looking for more trouble. I'm not here for that. If it makes you feel better, I'll just walk away."

The men didn't answer, only stared at him with dark, plotting eyes. Esteban could read it; they weren't finished. He glanced at Amanda, then suggested they move to the other side of the room. For a while, they talked again, but Esteban's instincts wouldn't quiet.

Finally, he leaned in. "It's time for me to go. I don't want this turning into something worse."

Amanda looked disappointed. "Don't leave yet. We just got here."

"I know," he said gently, "but I don't want trouble. And I don't feel right leaving you here alone with them watching."

"I've been here plenty of times," Amanda insisted. "They won't do anything."

Esteban shook his head. "You never know. But I need to go."

With that, he left the bar and walked toward his borrowed truck. Amanda stayed behind for a short while, but the ranch hands never took their eyes off her. At last, she sighed, finished her drink, and decided to leave.

She hadn't gotten far when she heard them behind her.

"Hey! Hey, where you going?" one of them called.

"Home," Amanda answered firmly.

"Oh, no, you're not," another said, stepping closer. "What's the rush? Is it because of us? Or is it because of him? What's so good about Esteban, huh? He's just a damn Mexican."

Amanda stiffened. "Leave me alone."

They laughed, fueled by drink and spite. One reached out and grabbed her arm. She shoved him back. Another stepped forward and, without warning, slapped her across the face.

Amanda gasped, stumbling. She turned, trying to run, but the men closed in.

Across the lot, Esteban hadn't left yet. He would not leave Amamda alone. Something had told him to wait. When he saw the men surrounding Amanda, anger shot through him. He started the truck and pulled up fast, jumping out before it even settled.

"Hey!" he shouted, his voice like a crack of thunder. "Leave her alone!"

The men sneered. "Well, if it isn't Prince Charming. Come to rescue your lady?"

One tried to drag Amanda toward their car while the others turned on Esteban.

That was a mistake.

Two men lunged, fists swinging, but Esteban moved with speed and precision. He struck one across the jaw, sending him crumpling to the ground. The other swung wildly, only to take a hard punch to the stomach and an elbow to the back that dropped him cold.

Meanwhile, the other two tried to rip at Amanda's blouse, holding her by the arms. Esteban charged forward, yanking one away and throwing him to the dirt. The second swung, but Esteban caught his wrist, twisted, and sent him sprawling with a sharp kick.

It wasn't a contest. Within moments, all four men were down, groaning, bleeding, or unconscious.

Breathing hard, Esteban turned to Amanda. "Are you okay?"

She steadied herself, shaken but strong. "I'm okay. Just get me out of here."

He nodded, guiding her gently toward his truck. He opened the door, helped her inside, and without another word, drove her home through the quiet night.

As Esteban drove Amanda home, she sat quietly at first, then the tears began to fall. She tried to wipe them away, but her voice broke. "I don't understand why this is happening. Why would they do this to me?"

Esteban kept his eyes on the road, his voice steady. "Don't worry. I'll explain everything to your dad. He'll understand."

Amanda shook her head. "No, you don't understand. There's more to it than that."

"Maybe so," Esteban said softly, "but right now I just want to make sure you're okay."

When they reached her house, Mr. Hamilton wasn't there. Esteban stayed long enough to be certain Amanda had calmed down. She thanked him through red, swollen eyes, and he gave her a reassuring nod before heading back to his trailer for the night.

***

The next day, Mr. Hamilton returned. Amanda wasted no time telling him what had happened.

Fury swept over him like a storm. He didn't hesitate. He climbed into his truck and went looking for the ranch hands. When he found them lounging near the bunkhouse, he didn't bother with pleasantries.

"Come here, you sons of bitches!" he barked, his face red with anger.

The men shuffled forward, uneasy, but Mr. Hamilton didn't give them a chance to say anything. "I trusted you. I gave you work, a place to sleep, and food on your table. And this is how you treat my daughter? You lay a hand on her?" He stepped closer, eyes burning. "You're lucky nothing worse happened. You're fired, all of you. Pack your things and get off my land. If I ever see your faces here again, I swear I'll kill you myself."

The six men muttered curses under their breath, but none dared answer back. They knew his word was final. Furious and humiliated, they gathered their belongings and left, their anger simmering as they disappeared down the road.

***

Afterward, Mr. Hamilton went searching for Esteban. He found him by the barn, tightening the bridle on one of the horses.

"Esteban," he said firmly, "I want to hear from you what happened last night."

Esteban straightened, respectful but honest. "Sir, I don't know how it all started, but Amanda was there. We had a few beers and listened to music. Then your men showed up, started drinking heavily, and things got out of hand. I decided to leave, but Amanda didn't want to go. She said she'd been there many times before. I stayed nearby because I didn't want her alone with them around. That's when it happened."

He took a breath. "They cornered her outside. One of them slapped her, and two of them tried to put her in their car. They'd already started to rip her clothes. I couldn't let that happen, sir. I stepped in, and I took care of them."

Mr. Hamilton's jaw clenched as he listened. His anger was sharp, but so was his gratitude. Finally, he put a hand on

Esteban's shoulder. "Esteban, thank you. You have no idea how much I appreciate what you did for protecting my daughter, and for respecting her. You've earned my trust. As long as you want to stay here, you'll always have a place."

Esteban bowed his head slightly. "Thank you, sir."

For the first time since coming to the ranch, Esteban felt something shift inside him. A door had opened, not just to trust, but perhaps to something greater.

***

Several days went by, and of course, Amanda was thinking about Esteban. That was all she thought about. Finally, she decided to go visit him. He was working at the barn when she arrived. The evening was settling in; the sky was painted with shades of gold and purple.

"Hey," Esteban said, glancing up from his work. "What are you doing here?"

"Well," Amanda replied softly, "I just came to see you."

"Oh, really?" He gave a half-smile but shook his head. "You know, every time you come to see me, trouble happens."

"That's not what I intend," she said quickly. "I'm sorry about what happened last time. But I really wanted to see you."

"Well, thank you," he said after a pause. His tone softened. "I really went over there to see you as well, and I'm kind of glad I was there. It could have ended worse."

"Yeah, it could have," Amanda agreed.

Then her eyes lit up. "Look, there's something I want to show you."

She led him up to the top of the barn. From there, the roof opened just enough to reveal the sky. The sun was sinking, and as the last light slipped away, the first stars began to appear.

"When I was a little girl, I used to come up here and look at the stars," Amanda said, her voice hushed with memory. "I'd think about all the places I wanted to be."

Esteban leaned against the wooden beam, gazing at the horizon. "I had something like that too. But in the city, it was harder to see the stars. Still, I'd imagine."

Amanda inched closer. Their shoulders brushed. She turned to him and looked into his eyes. Esteban could not resist. Their lips met in a quiet, lingering kiss, and soon they were lost in each other. For a while, nothing else mattered.

Later, they talked about dreams, about the paths they wanted to take individually, and about how strange it was that their lives had crossed.

"You know, we come from two different worlds," Esteban said at last. His eyes grew distant. "There are so many things I have to do."

"Well, what exactly?" she asked.

"I cannot tell you. There's just too much."

Amanda frowned. "How come you're not closer to me? I've tried so hard to get close to you."

He hesitated. His jaw tightened. "You remind me of someone... someone very close. I had a fiancée. She died. She reminded me a lot of you. Almost exactly like you, except... she didn't have blonde hair and blue eyes, like you. But the way she smiled, the way she carried herself... It's just...it's uncanny."

Amanda's voice softened. "What was her name?"

"Her name was Isabel," he said.

"What happened?"

He shook his head, pain flickering in his eyes. "I'd rather not talk about it. It's still too painful."

"Okay," Amanda whispered. "I understand."

They stayed there a while longer, speaking quietly about life, about what they wished for, about the future they weren't sure they could share. Then Esteban stood.

"You need to go back," he said gently. "And I need to go to my trailer. I've got to get up early in the morning."

Amanda nodded. They climbed down from the barn, their steps slow, as if neither wanted the night to end.

***

Several days passed after the trouble at the bar. The men Esteban had humiliated nursed their anger. They gathered, bitter and drunk, and hatched a plan to strike back. Their target was not Esteban directly; it was the barn, the pride of the ranch, the home of Hamilton's finest horses, and also conveniently, it was the place where Esteban worked.

Late one night, they came with fuel cans and matches. Shadows flickered across the wooden walls as flames began to lick upward. But Esteban had suspected something. When he spotted the glow in the distance, he raced to the barn.

Inside, the fire spread fast. Horses screamed, thrashing in panic. Esteban moved quickly, throwing open stalls, driving the animals out into the night. But the blaze was growing, threatening to take the whole structure. Then his mind caught a memory, something he had once read about the blast of CO_2 extinguishers.

In the back room hung a line of heavy red fire extinguishers. He dragged several together, wired them tight like a daisy chain, and aimed them toward the inferno. There was a rifle in the room. He quickly grabbed it and aimed at the center extinguisher. With one strike, the canisters erupted, a white storm of gas flooding the barn. Flames hissed and shrank. The roof groaned but did not fall. Against all odds, the barn was saved.

When Mr. Hamilton arrived, his face went pale at the sight. He saw the smoke, the scorched beams, the horses trembling in the pasture. Then his eyes found Esteban, blackened with soot, standing firm.

"I can't believe this," Hamilton said, his voice trembling with both fury and relief. "Those sons of bitches... they tried to burn me down. My family, my livelihood. Esteban, if it wasn't for you, it'd all be gone."

30

Far beyond the ranch, another fire was spreading.

In Mexico City, the hum of ceiling fans mixed with the rustle of papers as investigators combed through Senator Fernández's files. His computer had been cracked open like a vault. Pages of coded notes, transcripts, and hidden recordings lay scattered across the table. But something was missing; key evidence had vanished.

Men in dark suits murmured in the shadows of the office.

"Who has it?" one demanded.

"Not us," another replied, his voice low, cautious. "But someone does. And whoever it is... Fernández died for it."

Whispers grew bolder in the cafés, in the streets, in the chambers of power. Some swore he had been assassinated. Others dared to say what no one could prove, that Esteban, the one man who had worked too closely with Fernández, had vanished with the truth.

The authorities scoured records, called in contacts, and retraced his movements. But Mexico had no trace of him.

What they didn't know was that, after the senator's death, Chávez had told Esteban to flee the country.

And so, as Esteban crossed the border under the weight of silence, his name already becoming legend.

But secrets never stayed buried. Somewhere, somehow, his trail slipped. A careless call. A number traced.

In Washington, D.C., behind oak-paneled doors, a man twisted a heavy ring on his finger, revealing the scorpion etched on it, as he leaned into the phone. "We've been compromised," he murmured. "The Mexican agent is here. In America."

Within days, every glowing screen bore Esteban's face. WANTED. Suspected Assassin of Senator Fernández. The narrative had been written for him, and it painted him as a terrorist.

***

When the news about a runaway terrorist reached Amanda and Mr. Hamilton, it felt as if the air itself had thickened. They saw the picture. They knew that the wanted man was the hand they had hired. They called the man who had saved their lives and livelihoods.

Esteban stood before them, his shoulders sagging beneath the weight of truth, eyes dark but steady. He told them everything: every secret, every betrayal, every reason the danger was closing in.

Amanda's hand trembled at her side, her voice breaking as she finally managed, "So it's true... all of it?"

Esteban met her gaze without flinching. "Yes." His answer was simple, but it carried the finality of a blade slicing clean. "But I am not what they say I am. I did not kill Senator Fernandez. I just ran because there was no way I could prove it and stay alive."

Silence spread through the room. Mr. Hamilton turned away, staring into the distance, too stunned for words. But Amanda didn't look away. Her chest rose and fell, her heart aching with a storm of emotions: fear, grief, relief, love. Then, with a kind of fragile defiance, she stepped closer and reached for his hand.

Esteban froze, every instinct telling him to pull back, to shield her from the ruin he dragged with him. But Amanda's fingers wrapped firmly around his, grounding him.

"You saved my life," she whispered, her voice cracking under the weight of her confession. "And somewhere along the way, you stole my heart too. I don't care about the danger, Esteban. I don't care about the past. I only care about you."

His throat tightened. He wanted to tell her it was foolish, that she deserved safety, that she deserved a life untouched by shadows.

"Amanda..." He almost begged her to stop, to let go, to run far from him. But he couldn't. Instead, he squeezed her hand, his mask slipping, allowing her to see the fear and longing he carried.

"Then we face it together," she said, her voice steady now, her decision unshakable.

Mr. Hamilton turned to face him. "You have my complete trust, Esteban. I know you are a good man. You would never do something like this, and you would never harm my daughter." He paused. "The two of you have my blessing."

Amamda ran to her father and hugged him.

For the first time in longer than he could remember, Esteban felt the weight on his shoulders ease.

***

Airports, buses, trains, every route was a trap. Instead, Esteban remembered an old friend's cabin hidden deep in the Mississippi woods north of the state. Remote. Off-grid. That was the place they needed to go.

Under the cover of night, he and Amanda drove the backroads until the headlights cut out and the forest swallowed them whole.

Once they reached the cabin, they got out of the truck. Esteban leaned back against the truck, arms crossed, trying to steady himself after the long drive. Amanda stepped closer, her eyes lingering on him, studying the sharp lines of his face, softened by the moonlight filtering through the branches.

"You know," she said softly, "I feel safer here with you than anywhere else."

He turned his head, surprised by her honesty. "Safe? With me?" He gave a short, humorless laugh. "Amanda, being around me is the last place anyone should feel safe."

She shook her head, closing the small distance between them. "You don't see yourself the way I do. You've been protecting me from the second this started. I trust you."

Her words struck deeper than he expected. For a moment, Esteban didn't reply, afraid his voice might betray what he was feeling. Instead, he reached for her hand, his thumb brushing against her skin.

Amanda looked up at him, her eyes searching his, and something in her expression cracked the walls he'd built around himself. He bent down slowly, giving her the chance to turn away. But she didn't. Their lips met, tentative at first,

425

then deeper, like they were both admitting what had been growing between them all along.

When they finally broke apart, Amanda rested her forehead against his chest, breathing in the scent of pine and him. "I don't care what happens next," she whispered. "Just... don't let go."

Esteban held her tighter, his heart pounding in a way that had nothing to do with fear.

"I won't."

For a time, they had peace. No phones. No radios. Just the wind threading through the pines and the crackle of firelight against the logs. Esteban almost believed the world had forgotten them.

But peace had never been meant for him.

One morning, the sky split open. The thunder of helicopters shattered the stillness.

Amanda bolted upright. "Esteban!"

He was already at the door.

Outside, black silhouettes filled the air. Men in tactical gear spread through the trees, rifles raised. A loudspeaker boomed:

"Come out with your hands up! You are surrounded!"

Several men came out at once, rifles raised. Esteban knew immediately there was no way to do anything. If he resisted, they would shoot him. If he gave them what they wanted, they would kill him anyway.

He stepped forward slowly, hands half-raised, his jaw tight. He had told the woman he had grown so fond of to stay inside, but she wouldn't listen. Amanda clung to his side.

Together they walked toward the helicopter, dust whipping up from the rotors. The men herded them closer, rifles pressing into their backs, shouting over the roar. Esteban kept his eyes ahead, his mind racing, every muscle tense, waiting for the moment when everything would break.

From one of the descending helicopters, a man stepped into the clearing. His jacket bore bold letters, FBI. And behind him... a familiar face.

Esteban's blood ran cold. "Chávez..." he breathed.

Amanda's eyes darted to him. "You know him?"

"He was my friend." His voice trembled between disbelief and rage.

Chávez raised his hands as if in surrender. "It's not what you think," he shouted across the noise. "Listen to me..."

But the words were hollow, drowned out by the agents fanning into position.

One of them called out, "You have something we need. Hand it over, now."

Esteban's hand brushed against the inside of his jacket where the drive lay hidden. He felt Amanda's eyes on him. If he surrendered it, their lives would end quietly in some forgotten cell. If he resisted, they would die here in the woods.

Then, the roar deepened. More helicopters, dozens of them, broke through the sky, not black, but white, red, yellow. News teams. Reporters. Cameras pointed down like watchful eyes.

The FBI agents hesitated. Their secret had just been dragged into daylight.

Esteban stepped forward, his chest rising, his voice ringing out. "If anything happens to me, the truth is already free. Every outlet you see up there has it. Every secret Fernández uncovered. You cannot stop it."

The agents looked at one another, uncertain.

Esteban pulled out the thumb drive. "Take it and leave."

The agent touched his ear, appearing to talk to his superior. "We have a problem." He explained to the man on the line that Esteban had made copies of the proof and that if he died, all news outlets would receive a copy.

A man wearing a scorpion ring and holding a phone in D.C. scowled as he heard what the agent said.

The agent said, "What do we do?"

The man holding the phone frowned. "Let them go."

One man moved quickly, snatched the drive from Esteban's hand, and fell back into line. The order came sharp and cold: "Stand down."

Guns lowered. Men withdrew. Helicopters lifted.

Esteban's eyes locked with Chávez's one last time. He searched his old friend's face for loyalty, for betrayal, for anything real. But Chávez said nothing.

As Chavez climbed into the waiting helicopter, he slipped a ring onto his finger, the gold scorpion on it flashing once in the light before he disappeared into the sky.

www.ingramcontent.com/pod-product-compliance
Lightning Source LLC
Chambersburg PA
CBHW062107290726

48975CB00001B/144